BLADE OF GLASS

A Dark Fantasy Adventure

THE SPLINTERED LAND
BOOK I

RICHARD PARRY

Contents

THE STORM WITHIN

Blade of Glass

Sorcerers are a blight. **Knight Adept Geneve was raised to end them.**

Now, one is on the run, carrying the **Tome of Lost Souls**—a grimoire powerful enough to **shatter her order in an instant.** Geneve's mission is simple: **track him down, seize the Tome, and bring it back to her masters.**

But truth is a dangerous thing. **Monsters brutalize the world, and the people Geneve serves are complicit.** Betrayed and hunted, she flees into the **blasted plaguelands**, damning herself through her choice of allies: a **Feybrind who keeps his own counsel**, a **renegade illusionist**, and a **creature she was trained to despise—a Vhemin.**

Her quest for the Tome's hidden secret remains. If she succeeds, she will **betray everything she swore to protect**. If she fails, not even the gods can stop what comes next.

Her armor has never felt so heavy.

You're Awesome

You could have picked any book, but you chose this one. That means a lot.

Your support keeps independent authors like me forging ahead, writing the stories we love (and hopefully, the ones you love too). Whether you're here for the characters, the worldbuilding, or just a little escapism, thank you for being part of this journey.

You. Kick. Ass.

Roll for Narrative

WHERE WORLDBUILDING AND OVERTHINKING COLLIDE

Love stories that linger in your brain long after The End? Ever wonder why some books hit like a natural 20 and others critically fail their way into the 1-star abyss?

Join *Roll for Narrative*, my hub for sci-fi and fantasy lovers. I explore storytelling like a rogue casing a dungeon, review movies, books, and games, and dish out writing tips like a chaotic-good bard with a grudge against bad prose. No spam, just good stuff.

Join the quest:
https://rollfornarrative.parrydox.com

For my Rae, always.

Dramatis Personae

KNIGHT ADEPT GENEVE

Geneve was raised by the Tresward from age five. She knows no life other than service to the Three gods.

Her skill with her blade Requiem is unparalleled, yet the Storm eludes her. She has mastered all 2,100 patterns handed to humanity by Cophine, Ikmae, and Khiton, but can't change the world with Sway.

She is a Knight Adept, a rank she only holds because she cheated. But as Israel would say, there are no cheaters in war, only the living and the dead. And Geneve wants to live.

MERIWETHER DU REEVES

A fallen scion of a noble house, Meriwether is on the run from the law.

This isn't an unfamiliar state.
Since leaving the questionably safe
harbor of Leander du Reeves' estate,
Meriwether's run from the Tresward,
royalty, and common folk alike. Why?

No one likes a sorcerer.

Not being a very good sorcerer
isn't a great defence when facing the
gallows, so Meriwether keeps running.
Starving, penniless, and friendless,
he's running low on dark corners to
hide in.

SIGHT OF DAY

One of the secretive Feybrind, Sight of Day leaves his forest home on a mission to the human kingdom of Or'sen.

Skilled with a blade, bow, and wit, he is friend to all except the hated Vhemin. Sight of Day is a craftsman of great skill, whether making weapons or pancakes.

He has lived many years longer than even the oldest mayfly humans and Vhemin. The Feybrind can't talk, so he communicates with the People's beautiful handspeak.

ARMITAGE

Hated by even his own Vhemin kind, Armitage is one of the reptilian warriors from the blasted plaguelands.

Cold of blood and heart, he journeys into human lands for the good of his people. The Vhemin won't thank him for it, but they never do.

He's learned the cost of life as weight by blood on the sands. No fear. No mercy. And no forgiveness.

VERTILINE

Knight Chevalier Vertiline commands the Storm in one hand, the bitter whip of sarcasm in the other.

She's in the Tresward for the wrong reasons, but she's still the second best swordswoman the world has ever seen. If she can hold on to her courage, Vertiline might just stop stupid people from doing stupider things.

If not, well. She wasn't a proper Knight anyway.

ISRAEL

Israel is a Knight Valiant of the Tresward. He has given his life in service to the Three.

Late to the sash, his skill at arms is only bested by his sense of honor. He is a mentor to Geneve and Vertiline, leading their small band on the Three's business. Israel sees each day as a lesson, if you have the wit to learn.

He has known Vertiline since before their time in the Tresward, their shared past a comfortable cloak between them. Israel accepted Geneve for all her lack of skill with the Storm, showing her the patience the world wouldn't.

Vigilance. Duty. Loyalty. These are the burdens he bears.

The Prisoner

They came to kill a sinner.

The cage's iron presence rode at Geneve's back. It was made of good Tresward Smithsteel; cold metal fingers waited to clutch their prize as it rode their creaky wagon. It knew how to carry prisoners better than she did. Two oxen pulled it with a trudging step. She rode her blue roan beside them as the cart made its trundling way toward Calterburry.

She'd named the roan Tristan. He was young and eager for the road ahead, just like her. Vertiline said *he prances too much*, but that's how Geneve liked it. Unaware of their grim duty, Tristan tossed his mane, harness jingling like silver bells.

The noise made Israel turn. He led from the front atop a massive charger that looked like it could eat a man whole. Road dirt dusted his honey-brown skin but couldn't cling to the white of his tabard. The Tresward's sun gleamed gold across his broad chestplate. He tossed her a lopsided smile. "It'll be fine."

"It'll be a hoax, is what it'll be," groused Vertiline from her rear-guard position. "The most exciting thing we'll get here is warm ale." Her chestnut mare seemed to agree, offering a snort.

Geneve laughed. "Warm ale wouldn't be so bad. After two weeks of Iz's cooking, I need something to take the taste away."

Israel *tsk'd*. "You're young and inexperienced. I wouldn't expect you to know what good food tastes like."

"She's not wrong." Vertiline urged the chestnut past Geneve to join Israel at the front. "Your cooking is a true misery. We used to call it the Lost Trial. Calterburry's just ahead."

"Please, let it stay lost." Geneve craned to see the town as the three rounded a bend. The rutted road swept down before them toward their destination, giving Geneve her first glimpse of Calterburry. Wooden walls ringed a town nestled in a valley. Perhaps a thousand souls called her home. The stone facade of Calterburry Stronghold stood like a stern older brother peering over the fortifications.

The walls were well-maintained, despite the weather here being cool enough to keep most Vhemin away. Queen Morgan's Lord Symonet had a hard but fair reputation, which made his keeping the prisoner from the Tresward surprising. *Perhaps the messenger bird went missing. The Justiciars tells us to look for mistakes over malice first.* Protocol said he should've sent the sinner to them directly, and yet here they were: eating Iz's cooking and two weeks of road dust.

A weak midmorning sun smiled on them, raising Geneve's spirits and her body temperature. The three Tresward Knights approached from the north, a river keeping pace with their travels to the west. Geneve didn't know its name and struggled to find a reason to care. Their mission was escorting the prisoner to his Judgment and subsequent death.

She winced. *We're here to see justice done, but he needs to be Judged first.* It's why they had a cage. The prisoner was rumored to be a wizard, which is why Israel and Vertiline kept their glass swords ready. Geneve's metal blade Requiem rested heavy against her spine. Cold iron wasn't as good as glass for killing the wicked, but it made a man bleed out well enough.

Calterburry's gates loomed closer. They were open—a good sign. Two guards waited outside, holding pikes like the weapons supported the sky. Geneve shifted in her saddle. She felt a stab of unease as the guards straightened. *Tresward Knights aren't a cause for alarm unless something's wrong.*

"Easy, now." Israel felt it too, patting the neck of his charger. The great beast tossed its mane, no doubt ready to eat one of the guards.

Vertiline rolled her shoulders. The dust of the road hadn't dimmed her ghost-white skin any more than her steady, even level of latent ire. "The day's looking up. We might get to knock some sense into someone."

Israel glanced back to Geneve. "Stay with the wagon." He urged his horse ahead, the beast surging toward the gates.

"Does this look like a plan to you?" Not waiting for Geneve's answer, Vertiline gave chase. The tail of her braid bounced in her wake, her white-and-gold tabard burning in the sun's light like a torch.

Stay with the wagon, huh? That's a special kind of bullshit. Geneve curled her lip. Iz and Tilly looked out for her, but sometimes it rankled. She could swing a blade better than most. *But not well enough to be a real Knight. I don't have a glass sword yet.*

She gave a grunt, which the oxen ignored. Geneve offered them a glare. "I didn't want your opinion, anyway." It didn't feel like anyone would try and rush her for a metal cage meant to take sinners to trial, but they taught her to be prepared. Still, the cleared area around Calterburry meant she could see for klicks. There wasn't anyone out here.

No one at all. Isn't it odd that there's no merchants on this road or people outside the walls? She squinted, focusing on the gate. Israel talked with the guards, making big gestures. Geneve could guess his meaning. *Step the fuck aside, or get stepped the fuck on.* Vertiline stood across from the guard Israel wasn't berating, hands on hips. She hadn't drawn her sword, but that didn't mean much. Geneve had seen Vertiline cut a man in half with a single strike from her glass sword, armor and all. He'd looked a little surprised while he bled out because her sword had rested in its sheath a heartbeat earlier.

Geneve drew close enough to hear. *Wagon doesn't need much guarding here.* The oxen continued their tread, unaware of the increasing odds of violence. Geneve swung a leg over her saddle, dropped to the road, then hopped up to the wagon's seat. She grabbed the reins, and the oxen deigned to take notice of her. One gave her a reproachful look as she gave a tug, but they came to a halt. She engaged the brake, slipped down, patted Tristan, and walked to stand a handful of steps behind Iz and Tilly.

Israel sucked in a lungful of air, brows closing in like storm clouds. "By the Three! For the last time, you *will* let us pass. We are Knights of the Tresward."

The guard, a man with a too-large nose beneath too-small eyes, hawked, turned his head, and spat. He wore chain armor beneath a tabard sporting the queen's black raven crest. "I don't care if you're Cophine, Ikmae, and Khiton themselves. You can pass *back* the way you came. Or, you can pass *around*. You can pass *up* the opportunity of a warm bed inside, though. By Lord Symonet's orders, you aren't passing *through* these gates." Each utterance of *pass* was slow, deliberate, as if he was speaking to a simple child. "Am I being unclear?"

Geneve winced as Israel's neck darkened in anger. Lips pressed in a thin line, the Valiant took a step forward. "We're here on Tresward business. Word was sent. There's a sinner here."

"Dare say there's many sinners." The guard shrugged. "But it doesn't change—"

"Fire!" The cry rose behind the guards. They spun, pikes at the ready, as if a length of wood and steel could cut flames down to size. Geneve saw a thin pillar of sooty black smoke rising from within the walls.

The guard clapped a hand to his helmet. "By the Three, that's coming from Elean's Masonry." He broke into a run, arms pumping, the head of his pike glinting in the sun.

The other watched his companion go, mouth open, eyes wide. Israel cleared his throat. "Elean's Masonry doesn't sound so bad."

"Hah. They break stone with black powder." He pointed to the dirt. "Stay here."

"No problem." Vertiline crossed her arms, watching the guard sprint off. "Idiot."

"Geneve, get the wagon. You know where to go." Israel vaulted onto his charger, then nudged the massive beast forward. Vertiline swung onto hers, sparks ringing from the steed's hooves as they clattered inside.

Get the wagon. Geneve sighed, then hopped aboard. She gave the reins a flick, wondering at what point being a Knight turned from *teamster* to *warrior*. Tristan shook his mane in agreement, prancing at her side as she drove the wagon inside.

No telling where Israel and Vertiline went to, so she drove the oxen to the Yellow Mug. The tavern doubled as a Tresward stable, paid in good coin to reserve space for Knights. It felt surreal to drive her team of oxen to a place that no doubt sold warm ale while Israel and Vertiline raced toward danger.

They're not alone. Villagers hurried in the direction of smoke, many carrying buckets. Fire was always bad, but one where explosives were kept would be devastating. The only thing tethering Geneve to the wagon was the cage, and their purpose. *Find the sinner. Bring them back for redemption.*

A short trip through panicked Calterburry brought her to the inn. The Yellow Mug's sign swung ahead. *Original: a mug, painted in yellow.* Rumors said the tavern was built atop haunted catacombs, which sounded extraordinarily unlikely, but it meant Knights were always welcome. Spirits didn't like coming into the Light. Geneve drove the team through the gates. A short man waddled outside, a mostly-clean apron identifying him as the likely innkeeper. Geneve wracked her brains. *What's his name? G-something. Grim? Grimson?* She tried a smile. "Gilbert."

"It's Gylbard, m'lady." He gave a tiny bow, returning her smile. His teeth were so bad they hurt to look at.

"Gylbard!" Geneve jumped from the wagon. She wanted to say, *Must be a mistake in our records*, but that would be a lie. "Sorry. My mistake."

"Gilbert's close enough. Most folk call me 'That Fat Fucker.'" He chortled, then cut off, as if seeing the golden sun on her breastplate for the first time. "I, um."

"You've got to admit, Fat Fucker's memorable." Geneve grinned. "Basically rolls off the tongue."

The innkeeper sagged in relief. *No telling when you'll get a Knight high on scripture, or one just wanting a place to rest their feet.* Israel said, *I never trust a man who won't swear,* and Vertiline elbowed him so he offered, *or woman.* It was the kind of thinking that kept Geneve's feet on the ground. "Will it be lodgings?"

"It will, Gylbard. Do you mind if I...?" Geneve trailed off, then jerked her head in the direction of the fire. "Best get in before it spreads."

"Aye, I'll see to your wagon. Leave your horse, too. Streets will get crowded, right quick."

Geneve turned to go, then swung back. *Courtesy.* "Thank you." Gylbard offered her another horrific smile, and she returned her more even version before sprinting onto the street, sword clattering against her back.

◈

SOMETHING WASN'T RIGHT. GENEVE'S FIRST INKLING OF IT WAS AS people passed back her way, looking confused, still carrying buckets.

The second was, as she looked at the now soot-laden sky, she realized she could smell no smoke. The odd hint of wood fire clung to the air as it did in any town, but a blaze of that size should make her dirtier than the road.

I hunt a sinner.

She shored up beside a bakery. Inside, the shopkeeper peered his concern at the sky through poorly-made glass. Fire could be the death of a town.

Geneve watched the crowd ebb and flow. People surging this way and that, looking for a blaze to quench. *Fire can also draw people to a place. Distract the eye and mind both.* She marked the place where smoke rose, then turned about, facing the opposite direction. She set off, shouldering through the crowd. Most parted for her tabard, but some were too confused or concerned to pay her much mind. A man clattered into her, bouncing off her breastplate. She kept her footing with ease, helping him with a steadying arm before he could fall to the street.

Geneve offered him a nod, then scrubbed red hair away from her face before looking to the sky again. She was close to the wall. The mouth of an alley led away to the right, so she took it. It'd get her out of the press of people.

Inside the alley, people noise dropped away. The sound of birds filled the air. She thought they sounded like bellbirds but couldn't see any. She craned her head trying to spot one but saw nothing up high other than walls and closed shutters.

"It's called Birdsong Alley." A strong male voice made her swing her attention back down, taking in a young man, lounging against a wall. He had a sparkle to his eyes, a hint of stubble at his jaw, and the kind of nonchalant attitude that made her want to punch him almost immediately. "No birds, though. No one knows why they still sing. Some say it's a curse, but as far as curses go it's not so bad."

Geneve gauged the distance between them. Ten paces, no more. The alley wasn't wide. Unsheathing Requiem would be a poor choice. *Fighting an unarmed man might be a worse one.* She lowered the hand that had risen unconsciously to the blade's hilt above her shoulder. "It sounds ... nice."

"Nice?" He laughed, pushing off from the wall. "I tell you of a flock of ghost birds forever singing, and you say it's 'nice?'" He shrugged, pulling a too-worn robe close about him. "Well, enjoy. I'll be off."

He made to walk past her. Geneve grasped his arm above the elbow. "Wait."

The twinkle didn't leave his eyes. "Normally, people ask for a name, or a quiet drink at a tavern, but if this is how the Tresward want to—"

"Why aren't you helping with the fire?"

"Fire?" He glanced at the alley mouth. She glimpsed his calm facade slip for a second. "Why, that's where I'm going."

Geneve tightened her grip. "I think—" Whatever she thought was lost to the roar of a beast. She spun, dropping her hand from the man's arm. In the alley behind her a black shadow hulked. Her mind tried to find a name for it, but came up empty. A bear? Whatever it was reared, pawing the air with malformed claws. She goggled for a moment, then drew her scattergun in a smooth motion. She'd named it Tribunal, and it spoke the Three's law.

She pulled the trigger, the hard *boom* silencing the birdsong. The shot blasted through the might-be-a-bear, then... nothing. The thing continued to paw the air, and not very well—it wasn't much of anything, let alone a real bear. Also, blood and viscera didn't blast out the back as expected.

I'm here to catch a sinner. I'm an idiot. Geneve spun, catching sight of the man sprinting for the alley's exit. She crouched, tossing Tribunal in a spin across the distance. The scattergun tangled in the man's legs, and he dropped to the cobbles with a grunt.

The not-bear vanished. Geneve gave a savage grin, all teeth, running after the sinner. She caught the man's panicked stare as he scrambled back like a crab before finding his feet and running. As sunlight touched him, she saw his clothing looked more worn, his skin pasty and sweaty. She scooped up the scattergun as she went, slotting it back into its holster, then bent her head and *ran*.

I'm here for a sinner, and he got the drop on me. She snarled, pushing herself harder. Her armor was heavy, bright Smithsteel weighing her down, but it wasn't like she could tear it off. The man wasn't weighed down by anything and buoyed by the fear of imminent demise. It made his feet lighter than air.

I will not lose him. She put on a burst of speed, vaulted a cart, and landed in a clatter of metal. Requiem lay against her spine, heavy, waiting, but running with a drawn sword was foolishness itself. She spied the sinner duck into another alley. She ignored it, running on. *Cut him off.* A porter stepped in front of her, and she plowed right through him. His burden of boxes scattered as if hit by a horse.

Geneve skidded around the corner of a clothier. Ahead, a small gap between buildings showed the alley's exit. The sinner backed out of it, looking for pursuit, and almost missing her until the hammer of her boots on cobbles drew his attention.

He spun, hand out, but she bulled on. Geneve crashed into him, the full weight of her armor bearing him to the ground. She felt the air and fight go out of him as he landed. Arm across his throat, she reared up, fist clenched and ready to strike. He raised his hands, turning away.

She got a moment to see what she'd missed before. His skin wasn't just pale. Gray cheeks sunken and sallow with malnourishment beneath a sparse beard. Unbridled terror in his eyes at the justice that came calling.

He is so afraid. She lowered her arm. *He is so afraid of* me. Geneve stood, holding a step away. She kept her stance ready but needn't have bothered. The sinner's coat was stained, a rent showing the cost of his temporary freedom. It looked like he'd been stabbed. She held her hand out, sunlight reflecting from her burnished gauntlet. *Sinners get a trial, and until then, they deserve our mercy.* "Come."

The sinner glanced about. A small crowd formed about them. Smoke no longer hung in the sky. He ignored her hand, getting to unsteady feet. He glanced about but found no escape. He plastered on a smile that came off as sickly rather than friendly. "I'm Meriwether."

"I don't care." She let her hand fall. "Let's get your injuries seen too."

"So you can kill me later? No thanks." He turned, gave a last burst of energy, and lunged toward the crowd. Geneve thought he might be trying for freedom, but he grappled with a man, snaring a knife. He faced Geneve, fear back in his eyes like it found a home there. "I won't go to the Three." He lunged for her.

It was a sloppy, slow strike. She saw it coming, predictable as sunrise, and stepped to the side. As the blade bit nothing but air, she straight-armed him. Her vambrace collected him in the face, and he slammed into the ground hard enough to make Geneve wince. The knife clattered free.

She bent to collect it. *Interesting. He went for* me, *not using anyone as hostage.* Geneve returned it to its owner, the crowd swirling like a shoal of fish. Geneve bent to lift Meriwether, hefting him across her shoulders like a sack of coal. He felt light, as if the sins had already left his body.

The crowd opened to reveal Israel, Vertiline in his shadow. The big man grinned, broad and bright. "Ah. You've found our little mouse."

Geneve adjusted Meriwether's weight on her shoulder. "He runs fast for a mouse."

Vertiline grunted. "Chains will slow him down." She led off, Geneve and Israel falling in behind. The crowd bled away, disappearing like a stain washed from cotton. Geneve was left with nothing but the fragile weight of a sinner. His blood dripped down her breastplate.

I'm here for a sinner, but all I found is a scared man. I expected lightning and got smoke, a poor mimic of a bear, and birdsong. Three's mercy, what is this?

Chapter One

"This is your tree." The big man stood beside the sapling, hand on the slender trunk, and looked down on Geneve. The timbre of his voice was chocolate rich, which she knew because she'd talked to him before, but this time it held something deeper, more insistent. This tree was important.

Geneve looked about the field. It lay inside tall stone walls that protected everything inside. The ground was turned earth, tended with exquisite care. She'd noticed that as the big man led Geneve down broad, worn steps to the flat ground. Her tree sat with hundreds of others in the field. They were well-spaced, so the sun's light could reach them all. Some were broken, as if by lightning, but no charring marked the wood. Other slots where trees should be were empty, the earth turned and ready for planting.

The big man had brought her here through a keep. Outside was nothing but rolling grassland. The keep stood on a small hillock. It was visible for klicks in every direction. The stone was white, without the staining she'd expect of marble left to the elements. This structure shone like new.

She couldn't remember from where she'd come, or what she was doing, but her clothes smelled bad and had rips. Her hands were smudged with old dirt. Geneve couldn't remember if the rest of her was dirty.

It was the not knowing that was bad, not being dirty. She was certain she'd been dirty a lot, and never died from it. But everything prior to the cart ride here was gone from her life and reaching for the memories brought nothing. No pain or discomfort, just an absence of anything.

The tree looked like it might fill a part of that gap. Geneve put her hands on hips. "So?"

The big man's face cracked, the stern facade allowing the smallest glimmer of a smile through. He fingered his necklace, a small stone crystal set in a length of silver chain. "So, you will break it one day."

"Why would I break my own tree?" Geneve took a cautious step forward, because she didn't know the big man at all. He was impressive in the way a huge rock might be if it could talk, all bedecked in gleaming steel armor, a golden sun on his breastplate. A black sash carrying the weight of three gold bars crossed his heart. A sword was scabbarded at his waist but worn in a rear-draw style. Geneve knew the blade was glass without knowing how she knew. She'd seen it, perhaps, before her memory was gone. Geneve felt like there should be blood on his armor, but it was clean like it'd been freshly forged.

She put her hands on the tree's young bark. It was smooth, without the knots and whirls time would bring. It was younger than her, and she didn't want to break it.

"The tree grows as you grow. When you're ready to live here forever you will come to this field. You'll break this with your bare hands." He crouched before her. "All Knights do."

Geneve bunched her hands into tiny fists. "I don't think I can do that." She glanced at the tree again, as if seeking moral support. "I don't think I want to."

"It's just a tree."

"It didn't do anything to me."

He laughed, stood, and gestured with a sweep of his arm. "These trees mark time. In ten years, you'll undergo the Trials. Your tree will be strong and wide."

"What about your tree?"

He raised an eyebrow. "My tree isn't here. I was a Novice at a different Tresward."

"I mean, did you break it?"

"That seems a curious question." He frowned, like he felt he'd explained this part already. "I'm a Knight. I passed my Trials."

"So many things could happen to a tree." She frowned right back at him, this strange, large man, with his armor, sword, and glittering necklace. "Lightning. A fire. Thieves and bandits." She rubbed her arms, which goose-bumped in memory. It wasn't chilly inside the keep, but outside the touch of the southern winds brought cold. Geneve didn't know why she wore only a shift without winter warms to keep her soul inside her body. "Thieves steal wood all the time."

The big man nodded, rolling the jewel at his neck between large, strong fingers. "No lightning strikes here. The Three," he held a palm to the heavens, where the moons would shine in the night, "keep it safe. To set fire to a tree, a villain would need to get past a fearsome collection of fighters sworn to protect them."

"It could still happen."

"It could." He nodded. "Do you know why we need people like you?"

Geneve bit her lip. She was tiny compared to him. Five years old, skinny, knock-kneed, uncertain, and hungry. "I'm not like you at all."

"That's right. We need all the difference we can find. The Vhemin roam, hunting people. The Feybrind hide in their forests and ice plains, ignoring us. Royalty wants control of everything, including the fires of desire inside people's hearts."

She thought about that. Vhemin seemed an old threat, well-used in her hearing. She'd never seen one and didn't think they were real. Feybrind were amazing, and she'd known one, but couldn't remember when, or how. If she was amazing like them, she might take herself away, too. "I don't know what that means."

"Difference left us. We need to remember it for ourselves." The big man spoke like he was reciting something he'd heard from someone else. "The Tresward hold the Light for our allies and against our enemies."

"How do you hold light?"

"With your heart." The big man offered her another smile. "Are you hungry?"

Geneve nodded so much she thought her head might pop off. "I haven't eaten in..." Her voice faded away, remembering—grr!—she couldn't remember. "I think it's been a long time."

"Do you remember who I am?" At her head-shake, he crouched again, taking off his gauntlet. Underneath was a hand like any other man's. Callused, a little *paler than the dark honey-brown of his face. Strong, though. She could see how a hand like that could hold up the very world. He held it out to her.*

She took it in her small one as best she could, wrapping her hand around two of his fingers. "Hello. I'm Geneve."

"Hello, Geneve. I'm Israel."

Chapter Two

That's the first and last time you'll underestimate a Knight. Consciousness returned to Meriwether like a forbidden tryst in the night: quickly, and with a lot of sweating and groaning. Light blazed, harsh as the forge of dawn itself. He squinted, holding a hand out to shade his eyes, then cried out at the pain in his side.

The gift from Symonet's lackies. Meriwether took a calming breath, then another as nausea leered at him. His fingers found his shirt, and tentatively made for the sword gash they'd awarded him with. Trembling and slow, he expected the harsh brand of rent flesh, but instead he found the brush of cotton.

You're not going to learn anything mewling like a babe in a bassinet. Strength, man. He lay on a bed, the mattress firm but not unkind. Another opening of his eyes showed the earlier brilliant flare was the meager glow of a lantern. Meriwether was in a small room with stone-lined walls. The lantern, now wanting to be his friend, sat atop a small wooden table. The table wouldn't fetch a high price at market; it lacked adornment or varnish but was well-made. *Check the door.*

He swung his feet over the side of the bed and let out a small whimper. His sword wound felt worse than he remembered. He'd danced aside from the thrust of a blade but caught the edge in passing. A clean enough cut with nothing vital severed, but it felt like Khiton's black sword of ending was lodged under his ribs.

Khiton's a long way off, but his Knights are here. Check the damn door. Meriwether grunted himself upright, staggering to the room's only exit. The door was sturdy and without an obvious keyhole. He tested the handle, fingers resting on cool brass. It turned easy enough, but the door didn't budge. Barred from the outside, no doubt. *Knights aren't known for being idiots or taking chances.*

With his face close to the timber, he caught the sound of footsteps. The tread was measured and even. Creaking wood belied the weight of the man coming for him. Meriwether stepped away from the door, hurried back to the bed, lay down, and closed his eyes.

He heard a rattle and clunk of wood, then the door creaked open. Heavy Footsteps entered. "If you're thinking to try something clever, don't." The voice was heavy, like a sack of gravel, but—like the bed—not unkind.

Meriwether risked winking an eye open. Before him stood a titan of a man. Skin the color of good mānuka honey. Pale blue eyes, hard as winter's ice. He wore faded clothes, but well cared for. A loose shirt did nothing to hide the musculature of his chest and arms. *Three's mercy. His biceps are larger than my neck. And he moves like a dancer. A big, unhappy dancer.* No armor, but Meriwether knew the stink of Tresward Knights whatever they wore. No sash either, so impossible to tell this one's rank. The titan held a steaming bowl. Meriwether's stomach gave a traitorous growl. "Is that for me?"

"Depends. You going to start something you can't finish?"

"Do I get the food if I do, or—"

"She could have killed you. I wouldn't have said a word." The titan put the bowl on the small table. The man didn't turn his back, always keeping Meriwether in sight.

He remembered a young woman chasing him through streets of uncaring people, her hair red like the blaze of a furnace. *She was young. Should have been easy enough to fool, but she had my number.* "Maybe. Do I deserve it?"

The titan pursed his lips. "That's a problem for a Justiciar."

"So, you don't know?"

"I don't *care*." The titan leaned on the word. "Before you start, there are three things you need to know."

"Start what?" Meriwether eyed the bowl. Steam continued its lazy rise, and with it the smell of stewed mutton assailed him. He hadn't eaten a meal in three days, and even then it was stolen bread hard as brick and cheese the mice wouldn't take.

"Your escape plan. I'm Israel, Knight Valiant of the Tresward."

"That's the first thing?" Meriwether talked to hide a flash of fear. *They sent a Valiant's four heavy bars after little old me. What's going on?*

"It is." Israel looked down at Meriwether, considering for a moment, then the grim facade of his face eased a hair's breadth to allow a smile. "You can't plead your case with me. There's no gold that'll buy me, and no cause that will bend my will."

Meriwether rubbed his face. "And that's—"

"Number two, right." A stern nod. "You catch on fast. Third thing is, no harm will come to you while you're in our care. Until we bring you to the Justiciar, you're our guest. Unless."

Meriwether thought about waiting him out, but he wanted the bowl of food more. "Unless what?"

"Unless you try to run. Then," Israel backed from the room, "we'll hit you until you stop moving."

"The Justiciar's said to be a real asshole."

"Which one?" Israel frowned, refusing the offered laugh. "No, you're right. They all are."

"Ah." Meriwether nodded, like they were old friends comparing notes. "Did you know the cellar's haunted?"

"Don't be ridiculous. Enjoy your dinner." Israel stepped away.

"Wait." Meriwether looked at his feet. "Why am I alive?"

That earned a silence long enough for his gaze to find its nervous way back up to Israel's face. Still no humor, but a little pity, unless Meriwether missed his guess. "Because she's young. New at this. Believes in the cause more than most. The Justiciar said *bring you back*, and back you'll go." He slipped from the room on easy feet, making to pull the door closed.

"Hold up." Meriwether stepped to the door, risking a glare and all that might follow. He looked Israel in the eye. "What's her name?"

"The one who didn't kill you was Geneve. The one who would have is Vertiline. Best remember the difference." The door slammed closed, the rumble of the bar dropping to lock Meriwether inside. Israel left the vaguest hint of sandalwood on the air, but it was insufficient to overpower the mutton stew.

Make the best of it. Meriwether descended like a ravenous army on dinner. If it wasn't for the inevitable death at the end of his journey, he could get attached to being a prisoner of the Tresward.

❦

IT FELT LIKE ONE, MAYBE TWO MINUTES PASSED SINCE MERIWETHER dimmed the lantern and put his head on the pillow to sleep. By all measures it was a good pillow, because he woke with a start to a pitch-black room and a hand over his mouth.

"Quiet," hissed the hand's owner. Meriwether couldn't make out anything but the smell of leather—*gloved hand*—and the urgency of the request. He tried for a nod and found the motion easy enough. The hand eased up. "We're here to get you out. Stay silent, and you might live to see tomorrow."

That sounds like an excellent deal. Meriwether sat up. There was the scratch and scrape of metal, followed by the red bloom of flame. A second figure by the door held a hooded lantern, allowing a tiny aperture of ruddy light to escape into the room. The dim illumination showed Meriwether's lantern, now out, and the person who woke him. Where the figure by the door was bulky, this one was slender. They wore leather armor and covered their heads with hoods. Both had cloth masks covering the lower parts of their faces. It lent them an unflattering appearance some—for example, those not about to flee imprisonment—might call sinister.

If you were busting a man from the Tresward's "justice" you'd want to look sinister, too. Meriwether got to his feet, biting back a cry at his still-healing injury. The bulky figure at the door left, leading the way, the small puddle of light vanishing with him.

He wondered how he was supposed to follow until the slender one grabbed his arm, hauling him along. This wasn't the gentle, easy pull of a lover leading Meriwether to a tumble in the hay. The gloved hand on his arm felt like it was made of iron, urgency in every movement. He followed, mostly because he had no choice, but also because being put in the Tresward's cage and taken to some asshole Justiciar wasn't on his things-to-do list. His shoulder banged on the doorframe on the way out, wrenching his injury, and he stifled a whimper.

The dim lantern light led the way up wooden stairs. There wasn't enough light to make out many details, but he smelled the faint hint of old wine, onions, and burlap. The walls here were the same stone as his cell. *Am I in a cellar? Did they imprison me in a* haunted basement? It didn't feel like a good place to be, and he picked up the pace.

A creak from ahead, followed by a sliver of light. A doorway, leading to a dimly-lit room. The bulky figure doused their lantern, then opened the door wider. Meriwether and his guard followed. They entered the common room of a bar. He'd never been here, but all inns shared the same folksy charm. A collection of drunks littered the space. A fire slumbered on its bed of coals above a wide hearth. No one stirred.

The three shuffled through the space toward a side door. Cool wind nipped at Meriwether's face. The door was held ajar by a small sliver of wood. The bulky figure paused at the doorway, head cocked as if listening, then eased the door open into the quiet night beyond.

Outside, stillness gathered like the world held its breath. The sky was lit with a thousand tiny stars. Cophine's pale face beamed down on the courtyard. Ikmae's gray huddled by her shoulder. Somewhere beyond was Khiton's black orb. The Three's moons held vigil, as if the heavens wanted Meriwether's freedom. Or waited for his fall.

The thin figure held a hand up, fist closed. Meriwether got the idea —*don't move.* He stilled, breathing as quietly as possible despite the hammering of his heart. A nod from the bulky figure and they set off, hugging the courtyard's tall walls. The gate at the end lay open, as if a careless stablehand forgot to shut it.

Beside the gate, the promised stableboy lay beside a dead lantern. He was stretched face-first on the cold stone cobbles, a small pool of something dark seeping from beneath him. *Did the Three want your freedom enough that this boy had to die?* Meriwether wanted to stop, to pull away, but the inn behind him held Tresward Knights, and their gross parody of justice.

They passed through the gate, Meriwether turning from the still form of the stableboy. Outside, the street was quiet and empty. A hanging sign out the front of the inn proclaimed it the *Yellow Mug*. A stylized mug was painted beside the words for the inbreds too dense to read. It was probably yellow, but it was too dark to wage a copper baron on it.

Two horses waited in the street. Meriwether would've figured them for their getaway rides except for the trifling detail of Israel. The Valiant stood by the horses, feet wide, with one of the Knight's glass blades in hand. The sword was massive, the tip resting against the ground. The weapon was almost invisible in the night, glinting its resentment at Meriwether. "Hold. By Tresward law, hold!"

The two hooded figures shared a quick glance. *They can't mean to fight a Knight. That's suicide.* The grip on Meriwether's arm tightened, and his slimmer rescuer broke into a run, dragging him along. He stumbled to follow.

Behind him, the night turned brighter than the day. The hiss of a bottled dragon broke the air, incandescent fury blazing behind them. Meriwether was blinded by the brilliance but followed as best he could. He tripped, knocked into something hard, and was pulled along by his savior, the hand on his arm tighter than ever. He thought he felt resentment in that grip. *They know the man behind us will die. He's tossed his life against glass, and there's only one end to that.*

He was yanked off-balance, their direction changing. Meriwether's sight was coming back, but he was still mostly night-blind. Vague shapes rose from the dark, resolving into walls, wagons, or barrels as they ran.

Shoring up in a narrow doorway, they caught their breath. His rescuer looked behind for chase. "Minkin's good. He'll be all right." A woman's voice, easy to make out now she wasn't whispering. From behind them came a high-pitched chime.

"I'm Meriwether."

"I don't care. Not paid to swap names."

"I just ... thank you." Meriwether put his hand on hers, where it clenched his arm. "I was a dead man."

Her eyes softened a degree. "Ritva." The night behind them still burned with the fierceness of the sun. Ritva squinted. "Minkin knows to get clear. The dragon's bottle doesn't last long."

A dragon's bottle is the blinding tool of assassins and thieves. Who's interest have I attracted? Who'd be fool enough to challenge the Tresward?

The flare from the dragon's bottle dimmed, the night returning like it knew the way. Another chime from behind them, then a scream, dulled by distance. Ritva's gaze hardened. "Come on."

Meriwether fell in behind her. They both knew Minkin was gone. Dead, cut down by Israel. He'd tested his blade against a Knight, and that was the kind of thing only the criminally insane did.

They found an alley heading between two old, tall buildings. The sky above was a sliver of stars. The Three were hidden from view, darkness shrouding all. Rounding a corner, Meriwether spied lamplight ahead. Ritva led him to a street, a lone street lamp holding watch until the dawn.

Beneath the lantern stood a woman. Lean and hard, skin pale like the dead. Her long hair hung in a braid down her back, and she too carried a glass blade. The lamp flickered, the glass capturing the yellow light, tossing it back to lay at Meriwether's feet. Hers was a shorter blade than Israel's: a broadsword, light and nimble. The woman wore full armor. The black sash and three gold bars of a Chevalier lay across her breastplate. A shield hung on her left arm, the golden sun of the Tresward hard and unforgiving in the night.

What had Israel said? *The one who didn't kill you was Geneve. The one who would have is Vertiline. Best remember the difference.* Ritva stiffened, her body rigid as if lightning struck her. She produced twin blades. Plain ol' steel, no good against Tresward glass, but the woman crouched like she was born for this fight. "Run."

"I ... sure, no problem." Meriwether caught a hint of surprise, as if Ritva expected him to say, *no, I'll stay and die with you.* But he had no weapon, and if he did, he'd no idea how to use one other than, *put the sharp bit toward the enemy.*

Meriwether broke and sprinted. His boots slapped against the cobbles. His heart felt like it might break free. He wanted to stop, the pain in his side dragging his steps, slowing him down. He spared a glance behind him and wished he hadn't.

Ritva circled Vertiline. The Knight followed the motion, her shield up, glass blade low. Ritva lunged, her twin blades going high and low. An impossible attack to block. Vertiline moved like flowing water, armor be damned. Ritva's attack, for all it was fast, precise, the lunge of a killer, looked like the clumsy lurching of a newborn babe compared to the Knight. Meriwether's rescuer cut nothing but air.

Vertiline swung her blade horizontally. The slash looked perfect enough to cut dawn. Her glass sword glinted, warm yellow light walking the length of the blade. *A trick of the light? Reflection from the street lamp?* Whatever it was, Ritva took two more steps, then her head toppled free of her shoulders to bounce on the cobbles.

The Knight pointed her blade at Meriwether. "Hold, sinner."

Fuck all *that shit*. Meriwether forgot the pain in his side, running as if his life depended on it. He prayed that a fully-armored Knight would be slower than him. Then he cursed himself for praying, because the Three wouldn't listen to the likes of him.

Ahead he caught the sound of hooves on stone. Horses came toward him at pace. He kept running. He'd rather face a legion of horses than the Knight behind him. He rounded a bend, spying Calterburry's keep hulking in the dark. It sat above the river, a massive bridge at its feet. Crossing the bridge were men bearing the queen's pennant.

Decisions like this shape a man. Run toward Symonet's thugs or face the glass? It wasn't a contest. He kept running, arms pumping, feet slipping a little on the cold stone. As he approached the mounted troops, he wondered if he could escape to their left near the water's edge. A leap, and he'd be in freezing water. It sounded heavenly, because Knights in armor didn't float. He might catch his death in the river, but he liked those odds better than what waited behind him.

He jinked, and almost tasted freedom before the butt of a pole arm collected him in the gut. Meriwether crumbled to the ground, fingers outstretched toward the low brick wall beside the river. Rough hands found his shoulders, hauling him upright.

The mounted officer who'd been too free with his pole arm spared a glance to where Meriwether came from. What he saw made him pale some. To the soldier holding Meriwether, he said, "Go. Take him to the Keep. Be quick about it."

Meriwether found his hands yanked behind him, rough cord binding his wrists as he was frog marched along. *Wait, what? Take me to the Keep? What about a nice, honest jail?*

Vertiline's voice broke over his confusion. "By Tresward law, stand down!"

The *whack-thrum* of crossbows followed. Meriwether tried for a glance behind him. The confusion of horses and soldiers obscured his view, but from Vertiline's position, golden light gleamed.

What are these Knights? How can they take a fusillade of crossbow bolts?

His guards hustled him over the bridge. The yawning maw of the keep's main gate awaited. Tall and strong, it was made from massive wooden slabs reinforced with good steel. The scream of a dying man caught up with him as his escort dragged him into the keep's court-yard. Burning braziers banished gloom. Guards hurried to shut the door behind them. Troops milled about, their chain armor jingling. He counted fifty before giving up.

I'm not sure fifty's enough for three Tresward Knights. Vertiline's out there threshing men and women like wheat. She's on foot, against mounted soldiers, and she didn't look like it bothered her.

His escort dragged him toward the Keep's entrance. These doors were smooth, polished wood, left wide open. Waiting inside was a man, not particularly thin, or particularly handsome. He wore a smile like laborers wore body odor, rank and sour. Bald, with green eyes that missed nothing. "Excellent."

"Hi," Meriwether said. "I—"

He sagged as a soldier gut-punched him, in about the same spot as the pole arm's butt hit him earlier. He whimpered. The green-eyed man kept up his putrescent smile. "Meriwether, I've waited so very long for someone like you."

"Handsome?" Meriwether wheezed.

"Gifted," the man corrected. "I'm Lord Symonet. We have so much to discuss." Symonet gestured to the guards. "Bring him."

As Meriwether was dragged into the keep, he remembered something else Israel said to him. Not the words about Vertiline or Geneve. A curious turn of phrase. *No harm will come to you while you're in our care.*

Meriwether struggled as he was dragged away. He knew what they wanted from him now, and the Tresward's justice seemed the easier death by far.

Chapter Three

Geneve cracked an eye. Her room was dim, but Cophine's light reached pale fingers through a curtained window, letting her see well enough. She saw Israel and Vertiline's cots were empty, sheets cast aside. The height of the Three moons suggested she'd been asleep a handful of hours at best. She sat up, teasing out red hair, fingers arguing with the stubborn knottiness of it. *By the Three. I've slept only a few hours and my hair's tangled worse than a briar patch.*

A quick inventory showed Israel's armor stacked as he'd left it. It was polished silver-bright. Geneve looked to where Vertiline's armor should sit and found it empty. She glanced back to Iz's armor. *His sword's gone.*

She was on her feet before her mind finished processing, snaring Requiem from the foot of her bed. Geneve kicked aside her pillow, grabbing Tribunal from its place of rest, and was out the door, leaving it banging in her wake. The Yellow Mug's private rooms were on the second floor. It took her a moment to clatter down two flights, bare feet slapping on the smooth, worn wood as she went. The common room was full of drunks, but all appeared still.

Geneve stopped to listen. She heard deep breathing and snores.

The terrified, shrill cry of cut metal came to her. Outside, someone with a glass blade fought against one with steel. She sprinted for the main door, barging it aside.

Light assailed her. The magnificent flare of a bottled dragon burned against the cobbled street. Israel stood, tall and strong, against a hooded man who held half a sword like he couldn't believe his bad turn of luck. Iz's eyes were shut against the brightness of the flare. The hooded man gave a frantic yell, lunging with his blade. The sheared end would be sharp enough to kill, especially as Israel wore no armor.

The Valiant turned aside, eyes still closed. His massive glass sword moved as if it had a mind of its own, sweeping a giant arc through his opponent's body. The hooded figure split in two, blood fountaining across the thirsty stone. Israel finished his swing, sword point resting at his feet as the two halves of his opponent slicked to the ground. "Geneve."

Geneve padded to him, scattergun and blade both held low. "Where's Tilly?" She didn't waste words on *are you okay* or *is the prisoner gone*. Both of those were self-evident. Israel wouldn't be on the street, blade naked as a newborn, if the prisoner was secure, and it would take far more than a common thug to bring a Valiant of the Tresward to his knees.

He cracked an eye as the dragon bottle's glare faded. "Buying you some time."

She growled. "Another test?"

"Life is a test." He offered a half-shrug, as if in apology, his massive shoulders rising and falling with the slow roll of an ocean swell.

"You could have stopped him!"

"But then what would you have done? Slept through it?" He stepped to his opponent, turning the pieces over. "Assassin. Poisoned blade." The weapon *tinked* to the cobbles as he rummaged through the dead man's clothes. "No coin. Light armor. Oh, my." He held up a hand crossbow. "Watch out."

Geneve rolled her eyes. "Thank the Three you warned me. An arbalest like that could really do some damage."

His lip quirked. "It is also poisoned."

"There's something else going on." Geneve looked toward Calterburry's keep, the dark tower nosing above the rest of the township's buildings. In the night, it seemed to brood, fires set in the upper windows blazing like ember eyes. "It's not just a sinner."

"That's right." Israel stood, stepping back from the fallen assassin. "Now, work out what it is."

"You could tell me."

"That doesn't sound like much fun." He squinted at the sky, as if measuring time. "Hurry. There's only so much time Vertiline can buy you."

Geneve gritted her teeth, then spun toward the Yellow Mug. Armor, and a horse. Israel cleared his throat. She cast him a glance. "What is it?"

"No armor. You don't have the time. And saddling your horse will take *far* too long." He watched her process that. "You've half a turn of the hourglass left at best before he's a dead man."

"Fuck!" She spun, sprinting for the keep. Geneve wanted to scream at Israel, but it would waste time and breath she couldn't spare. A word lay in her mind: *Harvest.*

He called to her back, "Everything's a test, Gen! Remember the mantra."

Geneve skidded into an alley, losing the dimming light of the dragon bottle. *The mantra, huh? 'We train hard, so life is easy.' I don't see him sprinting through unfamiliar streets at night.*

She lowered her head, charging like a bull. The sinner's fate was the Tresward's to decide, and if Israel was right, Lord Symonet would do a terrible thing this night.

HER HEADLONG RUN TOOK HER PAST A HEADLESS CORPSE BEFORE SHE found Vertiline. The Knight stood in the middle of a street before the keep proper, dead men scattered like fallen logs. A collection of horses milled about, getting in the way.

She didn't stop to talk. There wasn't time. In passing, she gave Tilly a wave with her scattergun. *Go.* She continued, breath rasping in her chest as she passed the Chevalier. Geneve couldn't help but mark the wry smile on Vertiline's face. *Three's Mercy, the two of them conspired to make me run through this town in my underclothes. The Trials weren't this hard.*

Geneve scampered onto the low stone wall of the bridge. Dark water moved slow in autumn's grip below her. The river wound its lazy way through Calterburry, unconcerned with what happened above. She brought her speed down, waiting for Vertiline to pass her. The other Knight approached the keep's closed gate. Tilly spread her arms wide, shield and sword aloft as if in supplication. "Lord Symonet! Open, by the Law of the Three."

Geneve held her breath. *This will go a lot easier on Symonet if he opens the damn door.* In answer, the thrum of a crossbow came from atop the wall. Vertiline stepped a half-pace to her left, cutting the bolt with her glass blade. It sheared in half to clatter behind her. "So be it." She strode toward the gate, shield up. Geneve spied other bolts sprouting like tall grass from the metal surface.

Vertiline made the gate, steps sure. She seemed to gather weight and substance as she came closer, her presence growing with each perfectly placed foot. When she reached the gate, she flung her sword back, the glass catching a twinkle of firelight for a moment. Then she swept it forward.

Geneve held her breath. She needed the noise and furor as a distraction, but seeing the Sacred Storm always took her breath away.

The glass blade hit the steel-reinforced bulwark of the gates. Light shivered down its length, the gates *booming* with the impact. A crack traveled up the tall height of the wood, dust and stone flaking from above. Vertiline swept her arm back, glass blade still bright and strong. *Boom!* The gates shivered again. *Boom!* Another bolt came from above, its noise lost in the cries of panic from men atop the walls. *Boom!*

The gates split down the middle, and Vertiline strode through.

Get moving. Geneve scampered along the bridge's wall, slinging Requiem over her shoulders as she went. The bastard sword banged against her back as she ran, urging her body for more speed. Tribunal's holster she slung across the other shoulder, then she jumped.

She sailed across the dark waters, crashing against the side of Calterburry keep. One hand snared old stone, the cold wall holding her like death's embrace. Her other joined it, and she pulled herself upward, one meager hold at a time.

Hurry. He may be a sinner, but no one deserves to die like that.

※

GENEVE CLIMBED TOWARD AN OPEN WINDOW OVERLOOKING THE water. It was ten meters up. Light came from within, warm like a lantern or fire. She wanted to be in there, not hanging over a drop into cold water of unknown depth. One of her hands slipped, old moss wicked like grease under her fingers. She dangled from one arm, chill wind plucking at her clothes.

Could be worse. You could be in the drink. With a grunt, she dragged herself further up. The window's ten-meter distance shrunk to five, then two. She waited, listening. Sweat drenched her. Her cotton shirt clung to her, wicking away her body heat. *Could be worse. I could be dead.*

No noise came from above, so she pulled herself to the sill. Inside, a meager fire tried to warm an empty room. Wasted effort with an open window, but she appreciated the thought as she swung a leg inside. Padding on bare feet, she huddled by the fire for a moment, rubbing her arms. Her sword and scattergun clinked together at her back, friends forever.

Do enough running and climbing, and one day I'll master the Sacred Storm. She snorted. *Sure. And one day, I'll ride a dragon and kill a demon. Get on with it.*

She padded to the door. Shoulder to the jamb, Geneve eased it open a crack. Outside, a stairwell curled both up and down. She stepped onto the stone, checking up. *Unlikely. Most assholes put their terror dungeons underground. They want to hide from the Light.*

Down it was, then. From outside, she heard the mighty *boom!* of Vertiline making her presence felt. Lord Symonet would need time to repair his keep. Queen Morgan would hear about this. The Justiciars wouldn't be thrilled and would want a conversation with the queen she wouldn't enjoy. None of that would stop what was coming.

A young man is about to die. Stop thinking about the things you can't control and save his life.

She hurried, feet slapping against stone. A door opened below her, a guard stepping out. Geneve didn't slow, running past him and clocking him across the jaw with her left arm. He slammed into the doorframe, beginning his lazy slump to the floor. She didn't wait for the clatter of his helmet hitting the ground.

A landing awaited below. A housecarl caught sight of her, checked left and right, and made to run. Geneve broke into a sprint, launching herself at the man. She slammed him against a wall. "Where is he?"

"I don't know—"

Tribunal was in her hand, the scattergun snuggling under the man's chin. "Friend, there are two ways this will go. Your lord is a sinner and walks away from the Three's light. He'll either take you with him, or you'll leave a free man. Choose wisely."

She was close enough to feel the *huff* of his breath. Young, like her. Wearing mail, but no weapon. Perhaps fled from Vertiline's wrath. Maybe his story told of a family hungry, needing the coin to fill their bellies, and taking work where they could find it. The risk of Vhemin was low this far south, and they never came in great numbers. Joining a lord's service would seem easy enough work.

Right until the Tresward came. Geneve watched him do his numbers, working to the inevitable conclusion. He jerked his chin to her right. "That way. There's a golden door. Behind, steps below."

Geneve eased up her grip, lowering Tribunal. "Thank you. Get on, now."

"What will you do?" The housecarl backed away, but curiosity vied with fear.

"What must be done." She looked at her scattergun. It was heavy, old, yet still gleamed with promise. "Away, now."

He didn't need to be told again, the clatter of his boots fading into the distance. Geneve hurried, finding the promised golden door. It lay open, torches in sconces leading their way into the belly of the keep. She ran down, taking the steps three at a time. Her breath was sure and steady, her body ready, her heart certain.

The steps ended at another door, this one also open. She could see old stone beyond, older than the rest of Calterburry's keep. Two guards stood ready, but she imagined more within. They drew swords as she ran at them. Geneve thought of the thousands of lessons she'd had and selected one. *Be like the howl of wind.*

She dragged Requiem from its sheath. The steel blade felt light, as if it wanted to leap forward. Geneve caught the swing of a guard against her steel, then swept underneath the crossed swords like a gust of dry air. From her position behind the man, she swung her blade like the eddy of autumn leaves. The steel slid through his chain amour and flesh like neither were stronger than spider's silk.

Her quick glance of the room as she'd spun confirmed what was going on. The sinner lay atop a stone slab, leather straps holding him in place. His chest was bare, showing the crisscrossed scarring of a terrible past. Above him, a robed figure with a black mask of wood held his hands aloft.

Around them were ten others in robes and masks, five aside. *Twelve including the remaining guard. They should have brought more men.* Geneve bared her teeth in a snarl, her steel whispering like wind through grass. It took the other guard's arm off at the wrist, blood fountaining like a geyser. She dodged the spray, ending his scream short as her blade took his head.

The central asshole chanted, his voice deep but shaky. The sinner on the slab writhed, a cry escaping him. Wisps of smoke strained free of his flesh. *Be faster. The Harvest's begun.* She leveled Tribunal, the scattergun booming. The central asshole quit his chanting, mask gone, nothing but gore left beneath it.

Another stepped up as if to take over. Geneve ran at him, swinging Tribunal. The scattergun roared a second time, shearing the would-be-hero's arm from his side. He dropped, screaming, other hand at the bloody stump. She let her firearm fall, its two rounds spent.

A third made to intervene. Geneve pirouetted as she ran, Requiem leaving her hand in a graceful whirl of steel. It sheared through the man's torso, cleaving him in half. He gurgled to the ground.

She made it to the let's-call-it-an-altar, bounding atop. The sinner lay beneath her, eyes wide. Geneve could almost feel the panic and fear coming from him. She turned a slow circle, eying the masked figures. "You will not Harvest him today."

A laugh from her left, clear and bright. A woman, with just enough sneer in it to confirm her as a noble. "You can't stop us. You threw away your sword. And it wasn't even *glass*." This last came with incredulity-meets-mocking.

"She's right," the sinner hissed. "I'm worried about this too. I don't want to appear ungrateful, but—"

"You think I need a sword?" Geneve straightened, foot either side of the sinner. "A baby with a rattle could take the coddled lot of you."

A rush of movement came from her left. She spun, bringing her left foot up in a crescent rise, then bringing her heel smashing down on the head of her assailant. Wood cracked, the mask breaking, and they dropped like a stone.

"I think that one's got a blade." The sinner pointed with his chin to Geneve's right.

"Which one?" She spared a glance to the sinner at her feet.

"That one. Tall. Wearing a hood and a mask. Yeah, that guy."

"I was beginning to miss the feel of steel." Geneve slipped from the side of the slab, heading for the slightly-taller asshole there.

Slightly-taller gave a look about as if seeking allies, then drew a sliver of steel. It was the length of Geneve's hand, and as wide as her index finger where blade met hilt. No crossguard to speak of, just a slip of metal to ease between someone's ribs. An assassin's weapon, not made for any honorable purpose.

A memory of training with Israel came to her. Geneve, on her knees in the dirt, blood coming from a split lip. He'd hit her with a wagon wheel, and she'd called it *unfair*. Israel had shaken his head and said, *there's no honor in battle. Just men and women, spilling their guts on the ground*.

It didn't stop her hating the slightly-taller asshole. She strode toward him, keeping her steps perfect, her body balanced. He lunged for her, and she met him like a lover, arms wide, then swept inside his blade, grabbing him about the middle. Geneve slammed her forehead into his mask, cracking the wood and hearing a *crunch* of bone beneath. He screamed, and while he was wasting good breath on that, she lifted him off the ground, slamming his length against the old stone.

The blade rattled free, chittering across the stone to rest at the foot of another. Geneve smiled like a cat. "Take it."

"Will you hit me if I do?" A man, uncertain, unsure if this was a joke or the final moments of his life.

"I'm going to hit you either way. Better to have a blade in your hand."

"Are you *mad?*" the sinner croaked.

The uncertain man scrabbled for the blade. Geneve ran at him. He swept the knife from the floor, swinging a savage rend toward her gut. She dropped the blade of her hand against the bones of his wrist, feeling the bone break. His hand spasmed, releasing the knife.

It kept rising as she knew it would, momentum carrying the bright dart of steel to her eye height. She spun, leg whipping around to catch her opponent in the side of the head. He and the knife fell at the same time. Geneve snared the blade from the air but left the man to slump against the floor.

She breathed hard, eying the remaining five. They stood on the other side of the sinner's slab. One bent, and with a grunt, returned upright holding Requiem. The bastard sword was a smiling gash of shiny red in the torchlight.

Requiem's holder placed the blade across the sinner's throat. "Don't come any closer. We'll kill him."

"By the Three," the sinner whimpered. "Are you a moron?"

The man with Requiem leaned close to the sinner. Through holes in his mask, Geneve could see the glint of his eyes. "She wants you alive, fool. If I open your throat, she doesn't get what she wants."

"To be fair, neither do I." The sinner rolled his eyes. "I know you're simple people, but she's a Tresward Knight. Death on two legs. The honed edge of the Three's will. They say just one Valiant can take a legion with a single length of glass in their hand. And here you are, making a bargain with one. That's not the funny part."

Geneve's fingers toyed with the blade she held, finding its balance. It was well made, if for an evil purpose. She stepped to her left, making her slow way around the slab. The man holding Requiem didn't move, but the other four shifted away, trying to keep the slab between them and the killer in their midst.

"What's the funny part?"

"They're going to kill me anyway, you imbecile!" The sinner barked a laugh. It looked convincing enough to Geneve, the right level of hysteria bubbling through cracked and bloody lips. "You cut me here, or she cuts me out there, it's all the same end. You're doing their work for them."

The man holding Requiem considered the blade for a moment, then lifted it from the sinner's throat. He stepped clear of the slab, sword low. *This one knows bladework*. Geneve held the assassin's knife so the edge lay against her arm. She crouched, placing her feet with care.

Her opponent pulled his mask free, revealing a man's face. Too-white skin, dark eyes, and short straw-colored hair. He wore the feral smile of a rabid dog. "I've always wanted to test myself against a Knight."

"It's your lucky day." Geneve remembered another of Israel's lessons. She'd been jumped in a market, a huddle of men with angry faces attacking her with lengths of wood. She'd left them about her feet, and when she asked Iz why they'd come for her, he'd shook his head. *When you wear gold, silver wants to feel it*. "Come, silver man."

They ran at each other. Requiem hungered for her flesh, but she knew her old friend. She remembered the weight of the blade, how it handled, and the sound it made as it cut air. She met its kiss with the assassin's sliver, running the edge down Requiem's length in a shower of sparks.

Geneve brought her knee into her opponent's groin. He lurched, falling against her. She slid down into a wide stance, her leg knocking his aside. He stumbled, and as he fell away, she swung her arm in a savage, tight arc.

The assassin blade slicked through his neck. He let Requiem fall, both hands trying to stop the tide of his life leaving him as he staggered away. She turned her face aside from the spray.

Four left. One stood at the head of the slab, using it for cover. She flung the assassin's blade in a tumble through the air. It *chunked* home as she wiped her face clean. Eyes clear, she looked at the three remaining.

One shook her head, a ringlet curl escaping the side of her hood. "Fuck *all* this. I'm not even with these guys." She ran for the door behind Geneve.

Geneve retrieved Requiem. The hilt remembered her hand, its long edge ready for what must be done. Geneve turned, tossing the blade again. It carved into the fleeing woman, knocking her from her feet. She faced the final two. "There is no redemption for Harvesters. It's written. It's *law*."

One dropped to the ground, returning to his feet with the assassin blade. "Your law, maybe. You keep all the power for yourself! The Tresward controls everything. All we want is a tiny spoonful. Where's the charity of the Three?"

Geneve stalked closer. "Charity is in the hearts of people. You just have to look for it."

"And what of your charity? You're cutting us down like animals!" Geneve reached him, dodging the wild swipe of the blade. She grabbed his arm, twisting away and rising tall. His elbow broke against her shoulder. He screamed as the blade dropped free. She caught it, turned, and stabbed him under the arm. Blood frothed forth.

The final robed figure ran. Geneve gauged the distance, tossed the knife up, and spun a kick into it. The heel of her foot hit the knife, steel flashing across the room. It *thocked* into the runner's spine, dropping them to the uncaring stone.

Geneve walked from the sinner to collect Requiem and Tribunal. Weapons secured, she began the slow return to his side. His eyes were wide and bright. "Say. I'm Meriwether. We met before, at the, uh..."

"I remember." She found the assassin's blade and used it to sever the leather straps binding him in place. Geneve helped him to his feet, watching as he massaged blood back into his wrists.

"You're not going to let me go, are you?"

Geneve shook her head. "No. You're for the cage, and Judgment."

The sinner gave a weary nod. "Just as he said, no harm will come to me. Although," he cast an arm at the ruin of bodies on the floor, "this was *almost* harm. It felt close for a while."

"It *was* close, sinner. They wanted the sweet, corrupt thing inside you. They wanted to suck it from your flesh." Geneve leaned close, whispering. "They say it's the worst way to die."

The sinner gave her a bright smile. "But we'll never know, right? Two reasons." He counted on his fingers. "First, you killed all these guys! Good job. Second, all the people who've been Harvested haven't been asked how it felt."

Maybe it was the adrenaline, or the feeling of a job well done, but she couldn't help herself. Geneve laughed, almost a snort, then clamped down on it. "What's your sin?"

"You tell me." He got off the slab, moving like his back hurt, or he was a hundred years old, or a combination of the two. She got a good look at the scarred marring of his flesh. *Who did that to him? That's not the Three's justice.* "Those are *not* comfortable."

She considered the knife in her hand. *It seems a lot of work to take him to a Justiciar for Judgment. But it's the hard way, so our world gets the easy path.* Geneve offered him the knife. "Here. A souvenir."

"Hah. Wait, you're not joking?" He looked at the blade resting on her palm. "Aren't you afraid I'll kill you with it?"

"Not even a little."

"I should feel insulted." He took the knife, lips pulling from his teeth in an expression of disgust as he wiped it clean on a robe of the fallen. "It's true, isn't it? Tresward Knights. The strong shield against the leeching tide of the dark. *And* you do all that in your nightclothes."

"There wasn't time for anything else."

He tossed the knife in the air, making to catch it but fumbling. The blade chimed against the stone. He huffed a sigh, then knocked back a groan as he retrieved it. "Are you a," he wiggled his fingers, "Chevalier?"

Geneve frowned. "No."

"Valiant?"

She shook her head. "No. I'm an Adept."

The sinner whistled. "Thirteen guys? And you're just an Adept?" At her darkening scowl, he held up his hands, one still holding the knife. He seemed to realize what he did, yanking the knife down. "I don't mean it like that. I mean, I did, but not like *that* that."

"You're wondering why the 'strong shield against the leeching tide of the dark' sends an Adept in her nightclothes into a keep against a hardened group of cultists, all intent on Harvesting the magic from your marrow? As opposed to, say, a Chevalier?"

He cocked an eyebrow. "Something a little like that, yes."

"It was what we had time for. Tilly held the keep's attention."

"Tilly's the one with the braid? Vertiline?" At Geneve's nod, he looked toward the steps leading out. "I'm so fucked."

"Come, sinner. Let's get you to your cage. You'll be safer there." She husbanded the man from the room but spared a glance at the fallen. *Lord Symonet, a queen's man. His advisors, all intent on Harvest. They claim they want equality. Is it true? Is this what Israel wants me to see? The weak and petty hearts of all men?*

Chapter Four

G eneve sucked her knuckle. *The skin was split, and the bright tang of blood lay on her tongue. She wasn't sure if it was from her hand, or the knock her lip had against her teeth.*

She wasn't sure of very much right now. Her ears rang from the blunt blow of a practice blade. Geneve had fallen onto her butt, legs splayed in front of her, but she hadn't gone all the way down, which she was certain annoyed Wincuf. The larger boy loomed above her, his wooden sword leveled at her face. "Yield."

Geneve thought about that. What yielding to Wincuf would feel like, and what it might feel like if she didn't. She felt rather than saw eyes on her. Perhaps Israel's, brows furrowed in a frown. The noises of the practice room faded to silence, the clack-clack of wood on wood vanishing like heat from a doused fire. Her peers waited for what she would do.

Yielding wouldn't bring her dishonor. She'd been bested by a larger opponent. More skilled, too. She'd been in the keep for a year, eating like a horse and training to be strong like the Knights who walked the halls.

If I yield to Wincuf today, it won't stop there. The clarity of the thought felt like benediction, a release from choice. She couldn't *yield, because it wouldn't be the last time. Geneve spat blood on the mat, then shook her head, angry red hair lashing.* "No."

Wincuf's face twisted in a snarl, and he swung the sword back to hit her

"Lying is a sin against the Three."

"I'm having trouble with all," he waved a hand at her, the room, her blade, and the world at large, "this. You're taking me to execution—"

"Judgment."

"At which point, I'll die, which is a *kind* of execution." He wiggled his eyebrow. "But before you kill me, you're buying me good food, nice mead, and keeping me safe. It would cost a *fortune* to buy a Tresward Knight's protection."

"It can't be bought."

"As you say." Meriwether took another sip. "Also, you're drinking."

"There is no sin in good food, drink, and company." She took another pull of her drink for emphasis. "Have you heard of Addler the cobbler?"

Meriwether blinked. "Who?"

"A sinner, like yourself." Vertiline shook her head. "Or not. He was framed. Knights took him to the Justiciars for Judgment. The Light found him free of sin. They let him go."

"To make more shoes?"

"I don't know. That's not the important part of the story." She eyed him over her tankard.

"You're looking after me in case I'm innocent?" Meriwether took another sip. "How many others were like Addler?"

"None."

He felt his hopes sink into a pit of nausea, roiling in his belly. The excellent mead turned sour and flat in his mouth. "This is why you didn't want her to give me the knife, huh?"

Vertiline put her mug down as if it were fragile. She took a moment before meeting his eyes. "I'm sorry, Meriwether. There's no mercy in hiding from you what lies at the end of this trail."

"You're right." His lips twisted into a snarl despite himself. "Of *course* you're right. You're a Knight. You can do no wrong."

She regarded him for a time. "We can all do wrong." Then she stood, striding toward the bar. He thought she felt guilty, but after thinking for a time, he realized it was more likely compassion. *They do a thing they think is terrible, because to not do it would be worse.* It was worth bearing in mind. These Knights were not unfeeling warriors of justice. They were *believers*, and that was worse.

He thought about the knife, and who gave it to him, and why she did that. *They believe, but it doesn't mean they don't care.* He wished he'd never come to Calterburry. It was the start of his destruction.

❦

DESTRUCTION WORKS BOTH WAYS.

The giant Israel said Meriwether was under their protection. He'd left him with the quick, slender Vertiline, departing with Geneve. Meriwether didn't know where they went. *Probably murdering sinner puppies.*

For all that Vertiline was the leanest of the three, she didn't look weak. Meriwether watched her walk the bar area. Her eyes were every-where, missing nothing. Though she wore heavy steel armor it didn't drag her steps. Vertiline looked like she could wear armor until the end of days and be happy about it. *What do they put in Tresward water?* Whether they drank strength or were given it by the Light, these soldiers didn't bow to the weight of the world.

Meriwether pushed his mead about. The bottom of the tankard scraped across wood. He felt vibrations through his fingertips. *Empty, like my hopes.*

Wait a minute.

He stood, a tiny flare of hope kindling inside. Vertiline's eyes snapped to him as he stood. Meriwether gave her a cheery wave with his tankard. *Need a refill.* She nodded, so he slipped toward the bar.

The Yellow Mug filled with the usual sort you'd expect. Drunks, working men, and working women. A man near the door looked at a lass serving drinks with a hungry stare. Meriwether glanced up, taking in the balcony ringing the common area. An older woman looked at a younger one below with unbridled hate. Laughter boiled up like a spring from a booth near the kitchen. Someone shouted a greeting. People, being people.

Some came full of hope, some looked for it. But a few sought the most common of things: trouble. Meriwether settled against the bar, raising his tankard. The barkeep, still not willing to meet the eyes of the Tresward's prize, managed to swap his empty for a fresh one without looking at Meriwether.

He sipped. *Still excellent. Seems a shame to waste it, but that's how it's got to be.* Meriwether chose a section of bar unremarkable in every way except for the surly, lump-shouldered man clutching a tankard like it was a throat to choke. Meriwether turned to face the man. Beard, none too clean, with a few hints of gray about the muzzle. Dark eyes, set against white skin. A scar, from a burn rather than blade.

Those dark eyes turned in Meriwether's direction. "Fuck off."

"Hello, good sir." Meriwether raised his tankard. "Buy you a round?"

The man straightened from his hunch, showcasing an impressive barrel chest, above a less impressive sagging gut. "Fuck," he stabbed a blunt finger at Meriwether's chest, "*off*."

Meriwether regarded the finger on his chest. Gnarled knuckles, thick wrist, callused palms. He could be a pit fighter as easy as a mason. Meriwether nodded, putting a little pity in the motion. "Elean's Masonry's put you out of work, hasn't it?"

A squint and a grunt, but the finger didn't move. "What do you know of it?"

"Only that Elean told me she'd thrown the, how did she put it, 'layabout rabble' out the door when she took over." Meriwether let his gaze travel the length and breadth of the man. "It felt odd that a woman would hire nothing but other women. Discriminatory, and that's a fact, but having taken the measure of you, I see she had wisdom."

The finger on his chest moved away, allowing its fellows to join the fun. The man grabbed the front of Meriwether's tunic, hoisting him onto his tiptoes. "What did you say?"

Lucky guess, and a good one. "That you stink of offal, are a fool, and your parents were brother and sister." He tossed his mead into the face of his antagonist.

Hush spread from the pair like ripples in a lake. The barkeep froze, tankard under a spigot overflowing to the floor. A bard, fingers still on his lute strings, gawped. The woman on the balcony above stopped staring her hate and turned curious eyes on Meriwether.

The silence wasn't complete. The steady *drip, drip* of mead leaving the stonemason's face, traveling the length of his tree-trunk arms, and trickling to the floor. There was a clink-scrape of booted feet, as Vertiline—previously near the lutist—made all speed for Meriwether's location.

The stonemason's other fingers, itching to join the fun, curled into a fist. Meriwether watched the motion, and as the fist cocked for a blow, he waited for it to land. It came, sure as spring rain, hard as an anvil, collecting Meriwether in the side of the head.

Stars and darkness. Red and black and white. A tumbling scuffle, Meriwether sliding along rough wood floorboards. Feet about him, then the silence broke like a storm. The stonemason roared, *"I'll kill you, you little shit!"* A man behind him swung a stool into the brute, splinters raining. Tankards flew. Wood broke. Across the bar, a grand melee erupted.

You have five seconds. Make them count. Meriwether lurched to his feet, feeling the floor shift beneath him like a ship at sea. *The floor's not moving. It's just that your brains are still sloshing about your skull.* His unsteady motion saved him as a chair hurtled through the space he'd occupied a second earlier. He jabbed a finger behind the stonemason toward Vertiline. "She made me do it!"

He spun—sloppy, like a thick soup—on his heel and made for the door. It was ten short meters and a lifetime away. He thought he heard Vertline's shout over the roar of the crowd, then a crash and clatter of wood on steel. *Don't look. Run.* Meriwether dodged a punch to his head, mostly by accident, and hurdled a prone fellow. He made the front door, pulling it partly open before a woman crashed into it beside him. The door slammed shut.

He glanced back. Vertiline stood in the center of the storm. Blood trickled from a cut in her scalp, but it did nothing to stem the murder in her eyes. She held a scattergun in a gauntleted fist, pointed at Meriwether's head.

A chair hit Vertiline in the side as her scattergun roared. It came from her right, a beautiful arc of flight over the bar. It shattered, wooden water against her steel rock, but enough to foul her aim. The scattergun's blast tore the woman at Meriwether's side apart, her blood painting the door. A circle of pockmarks sprouted on the wood around the silhouette of her body.

Good-natured brawling turned to fear. Fear went straight to panic without pausing for thought. A surge of humanity came for Meriwether, sweeping him up in its tight, urgent embrace. The door creaked, then popped with a crack of scattergun-weakened wood. Meriwether spilled outside into the cool night, crowd dragging him along like a deep-sea current.

He let himself go with it. Meriwether wanted to run, felt the panting *need* to flee, but didn't want to draw Vertiline's eye. She'd be outside faster than a Feybrind's sprint. Angrier than a Vhemin war party. So, he drifted with the masses. Got swept about a corner of a building. Resisted the urgency of the throng as they moved toward the keep—*I've had enough of that tonight, thanks*—and ducked into an alley empty of souls or their fears.

He hunkered low. His heart beat so hard he feared Vertiline would hear the war drum thunder of it. The night turned cold now he'd stopped moving. Without the warmth of the Yellow Mug's arms about him, he felt it seep through the rough cotton of his shirt. Meriwether had no coat or cloak. No coins in his pocket, not the bright yellow of a sovereign or even the brittle, tarnished brown of a baron.

I've been in worse scrapes. The cage they brought is death. It's an end to everything, even the cold, so get moving. Meriwether crept along the alley, hugging a wall. His fingers trailed against old wood, cold stone, and slid against wet moss. His boot *tinked* against a bottle, and he froze.

Nothing. No movement in the alley. No hint of pursuit. The cries of the crowd, fading. He heard no clink of armored boot and didn't see the terrible gleam of a glass sword hungering in the dark.

Meriwether was free.

⁂

THE PATH TO CALTERBURRY'S MAIN GATES WERE EASY TO FIND. THE north gate was the common trade route with the baronies and merchant cities that hugged the mountain's spine. The west gate was smaller, leading to Three knew where, but it would have guards. Patrols, stern men with an angry purpose now Lord Symonet was gone: find the sinner. Bring him to the Tresward.

That's why he didn't go that way.

Calterburry was bisected by a river. Spring rains were far behind them, so it wasn't flowing with the massive torrent of warmer times. Diving into the current was borderline suicide, but it was *also* less likely to be policed by Knights. Their armor wasn't known for its buoyancy.

Meriwether hurried though the streets. A foul, reeking pile afforded him a castoff cloak barely more than rags. It was shit-stained, but it was better than death, and where he was going would clean it better than an hour against a washboard.

Shivering, he picked up speed, blowing into his hands to get some feeling back. *I need to save my strength. Kindling ancient embers while planning a dive into icewater isn't a good use of time.* He made the low stone wall lining the river near the northwest of Calterburry. It flowed from here to the southeast, a long, mostly-straight, mostly-freezing run toward its eastern exit, and then to the salty throat of the sea.

Meriwether glanced about. Still no sign of chase. Perhaps Vertiline wasn't good at finding people? Maybe the Tresward Knights were exemplars at combat, but sucked at tracking? He clutched his stinking cloak close, then dived into the water.

The frigid wake welcomed him in. It was so cold he felt like he'd been punched. He tried not to scream, or inhale the water, thrashing in the water's dark depths.

A moment later, his head broke the surface. The city's tanners had their outlet closer to the southeast, and he prayed they wouldn't be operating at this hour. He didn't want to be cold *and* swimming in a mire of pollution.

The current pulled him along, just one more piece of flotsam making its way to the sea. He knocked against stone, the current ungentle with him. Ahead, he spied the exit. The river ran beneath the walls. Bobbing along, feeling the cold leach the life from him, he wondered how he'd arrived at this point.

I've done nothing wrong.

The river swept him under the tall walls of the keep, and he was into open countryside. The bank of the river widened outside the stone confines of its funnel through the city. He struck toward the northern bank. To the north were towns. Villages, with commerce, and fires he could warm himself against. Loose coins might find his pocket, and he could head far away from the burning need of the Tresward.

His fingers found stone, and he dragged himself from the freezing water. Meriwether felt the cold like an anvil atop him. A weight, trying to hold his head beneath the water. He fought it, shivering uncontrollably. He staggered from the water, breeches dripping, the sodden fabric clutching him with the cold fingers of the grave.

With waterlogged boots, he made his way up the bank to the grassy verge. He thought of resting, then remembered the Knights after him. Their cage waited. Meriwether clutched a fistful of grass, hauling himself over the bank's verge and into the night plains beyond Calterburry.

"Hello," Geneve said. "Did you remember the knife?" She stood in armor, starlight reflecting from it. Beyond her, a horse grazed, tail swishing in the night like it was offended. No light of a warming fire. Just a woman clad in steel, and her horse.

Meriwether looked to the river. "How?" Back to Geneve. "But… the river!" And the horse. "I was free!"

"You're cold," she corrected. "It's addled your wits."

Beyond Geneve's horse Meriwether thought he spied a figure. Beside a tree with a trunk wider than the giant Israel, a slip of shadow watched. He caught the glint of eyes in the dark. A monster, hunting prey. He wanted to shout a warning, but he shook uncontrollably with cold. Teeth chattering, he raised a shaking arm.

Geneve didn't move, not to look over her shoulder, not to apprehend him. *Fine. If she's not going to do anything about monsters in the dark, I'm out of here.* He broke into a run. He made it four staggering steps before his limbs gave out. Stretching his length upon the ground, he marveled at how warm he felt, like his body remembered the heat of the sun and gave it back to him. The figure beside the tree watched, perhaps waiting, and Meriwether wondered if he would die here, either from the cold or from fangs against his throat.

He spied a plant before his eyes. In the north, they called it *angel's kiss*. He'd no idea what the inbreds in the south called it. A tiny shrub, the soft leaves tickling his nose. He lurched forward, fingers snaring at the plant. Meriwether couldn't feel his hands, didn't know if he'd plucked the herb, or left it on the ground beneath him.

Then he thought nothing at all as darkness lapped his cheek, traveled down his body, and dragged him below.

Chapter Six

The sinner lay in his cage, still out for the count. His lips remained blue despite the swaddling of blankets about him, a bustle of heated rocks within. Geneve didn't know if he'd live and wasn't sure if he deserved to.

That's not for you to decide. The Justiciars will make the call.

Tristan shifted beneath her, eager to press on despite spending half the night beside a freezing stream in the dark. The horse nickered, raised his front left foot, and tossed his mane.

Geneve concured. Calterburry didn't agree with her. Not Lord Symonet and his cult, the guard, or the scenery. Even Birdsong Alley hadn't kept her interest, perhaps because the sinner had lied to her there. He'd picked her to whisper his deceit to, and she wouldn't forget it.

Gylbard, the short innkeeper, spoke with Israel a distance away. A respectful handful of paces back Vertiline waited, hands clasped before her. The three Knights gathered in the inn's courtyard, horses saddled and ready. Geneve was the only one mounted.

All wore armor. The burnished surfaces tasted fire in the early morning light. Even Vertiline's shone, despite her ... vigorous evening.

The Chevalier wore a sour look, mouth turned down at the

corners, brow pinched. Her hair lay in its customary braid down her back, glass sword at her hip. Her shield was lashed to her horse's saddlebags. Geneve saw no indication she'd fought last night other than a tiny nick at her hairline.

The people of Calterburry will remember her far longer than she would them.

Gylbard wore his horrific smile, perhaps unaware of its effect. "Four solars."

Israel gave a soft cough, leaning closer as if he hadn't heard correctly. "Did you say *four?*" He put hands on hips, armor *clinking* like it was upset. Iz craned to examine the Yellow Mug. The inn stood as it always had. A modest trail of smoke trickled from a chimney, a reminder of the morning's excellent breakfast. "I could *buy* a tavern for that."

Gylbard blinked. "Only if it was already on fire. My inn," he gestured behind him, "is not aflame. It *is* missing a front door. Tables, broken. Chairs, reduced to matchwood, or taken by miscreants." He rubbed his nose. "Miscreants now afoot, because the good lord's guard are dead or worse."

"What's worse than dead?" Vertiline broke her stillness to turn a jaundiced eye on the innkeeper. "Being a guest of your tavern? I'll remind you of the contract with the Tresward. Safe and secure facilities for holding prisoners. And strong walls, to keep *miscreants* out."

"I've got this," Iz said.

"As you say, Valiant." Tilly's tone suggested she doubted if Israel had this, or anything at all, really.

"Ah," Gylbard offered. "To be fair, and Knights are known for their equitable views, our small township isn't equipped to deal with the Scarlet Shadow."

Geneve patted Tristan's neck to calm him. *Scarlet Shadow? Here? Is that who stole the sinner away?* It made sense. Israel sending her to get the sinner, with him and Vertiline tackling the assassins one on one. *Everything is a test, but sometimes tests can be a shield against a greater darkness.*

Israel reached into his belt pouch, retrieving two bars of platinum. "I will offer you *two* solars."

Gylbard puffed up like an angry bird. "But—"

"Two solars is more than fair for a door and some tables." Israel dropped the coins from one hand into the gauntleted palm of the other. They chimed, *tink tink*. "Would you prefer interdiction?"

The horrific smile arrived back on Gylbard's lips, like it'd taken a moment for a tryst out the back and was satisfied with affairs. "No, Valiant. Of course not."

Geneve shifted on her saddle, feeling a twinge from a muscle abused during the sinner's rescue. *Interdiction might be the right approach. Ask the Clerics to root out corruption here, find who was responsible, and burn it to ash with the Light of the Three.* But Iz was the senior Knight. It was his call, and in all their time together, she'd never known him to make the wrong one.

Israel gave the coins to Gylbard, who scuttled like a sand crab back inside. The Valiant strode to his black charger, walking like his armor weighed less than gossamer. He paused, hand on pommel. "Something to say?"

"No, Valiant." Vertiline hadn't moved.

"I can *feel* it, Tilly. It seeps from the rocks. It radiates from you like the damn cold in this place."

Vertiline shifted. "The sinner should be dead."

Geneve winced, and wished she were somewhere else. Tilly and Iz went back a long, long way. On the road, they were less formal than in a Tresward keep. Friends, sharing the road. Vertiline almost never called Israel Valiant, and she'd just done it twice in as many minutes. His title was reserved for other places policed by Clerics with their robes and musty tomes. "I should ... check something. Perhaps out in the main street." She made to turn Tristan for the courtyard's exit, bridle clenched in too-tight fingers.

"Hold." Israel let go of his pommel, walking to Vertiline. They stood two paces apart. Two armored figures, faces impassive, all weakness hidden on the inside. "It's not your fault."

"I was on watch."

"It's my fault," Israel continued as if they were discussing the weather. "This sinner is ... tricky. A good judge of his fellow man, a better judge of situations, and willing to risk all for a hint of freedom."

"I left him to—"

"And when we're with the Justiciars, sinner in their care, I will make a report." He looked to the sky, watching thin wisps of cloud for a few heartbeats. "They'll understand who made a bad call."

Vertiline unclasped her hands. "I wanted—"

"You wanted to take his hope but leave him kindness. A few days of mercy before the end. There is no crime in the eyes of the Three for that, Tilly." He bowed his head a fraction, as if in acquiescence to something unspoken between them. "There are greater crimes."

The moment held. Vertiline, her hands empty of a blade but ready for action. Israel, still and quiet, massive and strong. Then Tristan tossed his head, chuffing. Israel looked, then laughed. "Young Tristan has the idea." He strode for his charger, vaulting to the saddle in a single, fluid motion.

Vertiline nodded, sparing a single glance for the sinner in his cage. Her face was hard, but her eyes didn't hold their usual coldness. She put a foot in a stirrup, getting astride her chestnut with the fluidity of a levitating sorcerer. Israel led the way from the Yellow Mug's court-yard, Vertiline in tow. The oxen, sensing a change in the winds, followed without urging. The cage jostled atop its bed of wood.

Geneve was left alone in the courtyard. It was time to put this town behind them. They had their sinner and putting Calterburry to rights could wait for another group of Knights.

THEY MADE CAMP ON THE ROAD. THE DAY'S JOURNEY WAS LONG. Geneve felt thin and pale like too-stretched taffy, transparent and bright in places, thick and slow in others. Her saddle did nothing to soften the road, especially with twenty kilos of Smithsteel on her back, and she thought wistfully of the Yellow Mug's beds.

The sinner was awake, lips no longer blue. She rummaged around the cart and by proxy his cage, hunting for tents and supplies. "Do I get one?" His voice was raw, cracked with remembered cold, but held a little more warmth than she thought she deserved.

"One what?" Geneve met his eyes. Blue, set in a pale face. They held fear, and hope, and made her look away.

"Tent. Fire. Food." His hands found the bars. They were clean, not a callus in sight. A far cry from her own, used to swinging steel to part a person's soul from their body.

"All of that, yes." She almost shifted away, then held herself still. "We put a tarp over your cage."

"*My* cage, is it?" He leaned back, staring about as if examining a fine room. "I see you've spared no expense."

Geneve snorted, about to reply when Israel's call brought her about. "It's time."

"By the Three," she whispered. "Can it not be?"

"I heard that," Israel said. "It's always time."

"Time for what?" the sinner asked.

Geneve shook her head, tramping back to Israel with weary feet. Their campsite was off the road's shoulder, a small hillock hiding them from other travelers. The grass seemed well used to this treatment, a small trail leading here from the rutted roadway. A circle of charcoal and ash remembered a previous fire.

Tristan was enjoying dew-sweet grass, grazing beneath a tree. Chesterfield, Israel's monstrous beast, shouldered next to Troubles, Tilly's chestnut mare. It looked to Geneve as if the two didn't care if their masters squabbled. They'd be friends anyway.

Israel and Vertiline waited by the circle of black in the clearing's middle. Israel held a deck of cards out. "Who's first?"

Vertiline reached for a card with a growl. "Three's mercy." She tossed the card to the ground, face up. It showed a Challenge of Might: a figure and a horse engaged in tug o' war.

Geneve took a second card. "Oh, come *on*." A figure on the card was frozen in an eternal sprint, a wind devil nipping their heels. *Of all the Challenges of Speed, and I draw sprints.*

Israel fingered the deck, then drew a card. His face broke into a grin of delight. "Cophine smiles, friends." He tossed a Challenge of Endurance atop the other card: three figures, one face-down, one crouched, and one leaping, hands in the air.

Vertiline wheeled on him. "This game is rigged. Every time—and I mean *every* time—you draw Prisoner's Punishment."

Vertiline and Geneve drew one more card each, completing the Challenges of Agility and Flexibility—summersaults and splits. Geneve dropped her load of camping supplies, reaching to unbuckle her armor. Israel shook his head. "Full armor."

Vertiline rolled her eyes. "Of course." She went to get a rope.

Geneve retrieved a rope from her own saddlebags. The Challenges were a Tresward game used to keep the body fresh on the road. The deck was officially called Destiny's Supplicant, and more enthusiastically known as Three's Bastard. It held a range of exercises to be done at the end of each day. The only escape was injury, and even then the leading Knight would often find ... *creative* options for an injured warrior. If your arm was in a sling, you got one-armed push-ups instead of the regulation form.

Israel once told her it encouraged the right mindset going into battle. She thought that sounded like a special kind of bullshit invented by a group of sadists but held her peace.

The last rays of the sun kept them company while they exercised. The ropes were tied to saddles, and each Knight tried tug-o-war with their horse. The horses, for their part, appeared to find this hilarious. Tristan dragged Geneve through the clearing, her armored feet digging up grass and loam while she gritted her teeth, sweat streaming beneath metal.

Only Israel looked happy. He went through the motions of Prisoner's Punishment like getting face-first on the dirt, climbing to his feet, and jumping was the thing he liked most in the world. His enthusiasm was infectious. Israel wore forty or fifty summers on him, yet grinned as he jumped or ran. Geneve tried to keep up, breath ragged, but couldn't manage it.

The sun's setting behind hills marked the end of Three's Bastard. Geneve tore her breastplate free with relish, the buckles difficult to manage in shaky hands. The cool of the night cut through the sweat of her undergarments, and she arched her back, breathing hard, relishing the wind's touch.

Vertiline collapsed on the ground in a clatter of metal, groaning.

Israel stood by them, armor glinting in the sun's fading light. "I'll make dinner."

"Gods, no," Vertiline whimpered. Israel answered with a laugh, unbuckling his breastplate, and bustling about for supplies.

Geneve bent, setting a fire. She spared a glance for the sinner, silent through all, his eyes wide like he watched the special works of the criminally insane. She turned away, a smile teasing the corners of her mouth. The smile faded as she remembered his role in all this, and the destination that awaited him.

Tossing wood on her fledgling blaze, she stood and walked away from the cage and the accusation hidden within. Tonight, she'd brush the horses down. Anything to get away from those silent, accusing eyes.

⁊

THEY SAT ABOUT THE FIRE, DRINKING TEA. IT WAS BITTER, THE taste rounding off residual hunger like a file against metal burrs. Not that Geneve had good reason to be hungry. Calterburry Keep's quartermaster restocked their provisions, which meant fresh food. Israel roasted a whole chicken over the fire while they shared weary silence.

She still felt warm from the Supplicant but sweat no longer beaded her skin. A quick splash in a brook nearby reminded her of what the sinner must have gone through in his escape. Geneve made herself wash despite the cold, thinking *it's because I don't want to reek like a three-day-dead dog tomorrow*, but wondering within the silence of her heart, *is it because I feel his pain?* The Tresward said empathy was important, but...

But nothing. He's a sinner.

So, she sipped her tea, and kept her thoughts to herself. The sinner had eaten too, but within his cage, because he'd proved resourceful, and none of the Knights wanted to chase a rabbit through the dark.

She had first watch. Geneve eyed her armor, breastplate gleaming in the firelight, then shook her head. It felt like too much for a place this small and cold. The Vhemin wouldn't come this far south. She struggled her way into a chain shirt, put Requiem and Tribunal in their holsters at her back, and stood staring at the dark.

"'WARE!" VERTILINE'S CRY JERKED GENEVE AWAKE. SHE'D FALLEN asleep, kneeling on the ground where she'd stood watch earlier. Her face felt numb, her lips heavy. She staggered upright, swaying, then spun to the sinner's cage.

Empty.

She almost fell as she spun, but flung a hand out. *Sorcery? Poison?* A malaise held her, limbs wooden, sluggish in response.

The rumble of many feet drew her eye. Through the trees came the horde, gray-green skin, eyes gleaming, horror teeth showing in snarls of rage. Heavy swords and motley armor, but that didn't matter. Not for these invaders. Their numbers alone were fearsome, but it was their *kind* that sent Geneve's blood cold.

The Vhemin are here!

She dragged Requiem from it scabbard, shouting a war cry, and charged. A Vhemin crossbow bolt hissed through the darkness. Requiem found it, slicing it in two. She vaulted the campfire's ember glow, dashing past Vertiline, who still struggled to raise Israel. The big man seemed slow, dopey almost, but Geneve had no time for that.

This was her watch. She'd failed, and her brother and sister Knights would pay for her mistake.

The first of the Vhemin met her with a snarl and a clash of steel. It towered an extra two hands over her. In the darkness it seemed black, only the red of its snake eyes giving any color. Its strike shuddered down Geneve's arms, Requiem shivering as it took the blow.

She ducked under the counter swing she knew was coming, rising into a strike that took both its hands off. Geneve dashed on, leaving the Vhemin to bawl behind her.

Holding Requiem in one hand, she drew Tribunal. The scattergun roared into the night, *boom boom*, and then it was empty. She dropped it, stepping into the throng of attackers.

Her limbs still felt lethargic, and she almost missed dodging the strike even a Novice could see coming. A rusty edge whistled past her face, taking a lock of red hair with it. She kicked low, boot hitting groin, but it had little effect. Her blade followed, eviscerating a Vhemin.

A strike came from her right. She brought Requiem about, but too slow by far, her limbs still stuck in treacle. The strike was from a club, the blow immense. Geneve should have dodged, not parried, but she couldn't *think* right. She couldn't find the perfect steps.

The club caught her in her shoulder, dislocating it. She screamed, Requiem falling to the trampled grass.

The Vhemin to her left backhanded her across the face. She spun, spreading her length upon the ground. Booted, massive feet ran past her. Something trod on her, and she felt the pop of a rib giving way. She struggled to rise, but a wheezing, slurring darkness pulled her back down.

Down, where she couldn't remember her failure. Down, to death, and judgment by the Three.

Chapter Seven

❧

"**K**ytto's an asshole," Vertiline admitted. "Try not to let it worry you." She dragged Geneve along like the girl might break loose in strong winds.

Geneve hurried, her smaller legs working hard to keep up with Vertiline's elegant strides. The Adept was lean and hard, quite unlike the usual bulk of Knights. Her frame seemed locked down against something inside coiling to be free. Geneve wondered if she'd be lean like Vertiline or big like Israel once she grew up. "Why are we going to see Kytto?"

"Because *he's* an asshole." Their forward march led them through the Keep's interiors, then down a flight of steps that looked well used, like most everything here. Globes within sconces gave off warm light without the eye-watering smoke of flame as they headed below the ground.

The steps didn't continue long, ending in a huge room filled with racks of equipment. Burnished steel breastplates sat alongside bright shields. Weapon racks held the glimmering glass blades of Knights, as well as more mundane steel weapons. The rows of equipment seemed to go on forever. The air smelled of oil and hammered metal.

It wasn't dim, despite the size. Light globes were everywhere. Vertiline towed Geneve left from the stairs. The far wall sported a modest hut, outside which stood a short, angry-looking man. His coffee-colored skin shone with *sweat, probably because he was sorting through piles of armor. He wore pants and a blacksmith's apron over heavy boots, but no shirt under the apron. The angry-looking man squinted at Vertiline.* "Fuck off, Tilly."

She let Geneve go, sweeping the angry-looking man into an angrier-looking hug. "Hello, Kytto."

"What part of 'fuck off' didn't you understand?" *Kytto escaped Vertiline's clutches and ran a hand through short-cropped black hair. It was wet with sweat, leaving his palm wet, but Vertiline's armor collected none of it.* "Who's the runt?"

"You'll like her. Grins when she fights. Takes a beating when there's no call for it." *Vertiline crossed her arms.* "We just spent time with Eleni."

"And what does Lucent," *Kytto leaned on the title,* "Eleni want with a runt?"

"Nothing."

"Ah. You're telling me this because the runt got hurt?" *Kytto pursed his lips, glaring at Geneve like this was all her fault.* "What'd you do, kid?"

"I—"

"Scratch that. I don't want to know." *He worried an itch under his apron.* "Was it worth it?"

"I—"

"Don't want to know that either." *Kytto frowned, before glancing at Vertiline.* "Why'd you bring her here?"

"Because Israel—"

"That asshole! Someone needs to knock his teeth in." *Kytto grinned like he was the man for the job.*

Geneve felt a jab of anger. "Don't talk about him like that."

Both Vertiline and Kytto swung to face her, as if she'd just sprouted an extra head. Vertiline patted the air in a calm down *gesture.* "Relax, kid, it's not like—"

"It is! You're saying bad things about him, and he's not even here. If you want to fight someone, say it to their face." *Geneve put her clenched fists on her hips, glaring up at Vertiline.* "He's kind, and nice, and tries to be the best Knight he can be."

Vertiline deflated a little. "Aye, that he does."

"What did Israel ever do to you?" *Geneve demanded.*

"You're right." *Kytto kept up his grin but with clenched teeth now, answering before Vertiline could.* "I do *like her.*" *He crouched down, offering a sweat-slick hand to Geneve.* "We haven't been introduced. I'm Kytto."

She took the hand. It wasn't the first time she'd touched a sweaty person. "Geneve."

"I'd love to say I'm pleased to meet you, but Tilly only talks to me these days when she wants something."

"That's not true. There was that time last year——"

"But it doesn't matter," *Kytto said, like Vertiline hadn't spoken.* "Let me guess. You're here because a bigger kid tried to knock your head off, and you wouldn't give in."

Geneve nodded. "It's not what Knights do."

He wobbled a hand in the air in a maybe-maybe-not gesture. "Eh. Sometimes that's right."

"Are you a Knight?" *Geneve still felt sullen anger at this angry man, and wasn't sure why, but he'd cast stones at Israel, and was now aiming for Knights as a whole.*

"Fuck, no. I'm a Tresward Smith." *He tugged his ear, then stood.* "Got no time or patience for the patterns. Can't call the Sacred Storm. Don't want to, really."

Geneve looked between Kytto and Vertiline. "But——"

"Thing is, when you make weapons for a bunch o' assholes who like to beat on injustice because it's fun, you need to be good at ... dispute resolution." *Kytto took a deep lungful of air, then blew it out.* "And nothing speaks to Knights like getting a beating from their lessers."

"Especially when they're short," *Vertiline offered.*

Kytto squinted at her. "Who's short?"

"I kind of——"

"If you want to say something, just say it." *Kytto crossed his arms.* "Don't feel like you need to save my feelings. Especially not when you want a favor."

Vertiline gave another small, bright smile. "I don't want a favor. She does."

"Nah. She doesn't even know what the problem is." *Kytto rubbed his chin.* "Doesn't matter, though. I'll help."

Vertiline gave a tight nod. "Thanks, Kytto."

"No problem. Now, like I said, fuck off." *He gave a smile to take the sting out of it.*

She nodded, then reached for Geneve. "Come on."

"No, leave her." Kytto turned from Vertiline like she'd already gone. "The kid and I have work to do."

"Like what?" Geneve asked.

"You think this armor's going to stack itself?" Kytto stretched his arms wide. "Let's get to it."

Chapter Eight

The long road left Meriwether plenty of time to think. The cold had got into his bones, so he spent much of the journey shivering, but the thick blankets the Knights draped over him served to keep him from death's door.

He'd found hot rocks sharing his blanket, which he kicked out once they started being cold rocks.

Meriwether's careful fingers found the angel's kiss nestled in a pocket. He hadn't been so cold-drunk to lose it, then. Stacked around the cage were the Knight's belongings. Not the precious ones—their glass swords, scatterguns, shields, or other means of wizard murder. Not coin, neither. But tents, pots and pans, and food.

Their eyes didn't linger on him. He was baggage. An item to be delivered, by pony express. It didn't bother him; he didn't much like them either.

It's hard to like people who think of you as a demon's instrument made flesh. But just imagine! They must be amazing fun at parties.

His quiet rummaging through their baggage revealed various things of note. Dried nuts, which he munched, and raw chicken wrapped within wax paper, which he didn't. A bottle of amber liquid, which tempted him sorely, but he figured he'd need his wits before too long.

No herbs, or coffee—*are these people savages?*—but, almost as he was at the point of despair, his fingers found a small tin. Inside, the bitter-sweet aroma of tea. He didn't fancy tea much. Too bitter, not enough honey in the world to take away the tongue-curling flavor. But good enough for his purposes.

He retrieved his twist of angel's kiss. The day was long, and he had plenty of time. Meriwether used the hours to render the kiss's leaves into tiny fragments, distributing them into the tin. He resealed it, gave it a shake, and packed it away where he'd found it.

The rest was in the hands of the Three, who were, in his experience, a pernicious bunch of pricks. He settled back in his blankets, stifling a cough, because he sure as hell wasn't getting sick, dying of the cold or black lung. Meriwether wouldn't give these Knights the satisfaction.

They made camp at journey's end, which was amusing not least of which because the fools spent more energy on physical efforts when already exhausted. His eyes kept straying to red-haired Geneve. She wrestled her horse, rope clenched in gauntleted fists while the beast dragged her across the clearing.

A weaker person might have sworn, or hit the animal, but he caught her fighting a laugh as the blue roan reared, then lunged forward, dumping her on her backside. Meriwether considered the angel's kiss for a moment but tamped down on his residual pity.

They hunted me without reason.

He considered that for a moment. *To be fair, there's some reason. You're a thief, a good one if a little pride's not too much, and you have a trick or two up your sleeve.*

The meal they gave him was terrible. The chicken was burnt, the seasoning nonexistent or also burnt. But there was plenty of it, and he was thankful for that. He watched, heart in mouth as they made tea, the angel's kiss roiling with the bitter leaves.

Night slunk in, tail between its legs. The giant snored first, which surprised Meriwether because he expected the big man to have a little more stamina. The ice woman nodded off next, her chin touching her chest, glass sword by her hand.

Geneve stood the longest, back to the fire, staring into the dark.

But even she settled, first yawning, then settling into a crouch, before slipping into slumber.

Now, the cage. Meriwether shook himself free of blankets, but carefully, quietly, like a ghost. He examined the lock holding the cage closed. It was a fancy affair, the Tresward's sun emblazoned in gold on good iron. The lock was the size of his clenched fist. There'd be no breaking it.

He closed his eyes. Touched the metal with delicate fingers. Felt inside, the tumblers and gears of Tresward-wrought metal a marvel to behold. *Get a grip, man. They make good stuff, but they're assholes, High Justiciar right to the lowest Novice.*

He reached with his mind and, with a flick of his fingers, tickled the lock. It snapped open. He eased it free of the metal hoops holding his cage closed, setting it against a blanket to avoid the *clunk* of metal on wood. So slowly it almost hurt, he eased the door open.

It didn't creak. Tresward Smiths made it better than a common blacksmith could. *Bet they'll regret that come the morrow.*

Meriwether slipped from the cage. His boots found dew-wet grass. He snuck toward Geneve's form, eyes on her blade and scattergun. Then he remembered the slip of steel she'd let him keep. It'd be poor form if he took her weapons after she'd given him one.

It wasn't like he could lift her bastard sword anyhow. It looked like it weighed as much as Meriwether with a good meal in his belly and winter furs about his shoulders.

Recharting his course, he made for the burlap sack of supplies near the fire. He helped himself to some dried meat, eyes watchful for the Knights stirring. *By the Three. It wasn't a lot of angel's kiss. I hope I haven't killed them.*

He shook his head. *I should cut their throats and leave them bleeding their last. If I was the sinner they claim me to be, I'd have done it already.*

Meriwether could tickle locks, and a few other tricks as well, but he wasn't a murderer. He'd be damned if the right arm of the Light would make him one. Making sure his stiletto was secured, he stuffed a sack with a water skin, a hunk of cheese, and a loaf of bread. Then he set off into the darkness.

THE DARKNESS DIDN'T LIKE HIM VERY MUCH.

Branches slapped him in the face. Twigs broke underfoot. He was good at being a padfoot, but only in city streets. The wilds weren't a home for him.

The night seemed to grow brighter ahead. He rubbed his eyes, feeling like the world conspired against him. He was going to die of the black lung, or on the unforgiving edge of Tresward steel, and to round it all off he'd had so little sleep he was seeing things.

Pressing on, he found his eyes hadn't lied: the night was indeed brightening. The murmur of drums grew louder. Meriwether crouched low beside a tree that smelled like sandalwood. He listened. Drums, no talking. The light was urgent, insistent, like a blaze.

Go the other way. Don't look.

Hells, but he *wanted* to look. He crept up a small rise, nosing over the top. Below him lay another clearing, but this one hacked from the belly of the forest. Trees were torn down, a bonfire of their bodies in the center of the clearing. Around the blaze, the massive bulks of Vhemin warriors stood. They beat drums as they watched the blaze.

He'd never seen Vhemin before. Feybrind, sure. Their quiet kind were welcome in the cities of humanity, their master artisans making Tresward Smiths look like bumbling novices. But the Vhemin? Never. Humans warred with them in the warmer north in all but the most brutal pirate city ports. They were ugly, brutish creatures, known for making war above all else. Meriwether heard the stories. Ones like, *They eat human babies for dessert*, and *they're five times as strong as humans, kilo for kilo.*

He counted twenty, but was left uncertain of the number as they moved about the flames. Their skin was gray-green and lightly scaled. Mouths wider than a human's, hiding a horror show of shark's teeth. They wore motley armor and carried no uniformity of weapons. This group stole their equipment from their victims and made no move to hide that.

Meriwether slowed his breathing. *Don't move. Don't make a sound.* There shouldn't be any Vhemin this far south, but clearly no one told them that. He wondered why they watched fire while beating drums, and patience rewarded his curiosity.

The Vhemin extended metal poles into the heart of the blaze. They dragged free slabs of stone, smoking and hot. The brutish figures tucked the stones into backpacks, lashing them tightly to their bodies. That put truth to one rumor at least: the Vhemin were cold-blooded, like lizards. The stones would keep them warm, like a portable basking rock.

But that means they're here for murder work. Meriwether wanted no part of that. He knew of no townships close to here. He was more familiar with the north. *No clue what their purpose is, but you want to be far away from them and their target.*

He backed away. His foot found loose scree, slipped, and he *oomph'd* on the ground. Twenty faces turned to him, then the group let out a communal roar.

Three's mercy. Meriwether dropped his satchel, turned, and fled. Branches lashed at him, and more than once he tripped on a root or stone. His face slammed against the coarse bark of a tree, but he pushed himself on. The pain was like an old friend, one that urged him on. *Keep going, old son. If I don't it'll hurt more, then stop hurting forever.*

If it'd taken him thirty minutes to get from the Knight's camp to here, it took him five to make it back. The Vhemin were on his heels, grunts and roars behind him. He spied the glow from the Knight's fire ahead. "Help!" Nothing. He kept going until a massive hand snared him from behind. Meriwether was hauled from the ground, feet dangling as a Vhemin brought him to its face. Fetid breath washed over him. "You should try chewing mint."

The Vhemin grunted, slamming a fist into Meriwether's gut. He curled up, a curious motion since he was still suspended in the air. "We have him."

Meriwether blinked. The Vhemin could *speak?* Truth, the words were rough, like listening to an anvil talk, but words they were. "You do," he wheezed. "I'm not sure why, though. The Knights are," he jerked a thumb, "that way. I'm not with those assholes."

The Vhemin wrenched its head away from Meriwether and his no doubt tasty insides, and toward the Knight's camp. From that direction, a cry came up. "'Ware!"

Vertiline, unless I miss my guess. The Vhemin ululated, then slammed Meriwether into a tree. He slumped to the ground, stunned, as the beasts ran past, roaring, blades out. Twenty Vhemin against three Knights.

What have I done? Nothing answered, not even the part of him that urged he cut their throats. *They cannot win.*

Chapter Nine

✦

Geneve woke to soft hands against her face. She tried to push them away, but it was like trying to ward against smoke. Her fingers found nothing, pawing air, and the hands found her face again.

She cracked an eye. Above her, trees waved at the sky. Between her and the trees, the unmistakable face of a Feybrind. It knelt beside her, hands checking her face, neck, and—with a stab of agony—her shoulder.

The Feybrind had light-brown fur, almost blond. Its cat-like ears were slightly rounded. It smiled as best its kind could, a slight twisting of the line of its mouth. Its fur-soft hands left her, moving through the air, the motion like poetry given form. *{Do you speak?}*

Geneve rose, almost blacking out at the pain in her shoulder. The Feybrind backed away, but not from fear. The cat people didn't fear humans except in great numbers. The Feybrind gave her space. Geneve touched fingers to her shoulder, instantly regretting it as pain jolted through her. "I handspeak the People's language." She gestured at her arm. "But I can't speak it like this."

{It's good you can understand. So many of your kind are simpletons.} It held its distance. *{There was a great battle here.}*

Geneve looked about, remembering Israel and Vertiline. As she turned, the Feybrind moved in, cat-quick, grabbing her arm and twisting. Her shoulder wrenched, *popping* back into place. She screamed, staggering, nausea rising within her like a wave. She vomited, then tried to straighten, trembling.

{I'm Sight of Day.} The Feybrind was once again at a distance, no doubt wanting to be far away from a potentially angry person. She measured how it stood, changing her view from *it* to *him*. This Feybrind was male. The women of its people stood a little shorter, a little less broad of shoulder. *{There were Vhemin.}*

Geneve moved her arm, biting her lip. It needed a sling, but she had no time for such. "I'm Geneve, Knight Adept of the Tresward. Were there ... others?"

Sight of Day shook his head. *{You're alone.}*

She bowed her head. *By the Three. I've killed my friends.* Her gaze found her fallen blade. She hefted Requiem, slinging it into its scabbard. Her scattergun was nearby, so she collected Tribunal as well. Geneve moved through the camp, finding many dead Vhemin. She counted eleven of their fallen, the burn marks of glass wrought on their bodies.

No Israel. No Vertiline. And no sinner.

Sight of Day watched her from the safety of the tree line. He made no move to help or hinder her, but Feybrind didn't approach humans without purpose. She made her way back to him without conscious thought, stopping five paces away. "Thank you."

He cocked his head, hands moving their beautiful path through the air. *{What for?}*

"My arm." She shook her head, angry with herself. *Give him your honest self. It's the People's way.* "For standing guard while I lay on the cold earth. For making sure I saw the sun again."

The Feybrind measured her with its golden eyes. Vertically slitted pupils should be alien, but his eyes held warmth, and sadness, and even a hint of pity. *{You've known the People?}*

She winced but brought her arm up to speak to him in his own language. *{Once. A long time ago.}* Her fingers felt clumsy, awkward as she fumbled through her human imitation of handspeak. Her finger joints felt rusty compared to the fluidity of his.

He nodded, perhaps in approval, perhaps just as acknowledgment. *{What will you do, Daughter of the Three?}*

She turned a slow circle. "I'm going to find my horse. Then I'm going to find my," she gritted her teeth, "fellow Knights. Free them, if they live. Avenge them, if not."

{And the sinner?} The golden-yellow eyes moved to the cage.

"I don't know," Geneve admitted. "It depends."

{I will make you a deal,} the Feybrind offered. *{I will help you. In exchange, you will stay your blade against the sinner.}*

Geneve watched the Feybrind. The cat man stood like the sea of death at his feet bothered him not at all. *It probably doesn't. They don't like Vhemin very much.* She wondered at the People's motives in this. Feybrind didn't come to human lands without purpose. But they weren't evil, not like the Vhemin. They were just ... apart.

"I can't do what you ask." Geneve sagged as the words came out. "The Justiciars demand the sinner."

The Feybrind touched his fingertips together lightly. *{Perhaps.}* He gave another slight smile, head at an angle, as if he believed a different truth but was too polite to say.

Geneve thought about the road ahead. A sinner, free. Two of her friends, dead or dying. About the weight on her soul if the sinner went free, and the debt in her heart if her friends died. Would Israel and Vertiline want to live if it meant a sinner went free? Could she live with herself if they died?

The Feybrind watched her with those wonderful, golden eyes. *{There is a storm inside you, Daughter of the Three. Storms can be terrible or wonderful. Shall we find out which you are?}*

"I don't command the Sacred Storm." Geneve bit her lip, fingers running along the black Adept's sash with its single gold bar. "There's nothing inside me."

{A woman in the eye of a hurricane might see as you do.} The golden eyes didn't shift. *{We have a duty.}*

"I ... can't." She shook her head, sharp and hard. "He's for the cage.

I won't kill him unless he leaves me no choice, because it's not my justice to give, but..." Geneve trailed off. "He can't go free."

{I understand.} The Feybrind turned to the trees. *{Come anyway. We can talk about the end of things once the middle is done. Vhemin live, and I cannot abide.}* It slipped into the dappled shadow of the forest.

Geneve stared after, then scoured the camp. It took her some time to don her armor; her shoulder swelled, a tight, angry pain inside it. She hissed as she tightened straps. It hurt but would hurt a lot less than dying.

Of the horses, there was no sign. *Vhemin don't take prisoners. What do they want with Tresward Knights?* It was a puzzle, but not hers to solve. Geneve grabbed a waterskin and headed in pursuit of Sight of Day. The Feybrind was right. They might not agree what would be done with the sinner, but they had common ground. *No Vhemin will live on human lands.* All else was secondary.

SIGHT OF DAY LEFT A TRAIL EASY ENOUGH TO FOLLOW. IT MEANT HE *wanted* to be followed; Geneve knew of no human who could track a Feybrind that didn't want to be found. He left her notches on tree bark. Tiny little arrows pointed her forward, no doubt scratched with the claws on the Feybrind's fingertips.

Geneve felt weak, wobbling through the dappled green of the trees. She felt sick, more than aftereffects of re-seating her shoulder. As the sun's midmorning stance took charge of the heavens, she wondered what was wrong with her. Was she sick? Had the Vhemin poisoned her?

Why didn't they take me with the sinner and my friends?

She imagined she may have looked dead to them. Her ribs ached. Geneve remembered more than one kick to her midsection leaving them feeling like that. The Vhemin might have kicked her, got no response, and carted off her companions. They were known to eat humans. Geneve shuddered, wondering if they saw her friends as a banquet with legs.

Sight of Day waited for her in a small clearing. The Feybrind had collected a soft leather backpack since she'd seen him last. A slender sword hung from his waist, and a bow hung from his shoulder.

He stood by four horses. Geneve held herself still, unbelieving. Her blue roan Tristan tossed his head, prancing for the Feybrind. Vertiline's chestnut grazed dew-sweet grass, holding close to Israel's black charger. The beast looked angry. It'd be best to stay away from him. He was known to bite the unwary.

The fourth horse nuzzled Sight of Day. It was a red roan, about the same size as Tristan, but without the attitude. The Feybrind and horse stood, forehead to forehead. Sight of Day's golden yellow eyes were closed, that small half-smile at his mouth.

Geneve was sure she made no sound, but the Feybrind turned to face her. He stroked the roan's face, then beckoned her closer. *{I found your horses. The black and I haven't come to terms yet.}*

She laughed, feeling joy at seeing the horses. She thought they must be dead and liked Tristan too much to lose him to the Vhemin. "Chesterfield doesn't come to terms. He's a bit like Israel." The smile left her face as she remembered why Chesterfield was riderless. *I slept instead of keeping watch.*

The Feybrind studied her, then gave his horse another pat. *{I thought Tresward horses fought beside their Knights.}*

"They do." Geneve broke from the tree line and headed for Tristan. The blue roan sidled away from her, wanting none of her armored bulk. The traitor made for Sight of Day's side. "Perhaps Israel sent them away. He's always had a soft spot for..." She tasted bitterness in her words. "For those who'd fall."

{There are always three.} He offered her a waterskin.

Geneve drank, nodding her thanks before handing it back. "Israel leads us. Vertiline's his second, and I'm..." She tried to find the right words. "The extra."

Sight of Day half-smiled. *{Let us find the Vhemin.}* He patted his red roan's flank. *{This is Fidget.}* Fidget wore no saddle or bridle. The Feybrind didn't need them.

"She doesn't look as feisty as Tristan."

{Try spending an hour on her back.} He slipped atop the horse, the motion fluid, like water pouring itself back into a bottle. *I've trained my*

whole life in the martial arts, and I don't have half his grace. {The Vhemin went north.}

"Then we go north." She didn't like the idea of following Vhemin to their territory. They were easier to fight in the cold. Hopefully they'd catch the enemy before they made it too far.

Tristan had no saddle or bridle because only sociopaths made their horses sleep that way. Geneve had trained to ride bareback like the Feybrind and could steer Tristan with her knees. She eyeballed her horse. He eyeballed her right back. She held her palm flat, knuckling two fingers into it. *{Kneel.}*

He nickered, prancing away. Sight of Day watched, an eyebrow raised in curiosity. *{You talk to him with the People's handspeak?}*

"It's less one-sided than you'd expect." Tristan pranced a circle, coming back to her with a toss of his mane. He sidled close, and she touched his neck. "I missed you too." The horse huffed. "I don't know where they are either, but we need to find them." *{Kneel.}*

The horse dropped to his knees, letting her swing her armored weight atop. Tristan stood, but found time for a reproachful stare before prancing in front of Sight of Day and Fidget. Fidget ignored him, but Sight of Day clapped with delight. *{Where did you find him?}*

"He found me, I think." Geneve patted Tristan's neck, wishing she could run bare fingers against his coat. Gauntleted hands weren't the same. "Let's go."

Sight of Day turned Fidget toward the trees and led the way. Feybrind were master trackers, and Geneve didn't mind following. There was no time for prideful displays while her friends lay in the hands of the enemy.

Chapter Ten

Geneve liked Kytto. Not because he was nice, but because he spoke to her like she was already fully grown, with glass in her hand and steel around her body. He didn't mind she was six years old, as long as she didn't mind him swearing and ordering her around.

She visited him as often as she could. Sometimes he got her to move armor. Other times, he gave her a hammer and let her beat glowing steel. Most of the time, she left tired, sweating, and happy. Kytto didn't take it personally his orneriness didn't leave a mark on her mood. He seemed to like her too, but never said. She got sore working there.

"Your first problem is you're small," he observed as she struggled to carry a breastplate to a rack. The metal was shiny, like all Tresward-forged armor. It didn't scratch on the coarse ground, and appeared to be newly minted. All Knight equipment from the hands of Smiths was like that. Strong, and bright, just like the Light.

"I can't help that." Geneve huffed as she dragged the armor along.

The scraping sound made Kytto wince. "That took me a month to make."

"Is that long?"

He pondered that while he leaned against a table. "I guess some could do it in less, but they're not here."

"Why am I here?" Geneve let the armor go, and the breastplate rattled on the ground. "What am I learning here that the Knights can't teach me?"

"You're not learning anything yet."

"But why—"

"You're getting stronger. Keep eating. Keep moving heavy shit from there," he pointed to a mount of greaves, "to there," his finger found a rack a heart-sinkingly long, long way away, "and you might be strong enough to punch wosshisface in his, uh, you know."

"Wincuf."

"That's the asshole, yeah." Kytto shook his head. "For one of my countrymen, he's a depressingly bad example."

Geneve felt her brow furrow. "Countrymen?"

"Tebrani. It's a long way from here. You need to cross the sea to find it." Kytto looked at the greave pile. "Those aren't moving by themselves."

❦

ISRAEL CAME TO KYTTO'S DOMAIN AFTER A MONTH OF GENEVE WORKING there. He stormed inside, armor gleaming, sword hanging at his waist behind him like the first day Geneve saw him. Unlike the first day, his eyes weren't kind. They were hard, and maybe a little bit angry. "Kytto!"

The Smith looked up from a large box of broken armor. "Ah, Chevalier Israel. I was wondering—"

"You're interfering with this Knight's training." Israel pointed to a wide-eyed Geneve without looking at her.

"Much as I hate arguing with a Chevalier, that's not correct." Kytto didn't look like he hated this even a little bit.

"How so, Smith?"

"Because she's not a Knight. She's a Novice."

Israel nodded. "The error of title was mine. Still, you're interfering with this Novice's training, and—"

"Again, humble apologies, but no." Kytto shook his head, but had no hangdog look about him. If anything, he looked like he was about to eat a cake. "I'm fixing her training."

Israel looked at Geneve, the hammer she held, and the stubbornly un-

hammered steel on the anvil before her. His eyes moved to the floor, where other scraps of metal lay, then to the racks of ordered armor, and finally to a pile of gauntlets Geneve was certain she'd have to move soon. "Ah."

Kytto look like his cake was leaving on a cart owned by someone else. "What do you mean by that?"

Israel gave a small bow. "I'll leave you to it."

"That's it?"

"Was there something else you wanted?" Israel countered.

"I was hoping for more of a fight, truth be told," Kytto admitted.

"We've no quarrel, Smith. I know you look for them among the Knights." Israel held up a gauntleted hand to forestall Kytto's eruption. "You are very good at putting things back together that we break." The Chevalier turned to Geneve. "Novice?"

"Yes?" Geneve put down her hammer, ready to leave with Israel. "Did I do something wrong?"

His eyes softened, then found his feet. "No. It was me that did something wrong. I brought you here but haven't been around to help."

"Seems like your job is going out. Spreading the Light. Killing the dark things of the world." Kytto sniffed. "Wouldn't be a good use of a Chevalier's time to train a Novice, would it?"

"Not a good use of a Smith's time, either." Israel tipped his head sideways, fingers playing with the crystal at his throat. "She's more precious than glass or steel, Smith."

"Aye."

"I'm in your debt, then." Israel turned on his heel, climbing the steps from Kytto's sanctuary.

When Geneve couldn't hear his booted feet on stone anymore, she turned to Kytto. "Did I do something wrong?"

Kytto watched the stairs and shook his head. "No."

"Did Israel?"

The Smith gave a small, tired smile. "Not really. He thinks so. I don't, and neither does Tilly." He clapped his hands together. "That steel's not going to hammer itself flat, is it?"

Geneve fingered the hammer but didn't lift it. "Vertiline doesn't like Israel."

"Like? No." The smith's eye twinkled.

"*Then why—*"

"*Not having this conversation.*" Kytto wolfed that grin of his like he wanted to punch someone. "*We'll have a different one instead. Tomorrow, I'm going to show you something.*"

Chapter Eleven

I'm an idiot. That's it! And it's all my fault. Meriwether hung by his hands and feet from a pole. It was lugged between two hulking Vhemin. He didn't like being trussed up and carried, especially since the Vhemin didn't have the courtesy of using locks. He couldn't tickle rope open. The strands were coarse and chafed his wrists as he swung like a dead hog. Above him, his knife skewered the wood, wedged in there nice and solid. Tied up as he was, he wouldn't be able to work it free without attracting a great deal of attention, which he supposed was part of the cruel joke.

If he craned his neck he could spy the giant Israel behind, and the slender form of Vertiline ahead. Both were trussed like he was, but also out cold, which was probably a mercy as otherwise there'd be no end of, *You're an idiot, Meriwether!* commentary from them. At least, he hoped that's what they'd say, as opposed to, *You're a dead man, Meriwether!*

He deserved to be dead. Meriwether drugged Knights of the Tresward and led a pack of ravagers to their camp. Despite being doped on enough angel's kiss to drop a stallion, the Knights fought against the Vhemin, cutting the brutes down. Meriwether watched as glass swords carved a path through the enemy, severing arms, legs, heads, and torsos. What *didn't* happen was use of their cursed Light magic. They fought like ordinary humans, albeit highly trained ones.

Does the narcotic stop use of their Sacred Storm? It felt like an important operational detail Meriwether should research further. Knights without the Storm were still vicious bastards. The red-haired Geneve killed thirteen people without using it once. Twenty Vhemin was an entirely different proposition though, and without the Storm at their call, the Knights fell.

The Vhemin hadn't been easy on them, clubbing them to the dirt, then hitting them over and over until their faces were bloody, noses broken, eyes swollen shut. Meriwether *almost* went to their aid, the little knife Geneve gifted him in hand. Then he reconsidered. *Meriwether*, he'd said to himself, *if two Knights can't win, what am I going to do?*

He'd turned, rabbited, and run straight into a Vhemin. He'd swung the knife, which the Vhemin laughed at, disarmed him, and punched him in the gut with the force of a horse's kick. The brute dragged him back to its fellows, ignored Meriwether's retching, tied him up, and rammed the little knife through the wooden pole. The Vhemin leered at Meriwether as he'd done it.

I'm getting tired of folk dismissing my threat level. If I stabbed someone with the blade, it'd leave an impression. He let his head sag back, watching the ground travel by.

This is my fault. He gritted his teeth. *Well, not all of it. The whole imprisonment-by-the-Tresward lark is on the Knights, but leading a pack of monsters to their door ... that's on me.* Under normal circumstances he wouldn't have spared a second thought for Knights getting their just desserts, but Vhemin weren't *normal*.

They also shouldn't have been this far south. *Still, give 'em credit: they've got a work ethic.* The Vhemin's marching speed was a slow run, and they kept it up, hour after hour, despite the weight of their armor, weapons, and those giant hunks of rock they carried.

About midday, the Vhemin broke from their forced march. They dropped Meriwether to the ground, then set about felling trees, building a pile of branches in the clearing they made. The wood wasn't seasoned, but one of the Vhemin poured oil on the branches before setting them alight. They gathered close to the flames, setting their stone weights into the heart of the blaze.

The rocks keep them warm. The cold-blooded bastards need hot rocks to stop freezing up. Meriwether hadn't heard of Vhemin using this trick before. It felt above their usual mental level and spoke of a darker future for the south.

A groan distracted him. He wriggled and caught Vertiline shifting. She woke, only one eye opening. The expressions of disbelief, anger, and acceptance went across her face in less than two heartbeats, before settling into an implacable mask. *Well, as implacable as you can be with a cracked lip, swollen eye, and split cheek.*

Her open eye roamed the clearing, marking the Vhemin, their fire, Meriwether, and finally settling on Israel's prone form. She seemed to relax a hair's breadth on seeing the Valiant with them, then looked at Meriwether again. "You." The word came out as cracked and broken as her face.

"Me," he agreed.

"What was it?" Her voice was like a saw sticking in wood.

"The Vhemin."

An eye-roll, a valiant effort considering her condition. "What did you drug us with?"

"I didn't—"

"What was it?" Her tongue probed her lip, found the split, and withdrew.

"Angel's kiss." Meriwether tasted his own disappointment.

She grunted. "Nice work, sinner."

"Hey. Hey! It was *you* assholes who—"

"No talking!" A Vhemin turned from the blaze, eyeballing Meriwether. "Boss said we get you. Boss didn't say we couldn't break your legs a little."

Meriwether rethreaded that line a couple times. "How do you break legs only a little?"

The Vhemin glared. "Frail, ugly human want to find out?"

"Who you calling ugly?" Meriwether bridled. "It's just—"

"Shut it, sinner." Vertiline closed her eye. "Or, don't. To be honest,

I don't care if they break your legs. The Tresward isn't particular about your state when we put you on trial."

"I thought I was under your protection?"

"No talking!" the Vhemin roared.

Her eye opened for another valiant roll. "You're *really* going to try that after slipping me angel's kiss?"

The Vhemin broke from its fellows, lumbering toward them. Meriwether shrank back, or tried to, but the pole-rope combo held him immobile. The creature made it to Vertiline, dragging the Knight upright by her throat. It didn't seem to mind she was hog-tied, bound limbs and pole between them. "Speak again, human. I dare you."

Face mottling as the Vhemin squeezed, she choked. It relaxed its grip a fraction. Her eye found Meriwether before going back to the monster. "Go fuck yourself."

It roared, slamming its fist into her gut, face, gut, and face again. She took the blows, shaking like a doll with each impact. Meriwether tried to get up, to do *something*, but he was tied fast. As the Vhemin rained punch after punch into Vertiline, Meriwether helpless not five meters away, he thought, *You're still under their protection. She's shielding me the only way she can.*

Yeah, he thought. *It's my fault.*

THE VHEMIN KNOCKED VERTILINE OUT. BEFORE SHE'D GONE UNDER, she hadn't whimpered. Made no plea for clemency. Didn't hold bound hands up to ward the blows. The Knight took the beating like it's what she was made for. Hardwood under the skin. Steel in her marrow.

Meriwether watched the whole time. He figured it was the least he could do after drawing the monster's attention. The sliver of good news was the Vhemin's heat stones readied quick enough, meaning the band set off once more.

He'd heard a hundred stories of the Vhemin. Immune to the kiss of the blade. Stronger than a horse. Faster than a Feybrind, and always, *always* angry. Or was it hungry? Meriwether once met a woman in a tavern, both of them worn thin by the cold, who told him her caravan were *eaten* by the monsters. She'd escaped, but showed her the smooth, rounded stump of her arm, cut off below the shoulder. *They eat you*, she'd insisted, hand rubbing the stump, *but not all at once.*

It's bullshit. They don't eat people. Meriwether jounced along, wrists numb, fingers purple above him. *Do they?* He glanced at the Vhemin he could see. Eyes front, focused like a predator. They had vertically slitted pupils like the Feybrind, but Vhemin didn't look playful or kind. They just looked *hungry.*

Okay. So, yeah. Maybe they're gonna eat us. Question is, what am I going to do about it? The problem with being bound by rope of all the backwater things was he couldn't get free. He'd need to wait until someone bought him a little time.

All the thoughts of being eaten reminded him he hadn't snacked since yesterday. Macabre it might be, but his stomach growled. He wondered whether he'd eat meat if offered. How could you tell whether your steak was human or bovine? His eyes moved to the bouncing load of Israel, still out cold. *The Knights would know. They're experts at knowing all the parts that make up a man.*

Day wore into afternoon, and then to evening without concern for Meriwether's wrists. The sun peeked through trees above, but the light never warmed him. A chill settled into his bones, an aching coldness that stopped at his wrists and ankles. The Vhemin ran on, their tireless rush suggesting at least one rumor was true: they really were strong as horses.

The forest ended suddenly enough that the late afternoon sun dazzled Meriwether. He blinked, eyes bleary for a moment, and was rewarded with the sight of a collection of Vhemin clustered in a clearing. A cave mouth leered, a gash in a stone wall stretching hundreds of meters above. The Vhemin didn't slow, carrying Meriwether and the Knights toward the cave.

The smell of roasting meat made his stomach roar. A massive fire burned, and he thought it was for more hot rocks until he spied a huge stake leaning over it. Strapped to the stake was the roasted body of a person, mouth open in a silent scream. The clothes and hair had burned away long ago. Meriwether felt sick. *That's what smells good. Roasted human's on the menu.* He wanted to throw up but swallowed it down. *Focus! There's got to be a way out of here. It's not like they attacked three Tresward Knights for lunch. Something else is going on.*

The cave swallowed them. Rough walls led inward, the chewed stone showing marks of recent expansion. Ten meters in the floor smoothed to large, square pavers. Another ten meters, torchlight eased back the dark, showing walls of smooth brick, faded by time but still standing tall. Had the Vhemin found an ancient temple? Expanded the entrance? That didn't bode well. The dark heart of the earth held secrets that should stay hidden.

Corridors stretched past. Meriwether saw old and broken doors, Vhemin by the handful, but no humans. He'd expected them to keep human slaves, but maybe they were fresh out. *Or maybe they've eaten them all. How's that for an incentive to keep the floors clean?*

The Vhemin took them to a room about ten meters long, half that wide. Rings were set into the walls. A skeleton moldered in a corner, chains from its wrists tethering it to a ring for all eternity. Meriwether *oof'd* as the Vhemin dropped him to the floor. They left him with the unconscious Knights, shuffling off and slamming the door behind them. He heard the unmistakable sound of a wooden beam sliding into place. "What's *wrong* with these people? Not a decent lock in sight."

No response. Israel and Vertiline were out for the count. *Perfect. No sense in proving I'm a sinner to the Tresward. If nothing else, it'd spoil the surprise.* Meriwether worked his hands, getting a little blood flowing back into them. He stretched his arms and shoulders as best he could while hog-tied to a pole, then eased his clever fingers around the haft of the knife the Vhemin so arrogantly left for him.

It was stuck well and good, but Meriwether had one asset on his side: he was *motivated*. He grunted, straining, then paused for a moment. *Leverage. You need leverage.* He got to his knees, then dragged the pole toward Israel's comatose form. The man was a mountain, no mistake, and while he no doubt personally contributed to at least half the Tresward's food bill, in this case it would prove useful.

Meriwether put the pole on the ground, humped Israel closer, and used the Knight's pole as a little lever under the knife's cross guard. He eyed his makeshift freedom device. *It'll do.* A hop, a huff, and the knife popped free to clatter on the cold stone floor. Meriwether fetched the knife, sliced his bonds, turned back to Israel, and found the giant had one bleary eye focused on him. He tried on a bright smile. "Morning. Or, evening, I think."

The eye moved to the knife. "You wait until we're fallen to bare blade against us?"

Meriwether tapped the knife's blade against his palm. It was sharp enough to shave with. "I can see why you'd think that."

Israel's eye roamed the room, coming to rest on Vertiline's supine body. "You owe her. Spare her life, at least."

Meriwether laughed. "Oh, I *know* I owe her." He tapped the knife's point against his temple, wincing as it pricked his skin. "That's why I'm getting you out. Both of you. Tonight. Right now, even."

"You're what?" Israel looked to him, the knife, then back to Vertiline.

"Before I do, I need a promise."

"We can't let you go." Israel stared at Vertiline for a long time. "No matter what the bargain might buy us."

"Don't insult my intelligence, big man. I'll look after myself." *It's what I'm best at, anyway. Times like this I appreciate why leaving home wasn't the wisest course of action.* Meriwether hunched over Israel's surprised face, blade bare, edge catching the dim light. "I'm going to cut your bonds. Before I put this steel to the rope tying you down, I need you to promise me you won't go hurt anyone until I give a signal."

"Why?"

"It's a surprise."

Israel growled. "No sinner is worth this much trouble."

"That doesn't sound like a promise." Meriwether sat back on his haunches. "You've got to ask yourself whether choking the life from me right now is worth dying for."

"It might be." Israel regarded him for a moment. Two heartbeats, no more. "I give you my word, sinner—"

"It's Meriwether."

"I give you my word, Meriwether. Until you give me the signal, I won't hurt anyone."

Meriwether regarded the Knight before him. It'd be so simple to end him here. Slit his throat, letting his blood pool and cool against the stone. Sidle over to Vertiline, ending her life too. Two fewer Knights running rampant on the 'sinners' of the world. All it'd take was a slip of his knife, and the job'd be done.

He thought of a red-haired Knight who'd given him that knife. A blade, given without concern for him hurting her. An arrogance behind the move, but something playful too. *Actions have consequences. Geneve put a blade in my hand, and here's a chance to repay the favor. Turn that edge on her fellows, and I'll damn myself. Also, it'd be a dick move.* "Good enough." Meriwether set to work on Israel's bonds.

The giant eased himself to a sitting position without wincing. He must be in pain, discomfort wracking him, but he gave the impression he'd just woken from a deep sleep on a feather mattress. Meriwether backed up, a healthy caution encouraging space between them, but true to his word Israel didn't attack.

He found his feet, swaying, before heading to Vertiline's side. His big hands were gentle as he turned her face over. "There are one or two chances in our short lives to make the world better, sinner. The best of us might have as many as a handful of moments, but for the rest, it's one or two." He sighed. "Don't squander yours."

Meriwether padded to his side, crouching. He sawed the blade through rough rope holding Vertiline. As her hands fell free, Israel massaged his fellow Knight's wrists, eliciting a groan but not a lot else. "My time for greatness is done, Knight. Your kind hunt mine to the ends of the earth. We don't have room to breathe, let alone change the world." Despite his words, he cut the bonds holding Vertiline's feet. Meriwether remembered her taking a beating from the Vhemin to keep him safe. *Until trial, at least.*

Israel nodded, but Meriwether wasn't sure which part he agreed with. "Geneve?"

"Not here." Meriwether wanted to be far away from Israel, and what might be in those eyes when the Knight next looked at him. He didn't want to say, *Probably dead, boss. Because I drugged you all, then led a horde of Vhemin to your camp.*

"Did you see her die?"

Meriwether took a step back, then held himself still. Israel's voice held concern, not hate. "No. I mean, it was dark. I was running—"

"From the horde of Vhemin you led to our camp."

"Yeah, those assholes. And when I burst in, she—"

"Geneve?"

"Yes. She was upright, swinging steel, but then she..." He backed away from the memory. "She fell."

"Because you drugged us all." Israel glanced at Meriwether, the ghost of a smile on his lips. "You know what this means?"

"You're going to hit me?"

"It means she's *alive*, sinner." He stood, stretching his arms. "Let's kill some Vhemin."

"She's alive?"

"She's a Knight of the Tresward. We don't die easy or quiet. We don't slip from the world without others remarking our passing." Israel touched his chest, over his heart. "I feel hope, so she lives."

"Uh-huh." Meriwether waggled his blade. "No killing Vhemin."

"What?"

"You promised." Meriwether beckoned with the knife. "Let's get you tied up again."

"You jest."

"This will be pretty funny, but not in the way you think." Meriwether sighed. "Vertiline said you were taking me to trial."

"That's right. We'll test you, and if you're found—"

"I get it. Burned alive, or something." Meriwether paced. "Until now, you've yet to see me sin, whatever that means. Right?"

Israel's eyes were calculating. "That's right. You're clever. Angel's kiss?" Meriwether nodded. "I don't know how you got free of the cage, but a skilled thief might manage it. So far, no magic. Why do you ask?"

"Because I'm about to sin, and it's going to save your life." Meriwether outlined his plan, watching Israel's expression go from incredulous to brooding, then moving to darker still, brows pulled together until his face looked like it would close entirely.

"No." The big man shook his head. "I can't allow it."

"You," Meriwether leaned closer, *"promised."*

"You're a very clever man. But I didn't promise to allow you to hang yourself." Israel glanced to Vertiline. "If you can do what you say and I see it, I *must* report it."

"One problem at a time." Meriwether offered the knife to Israel. "How'd you put it? One or two chances to change the world?"

"I thought Geneve the only one to use my words against me, but perhaps it's a problem with youth." Israel stared at him, eyes so hard it felt like a weight pressed on Meriwether's chest. The Knight reached his hand out, nice and steady, and took the blade from him. "I owe you one promise, sinner, and a promise you shall have."

Chapter Twelve

Following the Vhemin wasn't hard. The Feybrind could have been a blind human and managed it. The creatures trampled a swath through the forest about ten meters wide. Geneve wondered at their motivations. They normally took better care to cover their tracks. Leading people back to their lair wasn't good leadership thinking.

To be fair, they left you for dead. She winced, rubbing her shoulder. It felt hot, packed thick inside her armor. Getting the plate off would be painful, but that was a problem for Future Geneve. Today's Geneve needed to get her friends back.

They found the ashy remains of a bonfire. Geneve swung from Tristan's back, the horse snorting as she clanked to the loam. She tried to avoid Sight of Day's eyes, the Feybrind watching her from Fidget's back. He leaned forward, as if observing a special case of stupidity. He radiated agitation.

"Go on, then." Geneve poked in the ash, finding coals within. "Say it." She glanced his way to see his words.

{You're burning daylight.} The Feybrind looked to the canopy above, as if gauging the sun. *{Your span is that of a mayfly's. You certainly don't have the time to waste.}*

"Did you call me a mayfly?" Geneve rooted through ash, hefting out a slab of stone. "What do you think this is?"

{It's obvious you didn't find time to study in your brief life.} The golden eyes moved, Sight of Day making a show of examining his clean nails, in contrast to Geneve's sooty gauntlets. *{The monsters learn, Daughter of the Three. They take blood heat with them.}*

"That's disturbing." She dropped the stone to the ash, coughing as a cloud erupted at her feet. "Say nothing."

{It's good you're disguising yourself. Clever, even. No one would mistake you for a Knight.} The Feybrind's eyes twinkled. *{Normally your kind are cleaner. Now you look like a...}* his fingers paused for a moment, *{stray dog.}*

She put hands on hips, drifts of gray settling about her. "We can go now." She stamped toward Tristan, who sidled away, clearly not keen on her getting back on, especially since she looked like a chimney sweep.

The Feybrind watched her, Fidget snorting beneath him. *{Did you find them?}*

She knuckled her palm. *{Kneel.}* Tristan sighed, casting a look at Chesterfield lurking behind, as if saying, *Don't make me. Not in front of my friends.* Geneve knuckled her palm again, but harder this time. *{Kneel!}* The horse dropped before her, and she slung herself aboard. She checked her sword, scattergun, and shield out of long remembered habit. "Found who?"

Sight of Day held a palm out to the fire's memory. *{Those you fear lost.}*

"Now who's wasting time?" She steered Tristan in a circle, following the Vhemin's trail. "Come on."

{It's not your fault.} Sight of Day held a hand out, palm up. *{You slept because the angels kissed your brow. I smell it on your sweat.}*

She touched her lower lip. "How did the Vhemin drug me?"

The Feybrind shrugged. *{Perhaps you should ask the sinner.}* He urged Fidget forward.

"You're not doing a very good job of making me want to spare him." If Meriwether drugged her, endangering her friends, she'd... *I'll do nothing, except take him to the Justiciars.*

{That's because I don't want you to spare him.} The Feybrind gave that half-smile. *{I want so much more than that.}* He set off, Fidget tossing her

mane and making a big show of not wanting to be near the dirt trail Geneve left from the fire pit to her horse.

"What do you mean?" she called to his back. Sight of Day didn't answer. She'd forgotten how capricious they could be. "Fucking Feybrind. All the same!" Sight of Day didn't turn, but waved a hand, as if thanking her for a delicious compliment. She grinned. Geneve found no human remains in the fire. Her friends were still alive.

HALF A DAY'S RIDING LEFT GENEVE SORE AND MISSING THE SADDLE. Still, Tristin probably felt worse. She couldn't imagine having hard steel armor against his withers much fun. She patted the horse's neck. Chesterfield and Troubles cantered in Geneve's wake, keeping an easy pace without their riders. She tried not to look at Chesterfield. The black charger looked angrier by the moment.

They made good time through the forest. The Vhemin's wide trail wasn't just easy to follow but free of scrub that would normally foul speedy pursuit. As the day drew to a close, Sight of Day slowed Fidget, holding his hand in the air, fist clenched. *Stop.*

The Vhemin's trail might not need his tracking skills, but she knew Feybrind had the eyes and ears of, well, a cat. She stopped Tristan, leaning forward to whisper. "Quiet."

The horse stilled beneath her. Troubles slowed, tossing her mane, and even Chesterfield looked about. The Feybrind pointed three fingers to the right, then two to the left. Geneve nodded. *Guards.* She'd seen and heard nothing.

Sight of Day unlimbered his bow, notching an arrow with absent-minded perfection. She didn't know why Feybrind weren't Knights. They moved so much easier than clumsy humans. It'd taken her thirteen long years of training to reach the rank of Adept, and here was a Feybrind making her feel like a clumsy toddler.

He slipped from Fidget, settling to the forest floor without sound. She made to follow, but he cast her a scathing look, shaking his head. Geneve rolled her eyes, but he wasn't wrong. She'd sound like a spoon convention hitting the ground.

Sight of Day drifted into the trees. She waited, listening, eyes everywhere. After a handful of minutes, she heard a *whistle-thud* of an arrow loosed to target, then two more in rapid succession. Geneve looked to the trees but couldn't make anything out in the dimming light.

Two more *whistle-thuds* came from her left. Half a minute later, Sight of Day re-emerged from the trees. The Feybrind loped with an easy, relaxed stride, as if he'd just spent the last five minutes drinking ale and flirting with the barmaid. *Do Feybrind flirt?* It felt the wrong time to ask. He shouldered his bow. *{There are five less Vhemin in the world.}*

"Just five?" Geneve felt uneasy. "There's no way that small a number could account for Israel."

{Just five here. No more. We're safe for now.} Sight of Day's eyes glinted in amusement. *{I believe there are plenty more in the world.}*

"Oh, good. I was worried I'd miss out—" Geneve was cut off by a bloodcurdling roar. Five Vhemin burst from the trees about them. She caught scaly skin and slitted snake eyes before fixating on one. *That's the one who brought me down.* The monster seemed to recognize her, mouth opening in a horror grin of shark teeth. Her bastard sword was in her hand, Tristan surging forward as if the horse had a personal ledger of accounts to settle.

Lips pulled into a snarl, Geneve crouched low. A crossbow bolt *hushed* through the air she'd occupied. Shield on her left arm, she raised it. A *chunk-chunk* sounded as bolts hammered it, the distance between her and the Vhemin shrinking as Tristan charged.

Then she was among them. She rolled from Tristan's back as the blue roan reared, hooves finding a home in a Vhemin's skull. Geneve took a mace against her shield, the blow's force sliding her boots across the leafy ground. She grit her teeth into a grin that would make Israel proud, hunching behind her cover, then surging forward. The shield caught the Vhemin under the chin, lifting the brute into the air. Feet off the ground, her blade Requiem sang, carving the Vhemin in half.

A Vhemin fired its crossbow at her, but Requiem was ready. The blade slashed an arc as Geneve stepped to the side. She continued her turn, sword taking a Vhemin's head away from its shoulders.

The air hissed, a Vhemin ahead sprouting arrows as Sight of Day fired. She counted six impacting it before it fell back, an arrow through an eye socket finally knocking the dead into it.

Geneve sensed movement from her left and ducked below her shield. She heard the *boom* of a scattergun, her shield slamming against her. She remembered this Vhemin was taller than the others, enough height to be troublesome. Six paces away. Geneve kept the shield up, trusting her memory as she closed the distance between them. The scattergun *boomed* again, her shield ringing like a gong, the sound pure and angry. Then she was on the monster, sword slashing from on high, carving a path through the monster's head, chest, and out the side of its ribcage.

One left. She turned to the creature that knocked her out what seemed like an age before. It crouched, massive shoulders bunched, ready to fight. *Vhemin aren't known for running.* She held her arm out at shoulder height, blade leveled, pointing at it. "You owe me a debt."

"How's the shoulder?" it leered. "Last time, you were easy. This time, I might—"

Chesterfield rumbled over the top of him, trampling the Vhemin beneath glossy, black hooves. The charger bucked and stamped until there was nothing left, then did it a little more before sauntering off. Geneve checked the remains, then looked around for Sight of Day. The Feybrind leaned on his bow, watching with those wonderful golden eyes. "Are you okay?"

He nodded. *{The storm breaks, Daughter of the Three.}* He spread an arm to the carnage of the Vhemin. *{One against five.}*

"I told you before. The Sacred Storm doesn't answer my call." She cocked her head, listening as a horn sounded alarm. A few hundred meters away, no more. "We need to hurry."

The Feybrind didn't move. *{It looked like a storm to me.}*

"It only works if you're ... *whole*," she hissed. She tugged her Adapt's sash. "You'd know the Storm if you saw it, Sight of Day. It's..." She trailed off, thinking of Israel. "It works for those in the Three's grace, is all."

{You seem whole to me. Now stop wasting time.} He grinned sharp teeth. They were pointed like the Vhemin's but where the monsters looked

like sharks or the big marsh lizards, the Feybrind's were finely pointed. Delicate, but no less dangerous. *{It's like you want me to do all the work.}*

"I killed four to your one!" she spluttered. "Also, you said we'd be 'safe for now.' Does this look *safe?*"

Sight of Day made a show of looking at the fallen, unmoving Vhemin. *{Safe enough, yes. You speak like one trying to avoid their fair share. The one I shot was worth five ordinary ones.}*

"I saw no such thing. He was like the rest..." Geneve narrowed her eyes. "You're joking."

{Life needs joy, Daughter of the Three.} Sight of Day stroked his chin. *{Especially when fighting monsters in the dark.}*

Geneve pressed her lips into a line. She checked her shield. The surface was unmarked, good Smithsteel unharmed by its encounter with a scattergun. *Wait. Since when do Vhemin have scatterguns?* She paced toward the fallen creature, retrieving the weapon. She knew it like the back of her hand.

Geneve held Vertiline's scattergun to the fading light. "It's time to get you back to where you belong."

THEY LED THEIR HORSES. TRISTAN SEEMED TO WANT TO FOLLOW Sight of Day, so Geneve hissed at him. The blue roan shuffled behind her, head down, as if in a sulk. Chesterfield, Troubles, and Fidget clustered around the Feybrind. Geneve could understand Fidget following Sight of Day, but the other two? *Traitorous bastards.*

Finding the camp was easy as finding crabs in a brothel. They emerged from the forest's canopy. Sight of Day slowed, then halted, as thirty pairs of Vhemin eyes marked them in the fading light. Warned by the sound of a scattergun's anger, they were arrayed before a cave mouth. All were armed; two held glass blades. One was the heavy length of Israel's weapon, the other Vertiline's thinner edge.

Geneve stiffened. She knew those blades like she knew their keepers. *It doesn't mean they're dead. But it means you need to help them.*

Sight of Day chuffed a sigh. *{There are many Vhemin. I think you're in trouble.}*

"Me?" Geneve glowered. "What about you?"

{I can run much faster than you.} He winked.

The Vhemin shuffled, not leaving the cave entrance. *Interesting. It's like standing guard is more important than killing us.* Geneve's eyes traveled to a fire burning merrily in the twilight. A stake leaned over it, showcasing the horrors of the Vhemin's last shared meal. "Do you know how to fight against glass blades?"

{I'll work it out.} The Feybrind gave her a little side-eye. *{Is there more to it than not getting hit?}*

Geneve snorted, ran a gauntleted hand through messy red locks, then put her helmet on. Visor down, the world narrowed to slits as she marched toward the Vhemin. She spotted a few grins, more leers, and one or two chuckles as she approached. Her sword and scattergun were at her back, and she carried the souvenir of Vertiline's scattergun hidden between her shield and arm. The severed head of the Vhemin who'd knocked her sideways she clutched in a gauntleted fist, hidden from view behind the shield for just the right moment. The shield's crescent edge gleamed comfort below her chin.

The last time she fought this horde she'd been drugged. She wore Tresward Smithsteel and righteous anger, both heavy. These monsters didn't know what they fought against. She stopped ten meters from the closest. The Vhemin's skin was grayed almost to black, gnarled ridges running along its skull. When it spoke, its voice made her think of cracking ice. Brittle and hard at the same time, and oh so cold. "You shouldn't be here, Tresward girl."

It couldn't see her face, but she figured it imagined fear. Thirty against one? And they'd bested her not one night past. The mistake of leaving her for dead they looked to correct. Geneve glanced around, taking the time to check their arms, armor, and state of readiness. There'd be no quarter from the Vhemin. Not this close to their prize. Not against one Tresward *girl*. "You're right."

It seemed surprised by that. "You what?"

"I shouldn't be here." She swept her open hand, taking in them, the cave, and the mountain at their back. "I should be at home, minding hearth, tending for a man, no? Or maybe you meant I should be at Tresward, learning the skills of the Three. Perhaps you mistake me for a Cleric, a body-weak Postulant yet to pass my Appeal. No." She shook her head, metal rasping. "I see it now. You mean I shouldn't be *here*, before *you*. I should be dead, yes?"

The Vhemin shared an uncertain look with a fellow at its side. "Something like that."

"Then you shouldn't have taken my friends, sirrah." She tossed the severed Vhemin head, watching as it bounced against the ground. Twigs caught in sparse hair. Leaves and gore matted the stump.

The monster before her did a double-take, then roared, brandishing a cleaver. Geneve unslung Vertiline's scattergun, blowing a hole in the creature's torso. The roar cut off, and it dropped the cleaver, pawing at the hole in its chest. Geneve saw through the wound to the other side before it toppled to the ground.

One rushed her from the right. She pointed the scattergun without looking, firing. The blast took the creature's head from its shoulders, the body continuing a slow lumber. Geneve stepped aside, the carcass traveling past to stumble, fall, and splay on the ground. She let Vertiline's scattergun fall, drawing Requiem. Geneve raised her voice, shouting over the Vhemin's rumble of hate and spite. "You carry the glass blades of Knights! You believe to test your edge against mine. Come, then." She slammed Requiem against her shield, metal clanking and eager.

They charged her. Not just two with glass blades, but the whole remaining twenty-eight. She felt fear touch her, claws in her heart, threatening to drag her down. Imagined, *prayed* that Israel was at her back, his hand on her shoulder like when she was small. *Don't worry about the fight's outcome. It'll end in its own time,* he'd have said. *Be one with it.*

She raised her steel. Requiem caught the fire's ruddy light against its cold edge, almost like a brand of fire in her hand. If Geneve commanded the Storm, she could make it burn, or a hundred other things. But it was just her, her blade, her injured shoulder, and almost thirty Vhemin. She pressed her lips into a line, refusing fear's cold embrace. Geneve spared a thought for Sight of Day, hoping the Feybrind was doing his part, then the tide of Vhemin washed atop her.

A slash came at her legs. She swung Requiem, taking the Vhemin's arm off at the wrist. His blade spun past her, lost to the dark. Another charged, making to tackle her, but he moved like a slow and clumsy toddler, albeit one that ate whole cows for breakfast. Geneve stepped to the side, swatting him on the rump as he passed by. A strike came from her left, and she ducked under the rim of her shield, the blow landing hard and heavy. The force rattled her teeth, so she screamed, sweeping Requiem in an arc. Vhemin fell back against the whirl of steel, and she stood clear. *For the moment, at least.*

The two with glass blades stepped forward. The monsters about her shifted, panting and urgent, hungry and restless, all wanting the sticky red inside her. She felt like Israel was still with her, that gentle hand on her shoulder. *Fights are won in the heart, lass. Break their will.*

Little Geneve might have looked at him, his tall frame and strong shoulders. *But they're Vhemin. They do not falter.*

He'd only have shrugged. *You are Tresward iron. You can break anything.*

Geneve grinned within the privacy of her helmet. *By Cophine, Ikmae, and Khiton, I will not fall.* She straightened, widening her arms. Shield to one side, Requiem on the other. Chest bared, burnished sun on metal breastplate gleaming under the stars. "Give it your best shot."

The one carrying Israel's blade swung. By the Three, he was fast. Even Israel wouldn't have moved like that. The glass blade hungered for Geneve's frame. She stood, still as a frozen lake, hard as winter's rock.

The blade hit her armor, shattering into a thousand glittering pieces. The fragments sprayed about her. Vhemin shielded their eyes from the storm of shards, and Geneve lunged forward. Requiem took the head from the one with Vertiline's blade, the heart from another, and the arms off a third. She stood on a small piece of earth, making it hers. Not backing away. Not giving ground. If she stepped away to dodge, she always moved back to reclaim it.

The earth trembled, a promise of things to come. The Vhemin looked about, then withered as a rain of hooves and fury rode over them. Sight of Day galloped past atop Fidget, the Feybrind standing atop the red roan. He fired his bow into the Vhemin, shafts *thunking* into bodies, limbs, and heads. He tumbled free, landing at Geneve's side, back to hers. He stood with her, his slim sword held ready against monsters twice his size.

Chesterfield and Troubles rumbled past, braying and kicking. The Tresward horses fought as they'd been trained, hooves marking skulls, back legs caving chests. Tristan was with them, Geneve's beautiful blue roan looking like a slip of cloudy night.

Not one of the Vhemin ran. They fought, and bravely, and just as bravely died. Whether to the song of Geneve's Requiem, or the sliver of light Sight of Day fenced with, or to the terrible, unstoppable fury of Tresward horses, they all fell.

Minutes past, and it was done. Geneve panted within her helmet, casting about for foes. Sight of Day padded like a panther, checking the fallen for survivors. Making sure there were none, his blade talking to upturned faces or pleading hands. His golden eyes burned, not with the warmth of a hearth, but the terrible blaze of a furnace.

Geneve looked at her feet and the hundreds of shards of glass. All that remained of Israel's weapon, gone, all to break the spirit of her attackers. He'd have said it was worth it, but she wasn't sure.

Sight of Day approached, pointing at Vertiline's weapon. *{Now you can have glass in your hand.}*

Geneve pulled her helmet free, red locks tumbling about her face. "I can't use glass any more than the Vhemin." She tasted bitter envy in her words, tried to spit it out. "I'm not whole." The Feybrind watched her, waiting. Letting the silence do the talking. "I ... know the patterns, but I don't ... hear the song." She shook her head, then retrieved Vertiline's weapon. "The sword is just glass. It will break like anything else made of melted sand."

Sight of Day touched the blade's edge, pulling his hand back quick at the nick on his finger. He sucked it for a moment. *{Then how?}*

"The Sacred Storm is the only weapon a real Knight needs." Geneve pushed the bitterness back down, buried it deep, patted the mound of emotions down with a shovel. "We don't fight with steel or glass. The Light of the Three lives in us. Strengthens our weapons. We use glass blades," she tapped Vertiline's edge with a gauntleted finger, the glass chiming like fine crystal, "because they're very sharp. But it's our wills that make them strong."

Sight of Day watched her a few moments more. *{That sounds like a lot of hard work.}*

She gave a harsh laugh, cut it short. "Spoken like one trying to avoid their fair share."

He half-smiled. *{It's like you've known me for a hundred years. You see the color of my soul.}* He sobered, facing the cave mouth. *{We have work to do.}* He favored her with those beautiful eyes. *{And by we, I mean you. Get in there.}*

She felt her lip quirk in a grin, bitterness be damned. She clapped her hands, drawing Tristan's attention. She crossed her wrists before her face. *{Hide.}*

Tristan seemed to mull it over, then tossed his tail, heading for the trees. Sight of Day watched him go, seeming surprised as Fidget followed, then Chesterfield and Troubles. *{You have bewitched my horse with your Tresward magic.}*

"Your horse doesn't want to die. Probably the only smart one here." Geneve shook a few glass splinters from her helmet, then put it on. "Stay here. I'll be right back."

{Are you going somewhere without me?}

"Yes. In there." She stabbed Requiem toward the cave mouth.

{How curious. I'm going the same way. Care to join me?} The Feybrind set off, tail swishing behind him.

Geneve watched him. She felt like she should trust him. Like he was trust*worthy*. As if she *had* known him for a hundred years and knew the color of his soul. She didn't know how, or why, but she felt Sight of Day might be pure, like a mountain stream. Geneve distrusted the feeling, because he wanted her to set the sinner free.

He stood at your back with Vhemin raging for blood. He did not run. And he guarded you while the angel's kiss ran its course. Still, he was Feybrind. Not human, and not Tresward. Geneve should be careful. Mind her step and watch her back.

But as she stepped behind him into the maw of darkness ahead, she felt a flutter of happiness he was here. She told her traitor heart to still, but it wouldn't listen. It'd been a long time since she'd been with Feybrind. There were so few of them, and she missed them very much.

Chapter Thirteen

While the years hadn't made Geneve into a mountain like Israel, at ten she was taller than at her pint-sized introduction to the keep. Her memories of life before her arrival remained a mystery. When she'd talked to Israel about it, he'd offered a kind smile, saying only, "They'll come back. Nothing that's yours stays away for long."

The Tresward fed the Novices well. Meat with every meal. Fresh baked bread, and fruits brought from the warmer north. It meant her ribs didn't show anymore, and with Kytto's help she'd got a little lean muscle on her frame. She'd asked why she didn't grow larger like the older kids nearing their Trials, and Kytto had laughed. Stop reaching for it. It'll come to you when you're ready, was all he'd said.

It was frustrating. Despite Kytto teaching her how to fight with a brawler's low-class tricks, bites and head butts mixed with arm bars and groin gouges, Wincuf still beat her. He was a lanky young man now, almost at his Trials, but the Valiants in charge wouldn't allow him to take them. Geneve didn't know why but wished they would. It seemed he got angrier with each passing day.

Kytto clicked his fingers in front of her face, drawing her back to the here and now. "Sorry."

"No you're not, but there's good news here: I don't give a shit." The small, angry man gave her a pearlescent smile. "The problem with the twelve million *patterns is they don't teach you one important thing." Kytto rolled his shoulders like he was readying to wrestle an ox. "How to hurt a man where he really, really doesn't want to be hurt."*

"And you know this secret magic?" She tried to keep the smile from her face.

"Don't joke about magic, kid. That shit'll get you a Cage and a Judgment all of your own." Kytto slapped his chest. "Come on. Let's see what you've learned."

Geneve narrowed her eyes. Four years hauling crap for Kytto left her stronger and harder than her classmates. The Knight's training put her feet on the path of sword and shield. She could use a morning star more effectively than any queen's man. Geneve knew all the parts that made up a person and how to swing her steel so they'd come apart fast, swift, and easy. They'd taught her unarmed combat too, and soon she'd learn to fight on horseback.

She still couldn't beat Wincuf, though. The larger boy had the same training she did, and while laboring in Kytto's forge made her stronger than any of her age, he had five long years on her, and the growth a young man gets. "I've learned strong people are strong."

"You've learned a wise-ass's tongue." Kytto circled her, arms low and ready. She rushed him. Geneve was smaller and lighter, and definitely faster. She slammed into the Smith, and he tossed her aside with contemptuous ease. But rather than throwing her length on the ground, he used her momentum to turn her body in a summersault, setting her feet back on the worn stone floor. "What did you learn just now?"

Geneve backed away. "I've learned you're strong despite your years."

He shook his head, sourness coming to his tone. "Don't sass me. We don't have time for it. This Wincuf asshole going to wait for you to be his equal?" At the shake of her red locks, he cranked out a grim smile. "Right. So, what have you learned?"

She thought about what Kytto did. How he could have hurt her, really hurt her, but set her feet down nice and gentle. Geneve cast her mind back to her first sparring match with Wincuf, when he'd banged her fingers just because he knew it'd hurt. "We can choose how we fight."

"You've got it in one. You know why they won't let Wincuf take the Trials, right?"

"He's not good enough?"

"He's plenty good enough, kid. He's kind of remarkable. No, don't screw up

your face. I didn't give you lemons to eat, I gave you truth. Wincuf might be a great Knight one day." Kytto shook his head. "But not anytime soon."

"Oh great oracle of steel and wisdom, tell me your secrets." Geneve gave a mocking bow.

He grunted. "How we choose to fight says a lot about us. It says what we're willing to do."

"To win?"

"No, just what we're willing to do." Kytto shrugged. "Plenty of assholes willing to make others hurt just because hurting can be done. There aren't enough who are willing to hurt themselves to stop another going down. That's the way the world is, and the way it's always been."

"You're saying I shouldn't hurt Wincuf?" Geneve scoffed.

"I'm not saying anything at all, kid. That's between you and the Three. I'm saying why he's still a Novice is because he wants people to hurt all the time. We need people who can turn their steel aside when it's needed. Like that smug prick Israel."

A handful of questions bubbled up. Geneve selected the first, choicest one. "What's between you and Israel?"

"A woman."

"That answer seemed to come too fast for it to be born by honesty."

"Okay. Maybe it's a woman." Kytto shook his head, weary. "That's enough for today."

"There's still breastplates needing—"

"I said it's enough, kid." Kytto's tone softened. "Choosing how and when to hurt isn't just done at war. We do it all the time."

Chapter Fourteen

Whenthe Vhemin came, they weren't gentle. Meriwether hadn't expected any special dispensation, but he also hadn't expected a kick in the guts to wake him up. He curled over his pain, retching. As he spasmed, he clutched his pole, knocking his forehead against it.

The Vhemin towering above him laughed. "Get up, tiny human." He was, like the rest of his kind, ugly as the sins Meriwether was accused of. *And, let's be honest, I'm guilty of as of a few hours ago.*

Meriwether groaned, rolled onto his knees, and with an effort found his feet. He watched as Israel and Vertiline stood. The Vhemin cut the bonds at their feet, and if they noticed their re-tied nature, frayed ends, or looseness they made no comment.

Hands bound, cumbersome poles fouling their movements, the prisoners shuffled out of their cell. Vhemin crowded on all sides, a musky scent rolling from them. Not the rankness of stale sweat, but something almost like nutmeg, if you mixed it with a little ass. He eyed one close to him, trying not to draw attention to himself. That scaly skin reflected no light, but it also showed no moisture. *I guess that makes sense. I don't remember seeing snakes sweat either.*

The Vhemin led the three into a large chamber. It was twenty meters a side, following a line of steps down toward an altar at the end. At least, it *looked* like an altar, but not to the Three. Plain gray stone, thankfully unadorned with the ugly stain of blood. A mirror sat atop it, but not a very good one. It glinted but gave nothing back to the torches set in the walls except blurred, ruddy smudges. The mirror was, while not good at its prime function, impressive: Meriwether judged its oval shape to be seven meters tall and three wide, and just the kind of thing that made you think of a huge, vertically slitted Vhemin snake eye.

The chamber had a suspended balcony above on the left wall, with another entrance there. Meriwether gauged the height to be three meters. Too high to jump, even if he wouldn't be cut down by angry Vhemin before making it five steps. This might have been a theater at one time, the balcony a private area for those paying with platinum solars instead of copper barons, but no one stood there now. Except, of course, most theaters weren't buried in a mountain with an altar at one end.

Before the please-be-a-mirror-and-not-an-eye stood a Vhemin robed in dirty rags. Might be the one he'd seen earlier. The robed asshole held a book, old and ratty, the please-don't-be-human-skin-leather cover worn smooth. Meriwether froze, fear momentarily taking hold of his feet. His belly felt cold, and he wanted to turn and run. The Vhemin beside him grabbed Meriwether's arm with a massive hand. "Keep moving."

"I was just taking in the majesty."

The Vhemin eyed him suspiciously. "You follow the dark masters?"

"To be honest, I find all gods to be huge assholes." Meriwether stiffened. "Please don't hit me."

The Vhemin laughed, then hustled Meriwether along. "I like you, tiny human. I hope the demons aren't too hungry today."

Through the brief exchange, Israel and Vertiline continued down the wide steps, making a sizable lead. Israel glanced back. Meriwether shook his head. *Not yet.* He put one foot down a step, then cocked his head, listening. "You hear that?"

The Vhemin growled. "Hear what?"

"Sounded like..." Meriwether frowned. "It sounded like someone screaming. But a long way away."

"Probably a prisoner." The Vhemin continued down, dragging Meriwether like an unwilling and not very effective anchor. Israel and Vertiline's gap between them grew, and Meriwether didn't hate that. It meant that whatever was happening with the altar, mirror, book, and what was probably a High Priest at one end would happen to the Knights *first*.

Another scream sounded, this time clear enough for all to hear. The High Priest glanced up the steps, then shrugged. *They must cause a lot of people to scream to be this relaxed about it*. The priest opened his book, thumbing through the pages, before turning to the mirror and setting the book aside. He cast his arms wide, the robe falling away from arms so muscled it looked like a walnut convention. *Probably give Israel a run for his money*.

The High Priest began to chant, that rough Vhemin throat speaking words in a language Meriwether didn't recognize. The mirror *shifted*, a ripple going through the metal surface.

Another scream sounded, this one not far at all. The Vhemin holding Meriwether glanced up toward the balcony, then back to his captive. "That sounded close."

Meriwether nodded. "You keep prisoners nearby?"

"No." The Vhemin looked uncertain. The main body of his fellows huddled about Israel and Vertiline ahead. The mirror swayed, discoloring to a dark, sullen red. Another scream, cut short. "I should go check."

"Good idea." Meriwether held up his pole, offering an encouraging smile. "I'll wait here, if you like."

The Vhemin nodded, then beckoned to a handful of his fellows. They trekked back up the steps toward the main door.

The mirror turned black, then with a *snap* turned into a glowing cut in the air. Meriwether's ears popped, a gentle wind stirring his hair. Within what was clearly a portal stood a silhouetted figure. *No, that's not a silhouette. That's a person made of shadow, and they have red eyes. I'm no expert but that looks like a demon.*

Israel spun to Meriwether. "Now?"

"Now!" At Meriwether's shout, the Tresward Knights *moved*. It was like watching water flow, or the sun cross the heavens. They were perfect, the two complimenting each other. They dropped their poles, bonds freed earlier—a bit of mummery with the cords kept the Vhemin from catching on. Meriwether's knife appeared in Israel's hand. The big man swung the tiny blade at a Vhemin beside him. In another time and place, the perfect beauty of the strike might have made Meriwether gasp.

The Vhemin's body exploded in a shower of gore. Meriwether goggled at what the tiny blade did in the hands of a Valiant. Israel didn't roar or flex. He *flowed*. Where the tiny sliver of steel hit armor, it shattered buckles and ruptured leather and metal plates alike. As it hit the Vhemin's hide and the flesh underneath, it was like a thousand horses kicked the brute at once. The blade didn't look like steel. It looked like a tiny sliver of the Three, a mote of purest golden-white that hurt to look at.

As pieces of dead Vhemin cascaded across the steps, splattering against the High Priest and the altar behind him, butterflies conjured into being by the Three's Light burst into flight. Meriwether stood speechless as they took to purple wings. For the first time in his admittedly short life, he saw the power of the Three. *Cophine's tits. An exploding monster with butterflies as a side-effect. How did I think to stand against them?*

Silence held the room for a moment. The dead Vhemin's blade fell as if through treacle. Israel spun, Vertiline at his back. She snatched the weapon from the air, giving it a twirl. Like everything the Vhemin had it was old, a hand-me-down from a dead human opponent. The blade looked rusted, pitted, blunt as a baby's ass. As the Chevalier swung the blade, it looked like life itself ebbed into the old metal. The pitted edge gleamed as if it remembered how to hunt. Light sparkled along the glimmering edge, Vertiline's single braid lashing.

If either Knight carried pain or hurt, it didn't show. Meriwether let his pole clatter to the floor, speechless. If it hadn't been for the angel's kiss, there was no way they'd have fallen. *I took this from them. I took away their grace, and the world almost lost this wondrous beauty.*

He shook himself. *I'm being stupid. They're a cult of murderers. But my, they're pretty.*

A Vhemin ran at Israel, thinking the big man's tiny blade a better match than Vertiline's gleaming edge. The Vhemin carried a two-handed sword, and rust be damned: it'd leave a mark if it touched flesh. Israel moved to meet his opponent, the little blade parrying the bigger one. Meriwether wanted to cry a warning because only an imbecile parried a greatsword with a butterknife.

There was a chime, the bigger blade shorn through, then the Vhemin's body shattered, the peal of Tresward bells filling the room.

The Vhemin that had been at Meriwether's side was in front of him again, fists bunched in Meriwether's tunic, slamming him against the wall. His head knocked against the stone at his back and he saw stars. Sound took on a distant feel as if he were using someone else's ears. Meriwether scanned the room, dazed. Israel and Vertiline carved a path toward the mirror. The High Priest chanted, arms still high, black light kissing his hands. The Vhemin before Meriwether punched him in the gut, drawing his attention. "I said, what's happening?" Feet dangling, Meriwether choked a laugh. The Vhemin roared. "What's so funny?"

"She is," he croaked, pointing with his chin.

The Vhemin turned, the motion slow, almost comical. Another Vhemin soared from the balcony above, falling on the steps with a crack, body twisted. Above, red hair peeking from under her helmet, Geneve stood, a Feybrind of all things at her side. It was a lot to take in. Meriwether wanted to know how she got here. How she found time to meet a Feybrind. Why the cat, one of the Vhemin's sworn enemies, defied sanity and reason to come into a pit of devils.

Most of all, he wanted her to come down and save him.

Meriwether saw the flash of green eyes within her visor. The Feybrind fired a bow, three arrows skewering the Vhemin holding Meriwether. The grip loosened, but the Vhemin didn't fall. Geneve threw her sword, the steel tumbling end over end. The weapon hit the Vhemin, knocking it from its feet and staking it to the wall like a particularly large insect in a particularly small collection. Meriwether caught a tiny glimmer of half-light along the blade's edge. It might have been the torchlight running rampant. Cinnamon touched his nose. *I was hit harder than I thought.*

She vaulted the balcony's rail, landing on the balls of her feet. The Feybrind dropped behind her, soundless, lithe, golden eyes everywhere, teeth bared. Geneve ran at Meriwether, shoulder-barging a Vhemin in her path. The beast flipped into the air to crash against the stone behind her. The Feybrind stabbed it through the eye with an arrow without slowing.

Geneve made Meriwether's side. She grabbed the hilt of her sword, yanking. The steel cried as it came free from the stone, the Vhemin slumping to the ground in a slick trail of gore. He gave a nervous smile. "Nice throw."

"I missed," she hissed. Her gauntleted hand found his chin, turned his face about. "Are you whole?"

"I'm great, thanks. Never been better—"

"*Are you hurt?*"

"I can run, if that's what you're asking." He pointed to Israel with his suspiciously unbound hands. Meriwether didn't miss how her eyes narrowed. "We need to help your friends."

"I know my duty." She spun from him, back turned, that arrogance at his weakness showing. *She's not wrong. Geneve just fought her way into a Vhemin stronghold with nothing but a cat for company. It's a big cat, though.*

Israel reached the High Priest. He brought his tiny blade in for the kill, but as the steel met the black light hugging the Vhemin, its light dimmed. *Definitely a demon on the other side. They stood against the Tresward in the last war that mattered.* The Vhemin grinned, but Israel showed no surprise. He grabbed the priest by the robe, bringing the monster in for a savage head butt.

The High Priest lolled in his grip. The mirror's black-red portal flickered, and for a moment, brilliant light cascaded through. Instead of a shadowed horror, Meriwether saw an older man, maybe nudging sixty but with the benefits of a good diet. A face that was probably kindly but looked like it carried more stress than was good for a man's heart at that age. He flung a hand out. "Israel! Vertiline! Geneve! To me. By the Three, hurry!"

Geneve skidded to a halt, spun, and clattered back to Meriwether.

He could smell the sweat of her, and something sweeter underneath. She grabbed his tunic, hauling him behind her like he was no more concern than a feather pillow.

Vertiline sprang on the altar, hand out to Israel. The Valiant took her hand, stepping up, then gestured in an *after you* motion. Vertiline stepped through the gleaming portal. Geneve and Meriwether were just steps behind. Israel stepped through, then held his hand out.

Geneve put on a burst of speed. Meriwether felt jounced like good ale on a bad wagon. The Feybrind loped beside them, looking like this human speed was very slow indeed. Five meters from the altar, the High Priest looked up. Four, he raised a hand. At three, he snapped his fingers.

Screaming, Geneve lunged. She made the altar just as the golden portal snapped out. They crashed into the slab of metal, her armor ringing against it like a gong. The mirror toppled with them to the stone behind the altar.

The Feybrind leaped atop the altar, tail swishing, back to them. Meriwether looked up, wondering just how bad his day was going to get. Sure, through a portal toward a Tresward haven wasn't a *great* destination, but it was better than being in an underground chamber full of very angry Vhemin.

At least the Feybrind was on their side. Three of them, dying together in the dark below the earth. It sucked, but not as much as dying alone.

Get up. He groaned, found his feet, and stood. Hand out to Geneve, he tried for a smile, losing it to the gloom around them. "Come on."

She brushed his hand aside, standing on her own despite the weight of Smithsteel. Clambering over the altar, she stood in front of him and the Feybrind. She pulled off her helmet to slick back red hair. Her back was straight, shoulders square. Sweat slicked her amber-honey skin, but there wasn't a hint of fear about her. Vhemin entered the chamber from above. Ten, then fifteen. Another five from the balcony above. Then another five for good measure.

"Stay behind me," Geneve hissed.

He realized she didn't even have a shield. Lost, or broken, it didn't matter. "Fuck that," he suggested. As the Vhemin drew closer, Meriwether slipped beside the fallen High Priest. He pulled a blade from his sleeve. It was like the one he'd given Israel, a small sliver, barely long enough to open letters with. But like Israel's, this one glowed with the Light of the Three. Brilliant, incandescent, gleaming for all to see.

Meriwether knelt beside the High Priest. The Vhemin's smile guttered out as the blade found his neck, light undimmed by the black seeping from the priest's skin. He heard a gasp from Geneve behind him, and imagined her thoughts horse-trading around the topic of, *How does a sinner call the Light of the Three?* The Feybrind made no sound, but their kind didn't. Meriwether leaned toward the High Priest, nice and close, and put his lips to the monster's ear. "Hello, friend. How do you feel about living to see another day?"

Chapter Fifteen

G eneve was alone.

She walked beside a Feybrind. She already felt the foundations of trust between them, or perhaps something more like friendship, but they needed to make it out alive first. She wasn't sure of Sight of Day's motivations, but his golden eyes made her feel warm. There was no malice there. The problem with the situation at hand was she wasn't sure if they'd get time to be friends. There were a lot of Vhemin between *now* and *five minutes from now*.

Ahead of her walked the sinner. His face was bruised, lip swollen, and he walked hunched around a pain he carried deep in his chest. But no part of him leaked red, so she'd see him to his trial. *Except, neither he nor Sight of Day want him to go to trial. It's just me trying to get him there.*

One problem at a time. Her steel felt heavier than she was used to. Requiem dragged in her hand as if it didn't want to be used in conflict against *this* particular sinner. But a sinner he was, because he'd magicked a knife out of the air, pushing it into the demon darkshield of a Vhemin High Priest without breaking a sweat. *Even Israel's Light couldn't break through.*

"I can *feel* you wanting to ask something." The sinner nudged the

High Priest with the blade, a lick of steel against the softer scaled skin beneath the Vhemin's throat. "Not you."

Geneve bit her lip. The Feybrind watched her with those golden eyes, a smile hiding in there somewhere. His fingers moved quiet and sure. *{I can feel it too.}*

"Shut up," she growled.

"What was that?" said Meriwether, turning to glance at her.

"Not you," she said, pointing at Sight of Day. "I was talking to the Feybrind."

Meriwether glanced between them, then returned to his vigil of keeping the High Priest focused on not dying. Vhemin capped the corridor they walked down, keeping a good ten-meter distance front and rear. All bristled with weapons and intent. Geneve had no illusions about their chances of survival if Meriwether's Light—*by the Three, he holds their Light!*—failed. She was good with a blade, but her shoulder ached right to the bone, and she was past tired. She'd left 'tired' at a fork in the road some time past, and realized a deep weariness was her traveling companion.

To be fair, the sinner also looked tired. Eyes hollow, almost bruised. Haunted, as if—

As if someone's hunted him his entire life, then when they found him, threw him in a cage.

"My question is, 'How did you get another knife?'"

Meriwether put a hand on the High Priest's arm. "Hold up a minute." His blade never wavered, which was good because Geneve could feel the hate boiling from both ends of the corridor. She held Requiem ready, Tribunal in her other hand. Both weapons had tasted Vhemin blood today, and if she waged coin on it like the dice-rolling reprobates in taverns everywhere, they would again. "You want to know how I got a *knife?*"

"Yes." She nodded, slow because she was uncertain. "Israel had the blade I left with you. You have another."

He pursed his lips, chewing the question over. "I stole it." He spun on his heel, nudging the High Priest forward.

The priest, for his part no imbecile, spat, "I will barbecue you on open flames!"

"I'd start with the cat," the sinner said. "She's too gristly, and I'm too small."

{I don't like this human.}

"Are you ... fools?" The High Priest's tone was a turf war between confusion and anger. Confusion was winning.

"I don't know." Meriwether considered their direction as they hit a junction. Geneve pointed with her scattergun straight ahead. He nodded his thanks. "I'm not the one with a knife to my throat. Let's go over today's events. You outnumbered us by a healthy margin, and yet here we are, knives to your throats. I really can't imagine the conversation you're going to have with the black shadowy asshole in the portal."

The priest swallowed. "There's yet time to recover—"

"Who'd you steal it from?" asked Geneve. "The knife, I mean."

"You."

Geneve looked to her belt. The sheath holding her small blade was empty. "But. Uh. How?"

"Sword. Wall. You were distracted. Don't blame yourself." He tossed her a wink, despite the paleness of his skin, the *worn-thin* of him. "There was a lot going on."

{It's true. I was there.} Sight of Day's tail swished as he padded beside her.

She wanted to stop and demand answers from the sinner. How did he steal a Knight's blade? Why had he given his other one to Israel? *What I want to know is why he didn't stab me in the back. I earned it, and then some, yet here I am, on a merry jaunt for freedom.*

"I didn't stab you because I'm not that kind of sinner." He tossed this at her feet, barely glancing in her direction.

"You can read minds too?" She pointed Tribunal at a Vhemin getting too close. "You. Back up." The monster glared as it retreated, resentment in every footstep.

"No. But it's the next thing you were going to ask." The tunnel rose before them. The air smelled different here. Cleaner. *Safer.* The Vhemin backed away, making space for them as they left the underground labyrinth. The smooth stone floor gave way to crudely hewn rock as they emerged into the night.

Three's Mercy, we're outside. Vhemin gathered around in numbers significant enough to make Geneve's blood chill to glacier ice. She felt fear's fingers running down her sweat-slick spine. Her armor wouldn't be enough to see her free of this. Her strength wouldn't last, and she couldn't wield Vertiline's glass. There was no storm inside her.

Meriwether gave a small, polite cough. Geneve tamped down her doubts. *If a skeleton of a man can be fearless before the horde, I need to step up.* The sinner faced the Vhemin High Priest, blade still at the monster's throat. "How do you think this ends?"

"With your bellies slit open, innards steaming on the ground."

"Sure." He nodded. "That's one way. What's the other way?" He pressed his knife against the priest's throat for emphasis.

The High Priest's eyes were full of hate, lip curled in a snarl. Geneve caught the rankness of his breath, even three meters back. "There is no other way. No hope. No escape!"

Meriwether turned to Geneve. "I've got a plan."

{I really don't like this human at all.}

Meriwether ignored Sight of Day's handspeak. "What we do is, knock this clown out, then run, but *with* him."

The Vhemin priest laughed. "That's your plan? How do you dare hope to best me with a clutch of my finest warriors nearby?"

Geneve closed the five paces between them and slugged him across the jaw with the fist holding Requiem. His eyes rolled back and he slumped to the ground. To his credit, the sinner followed the Vhemin down, blade never far from the monster's throat.

The other Vhemin hissed but stayed back. Geneve saw their eyes on the sinner's glowing blade. The sinner, for his part cooler than anyone with no friends should be, gave Geneve a wink. He took his hands away from the dagger, but slowly, like he'd carefully balanced a teacup on a frisky horse.

The knife held upright by itself, tip suspended a hair's breadth from the Vhemin priest's throat. Meriwether straightened, arched his back as if working out the kinks, then dusted off his hands. "That'll just about do it, I think."

She goggled. "You ... how are you holding the knife in place?"

"Evil," he suggested. "Pure sin. The souls of the damned hold it in place. They harken to my every whim. Three hundred babies died to make it happen."

"Really?"

"No." He looked weary, like he'd spent all this energy on a joke that wouldn't land. The sinner stepped back from the comatose priest, heel catching on uneven ground. He stumbled, hands out, but Sight of Day was beside him fast as thought.

The Feybrind held the young man upright, and once the sinner found his balance, brushed him down with a half-smile and a nod. *{He can do amazing things but is clumsier than one of your ugly human babies.}*

"Ugly?" Geneve wasn't quite sure when she'd lost control of things. *Khiton's empty hearth, I need to get my head back into the game.*

{Furless, like infant moles. Shriveled and mewling.} The Feybrind shrugged, turning those wondrous golden eyes on Geneve. *{It's not your fault you were made that way. It will be your fault if we all die horribly because you didn't call our horses.}*

Geneve gritted her teeth, then holstered Tribunal at her back. She put fingers to her lips and blew a long, shrill whistle. The *clump-clump* of hooves on loam came across the night air, Tristan bursting from the forest's edge with Fidget, Chesterfield, and Troubles behind him. The horses huffed the night air as they cantered closer. Geneve sheathed her blade. *{Kneel.}*

Tristan considered the request, looked to the Vhemin and the glowing dagger above his throat, then crouched. She turned to Meriwether. "Up you get." Tristan glared, but held still.

Meriwether clambered with the gracelessness of those not just unfamiliar with horses but distrusting of them too. He eyed the horse beneath him with narrowed eyes, as if expecting Tristan to sprout an extra head. "Where to?"

"We need equipment. I know just the place." Geneve looked to Chesterfield. She pushed her wrists out from her body. *{Protect us.}* The giant charger tossed his head. She gestured to Troubles. *{Kneel.}*

Sight of Day leaped atop Fidget. Geneve mounted Troubles. They rode off with Chesterfield at their rear. The Vhemin howled in response but held their ground. Geneve felt half the eyes watched them leave, and the other half watched the mysterious, glowing dagger.

Danger took a breather but hadn't left. It would re-enter the fight soon enough.

❦

GENEVE PUSHED TROUBLES AS FAST AS SHE DARED. THE FOREST WAS dark, dawn's light far away. Sight of Day rode in the trees to her right, his horse keeping pace with ease. Feybrind could see as well at night as during the day, and his natural reflexes and grace would keep him safe from the branches that tried to tear Geneve from her saddle.

A silver lining is the sinner's having more trouble than me. She hated the thought as soon as it arrived. It wasn't the kind of thought a Knight should have in the quiet of their heart. *To be fair, your heart's far from quiet.* Part of it was riding an unfamiliar steed, but she'd figured Tristan would do as Geneve asked, but Troubles' flexibility in who she'd let ride her was limited by Vertiline's absence.

Thought of her missing friend cut Geneve, a lance of anxiety so bright it hurt. She'd seen Vertiline and Israel step into a portal, the Justiciar Ambrose beckoning them through. She knew her fellow Knights were safe. Safer than Geneve anyway, with a wily sinner to watch and a horde of Vhemin at her heels.

Focus on the task. Get equipment. Find safe haven. Fight when I must, run at all other times. Geneve was just one Knight, and not a very good one at that. The Storm wouldn't come to her aid, and that knowledge was heavier than the armor she wore.

"Where are we going?" Meriwether gasped from behind her.

She spared him a glance. The sinner clutched Troubles, face miserable. Geneve pointed ahead, then ducked a branch that threatened to toss her from the saddle. "Camp!"

"Are you mad?"

She ignored him. Geneve wanted more speed from Troubles, but she didn't want the horse to lose footing in the dark. An accident injuring Geneve and crippling Troubles would be disastrous. She put her armored hand on the horse's neck. *Be easy.* Troubles ignored her, intent on the task of not tripping and killing them both.

They rode hard until dawn brushed the leaves around them to a pale green. They broke into the clearing holding yesterday's camp. *By the Three, only yesterday? It feels like it was a week ago.* Geneve swung herself from Troubles. The horse stamped in agitation. "I know. We need to hurry." She ran her hand down Troubles' flank, then headed to the tents.

They still stood undisturbed. Night's dew covered their surface. The fire was long spent, black charcoal cold and damp. She worked her way from tent to tent, gathering bags and equipment. Supplies for the road. By the tree line, she caught sight of Sight of Day helping an exhausted sinner from Tristan's back. Geneve ignored them. *We need to move, and move fast. But where? We shouldn't go to Calterburry. We've no friends there, and besides, bringing Vhemin to their gates is no favor.* She exited Israel's tent, saddlebags draped over her shoulder, and almost ran into Sight of Day.

The Feybrind stepped aside as if human clumsiness was just one more thing to remember like water being wet. His golden eyes weren't on her, though. Sight of Day watched the sinner. Meriwether stood before the cage. He hugged himself, shoulders rounded, shrinking before the implied threat of the wagon and its burden.

She took a step toward the sinner. Sight of Day touched her arm. *{Carefully, Daughter of the Three.}*

Geneve shook him off, dumping the saddlebag to the ground. "He is a—"

The quick flick of the Feybrind's handspeak cut her off. *{You'd call him sinner and put him in that box.}* Another half-smile. *{He's stood shoulder by shoulder with us. I trade truth with you: he saved us. Perhaps breakfast before the cage?}*

She glanced to the sinner, then nodded, but slow, the movement rustier than armor left in the rain. Geneve walked toward Meriwether, stopping two paces from him. "Sinner." She bit her lip as soon as the word left her lips. He deserved more from her.

More? He drugged me. My fellow Knights almost died. If he hadn't done unspeakable things, none of this would have happened. The thoughts wanted to burst to the surface, break the tension in the air. Geneve hungered for them, how they would taste on her lips. The sinner turned to her and she saw pain in his eyes, deep and real. Weariness sat there too, not just from the road, but of the world. He gave her a bitter smile, lip curling like he could feel the acid of it. "At your service, m'lady."

Geneve took a step back. Her armor creaked, reminding her of who she was. A Knight of the Three. She straightened her shoulders. "We should have breakfast."

He snorted. "What do we eat?" The sinner tossed a hand past the cage. Her eyes followed the direction of the movement. The oxen that pulled the cage lay slaughtered on the cold ground. Dead eyes looked at a dawn they'd never see. "All the meat is spoiled." He looked back to the cage. "I guess it means I won't get back in there."

"Happy about that, are you?" she snapped.

The sinner shook his head. "No, Knight. Because two creatures had to die for it to happen, and even the cost of their lives has taught you nothing." He spun on his heel, walking back toward the cold remains of their fire pit. "I'll get water boiling."

Geneve watched him go, then looked to the oxen. Dead, and not by her hand. And not, if she was honest, by the sinner's either. Vhemin came here, slaughtering beasts they couldn't take with them. It was the kind of petty, vicious act of their species. But the oxen wouldn't be here if they hadn't been needed to take a sinner to Judgment. *Is that what he meant? That it's my fault?* Her lips pressed into a flat, hard line at the thought.

Sight of Day crouched by the remains of the fire, placing kindling like he were building a merchant's mansion one stick at a time. The sinner joined him, helping. The Feybrind watched Meriwether for a moment, accepting his help, but when the sinner's head was turned, Sight of Day replaced a few of the sticks. Geneve thought about how the Feybrind accepted help that wasn't needed, and why he might have done it.

I'm wasting time thinking about things that aren't important. We need to eat, then get on the road. The Vhemin will come. Thinking of the monsters in their wake made her wonder about the glowing dagger the sinner left at the priest's throat. How long would it stay there? What would happen when it fell?

She clanked toward the pair. Sight of Day turned his beautiful eyes on her. The sinner ignored them both. She crossed her arms. "Sinner. How did you do the trick with my knife?"

He shook his head. "Is this part of my Judgment? Ask me my crimes, so I set myself alight? I'll allow it would save you some trouble." Sight of Day studiously looked away, setting flint to tinder, coaxing a tiny flame to life. Meriwether readied a pan.

Geneve growled. "This isn't Judgment. Also, I'll make breakfast."

"How kind."

"It's not kindness. Last time I ate something you touched, I fell over there," she stabbed her arm toward where she'd been knocked aside last night, "and we almost died."

"Fair." He stood, bowing to their miniature fire with a flourish. "I await the marvel of Tresward breakfasts." He rubbed his chin, fingers rasping over the stubble growing there. "To be honest, I've never eaten so well as in your captivity."

"Never?" Geneve rummaged through Israel's saddlebags. She found a shank of good salt bacon, a wooden box with packaged eggs, a round of cheese, and bread that would serve if no one looked too closely.

He didn't reply, and she wondered if he was ignoring her. When she glanced up, he was still as stone, hand still on his chin. "Not for a long time, anyway." She retrieved his skillet.

Sight of Day headed toward the trees. *{Water.}* She nodded agreement, watching his almost accidental grace as he moved through the camp toward the nearby stream. *The sinner saved my life. The least he deserves is my kindness.* Geneve watched the fire until she was sure her voice held no more grit. "How did you do it?" Once she'd stamped the anger away, it almost sounded like her voice held wonder. *Ridiculous.*

Meriwether tossed a crooked eyebrow in her direction as if measuring whether she were mocking him. Then he let out a pent-up sigh, reached into his sleeve, and drew forth her dagger. "Here."

She scrambled to her feet, backing away. Her sword was half-drawn before she realized the ridiculousness of it. "How?" She rammed Requiem back into its scabbard, then took the knife from Meriwether. It was hers, no doubt about it. Geneve pressed the point to her finger, wincing as it pricked blood, then slipped it into its sheath. "I don't understand."

"It started when I was young." He crouched by their growing fire, huddling close to its warmth. "Isn't that always the way with sinning?" His eyes took a far-off look, like he was remembering a thing for someone else. "None of that matters. You want the how of it, and here it is. I can make anything I've seen appear."

"Illusions of light?" Geneve looked from the sinner to the forest behind them. "So—"

"So the unholy monsters will eventually work out there isn't a knife. Wasn't ever one, really. I mean, sure, there was a blade, but—"

She lunged for him, grabbing his shirt, and hauling him forward. His eyes were wide, a handspan from her face. *Close enough to kiss, if he were a different person, in a different situation. And I was not who I am.* "You imbecile!"

"I ... what?" He glanced to the trees as if hoping Sight of Day would return, or the Vhemin, or *anything* really.

She let him go, and he sagged away. "You had *nothing* on the Vhemin," she spat. "If they'd found out—"

"We'd be dead." He nodded. "But we were dead anyway."

"I could have—"

"What?" The sinner spread his arms, turning for an imaginary audience. "Fought your way out? You and the cat, back to back? Even if you gave me a blade—"

"Which I wouldn't. Certainly not after this!"

"Which you wouldn't, but *if* you had the three of us would've died anyway. Your precious trial and its Judgment wouldn't have happened. Your fellow Knights would have been fucking *barbecue*. Now, you've got the freedom to shout at me. Breathe air you'd never have felt again. And," he pointed a finger at the fire, voice rising, "make me breakfast."

Geneve seethed. She wanted to punch him with an armored fist. *I want to be the hand of Judgment.* Her fingers curled with the need to hold Requiem. It wasn't *what* he'd said, how *how* he'd said it. She'd had plenty of people say unkind things to her. No, it wasn't that at all.

It's that he's right, isn't it?

An overloud rustle drew her attention. Sight of Day waited at the tree line, hand shaking a branch to make noise. She saw he had a brace of fish with him. *How did he catch three fish in the time it's taken us to get nowhere at all?* She relaxed her fingers. "I thought..." Geneve trailed off. *What did I think?*

"You thought I held your precious Light of the Three." Meriwether nodded. "It was what you were supposed to think. But better. *Stronger.* The giant asshole—"

"Israel."

"Israel had a tiny blade and the power of the waves or whatever you call it, and he couldn't stand against the priest. I had to make them *believe. You* had to believe."

She looked down. Her voice sounded like crushed leaves. "I did."

Sight of Day joined them, golden eyes moving between the two humans. He handed his fish to Meriwether. The sinner looked at them like he'd never seen a fish before. "What am I supposed to do with these?"

{Clean them.} The Feybrind put his hand on Geneve's arm, drawing her attention. *{The storm almost broke, didn't it?}*

Meriwether's eyes narrowed. "What's he saying?" He held the fish out from his body. "Really. What am I supposed to do with these?"

Geneve kept her eyes down. *{There's no storm inside me.}* To Meriwether, she said, "You don't know the People's handspeak?"

"The what now?"

{This is surprisingly good news.} The Feybrind gave a half-smile. *{Imagine the things we can say about him.}*

"That's not very kind." Geneve felt her lip quirk anyway.

"What's not very kind?" Meriwether shook the fish. "Will someone please tell me what I'm supposed to do with these?"

"Clean them." Geneve drew her knife from its sheath, offering it back to the sinner. "Try not to lose it this time."

"You're giving me another knife?"

"Be hard to clean fish without one."

"Right." He nodded, taking the knife. "Wait. How'd I get suckered into cleaning the fish? And why are we eating fish when we have bacon?"

{Fish wrapped in bacon is delicious,} suggested Sight of Day. *{It will also shut the noisy one up for some time.}*

Geneve considered that. "Which one of us is the noisy one?"

"Aren't you worried about me poisoning you again?" Meriwether shook the fish. "Think of the things I could do while I'm cleaning these."

Geneve stepped toward the sinner. He leaned back, like she was living flame. "I'm not worried. Do you want to know why?" He nodded, like a pecking bird. "There are about a hundred Vhemin behind us. And they want you, sinner. Not me."

She left him to his fish, going about the business of squaring away the camp. Many things they couldn't take on horseback. Someone would find what they didn't need and make use of it. Nothing was wasted in the world.

SIGHT OF DAY FOUND HER AFTER BREAKFAST. THE SINNER WAS OFF trying to put a saddle on Tristan, which was amusing enough to watch. The young blue roan would wait until Meriwether drew close, then dance to the side as he tried to throw the saddle on the horse's back.

{We must go.} The Feybrind cleaned his teeth with a stalk of grass while he watched the young man. {Much as the entertainments here satisfy the soul.}

She eased her gauntlets off to speak with him easier in his own language. Her shoulder hurt, and she knew her skin would be mottling with bruising beneath her armor, but she owed the Feybrind the simple respect of the People's ways. {You want to take the sinner.}

Sight of Day nodded. {Yes, but that's not important yet.}

{It's pretty important,} Geneve insisted. {He must go to Judgment.}

{What is important is the storm inside you.} The Feybrind looked to the sky, sun climbing as it always did. {You told me you didn't hold it close.}

She grunted, hands falling to her sides. "There's no storm. There never will be. Only the whole get to see it."

The Feybrind stepped back, eying her up and down. {You look normal enough. For a human, I mean.}

She laughed, but it quickly died. "The Sacred Storm is about perfection. If we have," she groped for the right word, "precision, it will join its will to ours."

{You look precise enough, too.}

Geneve turned from his golden eyes. "I remember nothing before my fifth birthday. The Clerics tell me it's because of tragedy, and that the memories will return. But without them I'm not ... whole."

She felt gentle fingers on her jaw, Sight of Day turning her face back to him. *{You are perfect, Daughter of the Three.}*

Geneve shook her head, angry with herself. She shouldn't be talking about this with him. It wasn't his business. "So. How will we solve the problem of the sinner?"

Sight of Day considered her a moment longer. *{We don't need to make a choice yet. Your Justiciars lie to the north. There is a village of the People that way. Perhaps we should travel together a while longer. You humans can warble at each other. Once we're safer, we can decide.}*

Geneve considered it. She hated herself for the thought, but it needed voicing. "With the People, you could ... *insist.*"

The Feybrind shrugged, taking no offense. *{Here, you could insist also. Trust is a fragile thing, but we've been shoulder to shoulder. Do you think I would steal him?}*

"I think if you wanted to take him, you would look me in the eye as you did it." Geneve smoothed red hair. "I don't want to lead the Vhemin to your People."

{I do.} The Feybrind narrowed his eyes. *{We do not suffer a Vhemin to live.}*

Geneve blew out a great sigh, shoulders relaxing. "Then we'll see your people. Are they good?"

{The best. They are my kin.} Sight of Day's fingers paused, as if holding the air for a moment. *{My brother is a little special. Perhaps you shouldn't meet him.}*

She laughed. "I'm sure it'll be fine." Geneve watched Meriwether throw the saddle to the ground in disgust. "Come, friend. We've got to keep ahead of the Vhemin."

Chapter Sixteen

Geneve visited her tree a lot. It was peaceful standing in the field, surrounded by other trees waiting for their Knights to be strong enough. She didn't understand how she'd ever be able to break hers. Five years of growth put thicker bark on the tree and it was now wider around than she was.

The trees were all planted from the same kind of acorn, yet flourished in a hundred ways. Hers was straight as an arrow as it reached for the sun. Israel said the trees weren't oaks, elms, or hickory. Nothing here carried a name from the outside world. They were just trees, and each belonged to a Knight.

Geneve expected all trees to grow strong and true, but many didn't. Some carried myriad branching limbs, seeking the sky in all directions of the compass. Others were low, hugging the ground, with thick, gnarled roots emerging from the soil. It seemed impossible they all grew from the same seeds, but she'd seen enough planted as Novices were brought here to know the truth of it.

Wincuf's tree was twisted, as if it'd tried to grow around a rock, but there were no rocks in this sparse forest. Ready as he was for his Trial, he hadn't felled his own tree yet. The thing was as ornery as the young man, and Geneve felt it would be difficult to shatter with a punch even if you were Israel.

Wind ruffled her red hair. Above her, leaves whispered their response. Like *the rest of the keep, it was warm here, untouched by the southern climate outside the walls. It'd be easy to drift off, relaxing while the trees watched over her.*

Geneve put her back against her tree. She closed her eyes, waiting for sleep to come. She used the tree's girth to hide herself from the steps. Privacy was difficult to find in the keep, and a Novice found not training was moments from vile chores. Geneve cleaned her share of privies, or the big kitchen floors, to learn hiding was the best approach for a moment's peace. Few came here unless it was to plant new trees.

Geneve never saw the magic of their growth. One day, an acorn went into the ground. The next, a tree was there, the same height as the Novice attached to it. The trees grew as their Novices learned and fell as their Novices took the Adept's black sash and gold bar. It didn't matter if a Novice was five or fifty when they joined the Tresward. Each got a tree and kept it until their Trial.

She heard a hiss. Nothing carried so far or so fast as a whisper. Talking in low tones was better for secrecy, but not everyone knew that. Geneve felt she'd learned that from a Feybrind but couldn't remember their face. Like the rest of her life before coming here, it was missing in action.

Craning her neck around the trunk of her tree, she saw four Novices coming down the steps. They looked about like they were stealing the queen's jewels. Three carried bundles in rags. She recognized them all. Bald-headed Hettie kept her head shaved like the rest of her people, the purple tattoos of her tribe walking their spidery legs down the side of her face. The broken nose of Barbet was unmissable, mostly because the break had been bad, and made him squint. He claimed to get it in a fight with six men before becoming a Novice, which seemed unlikely, because he'd joined at four years old. He was quick with a laugh.

Raja's signature braids were bound together into a single rope that hung down beside the girl's face. She looked lost, like she shouldn't be here. Geneve knew her to be kind most of the time and wondered how she came to be in this company. Indeed, all three were mostly decent. She'd had no trouble with any except their leader.

He was empty-handed, but it didn't stop his fingers clenching as if hungry for the hilt of a blade. Wincuf.

The group headed toward Wincuf's twisted, misshapen tree. They cast furtive looks about before setting their bundles down. Fabric cast aside, Geneve spied drills and bottles of green glass corked tight. Wincuf gave a last look around, and Geneve shrunk behind her shelter. "Okay. We're alone. Let's get to it."

Geneve peeked from cover. Each hefted a drill and set it to Wincuf's tree. They rotated the cranks, wood shavings falling to the ground. They worked for a handful of minutes, fast and sloppy, until they'd drilled three or four holes apiece. Wincuf retrieved a bottle, uncorking it. He held it out from his body, whole face puckered as if he smelled a latrine.

Tipping the bottle, he poured a little into his drill holes. His companions followed suit. Geneve didn't know what was in the bottle, but she could guess its purpose. They'd come here to poison Wincuf's tree. Weaken it, so it was easier to break. Or perhaps make it fall by itself. The Light protected against many things, but poison wasn't one of them. She didn't know if the protection for Knights spread to their trees, but if her mind walked the nasty little trails Wincuf's did, Geneve might try the same trick.

If she was a cheat, that is. She wondered if she should get someone. A Knight would be a call away. Israel was at the keep, back from his latest task. Help was at hand. Geneve looked at the four, taking in Wincuf's sneer and the others obeisance. No, she wouldn't call for help. If she did, shy Hettie, brash Barbet, and gentle Raja would be caught in the net. What had Kytto said?

Choosing how and when to hurt isn't just done at war.

Geneve stepped from the shelter of her tree, calling out, "Hello, Wincuf."

All four startled, like they were rabbits and she a very surprising fox. Wincuf spun so fast soil scuffed from his heels. Hettie looked like she wanted to run but was anchored to the ground by steel chain. Barbet squinted more than usual, and Raja just looked at her feet, like Geneve was the end of all things.

"Where'd you come from?" Wincuf marched toward her, his long legs eating the original fifty meters down to thirty, then ten, and before Geneve knew it he was before her, sneer in place. "Looking for trouble?"

Geneve shook her head. "I was looking for peace."

"Today's not your day, is it?" Wincuf loomed. His frame bulked out over the years. Fifteen, with a teenage boy's restlessness in every movement. He seemed agitated while standing still.

"It might be today's not yours," she countered. His eyes locked with hers, which was good, because it let her make shooing gestures with her hands. She hoped the other three would run. Get clear, so a call for help wouldn't get them snared. "What would someone be doing near their tree with drills and poison?"

"Poison? You mistake your position, Novice." He leaned on the title, like he *was so much more. But he wasn't yet an Adept, his Trial incomplete. "I came to tend the tree. Nurture it, to make it grow bigger."* He slapped his chest. *"When I break the tree, all will see Wincuf's might."*

She nodded as if agreeing. "It's funny how nurturing can be mistaken for something else. I've never seen someone nurtured to health by use of a drill."

He lunged for her. Geneve wasn't sure what he meant to do—it wasn't a punch, or even a proper grapple. Both hands out, fingers stretched like claws. If he'd swung, his strength might have beaten her, but her smaller, lighter frame slipped out of his grasp. Wincuf tried to snare her again, and she darted under his hands. Geneve saw his companions were gone, like leaves on wind. It was just her, Wincuf, and the trees.

She sucked in a lungful of air to cry for help, and he sucker punched her in the solar plexus. Geneve felt the awful feeling of it, her diaphragm spasming before locking up. Wincuf tried to sweep her feet, hand on her chest, leg scissoring in from the side, but she tumbled aside.

Go on, *she urged herself.* Take a breath.

Nothing like that happened. She needed to breathe, but her body wasn't on board. She backpedaled, trying to get a little distance from Wincuf, but he was Knight-trained and as relentless as they'd made him. He clocked her a bruising blow to the cheek, her vision going bright with red stars.

Patterns. Remember the patterns. *She wasn't a Knight. Couldn't command the Storm like so many others. But she danced better than most when her feet were on the practice mat. She found one of Ikmae's patterns coming to mind. The name escaped her as much of her sense did at Wincuf's punch, but her feet remembered well enough. Her left foot swept back, bringing her retreat to a halt in a spray of dirt.*

Wincuf jabbed for her face again, lightning-quick. She felt the Storm in it and smelled salt spray. But the pattern knew what to do. Geneve swayed like the younger trees around her, hands enclosing his wrist with sticky fingers. He pulled back, and she went with him, right foot coming against his instep. Wincuf stumbled, and she rotated with all her strength, bringing her elbow into his jaw with a crack.

He laid his length along the ground, the air going out of him in a rush.

I should finish him now. End it, because there will always be another time, then another. *Geneve sucked air, diaphragm finally remem-*

bering how to breathe. She thought about whether she should hit him again or leave him be, and the delay was enough. He scrambled back, coming to rest against her tree. His face was twisted in spite. "I'll end you."

Geneve sighed. "What did I do to you?"

He spat, then scuttled upright. Wincuf ran to his tree, and she let him go, suddenly tired. She shouldn't be. She'd trained day in, day out. Kytto had her dragging 'heavy shit' from one end of his smithy to the other. But today, the fight of moments felt like a battle of ages. It was as if this moment made it all real. One against another, with no witnesses but the trees.

Geneve walked back to her tree, putting a hand on its smooth bark. Wincuf scrabbled to gather the collection of potions and tools at his feet, no doubt to get away before someone came. Geneve didn't know if Hettie or the others would get help. She didn't know if she wanted them too. It'd bring questions, and she was too tired for answers.

Wincuf wasn't done. She heard the scuff-scuff-scuffing of his feet at the last minute as he charged her. Geneve looked up, seeing him framed against the trees and sky beyond. One hand held a green bottle, the other a drill.

He tossed the bottle not at her, but her tree, then screamed as he dived on her, both hands trying to plunge the drill through her head. The bottle smashed on her tree, viscous, pale-gray liquid splashing on its bark. The drill wasn't the best of weapons, but they were training to be Knights, and anything with a sharp point would do.

Geneve flung herself aside. Wincuf's eyes were bright with rage, the young man slashing with ferocity where patterns would have worked best. Despite her speed, he got fingers through her red locks, dragging her backward. She landed on the ground with an oomph, and then he was atop her, pinning her down.

The drill came for her face. Geneve twisted, the drill biting earth by her ear. She writhed, desperation getting her arm free. Wincuf stabbed again, and she threw her hand up to ward the blow. The drill bit into her hand, the corkscrew teeth finding a home in the small bones of her palm. Geneve screamed, bucking, and Wincuf fell back.

She crab walked backward, crying out as her injured palm found dirt. It felt like someone sandpapered her flesh. Geneve felt sick with the pain, her breath coming in short pants. Wincuf found his feet, a trick of the light throwing his face into shadow. All she could see was his smile, all white malice.

The drill in his hand dripped red. "It's got a taste for your flesh."

Geneve rolled over and tried to stand. He made it to her side, kicking her in the ribs, and she went down, groaning. Wincuf stood above her. Strong, bigger, older Wincuf. More training than her, and the first glimmer of the Storm at his fingertips. He raised the drill.

The air ... popped. One minute Wincuf stood against the trees and sky, and the next a red, drifting mist floated on the breeze where his arm was. The drill fell beside Geneve, and a heartbeat later the older boy screamed, a long, keening cry of loss. He clutched the stump of his arm with bloody fingers, face pale with shock.

Beside him, glass in hand, body paused at the downstroke of his blade, stood Israel. Geneve hadn't seen him arrive. He moved like the Light itself. The air smelled of coconut and poppyseed, and tiny blue butterflies fanned their wings from their roost on the edge of his sword. One took flight, then the rest, vanishing on the wind like the blood spray from Wincuf's injury.

The boy stumbled back as Israel straightened. The Chevalier leveled his blade at the Novice, the tip wavering less than the stones of the keep. Wincuf scampered back, blood seeping through his fingers. Israel's voice, like the warm touch of golden sun, broke the silence. "Novice Wincuf, I find your behavior unbecoming of a Knight of the Three." He shook his head, as if disgusted at what he saw. "See Lucent Eleni before you bleed to death."

Wincuf nodded, pale and shaky, turning to flee. Then, blood loss being a natural consequence of his injury, he fell flat on his face. Israel sighed, sheathed his immaculately clean glass sword, then hauled Wincuf up by his shirt. He turned for the stairs, then paused. Israel didn't look to Geneve. "Are you okay?"

Geneve shook her head. Her hand bled freely, and it hurt like it was on fire, but all that paled beside her tree. The bark was ash-gray, peeling where the liquid Wincuf threw scorched it. "My tree."

"There will be questions. I need to deal with this," he shook Wincuf's body, blood spattering the soil, "but I'll send help."

"Who?" Geneve didn't want to be seen in defeat. Not by Wincuf, and not again.

"A ... friend. Perhaps the best of them." Israel marched off, armor gleaming as light found it. Geneve huddled on the ground, hugging her knees, then made her way to her tree, where the bark smoked and flaked.

Chapter Seventeen

I srael stood on a balcony overlooking Tresward grounds. Below, Clerics bustled to and fro, more than one or two embracing a waddle. Clerics weren't known for keeping up with Destiny's Supplicant, and once past their Appeal many faded to softer lines. He didn't mind; each had their role within the Three's Light. Knights stood against the dark with shield and sword. Clerics fought with word and censer.

This Tresward keep was a small one. It was barely an outpost, but the gardens were well-tended. Bees hummed a tune through flowers fat and heavy with pollen. The sun's radiance felt warmer here than the cold southern climes should allow. He closed his eyes, feeling its golden touch on his skin. If he kept his eyes closed, thinking of nothing but sunlight, he could almost forget he'd left Geneve to die.

Behind him, he heard—*merciful Three*—a gentle groan. He turned his back to the sunlight, stepping into the shaded interior of the Tresward's hospital ward. Beds lay in neat rows, white cotton sheets pressed and corners neatly tucked. Just one bed was occupied, and on it lay Vertiline. Her face was a ruin of bruising, but while she was out the Clerics had re-broken and set her nose.

The damage didn't stop there. They'd told Israel the Chevalier had four broken ribs, fractured clavicle, and cracked cheekbone. The fingers of her left hand were splinted. She woke to pain, one bloodshot eye beside a clear blue one. Despite her discomforts, she made no noise other than a grunt as she pried herself upright. She made to swing her legs over the side of the bed as Israel reached her side, putting a gentle hand on her shoulder. "Hold, Vertiline. You need rest."

She turned to him, her bloodshot eye angry, the blue one hard like ice. "Is Geneve with us?"

He looked away. "No."

"Then there will be no resting." Vertiline pushed his hand aside, rising. She swayed, putting her hands on his arm for support, then stepped clear. "Where are we?"

"Brightwater."

"*Brightwater?*" Her voice rose several octaves. "How did we get to Brightwater Port? It's five hundred klicks north of Calterburry."

"Sit and let me tell you."

"I'll sit when—"

"Chevalier, sit!" Israel bellowed. Vertiline stilled, then gave a stiff nod. He wasn't sure if it was her injuries or rebuke at his tone, but he'd put good silver regals on column B.

She settled on the bed. "What is your will, Valiant?"

"Three's Mercy," Israel grumbled. "Must you?"

"Whatever do you mean, Valiant?" Her jaw jutted.

Israel felt inside for a shred of calm. He fingered the pendant at his neck. It was old like him, and if he didn't think too much on it, he almost forgot where it came from. Ignoring Vertiline's question, he spoke of what she wanted to know. "Geneve is alive. The Justiciar—"

"Left her to die."

Israel winced. "Perhaps you could keep your voice down."

"Is he here?"

"Ambrose?" Israel shook his head. "He pulled us clear, then left."

"Then I'll speak as loud as I like. Unless, Valiant, your will says otherwise." Her words were a model of obedience, but her tone could break rock.

"What *is* here are a hundred Three-fearing Clerics of various ranks.

Two of them are posted," he jabbed a finger at the ward's stout door, "out there."

Her eyes made a slow circuit of the room. He saw what she did: empty beds, but there was never a want of Knights needing care. A closed door, stout wood, no doubt reinforced with Divine Sway. Her gaze found the open door and its balcony, and while she couldn't see it, he knew of the five-story drop to the gardens below. She continued looking about, finding the table beside her bed carried no items of interest, and certainly no glass swords. While their blades were lost on the road, there would be supplies here. Brightwater Port was one of the Tresward's holdfasts. She breathed in and out. "We've done nothing wrong."

"Do you wonder why you still hurt?" Israel made to touch her jaw, but she shied away. "Clerics heal the sick and wounded, yet you carry injuries."

"Are there Knights?"

"Some," Israel admitted. "None will speak to me."

Vertiline put her hands in her lap. He didn't know if she looked at her fingers, or the simple cloth covering her legs. No Smithsteel held her body safe. "Where is Geneve?"

"Ask a different question." He sniffed. "One I know the answer to, perhaps."

"My way's more fun." Israel caught the ghost of her smile. "They didn't want to heal me with Divine Sway?"

"They said they *couldn't*." Israel scratched his chest. "Ambrose pulled us from that Three-forsaken pit—"

"Where we left Geneve!"

Israel's voice failed him for a moment. He opened and closed his mouth a couple times. *Speak truth.* "I know it. I *feel* it."

Vertiline turned away. "I'm sorry. I know. I'm confused and angry. Help me understand."

"I don't understand much myself." He held up a hand at the bright glitter in her glare. "Save your fury. I'll get to the heart of it. Ambrose says the pit was an old temple. The sinner, an agent of evil. Geneve, corrupted."

"By the sinner?"

"By the place." Israel shrugged. "Us, too. It's why the Sway won't work. They tried to mend you, but ... nothing happened. The Light wouldn't touch you." Israel remembered fighting the High Priest. How the Sacred Storm couldn't pierce the monster's dark aura. "He has said how we might fix it."

"This is why he didn't send another Gate for her?"

Israel nodded. "Ambrose can't see her, Tilly. He," Israel's fingers clenched, "said maybe if she'd worked the Storm herself just once, she'd be easier to find. The man exhausted himself trying to find her."

"And we're five hundred klicks from her last location."

He nodded. "Five or ten days' ride, depending on horses. I don't know what happened to Chesterfield or Troubles, but we'll only ride what the Tresward can spare."

"*Spare?*" Vertiline stood, iron in her spine. "No, save your words. They bring no clarity. I'll not sit a moment longer. We must find Geneve."

Israel clutched his pendant. "Aye. But I haven't finished giving you truth."

She turned at his tone. "What more is there? Our fellow Knight lies no more than ten days' ride, while we holiday in Brightwater."

"Ambrose said Geneve must be Judged. He said she may have been marked from before we found her. That she's fallen. Her lack of Light..." He trailed off.

Silence gathered between them. The hum of bees seemed to fade away. When Vertiline spoke, her voice was a whisper. "And what will you do?"

"I'll find her." Israel let his fingers fall away from the pendant. "She is a Knight of the Tresward. We must do our duty. You, on the other hand, will stay here."

"You're joking, of course."

"You're injured," Israel insisted. *My heart aches to see her like this.*

She didn't seem to care about the state of his heart. Vertiline held her splinted hand up. "Is it because of this?" She grabbed the binding, and with a grimace, tore it away. "There. No more injuries. Let's go." She held her injured hand up again as he looked about to speak.

"Knights can't *fall*, Iz. We're not pieces on a board to knock over. You of *all* of us should know this. You've known Geneve for ten years."

"Closer to thirteen."

"And I've known you for twice that. We've lived in the Tresward. In all that time, have you *ever* heard of the Light failing?" Her eyes glittered, one sapphire, one ruby.

"No, but I know what I saw." He shook his head. "It doesn't matter. I'll find her."

"We'll find her, you mean."

"And then we'll do what must be done."

She eyed him, measuring, weighing, and discarding the chaff. "As you've always done."

"What's that supposed to mean?"

"It means we need to get out of here before your brain rots." She put her hand to her mouth in mock surprise. "I apologize, Valiant. That was my outside voice."

He grinned. It felt good. Israel thought he'd have to do this black task alone, but his oldest friend insisted on sharing the journey. *I've seen more summers than's my due. This may be my last crusade, but there's no one I'd rather share this final one with.* Geneve was with a powerful sinner, and the Light didn't walk with her.

There was no way this would end well for her, and he wouldn't let her go into the dark alone.

ISRAEL KNOCKED ON THE WARD'S DOOR. "OPEN."

After a pause, the door creaked a finger's width wide. "You're to stay in there until—"

"Open this door, or by the Three, I'll knock it down." Israel squinted through the gap. "I'll allow it's a difficult time, but I won't ask twice."

"Aye, Valiant." The door opened in a rush, revealing two young men standing guard. One shared Israel's dark honey-brown skin but had a nose big enough for two men. The other was darker by far, with hair braided down his back. They both wore good Tresward Smithsteel. Braid gave a half-bow. "Apologies."

The corridor outside the ward looked as it had when Israel entered. Old stone, but pale and clean. The odd door down a corridor stretching the length of the Tresward building. Wooden beams as thick as Israel's legs shouldered the load of the ceiling, and small globes holding the Three's Light provided warm illumination.

"I need steel and glass," Israel said. "Where?"

"The Justiciar—"

"Isn't here," Vertiline breezed. She considered Big Nose's black sash and its two meager stripes, then looked to Braid's single gold bar. "Come, Chevalier, Adept. There's no need for us to quarrel."

Big Nose grunted. "It's not you who'll pay when he comes to settle his account."

"Might be you who pays now," Israel suggested.

"A fair point, Valiant." Braid pursed his lips. "You'll find the armory down on the ground level. Steward Willis is a miser, so don't believe him when he says he only has short swords." He shook his head, rueful. "You'd think he paid for them himself."

"Now, brothers," Vertiline chided. "Let's not be unkind. It's possible he did."

That got a short laugh from Big Nose. "I like your optimism, Chevalier. Go with the Three's blessing."

"Likewise." Israel moved through the door, Vertiline shadowing his heels. He hadn't wanted to hurt his fellow Knights, but an urgency roiled in his gut he hadn't felt in years. It wasn't excitement, nor anger.

Israel didn't know what was coming, but fear's cold fingers ran down his back. He felt a whisper on the wind, a promise of what would be. *Death*, he thought it said. *Death, and the end of all you hold dear*.

Israel touched his pendant again, then pressed his lips into a thin line. Fear was for Novices and Postulants. He thought of Geneve, her lack of Light, and the sinner she traveled with. *I'm a Valiant of the Tresward, and I will not fail.*

Chapter Eighteen

This saddle's going to kill me. Meriwether felt little was going his way. The sun was too bright, perhaps because he hadn't slept. He sat on a horse that wanted him dead, and the only insulation between him and the beast was a saddle designed for an armored Knight. He wasn't armored, nor was he a Knight.

That's right. I'm a sinner. He winced at his internal monologue. *How can it be a sin if you're born with it? It's like being a sinner for having red hair.* The thought made him glance at Geneve riding at the head of their meager column. The cat rode at Meriwether's back, making riding look *easy.* He hated the Feybrind just a little for that, but Sight of Day didn't seem to care. If anything, the Feybrind didn't look like he cared much about anything, until you looked into those golden eyes. They held your gaze, commanding attention in a way the flickering fingers of his handspeak didn't. The cat's horse looked the happiest of their group, just as the huge monster of a charger that moved at the rear looked the least. *Probably hasn't killed enough people recently.*

Geneve was all business. Nothing resembling humor leaked from her when she spoke to Meriwether. Her back was ramrod straight, armor glinting in the dappled light making it through the trees. Her concession to the hot work of riding was a lack of helmet, letting her red trusses fall free. They were thick, slightly curly, and if this had been a different place, perhaps a tavern, with a different person, perhaps a by-the-hour doxy, he might have wanted to run his fingers through it.

But running your fingers through a Knight's hair was like running your fingers along a Vhemin's gums. Unless the Vhemin was dead, you were like as not to come out with fewer fingers than when you started. This here? Same deal.

Meriwether let his eyes leave Geneve for the cool greens of the forest. The road they were on was more *rutted track* than *cobbled thoroughfare*, and he harbored a dark suspicion it was a smuggler's route. Southward lay Calterburry and its handy river, ideal for shipping wares and escaping sinners. North lay a world of bullshit in the form of Judgments and Justiciars, but also the wondrous cities of the kingdom, ripe for a savvy trader, whether their goods were honest or restricted. Traveling the main road north would expose a fellow to the relative safety of patrols, assuming you weren't an escaped prisoner seeking release from the long arm of the law.

"Say." He shifted a cheek, trying for relief from the saddle. Troubles shifted under him, re-seating him right where he'd been. "Why don't we take the road?"

Geneve didn't bother looking at him. "Because there are patrols."

"That's kind of what I mean."

That earned him a backward glare. "Are you simple as well as a sinner?"

Meriwether frowned, staring at his hands. *Unbound, thank the Three, or whichever gods are unlikely to want me dead.* "I like to think I'm brighter than most."

"Of course you do." If there was a sneer trying to curl her lip, she didn't let it show. "There are two problems with patrols. First, Vhemin will kill them, and all other travelers besides. You would call it a good distraction. It would be a tragedy."

Meriwether glanced at Sight of Day. Pivoting in his saddle made his back pop, and he wondered how Geneve made it look so simple, especially since she was encased in Smithsteel. "It would be a good distraction, wouldn't it?"

The Feybrind shrugged, a half-smile showing a few teeth. His fingers flicked, but Meriwether didn't know the People's language.

"The second problem is you." Geneve's voice drew him back around, Troubles shifting under him again, but with a snort, like her cargo showing free will wasn't part of the deal. "You're a sinner. Prisoner of the Tresward. If we go by the main road, it will bring questions. I can respond to allegations, but I've a feeling someone like you might use such a distraction to ask for a stranger's aid."

"Meaning you'd be forced to murder some poor guardsman, whose only crime was diddling his sister." Meriwether nodded. "I get it. Casual murder's fine, as long as it's sinners. Unless there's a third angle." He leveled a finger at her. "You don't want to be seen wandering free with a sinner. That's a different line of questioning, with a harder set of answers."

Geneve's eyes flicked past Meriwether to the Feybrind, no doubt taking in Sight of Day's handspeak. "He is *not* right."

Meriwether let a few teeth show as he smiled. "Even the cat agrees."

"He's not a cat." She shook her head, lips firming into a line. "That's all beside the point. *This* road leads to a Feybrind village. The Vhemin on our tail won't follow us there."

"If they do?"

Geneve answered with a grim smile, fashioned of sharp edges and broken steel. "Then they'll find their deaths." She shifted her eyes front, her horse unconcerned in a way Meriwether's wasn't.

They rode on through the morning. The pace was brisk, the horses moving at a trot for much of the time. This wasn't doing Meriwether's butt or spine any good at all, but no one seemed to care. They didn't stop for lunch. While there were no Vhemin in sight, even Meriwether agreed they'd burned too much time at their breakfast camp.

Meriwether knew the Vhemin could run a mean pace, but they also needed hot rocks, and that would slow them some. The need to keep their speed up kept his lips shut when he felt like complaining about his condition. *To be fair, I've not had it this good in some time. Good food in my belly, traveling companions who can murder pretty much any bandits, and no one's threatened to kill me for at least a couple of hours. Let's not forget they left my hands untied.*

He nudged Troubles faster, pulling abreast of Geneve. "Thanks, by the way."

Red hair jounced as she glanced at him. "For what?"

"For not killing me. For coming for us." He looked at the trees above, branches from each side reaching to their companions opposite. *Trees yearn for their friends, kept separated by our need to smuggle stolen cargo on an old road.* "For not being more of an asshole than you have to be."

She studied him. Green eyes cool like a quiet pond. Geneve didn't look down her nose at him. "I should thank you."

"You should," he agreed. "For what?"

Meriwether sensed she *almost* laughed. The hint of a smile, the warming of her eyes, but only for a minute. "For the knife trick." She looked away. "It's a sin to use magic, but you saved my life, the lives of two Knights, and a Feybrind."

"It won't earn me clemency, will it?" Meriwether tasted the sourness of his words. "No, I get it. Sinning's sinning, and that's all there is to it."

"You could try running," Geneve suggested. He couldn't tell if she was joking. The Knight was as hard to read as a stone. *Never play cards with this one.* "See if it works better this time than it did last time."

"What will happen at the Feybrind village?" Meriwether kept his voice even, despite his nervousness about his future.

Geneve looked away. "We'll defeat the Vhemin."

"Not that part. I'm talking about the most important thing in the world." He jerked a thumb at his chest. "Me."

She didn't respond straight away, the trot of hooves doing the talking for a while. "If you can make a glowing dagger, why not a dragon? Scare people. Make them run."

He watched her, watching him. "Because I can't do living things. My fa... I knew someone who could, but he thought he could do anything. Felt the ancients were amateurs. Also, dragons aren't real."

"Sure they are. You're only saying that because you haven't seen one. How can you believe in stories of the ancients, but not their dragons?"

"Because I can't imagine a dragon being owned by someone. That's what they said, wasn't it?" Meriwether shrugged. "Maybe if you spent your life on the run, you'd understand. Always fighting, or running. Two steps ahead of death in a three-step race." He eyed her armor, taking in her sheathed blade. The *strength* of her. "Hmm. Maybe you get it."

"What's that supposed to mean?"

He sniffed, then twisted his back, trying to work out a kink. Troubles' gait put it right back in. "I mean, you're used to strength. What it can give you, and what it can take from others."

"I've trained my entire life to be a Knight—"

He pushed out his palms in a *calm the fuck down* gesture. "I don't mean anything personal by it. You worked for your strength. It wasn't feely given. But it's there all the same." He looked to the trees for support. "It doesn't matter. I can't make a dragon."

"Because it's living?"

"That, but also because I haven't seen one. Need to see it to make it." He concentrated for a moment, remembering the knife she wore. How it looked, how it shaped the world around it. *A bit of effort, and... done.* Meriwether handed Geneve her glowing dagger.

She startled, checking her sheath where the dagger still lay. Eyes wary, she took the knife from him. "It feels heavy. Has weight."

"It wouldn't be a good illusion if it didn't." She pressed the edge against her skin, finding the glowing tip passing through her skin. "It's not really there. You just ... *think* it is."

Geneve tossed the glowing dagger to the ground, eyes front again. "Then why not an Artifice? Surely you've seen one of those."

"Too big." Meriwether shook his head. "Also, I can't make *living* things."

"They weren't living."

"Apparently. But no one's seen one move. How do I make that happen?" Meriwether gusted a sigh. "Sinning's not as useful or as fun as it's made out to be."

He caught her snort, quickly tamped down. "So ... you just make small, immovable objects? It seems a silly reason..." Her voice trailed off.

"Silly reason to what?"

"To die," Geneve said.

They trotted beside each other in silence for a while. *Best not brood on that.* Meriwether handed her another knife. This one wasn't glowing. "Here."

She eyed it. "Why do I want another illusion?"

"It's not an illusion."

She glanced at her now-empty sheath, then glared. "How did you—"

"What you really want to be wondering is how you didn't see me, not how I did it. We're riding on *horses*, Geneve. I had to reach across, all while this vile beast," he nudged a knee into an uncaring Troubles, "tried to toss me off. It's a wonder the Feybrind didn't see it."

She snatched the knife from him, rammed it into her sheath, then looked at the Feybrind. Geneve grunted. "He says he saw it."

"Then you want to ask why he didn't say anything."

"Probably because he thought it was funny. They're like that. Also, they can't make sound."

Meriwether looked at Sight of Day, who nodded, golden eyes twinkling with mirth. "You've known a lot of cats?"

"They're called Feybrind." She shook her head. "Not many. A few. I just … don't remember them."

Meriwether heard a slight rasp in her voice, a tiny catch you'd miss if you weren't listening for it. He wondered at it, that tiny hint of pain-meets-frustration, and kept his peace. Maybe, just maybe, there'd be time enough before he died to learn her truth.

NIGHT DRAPED A GOWN OVER THE FOREST, DRAWING HER SHADOWS close. Meriwether felt tired beyond exhaustion, not helped by the hammering his spine got from Troubles. *Be easy. The horse hasn't slept either.* As visibility dropped to near zero, Meriwether called out, "Can we stop?"

Geneve reigned in her horse. Sight of Day drew closer, his horse's liquid black eyes staring into the evening. "We must press on. The Vhemin—"

"Will find our unconscious bodies if we keep going," Meriwether finished. "We'll knock ourselves out on a low branch. And the horses are tired." For once, Troubles didn't try to shift him away, the mare either too tired, or in firm agreement with the idea of rest.

Geneve's skin was a charcoal rubbing in the dusk. "They'll find us."

"It takes them hours to cut enough trees, build a big fire, and heat their rocks. They can run fast, but they're still behind us." Meriwether put a little pleading in his tone. "Also, it's cold. A fire would help us, too."

Sight of Day slid from his horse, making exactly zero noise despite harness and saddle. The cat moved like a solid shadow, disturbing nothing. His handspeak in Geneve's general direction was sharp, the meaning clear. *We should stop, imbecile.*

Geneve gave a reluctant nod. "A few hours. Enough time for a meal, and to gather our strength." She clattered from her horse, who for his part pranced a little in relief. Meriwether empathized; there's no way he'd want to carry a Knight, armor or no.

They went about the tasks of building a small camp. Meriwether dug a pit for a fire while Sight of Day headed into the trees, bow in hand. Geneve crouched by fledgling flames, amber-honey skin kissed by the warm light. Meriwether held his distance, watching her. The tension in her shoulders, the way her gauntleted hands held each other, and how her eyes held the firelight. *She shoulders the concerns of a whole Tresward.* In other circumstances, Meriwether would have taken the few steps to draw closer, crouched beside her, and asked her what her cares were.

But he knew them. They were *get the sinner to his funeral,* and perhaps, *find Israel and Vertiline to help me burn the evil from his flesh.* He found it hard to care about those things.

Vertiline took hits for you. That's a thing you've not seen before. Meriwether didn't want to unpick his feelings about that, because he was pretty sure inside that box of confusion were uncomfortable truths. Truths like *I owe a Knight my life, if only for a different death,* and *she took a beating, despite the likelihood of my death, so I'd be unharmed.* Vertiline did her duty, but Meriwether sensed it was something more. Maybe Vertiline didn't like killing sinners. Maybe they weren't all constructed of hardened steel, unflinching and unfeeling.

Maybe I should stop being an asshole. "I'm going to regret this."

Geneve jerked, hands unclasping, head whipping toward him. "What?"

Meriwether did the best saunter he could, which was in his view a pretty poor example. A day's riding left him feeling hammered like an unlucky anvil. Crouching beside Geneve, the movement the slow, rickety one of an elderly man, he fished around for a smile. "Copper baron for your thoughts?"

Her eyes searched his face. He could see her wondering what to say, or perhaps whether she could talk about it at all. "I..." The one word robbed her of speech.

"I get it." He handed her knife back to her. She started, then checked her empty scabbard. "You dropped this."

She laughed, then closed her armored fingers around his hand, pushing the knife back. "Keep it."

He shrugged as best a weary traveler could, then tucked the blade away. "Not afraid I'll kill you in your sleep?"

"Not at all." She turned back to the fire. "I think the Tresward owes you a knife, anyway. Israel took your last blade."

"Easy come, easy go." This close to Geneve, he could smell the flat metallic scent of oiled armor. It mingled with the dry smell of the road, the dust that clung to him but avoided her. Deeper still he could smell *her*, not sweat or candied oils like a lady of court, but earthly. Solid. *Honest, in a way I'll never be.* The fire crackled its hunger, so he fed it another branch. The wood settled, sparks rising on a tide of heat toward the heavens. "It'll be okay."

He felt her tense and turned to watch her rise. Her jaw was set in a hard line. "You want to cozy up to me? Make me let my guard down?"

Meriwether looked away. He didn't have the strength for this after a day's saddle-hammering. "I just don't want to *fight*, is all. Been doing it most of my life. Wasn't built for it though. Not armored, no blade of glass in my hand, let alone one of metal. Tomorrow brings the cat village. Help, if we want it, and decisions we don't need. Tonight, it's just us. The trail, and these trees. They don't talk much, and I hoped you might."

"That so?"

He nodded. "Aye. Also, I want to know how your armor is so clean after riding all day."

No laugh this time, but she crouched back down. He studied the line of her face where cheek met jaw. It didn't hurt to look at her there. It was just a part of someone's face. Impassive, without accusation, unlike the green agate of her eyes. "Why do you think?"

"Because you rode at the front and left me at the rear with the cat."

"The Feybrind's not dirty."

"Cat's an asshole," suggested Meriwether. "Talks about me behind my back."

He earned a snort for his troubles. "It's the Light of the Three. While we hold true to our purpose, Knights are ... I guess you would call it *protected*."

"What would you call it?"

She tugged the clasps on a gauntlet, then tossed the steel to the ground beside her. Geneve clenched and unclenched her fingers a few times, then ran her hand through tousled red hair. "Burdened." She held her still-gauntleted palm toward him, stilling his objection. "Not all who are burdened are unwilling, sinner."

"You'll need to unpick that for me."

"We can't get sick. No disease touches us. We don't bend with old age until the very end."

"But you can be poisoned."

She offered him a wry smile. "We're not immortal. A blade can bleed us back to the earth. Fire burns. We can drown. And," she glanced at the fire, "the angel's kiss makes us sleep."

"Seems a shitty kind of Light."

Geneve shook her head. "The Tresward trains us for the rest. Part of us is the Three's gift of Light. The rest is up to us. And I let us down."

Meriwether sensed the trap ahead and attempted to drag the conversational reins. "You want me to say, 'Oh no, Geneve, it was I.'" He raised an eyebrow, and at her nod, shook his head. "You fuckers tried to put me in a cage." It was his turn to hold his palm out. *Hold up.* "If it makes you feel better, though, it was *kind of* me."

"Kind of?"

"When I put the angel's kiss in your tea, I made the torn fragments look like the tea you already had."

She nodded, a grudging respect in it. "But you wouldn't have had to if you weren't in the cage."

"Sounds like an admission."

Geneve shook her head. "It's just the way it was. The Tresward teaches us to see the truth. Speak it, even when the words are heavy."

He wanted to spit. *The Tresward teaches you to slay the innocent.* The words were on his lips, a moment from leaping forward and burning their growing whatever-this-relationship-is to the waterline. He held his peace. Counted to ten. She waited, eyes back on the fire. "What if it didn't?"

A raised eyebrow. "The Light's a lie?"

Meriwether shook his head. "The Light's not a lie. I *saw* Israel carve a bunch of Vhemin into cubes with a butter knife. That's a … gift from *someone*."

"The Sacred Storm." Her voice was a whisper. "I can't … not all of us command the Storm."

He waved a hand, dismissing her comment because he sensed more emotional baggage down that path than he was equipped to carry. "Not my point. What if there was a bad person making good people do bad things?"

"Then the Light would leave us." She shrugged. "The Light is from the Three, not from people."

"But you haven't always hunted sinners." He stood. "Where's the damn cat?"

"Hunting. Don't change the subject." Geneve rose too, freeing her other gauntleted hand. Shining Smithsteel fell to the ground. It didn't gather a speck of dirt. "We've hunted for as long as I've been at the Tresward."

Meriwether pursed his lips. *She's eighteen, tops. My age but hasn't traveled the same klicks.* "A long time, then?"

"We've records. It's been over a hundred years."

"Not hundreds, but a hundred? Singular?" Meriwether looked to the sky. Above him, trees canopied the sky, but he knew the three moons waited up there. Pale Cophine. Ash-gray Ikmae. And dark, shadowy Khiton. The Three watched the world, marking time from the heavens.

"Even a singular hundred is a long time." She released her breast-plate with a sigh of contentment. The steel clanked as it hit the ground. Her under-armor padding was worn but also free of road grime, if a little sweat-stained. Geneve's red hair framed her light amber face. "Where *is* Sight of Day?"

"Hunting," said Meriwether. "Don't change the subject." But he said it with a smile. Partly because Geneve didn't look at him like he was evil made flesh. Her eyes now held a trace of pity, and a kernel of understanding. But also because a hundred years wasn't that long, all things considered. It wasn't entrenched in the Tresward's of the faith— more like a policy decision. And something like that he might be able to work with. "Get some rest."

"I don't need rest." She sat with her back to a tree anyway, removing her greaves and boots, stretching socked feet toward the fire. Meriwether stood apart, back to another tree, watching. The crackle of flames kept him company while he waited for Geneve's eyes to close.

⁑

SIGHT OF DAY RETURNED A HALF HOUR LATER. HE CARRIED THREE birds, fat and plump, and quite dead. The Feybrind looked at Meri-wether and his vigil by the tree, then to Geneve, out like a three-days-dead campfire.

"Relax." Meriwether kept his voice low. "She's tired, not drugged." He fashioned a wry smile, heart only half in it. "I couldn't find any more angel's kiss."

The Feybrind watched him for a moment, those golden eyes unblinking. Then his lips curled into a half-smile, a little glint of teeth showing. He pointed to Geneve, then placed a palm over his chest, giving a slight bow.

"I've no idea what you're saying," Meriwether admitted. "It's like watching Tebrani merchants haggle. You don't know whether they're buying coffee, selling slaves, or arguing whether the weather's going to be bad in the afternoon."

Sight of Day shrugged, as if people not understanding him was just the way of the world. He settled beside the fire and set to work on feathering the birds. Meriwether set a pan above the flames, pleased there was a little bacon left in a saddlebag. Bacon was above his usual means, and he thanked the Tresward they believed in treating their prisoners so well right up to the point they became human sacrifices or whatever happened at the end of Judgment.

Flames licked and crackled. Sight of Day removed Meriwether's pan from the fire, shaking his head like one might when teaching a small child something very simple, and set one of his birds to roast on a spit. The act of turning it every so often wouldn't take a lot of mental energy, and the cat looked to have things under control anyway. It left Meriwether time to reflect.

The smart money would've been to run. Once she was asleep, head for the trees, and freedom. Silver regals to copper barons said it wasn't just the clever thing to do, but the necessary one. What a survivor might do. And yet here he was, roasting pheasant with a cat while a murderer slept beside him.

It's been a difficult day. Part of the problem was if Meriwether ran, he was pretty sure the Vhemin would find him, and they might eat him, but not all at once. He glanced at Geneve. *It could be they want a two-for-one deal now. I doubt Vhemin care if their prey come in Smithsteel or linens.* Possibly they'd eat the cat too; the scaled monsters of the world didn't hold covenant with the furred. So, sticking together made the monster's jobs easier from a tracking perspective, but also upped their odds of surviving an attack.

The fire sparked, and he jumped. Sight of Day half-smiled and went back to turning the bird. "You can't speak, right?" The golden eyes found his, and the Feybrind shook his head. "That's got to suck." A shrug and what could only be called a smirk. "Oh, you don't *want* to speak?"

Vigorous nodding. Sight of Day tapped a finger to his pointed ear. The meaning was clear. *You're noisy.*

"I guess," Meriwether agreed. "We're loud, and don't look where we're going." He cast a glance at the Feybrind. "I'm sorry humans are such assholes." Sight of Day nodded, then put a hand under a palm, finger outstretched, and swept it away. He raised an eyebrow, making it a question. "I still don't know what you're saying, but if you're asking if I'm going to run…"

Meriwether glanced at Geneve again. Asleep, she looked like anyone else. Not a Knight of the Tresward, encased in steel and burning with desire to run him through. Vulnerable, like any of the Three's children. "No. Not tonight." He considered. "I'll save that for tomorrow. Once we're free and clear of the Vhemin."

Sight of Day went back to tending their dinner. They didn't speak for a while longer as the bird roasted. The smell was divine. The Feybrind swapped the cooked bird for another. Meriwether reached for the pan, and after a moment's hesitation, Sight of Day nodded.

"I *could* run. Tonight, I mean." Meriwether looked to the trees for help. "I should. Head for the road. Find a guard. Reach a settlement." He sighed. "She's right, you know. The Vhemin would come. There were a lot of them, and they didn't look ready to pack up for home." *I could take warning to others. Save people. Whole villages. Get word to Queen Morgan, somehow.* His lips twisted in a sneer. "But the queen won't listen to the likes of me."

Sight of Day shrugged, like he understood what Meriwether had both said and left unsaid. The cat seemed patient and was a very good listener. Meriwether pursed his lips. *This one-sided conversation doesn't seem right.* He sat up. "Teach me."

The Feybrind's golden eyes narrowed. He rotated his palms in the air facing each other, then drew a triangle with them.

Meriwether watched for a moment. "If that's 'the People's hand-speak,' then yes. Teach me." He shrugged. "I know, it probably seems a waste of time. I'll be dead in days after a trial, and I'll be one more short-lived human you didn't know very well."

Sight of Day watched him over the flames. Something close to sadness crept into his golden eyes. He touched his chest, clapped his hands softly, and pressed his knuckles together. Then he watched, waiting.

Meriwether nodded. "I get it. You're pleased about something." He pondered. "About me?" An encouraging nod. "You're pleased to meet me?" At the Feybrind's next nod, he laughed. "Me too, friend."

THE LESS SAID ABOUT THE MORNING, THE BETTER. GENEVE WAS furious they'd let her sleep, more furious she'd missed a hot meal, but somewhat mollified they'd saved an entire pheasant and some bacon for her. They hit the road before the world had risen. A fake half-light seeped through the trees. The camp was cool, embers in their fire pit doing almost nothing to keep their bones warm this far south.

Breaking camp took little time, and then it was back in the saddle, an ornery Troubles beneath Meriwether's aching buttocks. A couple hours into the day, as true light stole among them to turn the leaves green, Sight of Day pointed off the trail. His meaning was clear. *That way*. The cat dismounted, preparing to lead Troubles.

Geneve scowled. "Not on the trail?" She watched his handspeak for a moment. "He says the village isn't fed by any roads." She watched him speak, frowning. "Our roads are *not* badly designed!"

Meriwether hid a smile. "This one is."

"That's because it's not a road. It's a track used by criminals and vagrants."

"Sounds about right," Meriwether agreed. "Like us."

She narrowed her eyes, but reserved comment, instead sliding from her horse and leading a slightly reluctant Tristan off the trail. Meriwether followed suit. Riding in dense trees would be madness. And while walking would be tiresome, it wouldn't be *sore*, and he could use a little less of that.

They walked for an hour before Sight of Day stiffened. The Feybrind raised a hand up, fist clenched. Geneve and Meriwether halted. The wind shifted, tickling the foliage, and that's when Meriwether smelled it: smoke.

Sight of Day broke into a run. The Feybrind was *fast* at a dead sprint. Geneve called, "Wait!" then powered after him. Meriwether stood among the horses, wondering what he was supposed to do. The black brute of a charger and the blue roan cantered after Geneve and Sight of Day, but Fidget and Troubles stayed with Meriwether.

"I'm *really* going to regret this." Meriwether broke into a ragged jog, heading after Geneve. The smell of smoke grew, and he coughed a couple times as it drifted around him, gray fingers about his throat. The trees thinned, and within five minutes, swept back entirely. Ahead, a moat of grass surrounded a tree city. Tall redwoods rose a hundred meters above the forest floor. Nestled within their branches were treehouses connected by rope bridges spanning the sky.

All of it was on fire.

Meriwether stopped stock still, eyes wide. Above him, the Feybrind village burned. There were hundreds of trees and their attached houses. Hundreds of *people*. The forest beneath the redwoods was littered with sad, crumpled bodies. Golden, black, and red-furred people, some with bloody wounds, others charred and smoking from the flames.

Ahead, amid the flames, he saw brutish figures. *Vhemin*. They loped about, blades in hand, hunting for more to slaughter. The haze of heat shimmered the air. A falling branch trailed fire as a redwood above gave up its hundreds-years vigil, surrendering to the flames.

"No," he croaked. "No!"

Meriwether broke from the tree line, running toward the Feybrind village. As he drew closer, he saw not all bodies were Feybrind. Among them lay the scattered bodies of many, many Vhemin. The monsters paid for what they cut down, but it wasn't enough. It would never be enough for this tragedy.

He hunted among the flames and smoke for Geneve and Sight of Day. A flash of fire-reddened steel drew his eye. *There*. Meriwether staggered closer, coughing at the smoke trailing him like a sick gown. The cat and Knight were back to back, her blade out, wet and hungry, his bow in hand. Three Vhemin lay at Geneve's feet. Her hair was wild, teeth barred. Ahead, hulking figures drew closer, walking from the smoke and flame like fire was a thing that could only harm lesser, *weaker* things.

A voice full of gravel and spite ground through the air. "We meet again." Meriwether recognized the Vhemin High Prist from the cave before them. The monster grinned a horror story of shark teeth as he marked Meriwether. "And *this* time, I know your tricks. Seemings won't save you."

More Vhemin stalked from the trees. Meriwether saw tears marked Sight of Day's cheeks. It could've been the smoke, but Meriwether thought not. It was the sight of hundreds of your family dead. Meriwether joined them, drawing his knife. The tiny blade felt inadequate for his future.

"Back, sinner." Geneve coughed. He thought for a moment she was concerned about his blade, and wanted to say, *I'm here to help.* But she didn't look to him or the knife he carried. "Run."

"Don't be so stupid." He ignored her sharp look, putting a hand on Sight of Day's arm. "Do you trust me?" The Feybrind looked at him, really *looked* at him, as if weighing his body and soul. Then, a tentative nod. "Then trust me when I tell you, you can't win this fight. *Hear me.* There *will* be vengeance, friend, but not like this. Not right now."

Sight of Day glanced at the Vhemin, then gave a short nod. He spun, hand to the small of Geneve's back. Her blade held steady in the grim light. She hissed, "I will *not* run!"

Meriwether moved in front of her, blocking her view of the Vhemin. Later, if he lived that long, Meriwether might wonder about putting his back to hungry monsters. Now, he needed her attention. "Your duty, Knight. Is it to see me to Trial, or to die here?"

Geneve glared at him, fury in her eyes. "Have you seen what they did?"

"I see. I *feel.*" Meriwether coughed. "One bow and blade will make no difference. We must run. *All* of us."

He stood, waiting, his back to the enemy as they advanced. The trees held nothing but the crackling rumble of flames. Waiting for her answer felt like the wrong thing to do, but there was never a better time to be wrong.

Chapter Nineteen

*P*rogress, not perfection. Take a small step each day. When you're ready, perfection will find you. Israel's words to her years back as he crouched before her, hands on her shoulders. Geneve was new to the Tresward, perhaps six years old, and holding a broken practice blade.

She'd listened, nodded, and taken the step. She was *sure* of it. And yet, no matter how hard she tried, the Sacred Storm didn't answer her call. Geneve's form was perfect, but no light glimmered along her blade. No thunder rang heaven's bell. A glass sword was beyond her reach, and she'd never needed it more than now, facing fifty Vhemin, bloodlust in their eyes, rage in their hearts.

She held Requiem instead, the skymetal honest, trustworthy, and totally unsuitable for the task at hand. Israel could have taken them. Perhaps even Vertiline, but Geneve suspected fifty Vhemin more than equal to the task of besting a Chevalier.

Geneve was an Adept, and the Storm didn't answer her call.

We're going to die. Smoke rode the air. She could smell the charr of burning wood and the sickly smell of roasting meat. The unmistakable scent of blood made her heart pound. At her back, Sight of Day was frantic. He didn't run about like a panicked human. Feybrind were forged of clear thought and steady vision, but for all that Geneve felt him *vibrate*. She knew he wanted to run at their foe, and Geneve wanted to join him. Make them *pay* for their terrible crime.

The sinner moved in front of her. Behind him, the Vhemin marched closer. They didn't run. She almost laughed; they didn't need to. She spied them south, east, and west. The north was clear, but it wouldn't be for long. A noose coiling about them, drawing them together. When the rope drew taught, there'd be no escape. "Your duty, Knight. Is it to see me to Trial, or to die here?"

Geneve wanted to punch him. She felt her fingers curl about Requiem's hilt, the tension in her wanting release. She wondered what Israel would have said, if the Valiant were here. Probably something like: *He speaks true. Your duty is to the Tresward. Once it's done, we can return. Fight this evil, and with the Justiciar's blessing. With the Storm above and Sway beside us, they will pay.* Geneve wanted to believe that was true. She hoped the Tresward would send help. Bring judgment in the form of glass and lightning.

But she knew it wouldn't. The Tresward wasn't an army. There weren't many Knights left.

Her heart wouldn't let her feet free. She couldn't move from here. Not this spot, but this *purpose*. "Have you seen what they did?"

Meriwether—

He's a sinner!

—nodded, his eyes wet. "I see. I *feel*." He coughed. "One bow and blade will make no difference. We must run."

Her eyes moved to his hands, and the tiny knife he held. The sinner stood this ground with her. She could see if she didn't move, he would make a stand with her, and he would die, because she wasn't doing her duty. *His lack of purity doesn't starve him of courage.*

Geneve felt her heart slow for a moment, its beat steadying, becoming less frantic, more certain. Blood surged within her, not the frightened gallop of a terrified stallion, but the sure tread of intent. She whirled, gauntleted hand on Sight of Day's arm. The Feybrind turned haunted golden eyes on her. "The sinner's right. We can't win this fight. We must go." She blew a harsh whistle.

The drum of hooves answered her. Chesterfield rumbled past at charge, mane flying. Troubles and Tristan were but a handful of steps behind. She moved to follow, but the sinner was still in front of her. Back to the enemy, eyes wide, but earnest, not fearful. "Geneve, not that way."

It would take too long to explain, but she had to try. "Ikmae offered the Tresward seven hundred perfect battle patterns. One is right for this fight. It will buy us a window to run."

"You'll die."

"We all die, sinner. You speak of trust to the Feybrind. Do you trust me?" She shoved him aside, feeling the fragility of him. In another place and time, she'd have taken him for a lordling's fop, all fancy clothes and meaningless life. There was *nothing* to him.

Focus. She loosened the straps on her shield. Geneve knew it was selfishness that made her walk forward, a hunger to see justice done at any cost. But it didn't mean she was wrong. There wasn't a way clear from merely running.

She let her shield hang from her fingers, low and loose at her side, its curved edge hungry. There wasn't light for the metal to catch, and that suited her fine. The enemy should be surprised when Ikmae's vengeance found them.

Israel spoke of progress, not perfection, but she needed precision now more than any other time. The Vhemin lumbered aside as the Tresward horses trampled their line. She couldn't see whether the horses took injury. The smoke thickened, swirling about her like a shroud. An arrow loosed from Sight of Day's bow hissed past her, seeking Vhemin, but missed.

That almost made her stop. *Feybrind never miss.* But it made sense— Sight of Day's village was a smoking ruin. All he knew and loved lay dead or dying. It didn't matter. She didn't need Sight of Day's bow. The pattern she wanted to use was a solo one for a single person facing an impossible horde.

She felt her lips part and wanted to hope it was in a savage grin. Geneve felt something ugly roil inside her and recognized it as hate. Not because the monsters were in the way of the Tresward's mission, but because they slaughtered so many of the beautiful things in this world. She drew back her arm, tensing her core. Geneve bundled up that hate and used it to power her throw. She torqued her arm, and sent the shield flying toward the Vhemin Sight of Day's arrow missed.

It spun through the air, hard and quick. The edge hit the monster's face, a stray beam of light breaking through from above catching the steel. A glimmer of golden-yellow shone on the metal before blood sprayed. The shield bounced with the sound of a gong, just as she'd known it would, flying back through the air. She caught it, readying her blade for the bloody business to come.

The Vhemin before her paused their advance. *That's surprising.* She didn't want surprises. Geneve hungered for their death. "Come on!"

"Geneve!" Meriwether's voice cut like a whip. "There are too many!"

"Get Sight of Day clear!" she hollered back. The horses came around for another pass. Geneve took the next three steps of Ikmae's pattern, tossing her shield once more at a brute in the smoke. This move needed her to be elsewhere on the return. As she broke into a run, sword behind and down, the edge trailing smoke, a Vhemin to her left roared and lunged.

Perfect. Her shield rang against her first target's skull before ricocheting to hit the back of the head of the Vhemin who'd lunged at her. As both monsters fell to the earth, Geneve's shield bounced heavenward. Its arc followed her run as she continued toward the High Priest.

Another came before her. She swept her blade up, skymetal parting armor and flesh. From the distance she heard the chime of Tresward bells and reached up to snatch her shield as it fell from above.

Four perfect strikes, and four downed Vhemin. Geneve hoped the sinner had Sight of Day clear. She risked a glance back. Meriwether was hauling the Feybrind along. Fidget stepped nervously behind them, the horse's eyes wild. She was no trained Tresward Knight's mount raised for battle and blood.

The sinner caught her eye. "I've got him. Clear the way!"

Geneve looked for a path as Vhemin drew close. To the south, hulking brutes marched in a line. West was the High Priest and his guard. East fared no better, the bulk of the Vhemin's forces breaking from the trees. The Vhemin there must have been part of a pincer movement.

She scanned north. That way lay human lands, and farther still, the desert. Vhemin lay thick as ticks across the sands, the heat a comfortable balm for their cold blood. But those Vhemin were klicks away. *These* Vhemin were a more immediate problem.

Geneve whistled again. Tristan galloped toward her out of the smoke. She sheathed her sword as the horse slowed to a trot, grabbing the saddle pommel and swinging herself onto Tristan's back as he continued on. He had a gash against his neck, blood running gritty fingers through the ash on his coat. It couldn't be helped. "Chesterfield! Troubles!" She ducked a crossbow bolt and raised her shield. Another *gonged* against the steel. "Sinner! We go north!"

She put her heels to Tristan's flanks. The horse, nobody's fool, dashed forward. The sinner pushed Sight of Day onto his horse. The usually cool Feybrind's golden eyes were distant, hands empty. Geneve couldn't see his bow and didn't have time to look for it. The sinner slapped Fidget's rear, and the red roan galloped north.

Geneve saw the alarm dawning on his face. She could imagine this thoughts. *I've just sent my only ride away. The Knight's going to run right by, leaving me to die at the hand of the Vhemin.* Geneve crouched low as Tristan bore down on the sinner. He looked at the charging horse, eyes wild at the pounding hooves, and seemed about to run.

Then he stilled and closed his eyes. *I've never seen such a thing.* Geneve reached low, snaring his shirt. A button popped, and the fabric tore. She caught a glimpse of scarred skin before hauling him up like a sack in front of her.

Tristan didn't seem to notice the extra weight. *By the Three, he's light.* Her horse charged north, toward cleaner air that smelled like freedom and cowardice.

⁂

THE HORSES CRASHED NORTH. TREES SWEPT BY. GENEVE HUGGED the sinner to her horse. *Why did I take my helmet off? Why did I trust a sinner with a Feybrind?*

Why did I trust a sinner?

She shook her head, gritting her teeth. She saw Sight of Day's horse ahead, red coat amid dappled trees. For all she wasn't a warhorse, Fidget kept her head, dashing between trees, the Feybrind clinging to her.

I've never seen a Feybrind lose it before.

Geneve wondered about that. Not Sight of Day crumbling in the face of his family dying; her heart ached for him. It was that she knew she'd never seen its like, yet couldn't remember the faces of other Feybrind. Someone taught her handspeak, but she couldn't remember their name.

They raced into cleaner air. They broke into a tiny clearing bisected by a stream. Their horses vaulted the stream, not slowing. Geneve pressed her hand to Tristan's neck. *Faster, friend. Faster.*

He seemed to understand. She felt his urgency as he tried for more speed. She glanced back but couldn't see any Vhemin. They wouldn't be able to run as fast as a horse. A hard ride, a little distance, and they could rest a while.

They pressed on.

PERHAPS FIFTEEN MINUTES PASSED BEFORE SIGHT OF DAY REIGNED in Fidget. Geneve slowed Tristan, Chesterfield and Troubles following suit. While Vertiline's chestnut looked edgy, Israel's black charger looked ... *angry*. He wasn't built to run from a fight. He'd been trained to face the enemy with his Knight.

Geneve knew how he felt. "Why are we stopping?" The sinner sat upright, hugging Tristan's neck, but swaying a little.

Weary, golden eyes turned to her. *{He's hurt.}*

"Who?" Geneve looked to Tristan's neck, seeing the blood there once again. "We don't have time to stop."

The sinner swayed, then made to topple to the ground. Geneve grabbed his shirt, steadying him. She felt the cold, hard hand of dread in her gut. She tried to turn the sinner about. He cried out, but not before she saw the quarrel sticking from his chest. *Three's mercy, no.*

She slid from Tristan's back, the sinner coming after like a sack of falling grain. They laid him on the ground. His face was paler than normal, his lips blue. The front of his shirt was torn from where she'd snared him from the ground, but also slicked with red. Geneve bit her lip, then looked to Sight of Day. "When did he get shot?"

The Feybrind eased himself from Fidget's back. {I don't know. I wasn't watching. I was...} He paused, fingers trying to find the air like a bird with a broken wing. {Missing.}

"We need to get the bolt out." Geneve reached for the shaft jutting from the sinner's chest. Her fingers stilled as she glimpsed scars on his skin. She drew back his shirt with exquisite care. The sinner's chest rose and fell with rapid, shallow breaths. His skin was marked by the furrowed lines of old injuries. Geneve's fingers hovered over a jagged mark that looked as if it were made by a short blade. A longer mark drew a line down his side. "The world hasn't been gentle with him."

Sight of Day crouched beside her. {We can't get this out here. He will bleed to death.}

"He can't ride."

{He must. There is a river ahead. The stream we passed meets it. There is a rope ferry.}

Geneve nodded. "Help me with him." She considered Troubles, beckoning the horse closer. {Kneel.}

They hoisted the sinner onto the horse's back. Geneve rooted through Chesterfield's saddlebags, retrieving rope. She and Sight of Day lashed the sinner in place. Geneve winced as fresh blood leaked from his chest. "How far is the river?"

{Why do humans ask questions they don't want answers for?} At her dark stare, the Feybrind considered his hands for a moment. {Twenty minutes at a safe speed.}

"We'll do it in ten." Geneve put her hand on Sight of Day's shoulder. "There are many things I want to say, but words aren't enough."

He considered her with those golden eyes. {Words may be all we have.} He turned from her, climbing aboard Fidget's back. His movements seemed more certain, assured, and steady. Like Sight of Day was missing as he'd said, but found his way back.

It was good enough. She vaulted to Tristan's back. "Let's go."

THEY SLOWED AT THE TREE LINE. SIGHT OF DAY POINTED. *{BEHOLD. One ferry, as promised.}*

Geneve followed the line of his arm, but not to the ferry. The river drew her eye. It was wide, but not a surging monster. Geneve knew that for an illusion; wade out too far, and you'd be swept away. The Three's blessings held: the ferry was on this side.

A cobbled road met the ferry at a worn but serviceable jetty. No one waited for the ferry, and Geneve could see no boatman loitered to exchange passage for coin. Two horses stood atop turntables on the ferry, patiently waiting for a driver. A looped line on a pulley anchored the ferry between riverbanks, stopping it from being swept away. She narrowed her eyes, looking for bandits. It wouldn't be unheard of for them to lie in wait, but the typical manner of their thievery involved a faux ferryman to hold up travelers while they waited in cover.

Nothing. She cast a glance at the sinner. His face was ghost-white, a stark contrast to the red staining his chest. *There isn't time to worry for things I can't change. Move.* Geneve urged Tristan forward with her knees. The horse stumbled. She marked the red leaking from him alongside the sweat on his flank. *I've been unkind with those in my care. The sinner and horse both would do better under Israel.*

Geneve slid to the ground, leading Tristan by the bridle. The horse dipped his head in weariness, following behind her. But he didn't stop, because he was young, prideful, and a show-off. Perhaps a little bit like the sinner.

The ferry waited, impassive. She led their small group along the jetty, wood creaking beneath Chesterfield's bulk. The Tresward-trained horses followed her onto the ferry without complaint. She examined the ferry controls. "I have no idea how this works."

{I do.} Sight of Day walked to the turntable's horses, stroking one along its face. It began walking, the ferry creaking as it began its slow traversal of the river.

"How do you do that?"

{I ask nicely.} The Feybrind didn't smile, though. He looked like he was fresh out of those.

The ferry picked up speed as it forged the river. About a third of the way across, a yell behind them drew her around. Vhemin broke from the trees close to where they'd come out. Two at first, then five more, and before she knew it the horde were at the bank. They surged toward them, heading for the ferry's line.

A Vhemin raised a crossbow, firing. Geneve swept up her shield, the bolt clattering aside. It was black, with a cruel barbed head, no doubt similar to what was in the sinner's chest. She turned to Sight of Day. "Can you get the sinner down?" He nodded, taking her meaning. Meriwether made an excellent target atop Troubles.

Geneve spun back to the Vhemin, lowering her stance. More crossbow bolts arced across the widening gap. Many she ignored, but those that looked to find a home in horse or friend she dashed for, sweeping aside with her shield.

The ferry horses, not trained by the Tresward, became alarmed at how their day was going. They picked up the pace, which wasn't a bad thing, but no good luck seemed to hold. A Vhemin reached the looped pulley and seized the rope. The first was dragged along by the strength of the horses' pull, but more joined the monster, hauling on the line like a sick tug o' war game.

The ferry slowed, then stopped. Vhemin swarmed the rope, scuttling hand over hand along the line. Geneve eyed the far bank. Five hundred meters away, empty and barren to boot. She felt her choices dwindling to zero. Sight of Day had the sinner laid on the deck, fussing over him, a small bag of bandages and unguents beside him. Geneve closed her eyes, feeling the sun on her face. The Vhemin would be here soon, and she needed her strength.

"The rope," came the sinner's croak. She turned to him. He was pointing with a shaking hand at the line. "Cut the rope."

"We won't make it to the other side."

"But we might make it to Tuesday," he said, before slumping back.

Geneve considered it. She wasn't familiar enough with local geography to know where the river went, but that didn't matter. He was right. Staying *here* would leave them a feast for monsters. Downriver was unknown, but with it came an inkling of hope.

She drew Requiem, strode to the ferry line, and swung skymetal. The rope was old and weathered, bouncing at her first cut. The Vhemin continued forward, the leader no more than fifty meters away.

He saw what she was doing and picked up his pace. Geneve swung her steel again. Fibers parted, but still the rope bounced, stealing power from her swing.

"Saw, don't slice," the sinner suggested.

"Do you want to do this?" she shot back. But he wasn't wrong—*again!*—and she didn't know why she hadn't thought of it. Perhaps among the seven hundred perfect stanzas given by each of the Three, there wasn't a single one for cutting a rope on a ferry.

Geneve set the edge of her sword to the rope and sawed. The fibers parted much faster. When the closest Vhemin was five meters from the ferry's edge, the rope snapped apart, hissing as it unwound. The Vhemin dropped into the water, the stone he wore for heat dragging him from view without a trace. The ferry turned in a sickening rotation as it lost its guideline. The bow faced downriver.

Then they *really* began to pick up speed.

Chapter Twenty

"*S*o *you didn't kick him in the balls?*" *Kytto seemed impressed.* "*I'd have kicked him in the balls.*"

Geneve hugged her hand to her chest. It throbbed. "*I didn't think of it. Ikmae's pattern didn't—*"

"*Ikmae doesn't* have *any balls. Leastways, not all the time.*" *Kytto tried to take her injured hand, and she drew away. He hissed.* "*Let me see.*"

"*It hurts.*"

"*Of course it hurts. A kid put a drill through it. Bound to leave an impression.*" *Kytto's voice was full of something Geneve couldn't place at first. A timbre she wasn't familiar with. She offered her hand, but cautiously. He took it, gentle as if it were a newly-hatched chick, and unwrapped the blood-soaked cotton around it. When the wound saw light, he winced.* "*Looks bad.*"

"*Aren't you supposed to tell me it'll be okay?*"

"*It'll be okay. Still looks bad.*" *He gave a cautious half-smile, looking like the Feybrind she knew but had forgotten.* "*You sure Iz didn't take the kid's head?*"

That tone again, and she understood what it was: real *anger. Kytto seemed angry almost all the time, but she'd worked out it hid something deeper. Perhaps being small and scared, like her, but he seemed too broad shouldered for that.* "*He took him to the infirmary.*"

"*That doesn't seem wise, but he's the Chevalier. I'm just a Smith.*" *Kytto* turned her hand over, nice and slow, but she winced anyway. "Wait here." He bustled off to his workbench's first aid kit, bringing the lacquered wooden box back with him. "This will sting."

"Aren't you supposed to tell me it won't hurt?"

"Nah."

"I'd like it if you tried," Geneve admitted. "I don't want to hurt anymore today."

He opened the box, removing a clean roll of cotton and a small wax-sealed jar. He eyed his catch, then set them aside, retrieving another wad of cotton and a clear glass bottle full of liquid. "Need to clean it first." He splashed the liquid onto the wad, and Geneve smelled the bite of alcohol in the back of her nose. "You ready for this?"

She was about to nod, and he wiped her hand with the cloth. Geneve hollered, pulling her hand back. "I didn't say I was ready!"

"Life sucks sometimes," he allowed. "We don't lie, you and I."

"To each other?"

"To anyone, I guess." He seemed thoughtful, then shrugged, splashing more alcohol on her hand. Geneve gritted her teeth, lips a snarl. "But definitely not to each other. It's why I don't tell you things won't hurt. They hurt all the time. They hurt a lot! There are Wincufs everywhere. Some use steel, and others a whip, but all of them are painful."

"I know this." She shook her head, then grabbed the wad from him. If her hand was going to hurt anyway, she'd be doing the hurting. Geneve moved to get better light from one of the globes above and wiped her wound. It was sore in an angry, insistent way, but throbbed less than it should. "What's in this?"

"A little boom-boom." Kytto looked away. "Don't drink it."

"Lucent Eleni says only the weak-willed drink alcohol."

"Lucent Eleni needs to get laid," Kytto said. "I'm not the man for the job, but I'm sure he's out there. I'm beginning to think..." He trailed off.

"I don't know why we're doing this. Lucent Eleni will fix it." Geneve thought she'd got the dirt out of the wound, holding it up for him to see. "How's that?"

"Not bad." He took her wrist, laying it on the table between them. His hands were callused like Israel's, but his fingers were gentle, like she was made of eggshells. He cracked the wax seal on the pot, revealing an unguent. It didn't smell of anything, or it was too faint to overcome the smell of steel and fire from *the forge. He rubbed the salve into her wound, then bound it. "The good Lucent will be busy for many days with Wincuf's injury. The boy will get his arm back, but it'll take time, and all her will, and not a little of her life. Your hand needs to wait."*

"I don't know if I want his arm to grow back."

"I definitely don't, but I'm—"

"Just a Smith. I know. I know! You say it a lot." Geneve winced as Kytto tightened the bandage. "You say it all the time, but I don't think you mean it."

"He doesn't mean what?" Vertiline's voice made them both look up. She stood at the base of the stairs, braid hanging down her back, a glint in her eye.

"Speaking of devils." Kytto curled Geneve's fingers on themselves, then patted her closed hand. "Vertiline, I'm going to tell you a story, and I don't want you to kill anyone. Can you promise that?"

"No."

"Then no story for you." Kytto winked at Geneve.

"Okay, I promise I won't kill anyone today. How's that?" Vertiline walked to where they sat, swinging an armored leg over the bench Kytto sat on.

"I don't want to be close when you hear the story." Kytto looked sour, shuffling away from her. "Here's what happened." He laid out the story as Geneve told it. How she'd been with her tree, seen the others, and fought Wincuf. Kytto omitted their names, because Geneve hadn't told him who the others were. He finished with how Israel sheared Wincuf's arm with glass and Storm, then put his hands on the table in front of him. Geneve thought he sat very still on purpose.

"Okay," Vertiline mused. "I'll kill Wincuf tomorrow."

"No! The whole point—"

"Please don't." Geneve rubbed her face. It still hurt from Wincuf's mauling. "I need to fix it. If I don't, he'll always be after me."

"Spoken like anyone four lessons into Justiciar Keel's Psychology of Warfare class," Vertiline said. "But he's a giant compared to you."

"It won't matter." Kytto stood, brushing his hands off against his leather apron. "They'll toss him out the door for this."

"Then we'll have a Knight—"

"Novice."

"We'll have a wannabe Knight outside, doing Three knows what." Vertiline frowned. "He can work the Storm. Not well, but a little." She glanced at Geneve

as if to say, and you can't. *Geneve knew that. The Storm never answered her call.*

Kytto looked like he was sucking a lemon. "Someone will—"

"No one will!" *Vertiline stood in a rush, the bench skidding back.* "That's the whole problem with this place! Just because you're old and command the Sway doesn't mean you can bend the rules. And the rules say excommunication, not execution."

Geneve watched, wide-eyed, trying to make herself small. Kytto patted the air in the People's way. {Calm down.} "That's the problem, though. Not the being old part, but the Sway. It means you* can *bend the rules and keep twisting them as long as the Three have your back."

Vertiline crossed her arms, turning away, braid lashing like a Feybrind's tail. "It's not how it* should *work."

"I'm not arguing." *Kytto sucked air through his teeth.* "If you're asking me, though—"

"No one asks the opinion of a Smith." *Vertiline tried for a smile, but it withered on her face.*

"Right. But this humble Smith says that kind of talk will get you thrown out, too. They've no need of argument at the top table, Tilly."

She shook her head, gauntleted palm out toward him. "You sound like Iz."

"Fuck." *Kytto sounded astonished.* "Right, you two wait here."

"Where are you going?" *Vertiline glanced between him and Geneve.*

"If I sound like Israel, something's wrong." *The Smith headed for the stairs.* "I'll find a bucket, fill it with water, and drown myself. Don't wait up."

Chapter Twenty-One

I've been shot before, but this time the assholes didn't have the courtesy to aim. Hitting me was accidental, and that hurts almost more than the barb. Meriwether felt the world came to him through flashes of too-bright light and too-muted sound. The only real thing was the pain in his chest, a deep, grating, *personal* fire that made everything else seem less important. In any other situation he'd marvel at Geneve's sweeping shield work as the Knight danced across the ferry's deck. Her red hair flew as she spun, and maybe it was the delirium setting in, but he thought she did it with her eyes closed.

Closed, for pity's sake.

Light glinted from the water. It felt like the blinding brilliance of the Three come for him at last. He felt the certainty of it, the hungering justice of angry gods wanting his end. *They sent Vhemin to find me.* "I'm going to die," he croaked.

Sight of Day crouched beside him. The Feybrind shook his head, putting a soft hand on Meriwether's shoulder. The meaning was clear. *Stay still. We've got this.* Then, like the implacable toppling of a burning building, the Feybrind slumped to the deck.

Meriwether looked to Geneve, but she was lost in one of the four, sixteen, seven hundred, or whatever-it-was battle steps of gods who wanted sinners dead. The Feybrind was *down*, but not *out*. His golden eyes stared at the sky, seeing nothing. Meriwether groaned, rolling himself onto his side. The pain as the bolt in his shoulder worried at his clavicle was exquisite and pure, and he needed a minute to steady himself. Nausea rose, but he stemmed the tide with a single thought: *if I puke on the cat, I'll never live it down.*

He waved a hand over Sight of Day's eyes. Nothing. Not even the twitch of an eyelid. His body was unharmed as near as Meriwether could see. No crossbow bolts sprouted from his fur, although it felt a disservice to the Knight's efforts to bother checking. Her dance was *perfect.* He almost got lost watching her for a moment, then the ferry listed, his elbow slipped on the decking, and his injury screamed blue murder inside him.

Right. Got the message. Do something useful. Meriwether looked past the sweeping grace of Geneve to the Vhemin on the bank. There, sure as Knights came for sinners, was the High Priest himself. The scaled monster grinned a grisly smile. His skin had the dark not-glow it had back in the underground temple. Meriwether looked to Sight of Day, then the priest. *They've got a trick to unwind the cats. That's how they took over an entire village. It feels like cheating.*

"Geneve," he rasped. She didn't seem to hear him, so he gathered a little strength, mere fragments really, and put it into his next words. "I need your scattergun."

That made her stop. Her hair settled about her face. She was sweating, breastplate rising and falling as she breathed hard and strong. "I need another two Knights, but wishing won't make it so."

"Just ... *trust me*," he urged. "It's for the cat."

She looked to the prone Sight of Day, then swatted a crossbow bolt from the air almost casually with the rim of her shield. The bolt shattered into fragments that rattled across the deck before slipping into the water. Geneve didn't do anything stupid like demand answers for what happened to the cat. She unslung her scattergun, cracked it open, and extracted a paper tube. Snapping it closed, she handed it to him. "One shot, sinner. Make it count."

He heard the challenge in her tone. Meriwether heard *try it* nestled in there somewhere. He let out a groan—couldn't help it, really, what with his lifeblood leaking all over the old wood deck of a ferry, pain in his shoulder so intense it felt like someone pushed the glowing tip of a brand against his flesh and left it there. *Poison*, he realized. *The fuckers poison their weapons.*

The ferry's timbers groaned and creaked beneath him. The vessel's motion shifted, edging back toward the Vhemin's side of the river.

"No one fights fair," he hissed, laying across the Feybrind. He leveled the scattergun across the water, lining up the High Priest. He pulled the trigger.

The weapon roared, a plume of white-gray smoke blasting from its mouth. A circular chunk of the ferry's deck vanished into splinters as the scattergun chewed on it. The High Priest ducked aside, a pointless exercise at this range, but Meriwether expected it. Intellectually a man might know the range of a weapon, but emotionally he'd still want to be out of the way just in case, right? Especially since there was no sure way of knowing what Tresward weapons could do, regardless of the range. The priest's black-tinged aura vanished.

Sight of Day gasped, sitting bolt upright. The movement knocked Meriwether aside, and he screamed in pain, dropping the scattergun. It slid toward the side of the ferry, but the Feybrind's hand darted out cat-swift, snaring it. He tossed it to Geneve and stood in a fluid motion, making both actions look like one.

Meriwether gave him a small wave, then slipped into blackness. It seemed the best place to be.

WHEN HE WOKE, THE SKY WAS DARKER, MARCHING TOWARD DUSK. The ferry still charted its course downriver, which was now significantly wider than it'd been before, but that was the way of rivers. Geneve rested in the shade of the ferry's meager cabin. Sight of Day prowled the deck. The horses looked unconcerned about pretty much everything, eying the banks and no doubt wishing for clover.

Meriwether touched his chest. The bolt was gone, a clean bandage hiding the wound. Where his fingers probed, he felt pain, but not fire. "Thanks."

Geneve's eyes slid in his direction. The dimming light made them the color of green actinolite. "Sight of Day pulled it while you were out. He said it was poisoned."

"I figured. But not with something lethal, right? Otherwise I'd be dead."

"Otherwise," she agreed. "I'm beginning to think the Vhemin want something with you."

"I'm beginning to think you didn't go to Tresward school or what-ever you call it just to eat your lunch." He hissed as his fingers brushed a more sensitive part of his injury.

Sight of Day's fingers flicked in his rapid handspeak, and Geneve laughed. "He says to stop playing with it."

"What else did he say?" Meriwether's suspicion was high because of the cat's half-smile.

"It was the way he said it." She looked at the far bank. "I think this voyage is cursed. We haven't hit the bank yet. The odds of that happening soon seem unlikely."

"Oh, that." Meriwether moved to a sitting position with a heartfelt groan. "It's because we *are* cursed. The High Priest," he waved a hand upriver, "worked his magic. Knocked out the cat, and I think was trying to lasso us to the bank."

Geneve stood, looking in the direction he pointed, then to the bank. "They can do that?"

"They're doing a lot of things they're not known for." He eased himself to his feet, feeling about a hundred years old. "Hot rocks. Massive incursions into the south lands. Burning villages." Meriwether looked to Sight of Day, then at his feet. "I'm ... so very sorry." He felt the Feybrind approach and dared a look into those golden eyes. There was sadness there as the cat laid a gentle hand on his shoulder. Meri-wether clasped the Feybrind's hand. "There are no words. I want time to sit with you. When we get to a village, we'll drink, and tell stories. The world should hear them."

He felt Geneve's eyes on him, so let his arm drop. "What do they want, sinner? What could they want from *you?*"

Meriwether sighed. "I've been wondering the same thing. No," he raised a hand in supplication, "this isn't a joke. I really don't know.

But I figure someone does." He jabbed a finger at Sight of Day. "Him."

Geneve looked between the two of them. "The Feybrind?"

Sight of Day watched Meriwether for a moment. He offered an apologetic shrug in Geneve's direction, his hands moving. Meriwether frowned. "What'd he say?"

"The oddest thing." Geneve strode forward. "He said he can't tell me."

"Us, you mean."

"Did I stutter?" She shook her head, red hair lashing her face. "He says there's a secret inside you. It is the key to the Tresward and the kingdom."

Meriwether rubbed his chin, feeling the rasp of unruly stubble. "Lots of secrets in me, I'll agree. They keep me alive." He eyed the cat. "What kind of secret's so secret even I don't know it? I think I'd know a secret that links Tresward and kingdom."

Geneve touched Meriwether's arm. Just the hint of fingers, then they were gone. "I think I *want* to know a secret that's cost me two Knights and a world of suffering."

"Not like that," suggested Meriwether.

"Like what?"

"You've got one speed. It's all, bash this, pummel that. It's awe-inspiring, but not the right tool for the job." Ignoring her incredulous look, he focused his attention on Sight of Day. The cat's left ear flicked but otherwise he made no move. "I think you want to tell us the secret your entire village died for. I think your people scream for peace, but the secret holds their souls to the ground. It's like an anchor, chaining them to this world. Or a sickness, I don't know. But I see it in your eyes. No," he touched the Feybrind's chin as the cat made to look away, "please. *Listen*. If I can help, I will. I just need to know how."

Sight of Day sagged a little, then his hands moved. As Geneve translated, Meriwether kept his eyes on the cat. "He says they want the Ledger of Lost Souls."

"Great. What's that?"

She snorted, drawing his eye. "You don't know?"

"I'm a sinner, not a scholar. I have no idea whose souls they are or how they got lost. Break it down for me." Meriwether raised an eyebrow.

She scratched her head, ruffling her hair. "It's a myth." The Feybrind's hands moved. "It *is* a myth! A fairy story." Geneve held up her hand to forestall Sight of Day's words. "Okay, okay. It's a book."

"Hence the term 'ledger,'" Meriwether said.

Geneve scowled. "Do you want to tell the story?"

"I wish I could."

She growled. "The Ledger of Lost Souls is a *mythical*," Geneve leaned on the word, "tome collecting the names of Tresward Knights doomed to die. It's a record of all of us stretching back in time and reaching forward to the future." She crossed her arms with a creak of armor. "It's said that writing a Knight's name in it will end their life."

"Oh, is that all?" At Geneve's blink, Meriwether smiled. "I've seen it."

"The Ledger of Lost Souls?" She glanced to Sight of Day, then back to him, before breaking into a hearty laugh. She braced hands on hips, head thrown back, cackling at the sky.

Meriwether pursed his lips, glancing at the cat, who shrugged, finger circling his temple, as if to say *humans are crazy*. "I mean, I'm not *sure* I've seen it, but I'm pretty sure I have. In Calterburry, where you found me. I was investigating a house—"

"Robbing it, you mean."

"If you like. Big place, lots of locks, for all the good they did. I found a library." Meriwether paused, glancing at the sky. "Some of the books were so old the dust made me sneeze. I'm pretty sure that's how they caught me."

"You were brought low by a sneeze?"

"Or the tremendous number of guards. Hard to say." Meriwether scratched his bandage, wincing at the pain. "It itches."

"Don't change the subject." She leaned closer. He smelled her armor, and that elusive just-Geneve scent. He thought he liked it, quite a lot. "You've *seen* the Ledger? The book that, should you write a Knight's name in it, they'll die?"

"Sure, why not?" Meriwether frowned. "Seems a handy thing for your enemies to have. You should go get it."

Sight of Day's hands swept the air, sure and certain, almost urgent. "He says they need to see it to destroy it. Wait. Who's 'they?'" Geneve took a step closer to Sight of Day, eyes narrowed. "Better question. You were *looking* for us?"

"That's obvious. I've got an idea! Why don't we let him tell the story from the start, without interruptions?" Meriwether faced Geneve's scowl with a bravery only skin deep. "Here's the thing, Red—"

"Red?" Her voice rose an octave.

"The thing is, he knows what's going on and we don't. Maybe not the whole of the thing, as I'll wager the Vhemin weren't part of the plan. He probably thought he'd find three Knights, and spirit me away at night."

"Under full guard?"

"Looks quiet on his feet," Meriwether mused. "Bet he could've slipped you some angel's kiss if I hadn't."

Sight of Day took one look at Geneve's face, then shook his head, the motion sharp and hard. His hands moved, and she translated. "There is a conclave of sinners. With a seeming of the book, they can transport it to a location. At this place they can destroy it, ending the tyranny against the Tresward." She frowned. "What tyranny?"

"There aren't a lot of you, are there?" Meriwether tapped his chin. "I've seen you fight. Israel and Vertiline, too. A force like that seems impossible to beat."

"The training—"

"Come *on*," Meriwether insisted. He thought about tapping her in the middle of the forehead, almost made the movement, but knew he'd end up on his back, probably with his arm broken. "Use your head, Knight. A bunch of assholes in Calterburry wanted to take my magic away. What if they really wanted to take the Ledger away? Stop the knowledge getting to this conclave?"

"That can't be it." Geneve's brow furrowed in confusion.

"It can, but the news is bad for one of us at least. See, if the cat's right—"

"He's a Feybrind."

"If Sight of Day's right, you need me unjudged... is that a word? You need me *alive,* and at the conclave, to gin up the book for them. But it gets worse."

She sank to her haunches. "It gets worse?" Her voice was faint.

"It does. Because the only way this gets fixed is with more sin. The conclave? I bet it's a collection of wizards, witches, and other unsavory sorts. A whole posse of sinners." He crossed his arms in satisfaction, the motion somewhat marred by his sharp intake of breath as he pulled his injury. "A conclave sounds like more than a couple people. It sounds like a horde. Sorcerers of old." He paused, thinking. "Oh."

"What else could be wrong?" She stared up at him, and for a moment his heart went out to her. She looked adrift, rudderless like their ferry.

"Something really, *really* bad must be going on if the conclave wants to help the Tresward. You guys are doing all the killing of the other." He tapped his chin. "Unless it's a lie, and they want the Ledger to write more names in it."

Geneve looked at her hands. They lay curled in her lap, empty of weapon and purpose. "There are too many things here that don't make sense."

"Yep," Meriwether agreed. "One of the biggest ones is, why are we still traveling down this river?"

"The curse. You said it yourself."

"Not great for teaching lateral thinking, these Tresward schools." Meriwether pointed to the ferry's horses. "Let's get these guys working."

Chapter Twenty-Two

He's not wrong, yet everything about him is. Geneve watched Sight of Day work with Meriwether. The Feybrind coaxed the ferry horses to higher effort, while Meriwether worked the craft's controls. She'd thought the vessel rudderless, but he explained it was merely *mostly useless*.

The ferry made slow yet steady progress to the far bank. The water swept them further with every moment, but she couldn't work up the energy to be concerned. She was exhausted, and not just by the sinner's prattle. Geneve had slept a little but worked harder. She'd worn full armor for days and felt ready for the knacker's yard.

What really wore on her wasn't physical ailments. The Tresward trained her to be their strong arm of justice in the world. To wear armor not to protect herself, but others. The weight she carried was something deeper and more personal. It revolved around a single question.

Why did the Justiciar save Israel and Vertiline, but not me?

It was a selfish thought, but one she needed to put to rest. She replayed the temple battle in her mind over and over. She saw the Valiant and Chevalier step through the glowing portal, then watched it snap shut. It left her and the sinner trapped with the Vhemin. Vhemin who wanted the sinner for the knowledge he carried.

Two things felt true. First, the Vhemin were part of *someone's* plan, and second, her loss was a convenient accidental victory for said someone.

Her brain felt sluggish, unused to this kind of work. Geneve was trained to see things as they were, but she had no special skills in politics. The work of words was given to Clerics, not Knights. Despite that, with the water lulling her body to rest and her mind to peace, she set her thoughts free. Adrift like the ferry, she thought of who stood to gain.

Demons were the obvious culprits, but proving their continued existence was as tenuous as the Ledger of Lost Souls. Demons were a catch-all. They would curdle milk, or cause cows to miscarry. If you found a dead bird in your house, demons must have done it. The Tresward trained Knights to face demons, but only because history claimed they'd faced them eight hundred years before when the world broke. The demons fell, and in eight hundred years no one had seen them again.

So, unlikely then.

The sinner's words nagged at her. *You haven't always hunted sinners.* What had he meant? To cause her to doubt her purpose? Idle speculation? It was hard to know the mind of evil.

Geneve glanced at the man. He worked with the Feybrind, sharing a laugh as the horses picked up speed, the bank drawing closer. He wore no shirt, just a bandage, and it let her see the ruin hands of men made of his flesh. She'd seen scars on this front, but his back was a lattice of deep lash marks. He was undernourished, and if she'd found him beside the road with a beggar's bowl she'd not have looked twice.

He isn't evil. Save me, Three, but he isn't evil. He knows its shape and weight. He's felt its hand, sure as the dawn will come tomorrow. But it's not inside him. She felt the heft of the thought and knew it for a deeper truth than the Tresward's teaching. Something inside her worried at the problem, because it meant one other thing was true.

Meriwether isn't a sinner. We've hunted his kind for a hundred years, but not hundreds, as he said. Like a puzzle box, something *clicked* in her mind, and Geneve felt she had it. She stood, muscles protesting, the sullen passive ache of overuse worrying at her. "Hah!" Meriwether turned to face her. The smile fell from his face, and it cut her. *I've done that to him. Made him fear the Tresward's Light.* "Israel taught me a truth."

"A truth, huh?" Meriwether looked doubtful, as if anything that came from a hulking Valiant could be wisdom.

"Aye. You can torture a man, but you'll get whatever he thinks you want to hear. Bargain with him, and you'll get what can be bought. Gamble with reprobates, and you'll tar your fingers with dirty nothings." Geneve arched her back, feeling her spine pop.

"That sounds like the kind of nonsense a Tresward-going sort might say."

{He's not wrong. Sounds like sermonizing.}

"Hush, you." She shook her head, her own half-smile forming, unsure of who she was talking to. "He told me the only way you can be sure of hearing truth is from those with nothing to lose." Water lapped the ferry. Tristan shifted, his big head nosing her. All else was still and quiet. "Meriwether, you spoke truth to power because you'd lost everything already. I treasure the gift."

"Uh, sure."

"We will find the conclave Sight of Day speaks of."

"That's good news." Meriwether brightened. "I mean, it's great—"

"When we find them, we will find more truth. They have nothing to lose, except their lives." She crossed her arms.

Sight of Day glanced at Meriwether, who glanced right back. "Great speech, but maybe I should do the talking when we get there." His brow furrowed in concentration. "You're not using this as a trick to get close to a bunch of sinners and kill 'em all?"

"I might be." She shrugged. "You'll need to trust me."

"Hah! Oh, you're not joking."

"The thing is, sin... Meriwether," she forced his name over the top of her train of thought, "there are many things that aren't right. The first thing is the Justiciar left you with the Vhemin. The second is he left me, too. This means—"

"You're a scapegoat." The young man nodded.

She raised an eyebrow. "I am?"

{You are, but unfortunately for this Justiciar, a very angry goat.} Sight of Day offered a half-smile. *{This isn't a bad thing.}*

She sighed. "The hidden truth you don't see is this: the Justiciar is in league with the Vhemin. I have seen Clerics work a thousand times. They can turn the sky blue at night, or a person love another. The Divine Sway lets those closest to the Light work miracles in the Three's name. Ambrose could've turned their bodies to ash or made them see fairy dust and moonbeams while we escaped."

"You suspect corruption?"

"I suspect I don't have all the information, so we'll find the conclave and get it from them, by word or steel." She offered Meriwether a small, tired smile. "It means another thing. I still need to keep you alive, for a while at least."

"Excellent. Wait. What do you mean, 'for a while?' What happens then?" He rubbed the back of his neck.

"Truth." She scanned the bank. It was very close. They'd be ashore soon. "They will send Knights after me. If we're very lucky, it won't be Israel and Vertiline. A different three would be best."

"Wouldn't Israel be *more* lucky?" Meriwether began readying the horses, dodging Troubles' attempt to bite him. "I mean, you know him. We could work something out."

"Israel is incorruptible." She gave a small shrug. "If he means to find and kill us, then we'll be found and killed."

{Sounds bad. Luckily, you have a Feybrind who is very good at not being found.}

Geneve thought about that for a while. She wondered at the High Priest's ability to render the Feybrind senseless, murdering their village. "We need to get a defense against their power over you."

"I thought the same thing." Meriwether walked a circle around Sight of Day, who endured the scrutiny by simply ignoring it. "Aren't Feybrind supposed to ignore magic tricks?"

{There is a not-magic that can bind us.} Sight of Day looked at his feet, tail lashing once. *{They know my name.}*

"What's he saying?"

Geneve rubbed her face. "He's not making a lot of sense. It's been a day for it. Let's get off this ferry, set its horses free, and find out where in the world we are."

WHERE ARE WE? WASN'T AN EASY QUESTION TO ANSWER. GENEVE'S reckoning said they flowed downriver fifty klicks, perhaps more. But her knowledge of this area was sparse to the point of being threadbare. First order of business was finding a settlement.

They tried letting the ferry horses free, but the beasts followed them. Geneve figured it a sign and let them come with. They would find a home for them ahead. The odds of the ferry master being alive were slim, so returning them to home was not just impractical due to distance, but because there'd be no one to hand them over to. Meri named them Casket and Britches. They were a matched pair of black geldings, and when she'd asked which was Casket or Britches, he'd shrugged in a way that suggested he *probably* couldn't tell them apart, but *might*, depending on which was more annoying.

Geneve let Sight of Day lead. The Feybrind took them through the scrub and trees that shouldered the river, finding a slender mud-slicked rut that might be, in a certain light, a road.

It looked like a storm was coming. Night marched toward them on faster feet with cloud to cover its approach. Meriwether stole a shirt from a scarecrow they passed. It was ripped in places, and smelled of straw, which she found funny, and he didn't seem to.

She spied the village by the thin spindles of smoke in the air, almost lost against the dark gray cloudscape. They made the town's verge as the light left almost entirely. The place was too small for a convenient signpost to mark its name, and well below the size that warranted lamps. She took over the lead, heading toward a larger low-slung building that had the look of an inn.

The front sported a trough for horses. A shady-looking lean-to on the right looked like something the overly optimistic would call a stables. Meriwether pulled his shirt close. "How you want to play this?"

"Play?"

{Play?}

"Yeah. We go inside, we've got a Knight, a cat, and—"

"Feybrind."

"One of those too. Inside, he'll draw attention. I think the easiest option is to call me your prisoner." He rubbed his ear. "It'll work."

"It'll be a lie." She stamped to the steps.

"All things are, at some level." Meriwether eyed the sky as a few drops of rain fell. "Fine. Not a prisoner, then. Leave it to me." He breezed inside.

{We're doomed.} Sight of Day followed the young man inside.

Geneve sighed. It felt like the sky rested on her shoulders. Pressing the door open, she was greeted with silence, woodsmoke, and the scent of cooking meat. A sour tang floated beneath it, almost like vinegar or spoiled vegetables. A portly man stood behind a sad-looking bar, the surface worn and stained. A collection of locals sat strewn about a common room, rude benches the only thing on offer.

"Hello," Meriwether said. "I'm Lord Meriwether du Reeves. Apologies for my dress. I was set upon by villains, and this fine Knight," he pointed to Geneve, "rescued me. We're en route to the capital." He offered a brilliant smile. "Would you have rooms?"

Geneve gawped. It was like a different man stood before her. Outside, Meriwether wore torn pants and a scarecrow's shirt. Now he was dressed in a silk doublet and fine purple pants. His boots gleamed, reflecting the fire's meager light. But it wasn't his attire that drew the eye. His posture changed. Meri's shoulders were straight, his head high. He almost looked down his nose at everyone. If she hadn't shared the road with him for days, Geneve would have sworn he was, in point of fact, the Lord du Reeves.

The innkeeper, also in a state of astonishment, bobbed his head. "Aye, you're lordship. Got a room. Not a good room. Bit small, to be honest." The man held a tankard and stained rag, moving the rag to mop his forehead before returning to polishing the tankard. "Not really up to hosting folk of your quality here."

"Think nothing of it," Meriwether insisted. "Tonight, you are all my friends. Why? Because the du Reeves house still has its heir, and he is happy!" The young man clapped his hands. "A round for the house."

He scattered copper barons before the innkeeper. "Would you have a boy to tend the horses?"

The innkeeper gave a slow nod, remembered himself, and turned to the back, bawling, "Ollie! Get out here." He gave a gap-toothed smile to Meriwether. "Apologies, m'lord. The boy's a bit simple. Doesn't hear too well, neither, since the horse kicked him in the head."

Meriwether leaned forward. "And yet you do him the kindness of offering him work. Many in your stead would have turned him out, or sold him. You, sir, are a good man."

"As you say, m'lord." The innkeeper bustled toward the back, sliding across a dirty leather drape. Geneve glimpsed an even dirtier kitchen, and a positively filthy boy within, before the leather fell back, obscuring all.

She sidled to Meri's side, leaving an astonished Sight of Day staring by the door. "Lord du Reeves?"

"The one and only." He smoothed his silk shirt. "I'd recommend eating nothing but salted meat. This place doesn't look clean."

Geneve opened then closed her mouth. *I feel stupid and slow.* "But, du Reeves."

"Aye." He nodded, encouraging. "What of it?"

"The du Reeves barony is real."

"The beauty of it is that it's also hundreds of klicks north." He broke out another fresh smile as the innkeeper returned. The man carried a small keg over one shoulder, setting it on the bar. "Ah. All's well, I trust?"

"Aye, m'lord. You offered a round to everyone, is all."

"That I did. And I wouldn't mind one myself, hey?" Meri winked.

"No, m'lord. I mean, of course, m'lord, but not this swill." The innkeeper beamed. "Got a bottle all the way from Tebrani. They say the wine's as tasty as the lips of their maidens." He looked too Geneve. "Beggin' your pardon."

Geneve felt like the world had turned upside down. She'd *never* seen anything like this. "Pardon given, of course." She gave a sickly smile. "Do you have food?"

DINNER WAS GREASY MIGHT-BE-CHICKEN SUSPENDED IN MIGHT-BE-broth. A few lonely carrots did laps about the bowl. It wasn't the salted meat Meri recommended, but Geneve was too tired and hungry to care. Her companions sat opposite her, a stained wooden table between them. There wasn't privacy in such a place. It was small, designed for locals who knew each other well enough to not mind sharing lice. Despite that, the locals previously at their table found places to be. Geneve imaged that might be her as much as the Feybrind. Knights had a reputation for murder, and folklore said Feybrind were all witches.

I don't know about them being witches, but they are marvelous. More appealing than the locals, for certainty. Earning a little space through fear didn't hurt at all, and she was too tired to talk with random people who were like as not inbred and superstitious to boot. She ate without lifting her face from her bowl and ordered a second helping from the innkeeper who's love of coin overcame his fear of Knights and Feybrind. As the man ladled might-be-chicken into a 'fresh' bowl within the filthy kitchen, she had a moment to watch her companions. Meriwether stared into a wooden cup, a kind of sick fascination on his face. He'd managed to finish his might-be-broth but didn't look up for a second round. Sight of Day was poking a spoon into the broth mixture, eyes narrowed.

"Something wrong?"

{Many things.} The Feybrind put down his spoon. *{Top of mind for me is I wasn't aware even humans could make food this bad. Also, I can't eat carrots.}*

Meriwether watched Sight of Day's handspeak without comment. "Try the carrots, they're not half bad." Geneve's second bowl arrived. She thanked the innkeeper with a nod and bent to her task of emptying it. After five mouthfuls, she felt eyes on her. Raising her head, she saw both Meri and Sight of Day staring at her. Meriwether swirled his cup of 'Tebrani red,' not looking interested in a second taste. "Try breathing this time."

Geneve jabbed her spoon at him. "Try not breathing."

Sight of Day rolled his golden eyes. *{While you're eating, spare some thought for our next steps. We need to head north.}*

"What's north?" Geneve wiped her chin.

"Fashion, good food, and doxies without disease." Meriwether shrugged as she raised an eyebrow. "It's easier to not worry about what the cat said and try to invent my own conversational fun."

{The north holds the capital of the human kingdom Ors'en. Queen Morgan is friend of the People.}

Geneve put her spoon on the table. "What kind of friend?"

Golden eyes considered her. *{The kind that offers friendship.}*

Geneve's brow furrowed. Meriwether watched her. "He being oblique again?"

She grunted, retrieving her spoon. "He's being Feybrind. It's kind of how they are."

{We are excellent conversationalists.} A small half-smile accompanied Sight of Day's handspeak. *{We are also used to using small words when dealing with your kind. It's nothing personal.}*

Geneve snorted. "We can't go north. There's a huge desert in the way. The desert is a wasteland of terrors. The Clerics talk of sand that can swallow a person whole in seconds. Parts of it hold relics of the old world, from when the ancients scorched the earth. We don't go there."

Meriwether took a sip of his wine, and his face told a story of many regrets. Lips puckered, he managed, "I thought you didn't get disease?"

"Our horses die from it easy enough, and in a sun-baked, waterless land, we die of thirst like everyone else." Her might-be-chicken didn't taste so good anymore. "We go north and west, or north and east."

"It'll take weeks."

"It will. It's how we got here in the first place."

{You mentioned monsters. You mean the Vhemin?}

Geneve shook her head. "Partly. The Vhemin live there. It's hot and dry. I don't know how they survive the blasted ground, but it's their home. I'm more thinking of the beasts said to roam the wastes." Requiem leaned against the table's end, and she glanced at the worn pommel. "When dragons flew the skies, they roosted in the desert. Stories say they also liked it hot."

"There aren't any dragons left." Meriwether laughed, a slightly pitying sound as if he'd heard a small child claim the sky was black during the day.

"The Tresward keeps records—"

"If there *were* giant, carnivorous flying monsters, they wouldn't hang about in a shitty desert, content with table scraps. They'd have knocked us right to the bottom of the food chain. Hell, there'd be one roosting in this town, because of all the slow-moving, stupid people."

The innkeeper chose that moment to arrive, cutting off conversation Geneve felt should best be kept quiet. The man wiped dirty hands on his dirtier apron, the movement obsequious. Close up, he didn't smell very fresh, and Geneve could see dirt seamed into the wrinkles of his hands and face. "Beggin' your pardons, but how's the food? The wine?"

"Excellent." Meriwether put his cup on the table. "So good, in fact, it seems a crime to horde it to myself. Perhaps share it among your regulars?"

The innkeeper looked aghast. "It's Tebrani red, m'lord."

"Ah." Meriwether's smile became fixed, like a seized cart axel. "I find myself in a good mood. It's being alive that does it, after facing certain death. It's like I've had the best theater show in the world, delivered right," he tapped his chest, "to my heart."

"If it's theaters you're after, you should stay for the execution." The innkeeper glanced to the bar, where his boy Ollie stood like a small post. "Bound to be excitement at an event like that. I'll be selling fresh sausages in hot bread."

Sight of Day pushed his bowl away. *{I find myself less hungry.}*

{Wait.} Geneve held her palm out to the Feybrind. "Execution?"

"Aye. We caught one of the monsters that razed Old Pencer's farm. Killed his wife, kids, and best cow."

"What monster?" Geneve half-rose. "Where is it?"

"In the lock-up." The innkeeper retreated a step as she shoved her bench back. "We caught a Vhemin."

Chapter Twenty-Three

Israel sat beside Geneve on a low bench. It was new wood supported by weathered stone. The wood must have been replaced often, but the stone lingered perhaps since the ancients walked the world.

The bench was in a market. He'd brought her here by cart. The sights and sounds were familiar, like she'd been here before, or someplace like it. Geneve half expected to see a raised platform with people on display, but there was nothing like that. Just fruit stalls, fish sellers, clothiers, and an enterprising blacksmith.

Israel wore no armor today. He held his hand out, palm up, to the blacksmith. They had a clear view of the man, all sweat and brawn, dark skin below darker hair, and wearing a permanent frown above a tough leather apron. "What do you see?"

Geneve watched the blacksmith a little longer. "Sloppy work. He's not a Tresward Smith. Not like Kytto."

Israel snorted. "Look deeper."

Geneve frowned. The blacksmith swung a hammer with intent, but not precision. He shoed horses, sharpened farm implements, and made small weld repairs to buckets. "He does little things. The workaday tasks that need doing, but not by an expert."

No snort this time. "Deeper."

She scratched red locks, ruffling them to fall about her face. "He works as well as he can."

Israel nodded, face impassive, but his voice held a little pride. "That's right. As do we all. The difference between him and Kytto is what?"

"He's not Tresward."

"Why is that?"

"Not good enough?" Geneve knew it wasn't the right answer, but she didn't have a better one.

"Not quite." Israel placed his hands in his lap. "The line separating good from bad is whisker-thin. It can be a moment of childhood opportunity, or a delicate comment made to the wrong person."

"He talked to the wrong person?"

"He didn't have the right person to talk to," Israel corrected. "Kytto is an excellent Smith." This came with a hint of grudging respect. "Perhaps the best. He has a great deal of talent, but he's made it to the top of our Smiths because we trained him how to get there. I'm a Knight. I could be good at fighting, but with the Three at my back, I'm a—"

"You can beat anyone."

He looked down at her. The sun was in her eyes, making his expression unreadable. "No one's unbeatable. All of us will meet our match. I'm a Chevalier. There are Valiants and Champions better than me."

"Better?"

He chewed on that. "In all ways. There are even Clerics whose skill with the Storm could break me open like overripe fruit."

"But..." Geneve trailed off. "Why try, then?"

"That's not the right question."

"Why do you try?"

"Because the Three need me." He pointed to the blacksmith. "This village needs this man. He'll never have the sacred knowledge of our Smiths. Higher arts are locked away in our vaults. He can't make Smithsteel armor that will never scratch. Glass blades are beyond his skill. But you don't need to make glass blades to help people." He stood, offering her his hand.

She kicked her legs beneath her, not taking his hand. "Are you saying I can be a guard for a lord? That without the Storm, I can still be useful?"

"Do you think Kytto needs the Storm to be useful to the Tresward?"

Geneve looked at her feet. "No, but he's not a Knight."

"Knights come in all sizes. Even little ones."

"How can I best Wincuf without the Storm?"

"By using something better. Your mind." His hand was still out, rock steady, *so she took it. It was strong, and warm. She felt like the Three helped her.*

"I don't know if that's enough," Geneve admitted.

"Doubt is the first step to mastery."

"It's not doubt, it's—"

"How do you know?" He walked her back to their cart. "Are you a master?"

"No, but—"

"Then become one." He winked. "One day, the Storm will answer your call." *Israel's other hand found the crystal about his neck. "We just need to find your way."*

Chapter Twenty-Four

Meriwether managed to talk Geneve down from the precipitous heights of instant justice by the simple method of explaining the jail *wasn't open*. The innkeeper confirmed it wasn't open, but also not much of a jail, which wasn't helpful, so he sent the greasy fellow away.

Tomorrow, he'd suggested. *We'll get in early. Bound to be all manner of people wanting to poke the bear.*

The three got the inn's single private room, which bordered on negligent advertising, because it was right next door to the room the innkeeper shared with his probably-wife, but possibly-sister, and the two of them made a lot of noise. Tomorrow dawned same as it did every day. Perhaps a little drizzlier on the weather front, and a little less bright, but cold like the south was. Meriwether's breath misted before his face from his lofty height of a straw mattress on the floor.

The cat was curled near the door, tail held in one hand. Geneve was asleep on the room's single bed, and he spent a long moment watching her. Her face was peaceful, like it never seemed to be when she was awake. Red hair framed her face, aside from a single, curled strand that lay across her cheek. Three days ago, he might have been tempted to run. Today, he wanted to tease the stray lock from her face far more.

Touch her hair, and you'll get a beating you won't forget. This is bad deci-sion-making, and you know it. Plenty of pretty faces in the world, and most of those don't work for a small army of sociopaths.

Meriwether sniffed, scratched his chest around the bandage, and wondered why it didn't hurt anywhere near as much as it should. The Feybrind must have bandaged his wound up well for it to be this good a single day on. Sight of Day opened an eye at his movement and yawned a maw of razor-sharp teeth. The cat offered a half-smile and some handspeak. Meriwether thought he said *food* and *now*, and a bunch of other stuff besides, and then he slipped from the room without a sound.

Standing, Meriwether stretched like a hero of old. He reckoned they'd be able to hear his back pop from the common room. Finishing a good stretch was its own reward. He scrabbled fingers through his hair and began the search for his scarecrow shirt and torn pants. Underclothes weren't warm enough for the day ahead, and besides, he found wearing something helped his illusion skills no end.

A quick twist of thought, and bam, there he was: Lord Meriwether du Reeves once more. He turned at a slow clap, finding Geneve propped upright in the bed. He noted the stray lock of hair had made its way to join its fellows and felt a passing regret he hadn't been able to help it complete the journey sooner. "Seeing you do that is…" She turned away. "Well, if I hadn't seen you do it, I'd have thought it impossible."

Meriwether wondered what she'd meant to say. *Seeing you do that is wonderful* would be a bit much to hope for, especially considering her sword was never far from her hand. It winked in the post-dawn light from the bedhead. "Sinning's easier than you think."

"I didn't mean that." She cast the covers aside, and while she wore her underclothes, he felt acutely uncomfortable regardless. "We have Vhemin to kill."

"About that." He held a hand up to forestall the inevitable *but the fate of the world* protestations that we're sure to follow. "We have *break-fast* to kill."

"Ugh. It might kill us." Geneve put her feet on the floor, bracing herself with hands on knees. "In all my Trials, they never said I'd have to face a bad breakfast."

"And once we've murdered breakfast, we're going to talk to the Vhemin. *Talk*, Geneve, not *cut*. They're different things."

She looked at him, eyes narrowed. "We're not in the business of saving monsters."

"We *are* in the business of working out where we are, and how we're going to get from here to somewhere more hospitable. Ten copper barons says the Vhemin can help."

"A silver regal says he won't want to."

"Real or fake?" Meriwether rubbed his chin. "Not that it matters much. They both spend the same. Also, a silver regal is the same as ten barons."

"I'd rather spend silver than copper." Geneve stood, obviously creaky from yesterday's exertions. She eyed her armor, and Meriwether swore he saw something close to loathing in her eyes. "*Ugh.*"

"Let me help," he said. "Carry your shield, or something."

Geneve looked at him for a couple heartbeats. He had the uncomfortable feeling he was being not just watched but *weighed*. "Thanks, but I can't."

"Afraid I'll sell it?"

"Afraid I'll get used to you carrying it for me." She turned to face her armor. "But I could use a hand putting it on."

"Done." Meriwether put a little northern cheer in his tone. "Armor, breakfast, and *then* conversation with bloodthirsty ravaging monsters. What a way to start the day."

⚘

THE COMMON ROOM WAS MOSTLY EMPTY OF CUSTOMERS EXCEPTING A drunk snoring by the hearth. The man hadn't thrown up, but managed to sleep through Sight of Day, Geneve, and Meriwether bustling about under the innkeeper's care.

The innkeeper seemed pleased they chose to dine here again, as if the village was rich with choice. They had a better breakfast than last night's dinner. Sight of Day had returned from a walk with three pigeons, which he offered to the innkeeper with a half-smile and an encouraging nod. Aside from freshly-roasted bird, tasty with fat and steaming hot, the innkeeper prepared a platter of eggs, sausages, and bread that wasn't too hard to chew.

Meriwether ate enough for three people. "I could *really* get used to being a prisoner."

Geneve slowed her chewing enough to point her knife at him. "You're not a prisoner."

"Oh, joy."

"For the moment," she corrected, before turning to Sight of Day. "Do you want to stay here?" Meriwether thought she meant, *so you don't go into a rage and kill our source of information.*

The Feybrind raised an eyebrow, then went back to his meal. Meriwether slapped him on the back. "I think if a Feybrind wanted a caged Vhemin dead, the Vhemin would be dead. In related news, if we find the monster dead with arrows in his eye sockets, we should have a good cover story."

The innkeeper provided them directions to the 'jail.' It was a wooden shack, well enough constructed, but in dire need of re-thatching. As du Reeves, Meriwether took the lead, looking like he knew the way. It was how lords worked: they took charge and bulled on regardless of whether they were going south when they should be going north. A good illusion was just clothes if he couldn't act the part.

Swinging the door to the jail open, Meriwether entered and stepped to the side, letting his eyes adjust to the dimmer light. The room had a narrow run where visitors could stand. There were two cells, the bars constructed of crosshatched wooden poles. To Meriwether's eye, they looked sturdy enough to hold a human, but possibly not a Vhemin, which was no doubt why the Vhemin in question was tied to metal rings on the rear wall with thick rope.

The Vhemin was awake, alert, and looked relaxed, like hanging on a wall was the perfect way to start the day. As alert as someone with a face that looked like it'd been used in kick-ball practice could, anyway. It smiled, lips over their signature wide jaw revealing the also-signature shark-tooth smile. When it spoke, its voice was like an anvil dropping on stone. "And now, I'm to be paraded before tourists."

Meriwether considered that for a moment while Geneve clanked closer to the bars. Sight of Day slipped between her and Meriwether, and he saw the Feybrind's hackles were raised. The fur on the back of his friend's neck stood stiff and rigid, and the cat's tail lashed.

Wait. Did I just think about the cat as a friend? That can't be right. I barely know him. Still, he has't tried to kill me. Meriwether rubbed his bandage through his scarecrow shirt. *He's actively tried to un-kill me, point of fact, so that's a plus.* Geneve engaged in a staring contest with the monster, chin jutting, but her hands were by her side, unclenched. She made no move for her scattergun or blade.

What's the best play? Meriwether joined her at the bars. *I need to regain control of this conversation. The monster took it from me when I entered, and that's no way to begin an interrogation. I should know; I've been on the other end of enough of them.* "How's a creature like you get captured by a bunch of inbred yokels?"

The Vhemin's eyes moved from Geneve to him, fixing those vertically slitted snake's pupils on Meriwether. It felt like being watched by a lizard, if lizards were very large. This Vhemin was a *massive* brute, with muscles on muscles. With his arms stretched wide by his bonds, shoulders up, it almost looked like he had no neck. "Accident or design." His voice was thick, a landslide with plenty of rocks in it.

"That's not very specific."

The Vhemin turned back to Geneve. "A Knight of the Tresward, in the company of a Feybrind and a lordling." The monster's gaze roamed her golden sun tabard. "An Adept, by the sash. Have you ever wondered why your emblem is a golden sun rather than three moons?" He nodded toward the roof, as if the three moons still stood above them. "It seems confused."

Geneve bristled. "It's because of the Light—"

"What's more confusing," the Vhemin rumbled on like he'd only paused to draw breath, and wasn't *done* yet, thanks, "is why there's only one of you. There are always three."

"There are three of us," Meriwether interjected. "If you can count that high."

"Tiny, feeble manling." The Vhemin smiled again, and Meriwether revised from *lizard* to *shark*. He flexed, the rope holding him creaking. "If things were different, you would be dead."

"If things were different, you'd be clever enough to not be caught by yokels." Meriwether spread his hands. "Sorry, but the evidence speaks for itself. What did you mean, accident or design? It feels like you should know."

"Doesn't it just." The Vhemin probed his lips with a flat slab of a tongue. "My secrets die with me."

"I'm fine with that." Meriwether tapped his chin. "I guess we're here for information, which puts us at a disadvantage."

"It does not." Geneve shook her head, red hair angry. "We need nothing from him. Come."

As she turned to leave, the Vhemin rumbled, "Have you wondered why the Feybrind were struck dumb?"

Geneve froze, hand half-way to the door. Meriwether saw Sight of Day's eyes widen, the cat's tail lashing the air so fast he thought it might crack like a whip. *This is getting out of control. Get in there. I'm a sinner; go sin a little.* "I've wondered many things, monster. I've wondered why my breakfast was better than it should be. I've thought long and hard on why horses don't like me. Sometimes, I gaze at the stars and wonder if the three moons really are Cophine, Ikmae, and Khiton, or if the gods left us as some claim." He felt Geneve behind him, her feet rustling on the rude straw covering the floor. But Meriwether didn't think she was angry at him, or meant to stop him. He felt like she, for a tiny, impossible moment, had his back. Or was *backing* him, if there was a difference. "What's bothering me this morning isn't the Feybrind or your special relationship with them. It's one thing, and one thing only. *How did you get captured?*" He spat the last words, clipping each syllable as if he sheared them from the air.

The Vhemin watched him, then made a curious noise. After a moment Meriwether realized it was laughter. "Oh, very good, manling. I came this way following traitors. They betrayed me, as is the way of their kind. I found myself overpowered, tied up, and left for the fools in his village of feeble creatures."

"Accident or design." Meriwether nodded. "I get it. You fell by accident, but feel they designed it that way."

The Vhemin squinted at Meriwether as if to take his measure better. "You are *not* a lordling. You dress like a dandy but speak like you've experienced a different flavor of lie. Truth for truth, insect. Why are you here?"

Geneve put a hand on his arm. "This is getting us nowhere."

"It's getting us a little to the left of nowhere." Meriwether touched the metal of her gauntlet. She wouldn't feel it but might see it. The metal was warmer than it had a right to be in the cold air. He stepped close to the bars and put his hands on them, making a special effort to *not* look at Sight of Day. "You mentioned Feybrind."

"I have a deal to offer," the Vhemin growled. "Get me free from this ridiculous jail. I will take you north to a temple of the ancients. In this temple you will find the secret of the Feybrind's," the snake eyes found Sight of Day for a moment, "weakness."

"I thought you were after betrayers."

"I still am." The Vhemin shrugged, ropes creaking again. "They stole the key to the temple." His eyes moved to Geneve. "There is more than one kind of key."

"Hold up." Meriwether let the bars go and held his palms out. "You want to take us north at significant risk of, and I'll borrow your word, *betrayal*. In return, we free you, as if it were that easy. The prize for us is a make-believe goal of anti-Feybrind fuckery."

"Yes." The Vhemin gave a short nod.

"Well, if that's *all*." Meriwether rolled his eyes. "What kind of door do you need a Knight to open?"

"I didn't say—"

"No, but you *looked*. I saw. I was right here." Meriwether crossed his arms.

The Vhemin gave a grudging nod. "The temple is a Tresward place."

Geneve crossed her arms like Meriwether. He had to admit, she did it better, what with the glinting Smithsteel. "We know all Tresward keeps."

"Not in the desert you don't." The Vhemin smiled, like he was hungry. "You never come to our home."

Meriwether laughed at the ridiculousness of it. It wasn't that he didn't believe the Vhemin. He felt like he was being *played*. Meriwether was about to leave when Sight of Day caught his attention. His hands moved, not with the smooth beautiful flow Meriwether was used to, but with agitated slashes at the air. Meriwether glanced to Geneve. "What's he saying?"

Geneve looked from Sight of Day to the Vhemin. "He said to take the deal."

Meriwether frowned, absent-mindedly finding the still-healing injury on his chest. He thought of the burning of a Feybrind village, and what it might mean to his friend to get answers. He looked to the Vhemin and its predatory smile, and to Geneve, her eyes harder than her armor. "Then we take the deal."

Chapter Twenty-Five

Geneve was torn. She felt the need to help Sight of Day. She'd been there when his village died. Geneve knew anything that would make a Feybrind share the trail with a Vhemin was serious. World-changing. The kind of thing the Three would see from their remote vantage high above.

She also knew Vhemin were monsters and not to be trusted. Going into the desert would take her closer to the enemy's home, and further from what her mission had become. It wouldn't be heading toward the capital and Queen Morgan's help. It would be going toward actual monsters that craved human flesh. The Tresward taught Knights well, and principle among their lessons was: a good Vhemin is one lying dead at your feet. Geneve didn't know who to trust within the Tresward, or whether there was a conspiracy higher up, but she knew, in the same way she understood good armor was hard Smithsteel, that her order wasn't *evil*. The Tresward held many good souls, and she'd worked with two of the best.

Israel and Vertiline would never countenance working with Vhemin. Her lips were about to move to the single-syllable response of *no* when a scream cut through the air. It wasn't near, but the early morning air was cool, and held the terror and pain of the cry well.

Meri jerked toward the door. "What was that?"

"Deliverance." The Vhemin grinned that ghastly smile. "Music."

"It's time to work." Geneve dragged the door aside, marching into the post-dawn light. Another scream came, closer this time. *From the south.* The village was small, a single street running north-south, bisected by another traveling east-west. The inn stood at the crossroads of the two. The jail was north of the inn. The morning air was clear. It felt like she could see for klicks in any direction.

What she saw was death. To the south, a Vhemin horde approached. Behind them, smoke rose in the sky, much more than could be accounted for by morning cookeries. The monsters came in a rush and burned everything behind them.

Meriwether appeared at her right side, Sight of Day taking the left. She felt bookended by sturdy supports. They weren't Knights, but they didn't run. Sight of Day stood fast even though he knew the monsters would take his will away. Meriwether held his little knife low and ready like he could fake it until he made it, or died trying.

She wondered what Israel or Vertiline would say about them, and what they would think of her favoring a sinner and a Feybrind over her order. She felt sick, unsteady on her feet, as if doubt were an anchor dragging her to the dirt.

{*I will take the high ground. We will make our stand, such as it is.*} The Feybrind touched her cheek with a soft hand. {*I am with you, Daughter of the Three.*}

Meriwether watched the handspeak, then moved in front of Geneve. He was close, and she could smell his nervousness, but also *him*, a scent like cloves and hearth. Meriwether stood with his back to the charging horde, and while they were nowhere near close, she thought, *That's the second time he's put his back to an enemy for you.* "Geneve! We've got to get the fuck out of here."

{*I am also with him,*} Sight of Day offered. {*Running has an appeal.*}

She felt torn by indecision. As an Adept, Geneve should be part of a Trinity. Israel to lead. Vertiline to back him. Geneve to do what was left. She wasn't a *leader*. Not yet, with her single gold bar, but she had to make a decision. Fight, and probably die, but standing with the villagers for justice? Run, encouraging others to safety? Her mind shied away from the question needing answers: *What will you do with the Vhemin?*

Geneve put her hands on Meriwether's shoulders. She held him firm, looking into his eyes. "*Why* do we go with the Vhemin?"

"You're asking this *now?*"

"Meri! I have to know." She gave him a small shake.

He nodded, like her touching him let him see all her doubts. He put one hand over her gauntlet. "Because I like Sight of Day. He's a nice cat. And everyone he loved is dead, and if we don't help, who will?" Meriwether squeezed her armored hand, for all the good it did. "I know liars, and the Vhemin isn't one of them."

She nodded, just once, then released him. Geneve drew her sword with a sharp hiss, then unlimbered her shield. Villagers were running about like they were starting to work out bad shit was about to happen, but they had no coordination. No captain of the guard joined her in the street, militia at their back. She hammered blade on steel to get people's attention. What she had to say wasn't a part of her training and its patterns. *But it's the only way.* "Run! Everyone, run! Take nothing but those you love and flee!"

The Vhemin horde drew close. She couldn't see the High Priest with them. Perhaps it was an advance party, or they'd split their forces, but either way it boded well for Sight of Day. The Feybrind held a freshly scrounged bow ready, golden eyes watching the onrush. He selected an arrow, then let it fly.

A Vhemin stumbled, arrow jutting from an eye socket. Meriwether whistled. "Nice shot."

"Get the monster." Geneve pushed Meriwether toward the jail. "Get him *fast*."

"Shouldn't one of you—"

"Get him!" she screamed. Meriwether turned and fled toward the jail. Geneve stood in the street with Sight of Day as the Vhemin hit the town outskirts. She could see the detail of their faces. The teeth, the snarling, and those slitted eyes so much like a Feybrind's, yet so very, very different.

The jail door slammed wide. The Vhemin stood in the morning light, stretching. *By the Three, but he's massive.* Unbound and standing tall, he was at least two handspans over two meters in height. He lumbered forward. Geneve felt dread, wondering where Meriwether was. *If the monster's killed him...* But no, Meri came out a moment later holding his knife. He offered it to the Vhemin. "Here."

The monster squinted at the blade. "What's that for?"

"Them." Meriwether pointed at the approaching horde, taking a nervous shuffle-step back.

"Don't need it." The Vhemin rolled his shoulders then charged his kin, roaring.

Geneve put a hand on Sight of Day's arm. "Be careful with your shots, friend." Then she ran in the monster's wake.

The first of the raiders saw the prisoner rushing them, then did a double-take, skidding to a halt. In an almost comical fashion, the raider tried to run the other way while momentum carried him forward, feet skidding on the mud and stone of the road. The prisoner clashed with him, swatting aside his enemy's sword like it was a baby's rattle. He lifted his kin from the ground, roaring, then *strained.* Muscles bunched in his back, and with a scream from his captive, tore the arm from his enemy. Blood sprayed, and the fight and life left the enemy Vhemin as if they'd never been.

The prisoner dropped the body, then tossed the arm beside it. "Roach." He lifted his enemy's sword, giving it an experimental swing, then looked at Geneve. She realized she'd stumbled to a halt in aston-ishment. "Adept! Get your horses!" Then he turned and resumed his roaring charge.

That's a good idea. She heard the hiss of arrows, and a Vhemin to her left sprouted three shafts, one from each eye, the third in his throat. Geneve saluted Sight of Day, but the Feybrind wasn't watching her. His teeth were barred, and he ran low and fast across the street to an alley. Bouncing from wall to wall, he scampered up between two buildings, then took aim from the roof. More arrows followed.

The inn. She glanced about for Meriwether, but he wasn't where she'd left him. Geneve felt a moment of panic, unable in the heat of the moment to put her finger on *why* she felt that about the illusionist. She spied him a moment later running *toward* the enemy. Geneve goggled, wondering why everyone was hurting the enemy except for her, before he zig-zagged around a Vhemin, heading around the cross-road's corner toward the inn's entrance. *Ah. He's already thought of the horses.*

Geneve charged after him. The Vhemin Meriwether dodged had turned to track the young man, hefting crossbow instead of getting his wind up. Geneve took his head from his body in a single perfect strike. As the Vhemin's head tumbled across the ground, blood fountaining in its wake, she caught the unlikely smell of cooking pancakes. It carried over the blood stench. Battle was full of tiny details, and she didn't have time to dwell on that one.

More by practice than good planning, she raised her shield in a sweeping arc. Three quarrels rattled off the surface. Monsters were everywhere. She barred her teeth, arms wide. "Come on!"

A dark-skinned Vhemin accepted her challenge and came for her. It swung and she caught the blow on Requiem's thirsty edge. Her block had the force of anger behind it, and her skymetal sword shattered the Vhemin's brittle, rusty edge. Geneve turned momentum into purpose, cutting off the monster's arm, head, and other arm. She kept her pirou-ette going, leading with her shield's edge. It hit another Vhemin in the throat, crushing the monster's larynx.

A third creature charged her. She ducked low, slamming her shoulder into it and surging upright. She smelled its sweet-sour stench, then it tumbled from her back. Before it hit the ground, she spun, slashing with Requiem. It landed with a scream as entrails pooled like spilled noodles.

The prisoner was roaring amid his fellows. Even in the massive forms of Vhemin he was a devil. He lay about with his borrowed steel like it was a club. Despite his lack of finesse his fighting style was effec-tive, and he brutalized the enemy without mercy. Geneve saw his shark-tooth horror mouth was grinning wide in glee.

"Geneve!" She turned at Meri's call. He had their mounts, and the ferry horses too, but as he reached the street Casket and Britches reared, tearing bridle from hand. They bolted. He spared them a glance before turning back to her. "Come on!"

She spun on her heel. *Time to take my own advice and run.* She vaulted on Tristan's back, and the blue roan reared, front hooves raking air.

Meriwether fumbled his way onto Troubles' back. Geneve gave him a tight nod, then called across the melee. "Monster!"

The prisoner swatted another of his kin aside in a wash of meat and blood. "I'll be right with you."

"Now!"

With a sour look, like he was a child being asked to pack his toys up, he turned and loped toward them. He made to mount Chesterfield, but Israel's black charger was having none of it. The big horse reared. The prisoner grunted. "I like this fucker. Okay, you ride, I'll run."

Sight of Day sprang from the rooftops to land on Fidget's back. He watched the prisoner run away, shaking his head, then urged his horse in pursuit.

Meriwether turned Troubles around twice before getting her oriented in the right direction. She gave chase. Geneve ducked another quarrel, but it had no friends. The Vhemin were fanning out, heading into buildings and homes. They would pillage and slaughter. She couldn't stop them all.

Geneve put her heels to her horse's flank. Tristan bolted forward. Toward her allies, a monster, and the hot, dry north.

THEY RAN THE HORSES FOR KLICKS. TRISTAN SURGED AHEAD OF Troubles, Meriwether clinging on like a terrified limpet, and nosed past an unladen Chesterfield. He couldn't catch Fidget, possibly because her rider made a mad-dash gallop look like a summer's casual ride. Sight of Day moved like water with poise on the red roan's back, as if the terrors behind them were nothing worth getting a sweat up over.

Geneve found the thoughts that bubbled up in moments of adrenaline the most confusing of all. She'd expect to be worried about pursuit, or the chance of one of their horses stumbling. Those would be sensible, useful thoughts at a time when fear threatened to ride her like she rode Tristan. Instead, she was thinking things like:

Can Feybrind sweat?

A couple klicks down the road, she held up an armored fist. Chesterfield slowed, flanks sweaty, but giving a little side-eye to Tristan. The bigger horse seemed determined to hide the effort it cost to keep up the pace. Troubles slowed soon enough, pulling close to Geneve. As she came to a halt, Meriwether slid from her saddle to slump with an *oof* on the ground.

Sight of Day circled Fidget around Meri, then returned to face her. *{Is there something wrong with him?}*

"I think he's better at running on his feet than on horseback." Geneve straightened, scanning the area. A set of low, rolling hills lay to the east. West held fields, the ground cold and empty in winter's grip. The road they were on was serviceable enough. *I have no idea where we are.*

"I think we're more lost," Meriwether croaked. The young man stood on shaky legs, absently patting Troubles' hindquarters. The chestnut bobbed her head, mane dancing in the wind, and gave him a gentle bite on the shoulder. "Ow!"

{Where is the monster?} Sight of Day's golden eyes held hers for a handful of heartbeats. *{I feel he's an important component of our plan.}*

"We have a plan?" Geneve gave a brittle laugh. *We ran. That's not planning. That's the opposite of planning. They'd strip me of my tabard for this.* She touched the golden sun on her breastplate. "We need to find the monster."

"We need to move the fuck," Meriwether jabbed a finger north, "that way. The Vhemin don't slow. They don't get tired. The only thing we've got going for us is their need for wood to build a fire, and we left an entire village made of planks behind us. I say we've got an hours' head start at best."

"You're scared."

"And you're not?" He blinked, looking up at her. She saw how fear held the color from his face. His shoulders were tense, but for all that he managed to pat Troubles' side as if he knew that horses didn't need to bear their emotional burdens as well as physical. "No. Of *course* you're not. You're a Knight of the Tresward! You know no fear."

"I've met fear." Geneve let her hand fall from the golden sun. "I know it."

"Really? When was the last time you felt it?"

"When I saw you shot." The words came out like wine from a smashed bottle, and she couldn't put them back inside her lips.

"Sure, sure. Losing a sinner would give you a bad rep." He turned from her, mistaking her meaning. "I mean real fear. The kind that holds your balls in a cold, firm hand. Gives 'em a squeeze every so often to—"

"I get it."

"And the thing is, fear holding your balls isn't like a doxy's touch—"

"I said, I get it." Geneve glared north. "Where *is* the monster?"

{He'll catch up.} Sight of Day gave her a half-smile. The expression held no mirth. It was the fixed grin of a person trying to laugh along at a funeral. *{I'm not sure if I'm happy about that.}*

"The Vhemin? He's making spokes from bones or similar." Meriwether adjusted his pants. He'd let the illusion fall. He stood on a dirty road in torn pants and a scarecrow's shirt, shivering in the cold. She saw again the thinness of him and as the wind lifted the coattails of his shirt, caught sight of the scars on his back. Meriwether glanced at her, then pulled his shirt close. "It doesn't matter. We go north. Either we hit the desert or a garrison. Staying here gets us dead." He hitched his pants again, frowning. "Where the *hell* are they getting all their guys from? That's a lot of Three-damned Vhemin. If they were coming from the north, we'd be up to our ears in assholes."

"We press on, then." Geneve glanced at a shivering Meriwether. She felt pity, sadness, and regret, and wasn't sure why. The world left marks on them all, but it'd been most unkind with him. Geneve was left wondering another peculiar thought, when her mind should have been focused on more important things:

What would the world be like if we helped those who sinned, rather than killing them?

THEY HAPPENED UPON A DESERTED FARM AFTER TWO HOURS' TROT. No smoke curled from the chimney. The stables were empty. There was no sign of slaughter; this hadn't been emptied by a force of Vhemin. Geneve led their group toward the old farmhouse. The building was wood, and not recently painted. The thatching was sound enough, but the porch leading to the front door held a broken plank or three.

"Hello?" Her voice fell flat on the ground. Cold, withered grass gathered up the noise, holding it close.

{Humans haven't been here for some time.} Sight of Day sniffed the air. *{Nor their animals. It's as if this place just ... forgot them.}*

"Isn't this cheery," Meriwether enthused. He half-fell from Troubles' back, dodged her bite like a pro, and creaked his way up the steps to the front door. He hammered on the wood. The door groaned wide. No light lapped at his feet. Inside seemed empty. "Could be plague."

"There aren't any animals."

"Could be conscientious farmers turning out the livestock so they don't starve." Meriwether's eyebrows met in the middle, like he didn't believe his story. "I'm going to see if they've got any clothes." He darted inside.

"Meriwether, wait!" Geneve grunted in frustration as Meri slipped from view. She slid from her horse. The cold ground was frozen, holding her weight like old stone. She marched to the door, throwing it wide.

The door opened onto a big room. A hearth sat cold and dark in the corner, and without ready wood on display. The rafters were bare; Geneve saw no dried herbs or salted meat. Stairs to the right led up. Meriwether was absent.

She tried the steps, resting her foot on the first one to make sure it would bear her armored weight. It creaked but held well enough. *The house has been empty so long, it doesn't smell of anything except cold.* There was no odor of old food smells or the tang of people.

The top of the steps held a landing. Three doors were closed, but a fourth at the end was open. Geneve clanked forward. "Meriwether?"

No response. Geneve curled her fingers into a fist, marching toward the door. She pushed it wide. Inside, she found Meriwether beside a small bed. Dark gauze hung over it. The young man's hand was stretched toward the gauze. As he parted it, the gauze tore, raining dust and cobwebs. "Ah," he said, the sound small, final, and impossibly sad.

Geneve held at the door. The room was tiny, and perhaps had been cozy. Once-bright paintings sat on a wall beside a window looking out over the farm's back paddocks. The shutters had long since failed, and leaves littered the floor. She walked to the window, unwilling to see the contents of the little bed. The fields beyond the window were overgrown, a sad testament to what had torn this family apart. She tried to speak, found her voice a whisper, and cleared her throat. "Was it plague?"

"It was."

"You should leave, then." She turned. "I can't get sick, but you can."

He didn't move from the cot, staring into the sad, old contents. "Nothing here can harm us anymore. It did all the hurting a long time ago. I wonder..." His voice trailed off.

Geneve took a cautious step toward him. "Wonder what?"

"Oh, it's nothing." His words shone with false brightness. "I guess I wondered what it'd be like to be loved so much the loss of you broke your family apart." Meriwether spun from the cot, avoiding meeting her eyes. "I'll see about those clothes. Meet downstairs?"

"If that's what you need." Geneve felt the words insufficient, because something unsaid sat in the room with them. "Is it what you need?"

"It'll do." He left her in the sad little room with its broken shutters and not-empty cot. She waited, listening to the wind ease through the eves, the scatter of leaves swirling at her feet. Red hair teased her face, far too vibrant for a place like this.

Chapter Twenty-Six

Kytto didn't look impressed. His gaze roamed her small frame. "Are you eating enough?"

"Yes."

"Sleeping?"

Geneve nodded. "Yes."

"Why are you so scrawny, then?"

She looked at her feet. "I don't know."

"I do. It's because you're not eating or sleeping." The Smith stalked about his forge, pacing like a caged animal.

"It's hard to eat or sleep. Wincuf's Trial is tomorrow. I'm to face him in his bout of fifty." Geneve felt the tiny size of her voice, a perfect match for her physical dimensions.

"So?"

"So, he holds glass and can cut me in half."

"Best you not let him do that." The Smith sniffed. "Okay, I agree, that's not the best advice. Lacks, what's the word..."

"Specificity," Vertiline suggested from her perch by the stairs. Geneve hadn't seen her come down.

Kytto jumped. Obviously he hadn't either. "Why, Knight Chevalier Vertiline! What a surprise. Have you come here to offer more sage advice, or to get on my nerves?"

"Why settle for just one?" She stalked forward, all lithe grace. Geneve felt crude and ugly beside her. Tilly could use the Storm. Her body held the raw might of the Three. Geneve would never be so fine. "She needs a blade."

"Plenty of blades about."

"She needs the blade." Vertiline stuck out her chin. "You know the one."

Kytto snorted. "Don't be daft."

"You'll never use it."

"I might."

"How long have we known each other?" Vertiline's armor gleamed, scattering the illumination of the light globes.

"A few years," Kytto said, in a way Geneve found unsatisfying and evasive.

"Fifteen years, Kytto. Have I ever asked you for anything?"

The Smith sighed, then looked at Geneve. "Here's how the conversation's going to go. She'll say she's never asked for anything—"

"I haven't."

"And I'll remind her about that one time—"

"I didn't ask."

"And eventually we'll bicker like two FOPs without teeth—"

"FOPs?"

"Fucking Old Person." Kytto didn't turn to Vertiline. "Keep up. Once we've whined at each other, I'll keep my sword."

"You will not."

"You're right." He stood. "I'll get it." Kytto trudged off, swearing under his breath, except louder than it might require.

Geneve, eyes round, watched him go. "What was the one time?"

Vertiline looked her up and down, as if noticing her for the first time. Her eyes tracked Geneve's small shoulders, down her frame, and landed at her feet. Geneve felt measured, and perhaps, equal to the answer. "I said he should kiss me. Didn't ask. Told. Big difference."

"And he didn't give you a kiss?"

"He said it wasn't his to give." Tilly shook her head. "I will never understand that man."

Chapter Twenty-Seven

Meriwether now wore good, sensible clothes that he'd not be seen dead in under normal circumstances. *My circumstances haven't been normal for most of my life.* So, they'd do. His pants were rugged, and he'd found a sweater of good wool. Mice made a home in it and appeared a little upset he evicted them. It was warm and dry, and he felt like he might get some heat back in his bones before day's end.

Even better, his new clothes didn't smell like straw. The scarecrow shirt he left behind after making a new home for the mice with it.

Boots and a cloak completed the image. The boots were trying to be black, the cloak edging toward red, and all in he felt he looked like a hobo, and that was fine. He pretty much was, just eating better these days. Sight of Day raised a majestic eyebrow from atop Fidget's back.

"I know. I look amazing." Meriwether tossed the cat a wink, which he caught and tossed right back. Sight of Day clapped his hands, which Meriwether remembered meant *pleased.* Or was it happy? Did it matter?

After an exciting couple of minutes trying to catch Troubles' bridle, Meriwether mounted. Geneve looked away when he caught her watching him, and that worked just fine, because there was nothing he wanted to talk about, and definitely not with a Knight of the Tresward. After the predictably sad deserted farmhouse, they pressed on. North, and north some more. They spent a little time walking the horses, letting them graze the meager grass by the roadside, before mounting up to keep ahead of the Vhemin. The grass hadn't looked satisfying, but today was full of disappointments for everyone.

Of their tame Vhemin prisoner there was no sign. Meriwether half-hoped the monster died. It'd solve one problem, in exchange for a handful of others, but they felt smaller. More manageable than, say, trying to figure out a watch rotation with a creature that fancied human flesh.

Night joined them soon enough. It stole color from the heavens, husbanding them for tomorrow. Meriwether squinted at the darkening sky, then jabbed a finger to a dark mound to the west. "Artifice."

Geneve gave a weary nod and nudged her horse from the road. He hadn't remembered seeing her tired. Not in the middle of battle, and not after. He paused Troubles by the roadside for a moment, staring behind them. *Nothing but the road. It's been a bad day all around, but she moves like she carries a mountain on her shoulders.*

Meriwether gave Troubles a nudge, and she obliged by giving a tiny half-kick to remind him who was in charge before following the Knight and Feybrind from the road. He patted her neck affectionately. "Sour bitch."

Fields gave way to ragged, scrabbly trees. Leaves had fallen from their boughs long since, and in the gloom they appeared to be monstrous skeletons. Monsters the world hadn't seen for a long time, and hopefully wouldn't again. Dead wood and leaves crunched under Troubles' feet.

Ahead, the Artifice loomed high. It was a huge one by Meriwether's guess. No expert, he'd seen a few of the relics across the land. Travelers used them for shelter, as the mighty metal carcasses kept the rain off. Some old trick or magic meant trees never grew close to them, which created a set of natural clearings across the countryside. A little spooky, but Meriwether wasn't afraid of ghosts. There was so much else worth being scared of than things already dead.

Geneve gained a little distance on them in the gathering dark. He followed the glint of her armor as it led the way. Of the cat, he saw nothing. His friend was no doubt in the trees above, waiting to jump out and scare Meriwether's soul right out of him. Or he was hunting. Whatever, he was either not here or invisible.

The Knight's silhouette merged with the scrabbly, pale figures of leafless trees. Meriwether slowed Troubles, who spent the time nosing the ground in a surprising display of hope. He patted her absently. "Geneve?"

He heard nothing. No night birds, no crickets, and no Geneve. Meriwether leaned down, whispering to Troubles, "Steady, now." She gave him an ear-flick, continuing to search dead ground for something worth eating. "Geneve?"

A light flared from the trees ahead. It wasn't brilliant coming-of-ages stuff. It was a steady, warm, yellow, exactly the kind of thing a lantern might give off. As the light bloomed, it showed Geneve holding a lantern. She fussed with it, no doubt letting out a little more wick, and the flame grew. It illuminated her armor, and while her back was to him, Meriwether imagined the golden sun on her breastplate challenging the night.

The lantern also illuminated the dead, blasted trees about her. *That's not right. Trees don't grow near the ancient's machines.* She was right beneath the Artifice. Six legs rose like pylons above her, the sheltering canopy of its body lost in the dark. What Meriwether first took for trees resolved in the lantern's light to bones.

Lots and lots of large bones.

It's okay! Don't panic. Bones means everything's dead. He nudged Troubles with a little more vigor, and she grudgingly gave up her search for a stray stem of grass. Getting closer to Geneve showed the size and shape of the bones about the Artifice. Troubles rode between curved arches that must have been a beast's ribcage. *But what a beast!* The bones arched high above him, so tall that even in death's sag he wouldn't be able to touch the top standing on Troubles' back. Geneve stared about in wonder, lantern raised to ward away the night. She slid from Tristan's back, debris under her boots crunching to dust.

"Where are you going?"

"I'm not sure." She tossed a look at him over her shoulder. It might have been, *come see*, just as it might have been, *do you want to see?* "The bones go for meters."

He slipped to the ground, steadying himself on Troubles. For once, the vile beast didn't bite him, instead joining Tristan for comfort. Chesterfield loomed out of the gloom, the massive charger pawing the ground. Where his metal-shod hoof struck bone, sparks flared. *What bone is hard as steel?* Meriwether hurried. He told himself it was to keep up with Geneve, but he knew it was simple fear. This graveyard wasn't a place to be alone.

The lantern's light and the gleam of her armor led him on. She stopped ahead, lantern held high. He joined her side, unsure of what he was looking at. Before them was a massive white rock. Jagged edges held pieces of Artifice. Thick metal braids ran across the ground like blood and veins. Meriwether blinked, took a step back, and his perspective shifted.

That's not a rock.

"It's a dragon," Geneve breathed. She pointed at the massive, ancient skull, and when she stared at him, her eyes were alight with glee. "Do you see? It's a *dragon*, Meri!"

The dragon's skull was larger than all of Chesterfield. It lay at the end of its long length of skeleton. Bones that must once have been mighty claws held fragments of the Artifice's metal hide in a fierce fist. He marveled at the size of that clawed fist. The dead bones stood taller than he did.

Meriwether tried to imagine what happened here so many years ago. He padded away from Geneve's side, light leaving him behind. He was used to hiding in the shadows and didn't admit to fearing the dark any more than ghosts. He left the Knight's side, following the metal braids that must have come from within the Artifice. Fifty meters on, he found another skull, no less massive. *Two dragons. By the Three.*

He didn't know how long he stood in the dark looking at the skull. It was broken, circumstance less kind to it than the other. A hole perforated what he liked to think of as its forehead, and jagged cracks ran down from the hole. Despite that, it still had all its teeth, and lay amid pieces of the Artifice's metal skin. After a while, yellow light touched it, Geneve joining his side. "There are three more."

"Five dragons?" Meriwether put his hand to his chest, feeling something inside him sink. He glanced back to where the Artifice's massive bulk lay. "Five dragons died killing this thing."

"You don't know that."

He gave a short laugh. "No one knows except the people who were here. They're dead. Long dust. Forgotten, like last Sunday's breakfast. Here, though, are *physical* memories. Look." He pointed. "Those look like metal entrails. Over there, a machine arm. The dragons tore this thing to pieces." He felt his heart flutter, in fear or excitement he didn't know. "Why?"

"I've a better question." Geneve strode closer to the damaged skull, walking the long length of the neck. Her lantern's light led the way. Where the wing bones sat, a ruin of steel and fabric lay. She set the lantern down, then pulled the debris. They snapped, coming away easily enough. She wiped her hands against each other, then retrieved her lantern. "Why do they have saddles?"

Meriwether realized his mouth was open. Before Geneve was, unmistakably, a saddle. For sure, it was made of different materials. Metals that still held their shine. Fabric that hadn't rotted to nothing. But for all the ancient's skill, they clearly made saddles in the same shape as people of today. "You know what this means?"

She nodded, eyes bright. "They rode dragons."

·❦·

MERIWETHER POKED THE FIRE WITH A DRAGON BONE. THE BONE didn't burn or char, which wasn't surprising—if legends were true, the dragons *breathed* fire. He'd expect 'em to be at least a little resistant on the inside.

Geneve dragged the dragon saddle to the center of what they called camp while Meriwether built up the fire. There was plenty of fallen wood, making the task trivial, but the quiet of the area around the dead Artifice was getting a little creepy. After he'd got the fire good and bright, and a stockpile of wood to keep it going all night, he'd spent a few minutes examining the saddle. It had a seat that looked like leather but wasn't. The saddle's padding was long gone. And while the ancient's faux leather withstood many of the ravages of time, it was still fragile and brittle. He'd poked and prodded the contraption, marveling at how the metal wasn't tarnished. But his fascination stopped there, because there weren't any dragons, and even if there *were*, there was no way he would get on one.

Sight of Day returned an hour after Geneve's discovery of the saddle. He brought two pheasants and two geese. The large birds were a surprise. "Geese?"

The Feybrind looked to the darkness, hands moving. Geneve ran a hand through red hair. "He says the Vhemin will arrive soon, and it's better to have something on hand to feed it."

"Good thinking." Meriwether set to helping prepare the birds. Plucking them wasn't fun but being eaten by Vhemin was going to be less fun, so he felt all his incentives were correctly aligned. That's how they spent a couple hours: plucking and roasting birds, while Geneve fussed with the dragon saddle. She appeared enchanted by it, as if being next to it would conjure a dragon from the ground.

For his part, Meriwether cast a nervous glance up. The bottom of the Artifice reflected back a little firelight. It was massive, and aside from six legs it also had huge pincers like a crab. He didn't know what this one was built for, but he suspected it wasn't for fancy parties.

About the time the dinner was close to ready, a stomping, crashing sound came from the trees. Sight of Day glanced into the night, cat eyes able to see just *fine*. With a sigh, the cat shook his head. Moments later, the Vhemin crunched from the forest verge. He was cut in about thirty places but wore a grin like it was his birthday. He led a bear, an actual *bear*, by a rope. The bear was seal brown and had what was probably blood matted around its muzzle. The Vhemin appeared to have resupplied en route, and wore piecemeal leather armor, including one of the hot-stone backpacks of his kind. He carried a large spiked club in one hand like it weighed no more than a toothpick.

The Vhemin let the bear's rope go. Meriwether scrabbled to his feet, aches and pains of the day forgotten. Geneve made her feet in a fluid motion, scattergun clearing its holster as if it had never wanted to be there anyway. She took a step forward. "Hold."

"Fuck's sake," the Vhemin offered by way of greeting. "If I wanted you dead, I wouldn't be standing here, balls dangling in the cold night air. You'd be dead."

"I think he's lying." Meriwether licked too-dry lips. "His balls aren't out."

Geneve didn't move. Her scattergun may as well have been held by a statue. "Will your bear hurt the horses?"

The monster scratched under his jerkin. "Depends if he gets anything else to eat before he gets hungry." He frowned. "But I think it's okay for now. Beck just ate."

"You named your bear?" Meriwether tried to keep the stammer from his voice.

"Sure. Even miserable fucks like you get a name, so why not my bear?" The Vhemin stretched, tossed the club to the ground, and spread his arms wide. "We going to fight, or eat?"

Geneve looked like the question needed serious consideration, then spun the scattergun around the trigger guard and slid it back into its holster. "We've got pigeon and geese."

"No man flesh?" The Vhemin offered a horror-smile. "Just kidding. That's a different tribe. I don't like red meat." Sight of Day gave a huge, obvious sigh, then walked into the night. "What's with the asshole?"

Geneve glanced at Meriwether. "Is he talking about you, or—"

"The cat." The Vhemin lumbered closer. "Sworn blood enemies of my kind, all of that. Where's he going?"

"Firewood," Meriwether suggested. "Could also be the boiling rage in his blood after your kind slaughtered his."

"Could be," the monster agreed. "I like how you're not pissing yourself, manling. Most of your kind do, and you're an especially runty example."

"Thanks." Meriwether glanced at Geneve, who'd made no move to sit. "I guess I'm glad you're not eating me."

The monster laughed like a smith's forge, a roaring, rumbling sound. "I like you. I promise not to kill you for at least a week. The name's Armitage."

"I thought we were going north." Meriwether's mouth was dry.

"Eh. I only need the Knight, and I'm not all the way sure she needs to be alive." Armitage wrinkled his nose. "Pretty sure she does, so she's got that going for her."

"Also, that she'd kill you if you tried killing her." Meriwether crouched by the fire, removing a spitted goose. He offered the smoking bird to Armitage, who took it with a nod. "She's good at it."

"Truth, I'm terrified, just too tired to show it." Armitage tore the goose in half, then started eating a drumstick. He crunched, bones and all. "You got names?"

"Meriwether. The Feybrind's Sight of Day, and she's—"

"Geneve, Adept of the Tresward," Geneve said. "It's taken you a long time to get here. What kept you?"

"Oh, that. I had a meet-up with my kin. Told them all about you. We've set a trap. They'll be along to kill you in your sleep." Armitage leered at Geneve, then tore another mouthful of goose. "Sound about right?"

She glanced at Meriwether. "It does."

The Vhemin coughed, hawked, and spat a fragment of bone into the fire. "I had to kill some fuckers for their wood. And their stones. Then I had to kill more fuckers who wanted it back. Other fuckers needed to die so I could get their weapons. Took a while to find a decent one, then I broke what felt like a good sword over someone's skull. Then I had to build a fire, heat my rocks, and find my good buddy Beck. I thought I might have lost you, but you imbeciles lit a fire you can see for klicks."

"It's cold." Meriwether heard the defensiveness in his tone.

"I ain't judging. I need the fire for the rocks. Also, I like a front-on fight. Calling my idiot kin here with a signal flare gets all the puss out in one go." He tapped the side of his scaled head. "Good thinking."

"I'll take first watch," Meriwether offered.

The Vhemin's snake eyes caught the firelight, holding it close. "You do that."

FIRST WATCH WAS COLD AND LONELY. MERIWETHER ALSO FELT IT carried a little more terror than he'd hoped for, because while the fire kept the chill from the bones, Armitage's assessment of it being a beacon for danger felt more or less accurate.

The wind picked up, tossing leaves about. Their rustling distracted him, drawing his attention, and what with being partially night-blind from the fire, he wasn't sure if he'd die because his hearing or eyesight let him down the most.

Geneve and Armitage dropped off to sleep without needing encouragement. Meriwether wanted to ask what weighed on her, but it didn't seem like the time or place with a Vhemin freshly arrived. He was surprised she'd been able to sleep at all, what with a flesh-eating monster five meters away, but she'd done all the work today. She was probably exhausted. Geneve and Armitage slept on opposite sides of the campfire. Armitage lay atop a hot rock, and his bear Beck snuggled his side like a dog of unusual size. Geneve had taken off her armor, but if Meriwether's assessment was right, her sword was closer to hand than usual. The horses, wanting no part of a bear, huddled in the darkness.

Sight of Day dropped to the leafy ground in front of him, and Meriwether let out a short scream. Geneve moaned in her sleep, rolled over, and drew her blanket with her. The monster Armitage didn't move at all; the creature slept like the dead, arms flung wide, mouth open.

The Feybrind gave a half-smile and waved his hand in front of his face. Meriwether knew that word: {Sorry.}

"It's okay." Meriwether watched the darkness again, letting his eyesight do a little of the hard work. He kept his voice soft. The cat could hear him whisper from thirty meters, and it was better to avoid waking the others. "I'm sorry, too. It's shitty you have to travel with a monster who killed your family."

Sight of Day nodded. {Still sorry.}

"Everything feels ... wrong. I should be dead, or at least ready to be judged. Geneve should be with her Knights, doing something important. You should be doing whatever cats do. On someone's lap, by a fire, I guess." He gave a brittle laugh. "I don't know if you do that. I figure everyone loves a fire."

Sight of Day nodded with his head and fist at the same time. {Yes.}

"I've been using my watch time to think. No, don't go." Meriwether held up his hand as the Feybrind turned away. "I could use a friend. I've precious few. It surprises me sometimes. Handsome, charming, and yet bereft of companions." He shook his head, rueful. "Mind you, the only people who say I'm charming and handsome are getting paid by the hour."

The Feybrind half-smiled, covering his silent snicker with a hand.

"I wish all my sinning could do something useful. I wish it could take back time. Bring people back from the dead. Move mountains, or save an innocent. But all I can do is steal, and make things that aren't real." His eyes found Geneve's still form. "It's a wonder I've not been killed before."

He felt a hand on his shoulder, and turned to see Sight of Day's wonderful, golden eyes on his own. The cat very slowly, very deliberately shook his head.

"Sorry." Meriwether tried for a laugh and managed to make it sound half decent. "I saw something today that reminded me of another thing I'd tried to forget. Or run away from. Makes no difference, really. Go. Get some sleep. All our problems will be waiting for us in the morning."

The cat nodded, then stroked Meriwether's cheek before padding toward his bedding. The Feybrind paused by the fire, looking at Meriwether's bedroll between the monster Armitage and Geneve, then shook his head. He picked up his blankets and put them between Meriwether's and Armitage before curling up to sleep.

Who'd have thought. There's one person in this world who cares who gets eaten first.

Chapter Twenty-Eight

The plague lands. Some called them a desert, others a misery, but all people agreed: if you stepped on the sands, your life was forfeit.

Geneve knew she *might* be able to walk the blasted steppes. The Light in all Knights kept them safe from disease and most of the ravages of time, but the sands were forbidden to all. No Knights came back from trying to cross them. The Tresward Great Library held no clues as to what lay in the middle. All maps ended at the border of such areas with a simple word: *DANGER*. The world was littered with plague lands. Vast stretches of scorched ground from the time of the ancients. Most were hundreds of klicks across, and without water or a horse, survival seemed tricky. Armitage snorted at her concerns. *You've never had a guide with balls, is all.*

She was nervous about her companions. Not the monster, of course: his people called the plague lands home. The hot, dry climate let them live in relative comfort, and they didn't seem to get sick. To hear him tell it, *the desert makes us strong! You feeble fucks could learn something from it.* The brute continued with snide, insincere comments, but for all that he did his part. He did his time over the cook pot and hunted with enthusiasm if not elegance. The Vhemin was worthless with a bow, but frighteningly fast over short distances. He ran deer to ground, knocking the life right out of them with his massive club.

It was the kind of speed it would be good to remember. Geneve was fast and strong, but she was only human. She didn't know if her training would be sufficient against a monster like Armitage without the Light, but it seemed he wondered the same thing. Their truce held. At least his bear was nice, as far as bears went. Beck showed affection for Armitage, and Geneve wondered at it. Her training said the Vhemin were evil to their core. Monsters who lusted for battle. And yet, Armitage play-wrestled with his bear, scratched under his chin, and talked to him in a low, gravelly voice when the night drew close.

The safety of Sight of Day and Meriwether when they reached the desert was more concerning. Feybrind didn't get sick like people did, but they weren't immune to disease. And Meriwether was just a man. Human, and without the Light's protection. She chewed her nails at night, watching him across the campfire. She wondered what dying of the desert sickness would look like, and if she'd have the strength to end his misery. These thoughts rode with her, weighing her down more than Smithsteel. Her feelings were born not from the teachings of the Three but from her heart, and her beliefs warred with a darker part of her that wanted him free and clear. She'd seen the good in him and knew for all his jokes of being a sinner, she'd struggle to set the edge of her steel to his throat in anger, and maybe not for mercy, either.

When they arrived at the plague lands, the ground didn't change all at once. The road they followed faded a klick or more past. Armitage led the way from atop Beck's back. Trees didn't try to grow here. Foliage stopped being quite the right color green. Firm ground became muddy, brackish water with an oily rainbow slick. The world stopped smelling clean, and a pervasive scent of rot floated on the air. Wind didn't rustle her hair.

Armitage held up a hand for them to halt. His bear grumbled, and he cuffed Beck. To Geneve's eye, it looked like a well-hidden pat. "This here's a swamp."

"No shit," Meriwether said. He made a great show of looking around, eyes wide. "Thank you for telling us. I wondered what the marshy ground was all about. The insects are feral, and the air smells of—"

"It smells like ass," Armitage rumbled. "Just remember your week's almost up. I might kill you tomorrow."

Geneve nudged a protesting Tristan forward. "And we all might die from sickness, too. What's your point?"

"My point is this. In five klicks, maybe a little more, the swamp dies. Everything dies. No more bad smell. The ground will dry out, like ground's supposed to. And then *we* might die. You step where I step. If I stop, you better fucking stop, too. I'm not pulling you out of swallowing sands." The monster squinted north, visoring his eyes with a hand. "And if we see other Vhemin—"

"Let you do the talking," Meriwether agreed. "Makes sense."

"Fuck, no," the monster scoffed. "Kill those assholes."

Geneve blinked. "Aren't they—"

"You have a funny idea of how we work," Armitage said. "We don't sit around a hearth singing songs and drinking wine. We spit our enemy's heads on pikes and drink their blood. The sooner you get with the idea we're not a family, the more likely it is you'll survive."

Meriwether scratched his chin. A short beard had taken root on his face, and Geneve admitted to herself she quite liked it. It wasn't patchy and highlighted the line of his jaw. "I'm curious about how you make baby Vhemin with that kind of society."

"We fuck," admitted the monster. "It's all in the fucking."

"That's not what I meant. I was thinking more of—"

"The point is, my tribe's not somewhere helpful, like *here*. They're," Armitage seemed to search for the right words, "taking a break. Anyone else is not my tribe, and that means they're fair game. Before you go all bleeding-heart on me, runt, it's worth bearing in mind they'll think you look *delicious*."

Meriwether shuddered. "Times like this I wish I knew how to use a weapon."

"Nah, you're all good without," the monster said. "You'd make a decent snack, and if it comes time to run, it's best to hamstring the helpless and leave 'em as bait on the sand." He nudged Beck, and the bear trundled in a northerly direction with a low, rumbling murmur.

Sight of Day offered a half-smile. Fidget followed the Vhemin without any obvious sign of direction.

The young man watched the Vhemin and Feybrind go. "I don't think I like Armitage." He bowed his head. "I don't want to get eaten."

Geneve brought Tristan next to Troubles. "I don't think he eats people."

"What makes you say that?"

"He'd have made a snack of you already." She felt an impish smile touch her lips at his astonished expression. "Don't worry, Meri. I've got you."

Geneve followed the Vhemin and Feybrind, leaving Meriwether to catch up. She almost didn't hear his whisper, but she caught it anyway. "Yes, but who's got you?"

⚶

ARMITAGE WASN'T WRONG. THE MARSH STOPPED, BECOMING A VERGE of dirt before the sand took over. It felt like it happened all at once. One minute their horse's hooves were trudging through muck, and then next sand was clinging to their still-wet fetlocks. Geneve swiveled in her saddle, looking behind. Marsh became sand in less than twenty meters. To the east and west, the line of marshland stopped like one of the Three drew a line in the ground and decreed *this is where the ass-water stops.*

She shook her head. Armitage's turn of phrase was getting inside her head. *I shouldn't think of the Three like that.*

'Desert' was the right term. There wasn't a hint of grass or green. Not even a tumbleweed had the decency to blow across the dunes, of which there were plenty. The sands rose like frozen waves. Armitage led them from the relative flat of the marshlands up the smooth slope of a miniature sand mountain. He got off Beck, and the rest followed suit.

The initial freedom from the cold south was welcome, but within an hour of the sun beating like a hammer of fire on her armor, Geneve wanted to be somewhere else. She walked like she'd been trained. *Stand tall. Don't bend, and don't break. I'm not glass. That's for blades.* She eyed

Armitage in the lead, taking a shrewd glance at his leather armor. It made a lot more sense now. You didn't want to encase yourself in a steel oven out here.

Meriwether looked to be suffering as well. He'd wrapped his cloak about his head to protect from the sun. Geneve felt it on her face too and wondered how long it'd be before she crisped. *Maybe I've burned already. At least my skin isn't pale.*

Sight of Day seemed to be having the best time of any of them. He padded along the sand like slipping was a thing that other people had to put up with. His tail was low, relaxed, and his eyes were bright. The Feybrind stepped back to her on feet that disturbed almost none of the desert beneath them. *{Are you well, Daughter of the Three?}*

"I'm great," she croaked.

{Oh, good. I asked because your skin is turning a peculiar color.} He offered her a small shawl. *{Here's something I prepared earlier.}*

Geneve nodded her thanks, wrapping the shawl about her face. Red hair strained for freedom around the sides of her makeshift cowl. "Is it just me, or is it hot here?"

"Did you get dropped as a baby?" Armitage scowled from the head of their column. "Of course it's hot. It's a desert. The sun," he pointed above, "pisses heat everywhere. There's no trees, or water. If your Three made a hell, this is it." He grinned shark teeth. "I kinda like it."

"How about a rest?" Meriwether rasped.

"How about we wait until the Vhemin behind us catch up and kill us all?" Armitage scratched an armpit. "I dunno. It doesn't sound great now I've said it out loud. What do you think?"

Sight of Day's tail lashed. *{Much as I wish all Vhemin done, it doesn't make this one wrong.}*

"No, and it doesn't make me blind, either." At Sight of Day's astonished expression, Armitage chuckled. "What, you think your flailing hand speech is hidden from us? Two people can keep a secret if one of 'em's dead, cat, and there's still plenty of you running about."

Meriwether put his hand on Sight of Day's shoulder as the Feybrind tensed. "Then we march on."

"We do," Armitage agreed. "We keep marching until the sun's at its zenith." He squinted. "A couple more hours, then we break. Beck doesn't like midday. Not on the sands."

They continued. The desert was featureless insofar as Geneve couldn't tell one dune from another. Their footsteps marked their passage, but she had no doubt a good wind would solve that problem. At the top of a dune, she caught the glint of metal from the west. "What's that?"

Armitage grunted. "Metal."

"I can see that. What kind of metal?"

"Why don't you go take a look?" At her glare, he shrugged. "I don't know, Adept. Could be an Artifice. Could be a dead Knight. Or a hundred other things. The sands spit up shit they swallowed hundreds of years ago all the time. Might be a dangerous relic, or a child's toy." He turned away, trudging on.

A dead Knight. A child's toy. Or a dangerous relic. Geneve wondered what life on the sands was like when you didn't know what lay a couple klicks away. Things outside the plague lands were predictable. The ground didn't vomit up history. The horrors were mostly just people. She bowed her head and followed.

The heat was oppressive. Geneve felt like she carried another on her shoulders. The air shimmered with it. The sand smelled hot and dry. It didn't smell of poison or death. It didn't smell of much at all. Scoured clean, as if the Three erased all memory of people from here. *They've forsaken this place. And what they turned away from, the Vhemin made into a home.*

The horizon ahead blurred, and she swayed, putting a hand on Tristan for support. The horse chuffed, but his head hung low. She spared a glance for Chesterfield. The big charger looked miserable, but also too damn ornery to let a bear have the upper hand. He stamped on, tossing his head every so often, but there weren't any flies. Nothing lived here.

The northern blur resolved into a smudge, and the smudge became a low range of coal-gray facades. "What's that?"

"That's a place we ain't going." Armitage arched his back. "That's one of your cities. Was, anyway. Pretty fucked up now."

"A city of the ancients?"

"Did I stutter?" The monster ran a finger under his collar. "We don't go there. Even Vhemin get sick where you left your footprints." He spat. "Humans spread across this world like a disease. And you poisoned the earth where you stepped."

"You don't know that." Meriwether coughed, the sound dry, like old leaves. "No one knows that."

"I know over there," Armitage jabbed a finger at the dead city, "the air kills anyone who breathes it. There's plenty more like it. Sometimes it ain't the air that's bad." He looked away. "Can be fun, though. Guardians remain in some of these places. We use 'em for training."

Geneve visored her eyes. "What kind of training?"

"The kind where we kill the guardians and wear their skulls as hats. You know what? This place feels as good as any to stop. Let's take five."

"Only five?" Meriwether paled despite the heat.

"It's an expression, runt. Might be an hour. A little more, if the heat sticks like it sometimes does." The monster patted Beck's hide, then rummaged in his saddlebags. He retrieved a tarp and some short metal poles. Armitage shook the poles, then with a grunt of frustration, slapped one against his thigh. It telescoped into a longer rod, which he rammed into the ground. In a couple of minutes, he'd assembled a sunshade. Beck ambled underneath, throwing himself on the sand with a huff.

Meriwether looked to the shade with longing, then shook his head before facing Geneve. "Let's get your armor off."

"I can't—"

"It's hotter than a forge out here. I've got sweat where I didn't know it could go. You must be miserable inside all that metal." He tipped his head sideways. "You and I both know you're too stubborn to admit it, so I'm suggesting it, so's you can yell at me, then take the steel off in a begrudging manner."

"Stubborn?" Geneve felt her voice rise an octave and tried to wind it back down.

"That's what I'm talking about." He grinned, like this was his plan all along. "C'mon, Red. You can holler at me while we get it off you."

Geneve eyed him. The wrinkle of a smile at the corners of his eyes, the easy grin he wore. *There's no deceit there. He's just thinking about* me, *and what it means to* be *me*. She'd not expected that from a sinner.

But then, she'd not expected to spend so much time with one who defied the Three's edicts. She certainly hadn't expected to *like* one. "Okay. But maybe I'll only shout a little bit. The dry air's making me hoarse."

⁊

GENEVE DOZED IN ARMITAGE'S COVER. IT'D BEEN A STRUGGLE getting everyone in there, but the monster himself didn't join them. He removed the stone tablet from his back, stretched, and rolled his shoulders before setting off across the sands. She didn't know where he went.

It didn't matter. The cold-blooded Vhemin relished this time of day. He left his bear behind, which she took to mean he was coming back. Beck didn't seem to care, laying like a harpooned furry whale, panting in the heat. She wondered about their partnership. Geneve hadn't seen other Vhemin riding beasts. Not horses, nor bears. They were foot soldiers. Tresward scripture said no beasts let the monsters near, which sounded correct, except here she was, sharing shade with a seal brown bear that played with a monster like dog and boy.

It didn't make a lot of sense, much like the rest of her life at the moment.

An hour passed and dragged its heels with a second. Huffing announced Armitage's return. She sat upright, fingers resting on Requiem's pommel. She spied Sight of Day sitting upright, bow in hand. They shared a look that asked, *has he brought enemies with him?*

The shimmering heat stole details from Armitage, but he seemed ... off. As he drew closer, she saw why. On his shoulders was a creature that looked like a dog crossed with a lizard. Scaled like the Vhemin, but much smaller. It looked dead, mostly because its skull was smashed in. She stood, bringing her steel with her. "What's that?"

"We call 'em dust hoppers." Armitage slung the carcass to the ground. Sand puffed up from where it hit. Geneve saw its feet we large and padded, each toe ending in a nasty-looking claw. "Usually they hunt in packs. This one wasn't with his friends, and that's why I've named this one, 'Lunch.'"

"I've given up eating raw dog, but thanks." Meriwether sat upright, watching.

"Suit yourself. It's pretty nice when dried into jerky." The Vhemin tore one of the dust hopper's legs off, crunching away. Geneve looked away, feeling slightly sick. "What?"

{You're a very vigorous eater.} Sight of Day showed his fangs. *{It upsets the children.}*

"Fuck 'em," Armitage suggested. He nudged the carcass with his foot. "Want some, cat?"

The Feybrind nodded. *{I've never had dust hopper.}*

Geneve shuddered. She'd known the Vhemin were eaters of flesh but forgotten the Feybrind were carnivores too—they just preferred their meat cooked. Didn't they? *I don't understand how the Three made both species meat-eaters, yet also made them different in every other way.* Sight of Day didn't tear a piece of the dust hopper away, instead choosing to use a slender, elegantly-made blade to skin the carcass, parting out the pieces within.

Armitage retrieved a small rack from his saddlebags, then hunkered down beside the Feybrind. The two set to work laying strips of skin on the rack. In the desert air, they'd dry into jerky in little time at all. They might have some ready by tomorrow. Geneve wasn't sure if it was a time of miracles, but she'd seen a dead dragon corpse, and found a saddle to match. The big surprise was a Vhemin and Feybrind working together.

Meriwether joined her. He looked like he might never stop sweating. "Can I have a word?" She nodded, and they walked away from the other two. They headed down a dune, the peak offering a little shade if you lay against its sandy back. Meriwether lay down, then patted the ground beside him. "I don't like it."

Geneve joined him. It felt like they were the only two people in the world. She glanced at him, but he wasn't watching her, choosing to stare at the cloudless sky instead. "Which particular part?"

"Those two. I don't like how Sight of Day feels he needs to protect us from the creature. Or, protect *me*, anyway." He turned to face her, propping himself on an elbow. "He's in danger."

"Armitage would be hard to kill," she admitted.

"Not just that." Meriwether scrabbled some sand from his hair. "Armitage knows what made the Feybrind fall. What if it's a spell? What if he knows the trick? I know the Feybrind are excellent fighters. Everything in this Three-damned world seems better at killing than us."

She sat up, feeling the sand shift beneath her. "That's why we have the Tresward."

"I'm not interested in a sermon—"

"Do I look like the preaching type?" She felt her cheeks flush and bowed her head. "Sorry. I'm hot, and it's making me irritable."

"So, you're going to be irritable for weeks?"

"I hope you fall into the sinking sands." Geneve felt the smile touch her face. "But I hear you. Feybrind are fast. A better, more accurate shot with a bow than any human or Vhemin. Precise with a blade. Did you know the Tresward asked them to come teach us?" Meriwether shook his head. "We have the twenty-one hundred patterns of the Three. We train for years upon years, and only once we get the sash," her fingers touched her shoulder where the black sash would have lain across her breastplate, "would we be considered better fighters than the Feybrind."

"They don't seem the fighting kind."

"They're not. They refused." She shook her head. "The first overture happened hundreds of years ago. It's a kind of ceremony now. Every ten years the Tresward asks Feybrind to come, and they always refuse. Or we can't find them. Their villages aren't on our maps."

"That must annoy the Tresward." He leaned back, staring at the sky again. "I like the cat even more, now."

She snorted. "In a fair fight, he would hold his own."

"It won't be a fair fight. That's my point. Sight of Day will drop like a discarded puppet. The monster moves fast, Red. He moves like lightning that someone let out of a bottle." Meriwether closed his eyes. "I like him. I don't want him to die. I know things between us are ... weird, but will you look out for him?"

Geneve listened to the cadence of his words. The softness of them, the simple request. He wasn't like most men she'd met. Outside the Tresward, men tried to show how strong they were. They'd have trouble asking for aid from a woman. Meriwether, not so much. He knew what he was, and he knew it insufficient to help a friend. Here he was, asking his enemy for aid. "I will."

"I would if I could, but ... wait, what?"

"I said, I'll look out for him. He's my friend too, Meri." She wanted to reach out, to touch his shoulder, to let him know it would be okay. But she was a Knight of the Tresward, and he was a sinner. They lived on two sides of a divide, and while they shared a temporary common purpose, she felt at the end of their journey was heartache. He'd have to run, and they might ask her to give chase. Geneve stood. "I'll try and look out for all of us."

WHEN SHE RETURNED TO THEIR SMALL SHELTER, THE DUST HOPPER'S corpse was gone, and Beck looked much happier, leaving no confusion about what happened to the bones and gristle.

"Vhemin waste nothing?" Geneve looked at the dark stained sand.

Armitage shrugged, the motion massive. "Vhemin are Vhemin."

Geneve glanced to the drying meat. "Are there more dust hoppers?"

"Sure, but we've got bigger problems." Armitage pointed to the west, the motion imprecise and vague. "I know what the metal was. I saw two armored figures heading toward us."

She took a step closer to the monster. "Two?"

"Leading horses. Had the holier-than-thou look of Knights." He grinned ghastly teeth. "Like the dust hoppers, many creatures hope we perish. Few are willing to make it happen. Knights are a danger we want to avoid, especially since you're," he pointed to her chest where her sash would have been, "a baby Knight."

"What's that supposed to mean?"

"It means you'll be beaten like a toy drum if they're after you. Been wondering what a Knight's doing out here alone. Not really my concern, and you know what? I don't give a shit. But if there are

Knights after you, it'd be nice to have that confirmed so we can make a plan."

Geneve gave a slow nod. "I can't confirm it. Not because I'm trying to mislead you, but because I don't know." She looked at her feet. "We were separated."

"They could be friends, then?"

Geneve didn't know how to respond to that. She held her silence for a moment longer. If it was Israel and Vertiline, would they be coming to help her? She glanced back at the dune where she'd left Meriwether. *What will they say when they see I've a sinner in tow? Could I explain it to Israel in a way he'd understand?* "I don't think so."

"Plan B, then." Armitage snarled like this was the *fun* part. "We'll set a trap."

"I won't kill Knights."

"Of course not. You couldn't, anyway." A little more feral made it into his shark smile. "But I know who might."

Chapter Twenty-Nine

Wincuf's Trial was like any other: bloody.

All were different, except for two things. The Novice must fight fifty peers and must also destroy their tree. There were no rules within those two constraints.

Tradition said the Novice selected their foes. They would normally pick the biggest opponents to prove their worth to the Three. Wincuf chose forty-nine opponents before his last: Geneve. That was why she stood in ill-fitting armor along with forty-nine others, waiting to cut Wincuf down.

Wincuf didn't have to beat them. He just had to survive. Get through them out the gates at the end, and then a clean run to his tree. That was the rule. It was the end of his Trial; two days passed with grueling physical tests. Geneve watched as he'd been kept without sleep. Waterboarded and beaten. If the Storm was within him, it would keep his body strong, his limbs straight, and he'd make it through.

Without the Storm, that would be a long, hard two days. Geneve didn't think she'd ever do it.

All other Novices carried glass blades. Geneve held Kytto's gift. It was a length of brilliant steel. He'd held it out to her, calling it star-fallen. A gift from the Three one night, cast from the heavens. Unsuitable for a god's battles, but sufficient for a human's. Kytto said he found the ore in a field when he was seven *and brought it with him when called to the Tresward. They'd told him they didn't need ore but had plenty of need for those with skill. He'd taken their oath to learn to forge it.*

It was light, but held a keen edge. When she'd taken it, he'd whispered its name in her ear.

Requiem.

Geneve didn't know what that meant, but wanted to learn. She wanted to beat Wincuf, or perhaps just survive today. She'd need more than a sword made of the Three's cast-offs.

Israel said her mind was stronger than the Storm. So, today she'd use it.

She stood at the end of Wincuf's opponents. Geneve could see the long line of them, clumped in pairs, threes, or even alone like her. She was the smallest.

Geneve's helm was too large, the poor fit meaning she couldn't see well. The visor let her glimpse parts of the room, but it didn't worry her. The Tresward trained them to fight without sight or sound, trusting in the patterns. Besides, if all went well, she wouldn't need to raise her steel more than once.

A noise drew her gaze. Wincuf entered the hall. He worked his way down his opponents. Novices fell, blood spraying in the thug's wake. He worked like a common butcher, hacking his opponents to pieces.

Clerics were on hand to stem the fall of life's flow, but the Tresward weren't gentle in their teachings. Novices could die here, either as the Trialist, or as their opponents. They needed only the strongest to be Knights.

Wincuf kept coming, unmarked by enemies. His armor gleamed, and his glass blade held a frosty glow of perfection. Geneve heard the Storm's footprints as Wincuf fought. The chime of tiny bells, or the susurration of the sea. A crow burst into flight at the end of one mighty swing that cut the arm from his opponent.

It didn't take him long to arrive before her. His glass dripped red. "You."

She nodded. "It's me."

"I owe you."

"You owe me nothing." *Geneve knew he couldn't see her smile.* "But you'll try to pay anyway."

"That's not what I—"

"The lesson here is whether you'll pay too much, or not enough. Behind me is your tree. You've tipped the scales."

"It's not against the rules." *Wincuf took off his helmet, smirking. He wanted all to see how he cut her down without the need for protection. Geneve, the little. Geneve, the weak. Geneve, without the Storm. Unworthy of the Three's Light.*

"There are no rules." Geneve raised Requiem, the skymetal catching light.

"A pretty blade. I'll take it when I'm done." He flourished his blade. *"Any last words?"*

"It's nice to have friends."

His sneer tightened. "Die, then."

Chapter Thirty

Meriwether felt uneasy, a sick, queasy feeling that seemed to go further than his belly. It seeped unto his diaphragm, making it hard to breathe, and tickled his heart, causing his blood to pound in his ears.

Knights are coming.

"This is bullshit," he offered.

Sight of Day nodded, golden eyes sympathetic. His right hand moved, fingers up, then splaying down as if tossing something vile on the ground.

Geneve ran a weary hand through red hair. "He says it's bullshit, too."

The special *flavor* of bullshit was Armitage's plan. He wanted to run them close to the dead city, drawing out some of its guardians, if they still lived. Not so close they'd get sick, but close enough to wake the sleeping dead. He was *fairly sure, runt*, that they could stay ahead of whatever they stirred up, leaving the guardians in their wake. The Knights following would need to detour around the fracas, buying them time.

The real problem wasn't the Knights, or that they were coming. They were *always* coming because of what he could do. What he *was*.

No, the real problem was Geneve. Meriwether wasn't concerned she'd turn on him, blade to his throat, and march him toward her fellows.

He was concerned not doing that would eat her alive.

It lay in how she held herself. Chin up, but not quite high enough. Eyes cool and hard, but always looking for the glint of sun on metal. Fingers clenching and unclenching. The hand that kept returning to her hair, smoothing it away from her eyes, no matter how much the wind teased it free.

Which meant, for all the high bullshit levels of the plan, he was on board. It would take them further away from their pursuers. Maybe get them out of this shitty desert, and into whatever temple awaited ahead. Armitage would get his prize, they could go on their way, and she wouldn't be burdened with choice. Not for him, and not for anyone else. Once they were in the capital, she'd be free of one more thing tearing her apart.

Once this mission was done, she'd be free of him.

Meriwether helped break camp. Armitage grunted acknowledgment as they broke down the poles that held the tarp up. Meriwether marveled at them for a moment. Their manufacture was fine, as if by a Tresward Smith. The Knights let precious few of their magnificent creations into other's hands, and Meriwether wondered whether Armitage had killed a Knight for these.

Beck grumbled to his feet, lumbering about and disturbing the horses. Chesterfield pawed the air in a movement that spoke through any species language barrier: *back off, clown*. The bear ignored the black charger, fretting at all this movement in the heat.

Rested but still hot was how they started the next stage of their journey. Sight of Day was changeless, implacable, his golden eyes watching all, missing nothing, but also unconcerned. The cat held no fear inside him. Armitage walked lighter without the hot rock in his pack. He'd donated the stone to Beck's saddle, the surface catching sunlight for the cool night ahead.

Geneve stood without armor but looked undiminished. Her hair flowed free from Sight of Day's borrowed scarf. She'd strapped her sword to her waist, scattergun on her back. Her pack yielded clothes, loose cotton garb that looked fitting for a fair, not the desert.

C'mon, admit it. She looks amazing. Despite all that wore on her, she faced the afternoon as if she was ready for it.

Meriwether shed some of his wool but kept his cloak for the sun. He led Troubles, the horse grumbling as they set out in the heat. The shimmer-haze of the dead city ahead beckoned them on. Meriwether heard stories of its kind. He expected sirens to call, hoping to draw them close, but no noise came from the north. Nothing came at all. The city was centuries dead.

Armitage led them at a trot. His speed carried urgency, but not panic. "We've got a decent head start. We can make this work, but the timing's everything. Too fast, and the guardians won't bother getting out of bed. Too slow, and the Knights catch us."

"You sure they've seen us?" Meriwether panted.

Armitage rolled his eyes. "They're *Knights*, runt. They miss nothing." Geneve nodded at this, red hair hiding her face, but kept on, footsteps sure. Meriwether wondered about the mysterious Trials. What did Tresward do to their Novices to make their hearts harder than stone? Two of her kind chased her down, no doubt wrestling with doubts about their mission, just as she ran from them, wrangling her own inner demons. Yet they did it anyway.

He realized something important: *those Trials are bullshit.*

The dead city loomed ahead. Closer, heat shimmer abated, Meriwether saw the buildings were broken like old teeth. Like the edge of the desert where marsh turned to sand, there wasn't the expected build up from small farms to big buildings. The city sprang fully formed from the earth. Around the edge of it rose a wall, crumbled and broken in many places. Behind the wall, the structures hinted at massive pride. The ancients built so high they wanted to shake hands with the Three.

"Steady, now." Armitage's eyes were everywhere, his head on a swivel. "If you see something moving, you move faster."

"Wait. I thought you said they took time to wake up?" Meriwether felt that queasy feeling of dread grow.

"Usually."

"*Usually?*" Meriwether's voice squeaked. "That's not reassuring."

"It'll be even less reassuring if they don't come at all. I haven't been to this place. Could be all the way dead." Armitage kept looking about like he didn't believe his words.

They made their way east along the dead city's wall. The Knights approaching from the west seemed indistinct in the heat haze, but the glimmer of their armor abated when they hit the shelter of the wall. Geneve kept casting backward glances. Meriwether hurried to her side, reaching for her hand. "You don't have to do this. You could—"

"I could what?" She didn't take her hand away. If anything, she squeezed it tighter. "If the Tresward is broken, I *have* to fix it. But to do that, I need truth."

"You could leave me here." He pulled her to a halt and turned her to face him. "It'd buy you time."

"I don't need time—"

"It'd buy you freedom."

She held still, then shook her head. "I wasn't made to be free any more than you were. I think—"

Whatever Geneve thought was lost to a massive, bass sound, like the world's largest trumpet. It vibrated the sand at Meriwether's feet, and he covered his ears to block it out. The horses' eyes went wild, tails flicking, but they held their place like Tresward-trained mounts should. Sight of Day lowered his stance, bow magically in hand.

Armitage looked at the wall. "Fuck."

"Fuck?" Meriwether asked. "What's that mean?"

"They ain't dead." The monster broke into a lumbering run as he half-turned. "Come on, then! Run!"

Sight of Day's tail lashed, then he headed after the Vhemin. Geneve held Meriwether's hand for a final squeeze, then she turned and fled. Chesterfield rumbled past in pursuit, leaving Meriwether and Troubles alone.

The horse lifted her head, as if confused at why everyone else was running away. He put his hand on her neck. "Easy, girl. I need to see." She jerked away, and he imagined her thought: *why'd I get the imbecile?*

A shadow stole over the wall. Meriwether was perhaps a klick away, but even at this distance he felt the size of it. It moved as smoke, sinuous and low to the ground. He caught a glimpse of red eyes within the shrouded haze of shadow surrounding it.

Another joined it. Then another.

"Okay." Meriwether took a stumbling step back. "I don't need to see anymore." He pulled Troubles' bridle. "C'mon."

The horse nickered, following. Meriwether looked back. The smoke creatures swirled a circle of shadow at the wall's base, watching, waiting. They didn't pursue. He supposed they knew he wasn't a threat. Too small, too feeble. Too ordinary, or perhaps too full of sin.

Instead of following Meriwether, they swarmed west toward the two approaching Knights. Meriwether watched them go but didn't feel happy. There wasn't any joy left in this dead city. Hell, there wasn't joy in the plague lands at all.

MERIWETHER RAN AFTER THE OTHERS UNTIL HIS SIDE HURT. HE didn't look back. The pursuing Knights would make it or they wouldn't. Looking wouldn't *change* anything and seeing the smoke creatures on his heels would just make his last moments more terrifying.

Troubles trotted along at his side, and he thought he sensed something snide in the horse's sideways glances. He imagined her thinking, *Is this the best you can do?*

His cloak billowed free of his head in the rush, but it didn't matter. A little sunburn wasn't the thing likely to kill him right this moment. He saw Armitage lead the group up a sand dune, their menagerie of horses in tow. Geneve kept an effortless pace on his heels, but the cat was plain annoying. Sight of Day loped along like the speed of both human and Vhemin was glacial. He had plenty of time to look around and enjoy the view.

Meriwether didn't want to run up a hill, and fate conspired to give him his wish. His foot slipped on loose sand, his other foot sank up to the knee, and before he could react he was rolling down the side of a dune. His view of Geneve and Armitage was replaced by a montage of earth/sky/earth/sky, on increasingly rapid repeat. On the way down, his face managed to find sand more than once, and it felt like someone was using a rasp on his eyeballs.

That was mere discomfort compared to the pain when he

starfished face-forward during his downward spiral, caught his injured shoulder, and was tossed into the air by momentum. His arm wrenched behind him, pulling his injury. Bright red pain lanced his shoulder, but when he opened his mouth to scream, he landed eyes-first, getting a face full of sand.

His downward fall was mercifully arrested by the arrival of level ground. He slid for a few moments, then spent a few more groaning. Meriwether sat up, testing his limbs for breaks. Nothing screamed especially loudly. Most of him hurt at a general low level, which was not ideal but also not terrible. Troubles took her time following him down the dune, picking her way with horsely care. She arrived at his side, nuzzling him. He took the offered help, rising to his feet.

West he saw a bright flash of light, then another. The boom of thunder rolled across the distance. *I guess that means the Knights are still alive.* He didn't feel disappointment, which spoke more to his character than the quality of his thinking.

He turned east, meaning to follow the party. The wall continued to track in that direction. He'd found himself at the bottom of a ridge of dunes. He stood on surprisingly flat and level ground. Meriwether couldn't immediately spy Geneve or Armitage, or the vast array of animals traveling with them, which no doubt meant they'd gone down the side of a dune. *It's fine. We're going east. No need to panic. Head the same way, and eventually we'll find each other. The important thing is to not be here when either the Knights or shadow guardians get here.*

Thunder nipped his heels, reminding him both teams were still going at each other. He gave a glance back and saw lightning arc from the sky to crack against the ground. He blinked in awe, taking a half-step in that direction before shaking his head. *There are things worth seeing in this life, but a pissed-off Valiant at the pinnacle of his power is not one of them.*

It was worth bearing in mind the Sacred Storm Geneve sought with all her heart was a power to behold. It conjured the might of the very heavens to fight at a Knight's side. Handy trick, that.

Spinning on his heel, he headed east. The ground continued to be flat, and more importantly, *firm.* His aching calves welcomed the lack of sandy give. He paused, scuffing the ground with a boot. After a few more scuffs, the sand parted enough to reveal ground. Not broken stone, or dirt. Meriwether bent, sweeping more aside with his hand. He cleared a patch, revealing an even, white material. It was coarse to the touch. He looked east again, seeing the smooth, flat sand stretching that way, then slowly turned west.

The ground was also smooth, flat, and no doubt solid that way too. *The ancients built a road before their city, and while they might have found it useful, it will deliver two Knights to us in record time.* If there was a silver lining in any of this, it was another four shadow creatures slipping over the wall. Their red eyes scanned around, marked Meriwether, then ignored him in favor of the westerly threat.

He scrabbled atop Troubles before the horse could bite him and put his heels to her flanks. She tossed her head but set off anyway. Troubles picked up speed, eating the klicks along the much firmer ground. Meriwether kept an eye out for Geneve's red hair, Sight of Day's tail, or Armitage's hulking form, but also the end of the road. If he hit unsupported sand, Troubles would fall, perhaps breaking a leg. She'd toss Meriwether, the outcome of which was probably death for both of them, and he was keen to avoid that.

To the south, he spied Geneve standing atop a dune. She had her sword out, the blade glinting in the light. It gave her position away, and he wondered why she did it.

I'm an imbecile. It's because she wants me to see her.

He reined in Troubles, waving. "Geneve!"

She saw him, waving back. "This way!"

He cupped his hands into a makeshift speaking-trumpet. "Trust me, but no. Down here!"

Geneve visored her face with a hand, surveying his position. She no doubt took his meaning because she vanished from sight. Meriwether sat on Troubles, more nervous than he'd normally be atop the vile beast. *Waiting sucks.* A minute later she came over the dune, Sight of Day and Armitage following her, as well as their horses and a pissed-off bear.

They hurried down the dune. Troubles shifted from foot to foot, perhaps sensing Meriwether's agitation, but more likely trying to make him *more* nervous. The beast was uncanny in her dedication toward his discomfort.

The Knight, Feybrind, and Vhemin checked the west. Lightning slashed the sky again, and Meriwether caught what might have been longing in Geneve's eyes, quickly hidden. *Take her mind off everything she's lost or never found.* He pointed east. "The ancients built a road. It heads that way." He jerked a thumb behind him at the light show. "It also goes that way, where there are two angry people fighting monsters. They'll be finished soon, at which point they'll want to fight us."

Armitage squinted at him. "So, you're not completely useless. Good to know." He patted Beck, then hauled himself on the bear's back. "The better news is there's a place I know. We can hide there." He sniffed, as if unsure of his assessment. "Maybe."

Sight of Day seemed to float onto Fidget. Geneve swung atop Tristan. "Then we run." She put her heels to her horse's flanks and set off. Armitage whooped in response, urging his bear after, but the race was lost. Chesterfield galloped past the Vhemin, followed by Sight of Day. There wasn't a contest. On smooth ground, horses were the fastest.

Meriwether kept Troubles' speed down, holding level with Armitage. The bear's gait was the unruliest thing he'd ever seen, but the monster kept to the bear's back with whoops and hollers. He looked like he was having *fun*. Armitage glanced in his direction. "Go ahead, manling!"

"You know the way!"

"I'll catch up." A shark-toothed grin. "Road won't last forever."

Truth. Meriwether saluted, then let Troubles have her head. The horses bent to the task, mane flying. Meriwether ducked low, holding on tight. But for the first time in a long while he felt something tickle the back of his mind. It sat there behind the fear and pain. It was mirrored in the monster's smile.

I'll be damned. This is kind of fun.

THE FUN DIDN'T LAST, BUT THAT WAS THE NATURE OF FUN.

The horses galloped but as Troubles began laboring under Meriwether, he reined her in, letting the foul-tempered brute walk it off. Geneve and Sight of Day waited for him. Geneve's cheeks were flushed, and it almost looked like a smile threatened to break free. Chesterfield pranced a ring around her.

Sight of Day's golden eyes were bright, and the cat half-smiled as Meriwether joined them. The three kept their speed low while Armitage caught up. Beck blew great lungfuls of air and let out a bellow that terrified Meriwether but didn't seem to bother the Tresward horses at all. Chesterfield slashed a hoof through the air, tossing his head, as if saying, *you want a piece?*

Beck didn't, as it happened. The bear was just being a bear.

They walked the horses for a while, then brought them up to a trot until they hit the sand's edge. It was marked by a massive slab of the white road material breaking from the surface like a jagged bone. Meriwether swung down to examine the material.

"Careful," Geneve warned.

"Yeah. Could be silk sands." Armitage didn't seem too worried.

Meriwether tested the ground as he walked forward, but nothing rose to eat his face, nor did he vanish beneath the surface, never to be seen again. The road material *looked* like stone, perhaps the finest quartz, but was clearly stronger. It'd sat here in the desert for over eight hundred years, and aside from this broken piece, looked like new. He glanced at the dead city, where the only thing living were shadow guardians. "What did they do to break the world?"

"Same thing you fuckers always do." Armitage jabbed a finger at Meriwether. "Started a fight."

"I didn't start a—"

"Sure you did," the monster rumbled. "Your Tresward is made for killing, and that's an organization dedicated to *worship*."

Geneve bridled. "I don't think—"

"And then there's your clown circus of royalty. They can't stop fighting long enough to make a credible defense against the Tresward, right? Like, Knights do pretty much what they want, when they want. Yeah, yeah," he patted the air in a *calm the fuck down* gesture, "I get the whole unstoppable force side of it. But there just ain't that many of you. Not enough if the rest of humanity decided they were well sick of you. But they don't stop reaching for each other's throats long enough to get a posse together. Fighting's what you know. It's what you are."

Meriwether rubbed sweat from his face. "And what of the noble Vhemin?"

Armitage guffawed. "We're about as noble as your horse's ass. We're killers, like you. Worse in every way, too. No tribe around here larger than about fifty guys, right? When we meet each other, it's a real struggle to work out whether we want to fight or fuck." He scratched his head. "No, that's easier, come to think of it—"

"Which raises the issue of our mission," Geneve interrupted. "We're trying to work out how the Vhemin raised a coordinated force."

"Got a bigger boss, most likely. Someone ornery enough to punch-drive the rest of those assholes in the same direction. It happens. To be chief, you fight everyone. Win, you're in charge." Armitage nudged Beck into motion. "Come on. Daylight's wasting."

Meriwether led Troubles, following the rest. Armitage slipped off Beck's back, even though the bear could manage well enough on the sand with paws instead of hooves. Meriwether wondered about the Vhemin's reputation as heartless monsters. This one at least cared for his mount.

Sight of Day said nothing to any of them, his hands still and silent. The cat's half-smile left, gone on a breeze, as he watched the Vhemin. Not suspiciously, or with anger. The Feybrind's head tipped to the side like he was curious. *Makes two of us. I don't understand that creature at all.*

They led their horses along the sands, heading east. Armitage squinted at the sun as if it held a map he could follow, sniffed the air, then turned them north again. The city was large, keeping to their west for a couple hours, but they eventually left it behind.

Meriwether hadn't seen lightning strike for both those hours, but he hadn't seen the shadow guardians follow. "I've been thinking."

"First time for everything." Armitage laughed. "How's it feel?"

Geneve rounded on the monster. She got right in his face, staring up at the Vhemin without fear. "This man," she jabbed a finger at Meriwether, "is one of the cleverest people I've met. He kept ahead of Knights after his blood. He contrived a ruse to get away from a horde of your kind. Meri's learning Feybrind handspeak, and he picks it up faster than anyone I've seen. You've chipped away at his pride and his courage for days, and I will *not stand for it!*"

Armitage didn't move. "That's because he's tiny."

"You think size matters?" She slapped her chest, giving no ground. "Would you like to test yourself, creature?"

"I don't think so." Armitage shook his head, nice and slow. "Not today, anyway." He took a careful step backward, then gave a mocking bow to Meriwether. "My apologies, manling. The squealing of your much stronger female convinced me. You are clever, oh mighty thinker. I stand ready to receive your wisdom."

Meriwether's mouth opened and closed a couple times without anything coming out. *Too many impossible things just happened.* He wasn't sure if it was Geneve standing up for him, or Armitage apologizing that was the most confusing. He looked to Sight of Day. "What just happened?"

The cat gave a half-smile, touching the closed fingers of both hands to his chin, then spreading them forward like cascading stars. *{Miracles.}*

Make the most of the moment. Geneve hadn't backed down, so Meriwether cleared his throat. The Knight glared at Armitage but swung aside without another word. Her cheeks were flushed, and Meriwether wouldn't have put a silver regal either way on whether it was anger or embarrassment. "Anyway. The thinking part is this. The shadow guardians seek the highest threats out first."

Armitage gave a last glance at Geneve, then nodded. "Okay, yeah, that sounds right. I mean, they wouldn't attack you—peace, Knight!" He held up his hands as Geneve rounded on him again. "I mean no disrespect."

"He speaks truth," Meriwether offered. "They saw me on the sands. No sword or armor. Just a man with a horse. They saw another two with glass ready and dealt with them first." He sighed. "It gives us a tiny piece of tactical knowledge. If we need to face shadow guardians again with a horde of Vhemin on our heels, we shouldn't keep our weapons."

"I don't know if that's the best idea," Armitage rumbled. His eyes sought the massive club lashed to Beck's side. "Weapons are useful."

"Or you could fight the shadow guardians," Meriwether offered. "That's a thing you could try. I don't think it'd be that useful a test, though."

"It's a good idea." Geneve nodded her agreement. "We don't need weapons."

"You might command the Sacred Storm, but the rest of us don't have the same sense of style." Armitage's shark teeth showed.

"You're the size of a house," she countered, but her eyes slid away, perhaps not wanting to bring up her complete lack of Storm-ability. "Let's press on. Night closes."

Armitage nodded amiably enough, taking the lead once more. *The monster doesn't seem to hold a grudge. Are all Vhemin like that, or is this one unique?* Meriwether followed, casting glances behind them, but he didn't make out the telltale glint of steel in the setting sun's light.

Maybe they'd made it after all.

Chapter Thirty-One

Geneve didn't know why she felt angry. Since leaving the partnership of her fellow Knights, she'd felt... *off balance*. Like the ground beneath her feet swayed, or she'd taken too much summer wine. The colors seemed different, and her heart was confused about true north.

It kept telling her there was something wrong with the Tresward, and it also told her the Tresward protected her. It'd taken her in when there were no other options. Knights fought the scourges of the world. Their Light kept the darkness at bay. Geneve glanced sideways at Armitage. *Darkness like the Vhemin.*

That was the problem, really. Here she was, sharing the trail with a killer. She'd seen Armitage fight. He was no stranger to violence. He spoke its language. By the Three, he whispered sweet nothings into murder's cold ear. Such a thing was far from what a Knight *should* do.

She felt the world tip again and tried to steady her internal turmoil. *We keep the road with the monster to get across the sands. We need to get to the capital, where aid awaits. When we get through the desert, we'll be free of the creature.*

It made good sense, an internal logic she could follow, but Geneve knew it was a half-truth at best. The whole of the truth was deeper, darker, and as uncomfortable as befriending a sinner, or thinking the Justiciars were corrupt. What her off-kilter heart whispered was, *I share the trail with a killer, but for all his vile words, I've yet to see him work casual murder. He's kept his hands from my throat, and doesn't raise arms against the Feybrind. Is he unusual, or are all Vhemin like this?*

She might have killed more folk than Armitage, and all under false orders. The figurative sands flowed beneath her, and she wasn't sure where to step.

Geneve shook her head, red hair lashing her face. *Focus.* The answers would arrive at trail's end. Israel would have said, *The journey is the destination.* Except Israel wasn't here. He followed her, she was sure of it. They'd set him on her trail. Geneve didn't know why, because he was a Valiant and she just an Adept. You didn't set Valiants on a task unless you wanted to be very, very sure it was done. *Tasks like catching sinners.*

A low keen almost escaped her lips, but she held it in check. Geneve clenched her teeth so hard they might break. To take her mind off the roiling church of her thoughts, she looked to Armitage. "How far?"

"I don't know."

"By the Three—"

"I'm not trying to be the asshole here." The monster straightened, scanning the horizon. "These things are tricky to find at the best of times."

"What things?"

"Don't know what they're called. Never been inside one either." He pressed forward. "Truth be told, we should have been there by now—"

He vanished from view.

Geneve gaped at the *absence* of Armitage before hurrying forward. His loss was explained easy enough as she skidded to a halt over a fresh precipice. *He's fallen into a hole.* Grains poured into the depths. "Are you okay?"

A grunt came from the darkness below. "I found it. Toss me a shovel. Should be one in my pack, unless the cat stole it."

She eyed Beck. The big bear didn't eye her back, completely unconcerned that his master fell from view, or that a tiny human approached.

The heat stone on Beck's saddle was atop the saddlebag flap, so she needed to move it out of the way. Her fingers found it warm, rather than hot as she'd expect from the sun. Closer inspection showed tiny markings around the outside edge, like letters, but not in a language she knew. *Not important.* She pushed it aside, then rooted through Armitage's saddlebags.

There wasn't a collection of skulls inside. A few wrapped packages of what was probably food. A small lantern, which surprised her because the Vhemin were supposed to see as well as Feybrind at night. The spars for his tarpaulin shelter. Knives aplenty. And there at the bottom—*of course it's at the bottom*—of the bag was a shovel.

She drew it out, fascinated. It was a folded design, and light in her hand. The blade was well worn but serviceable. Geneve hefted it, then approached the hole. Meriwether stood an uncertain pace or two from the edge. "Careful."

"I'm always careful." But she offered him a smile as thanks for the thought before facing the hole. "Ready?"

"No, I decided to take a piss. Of course I'm ready." She tossed the shovel into the hole and was rewarded with a *clank*. "Ow. Thanks."

"No problem." She backed away from the hole. "I guess we wait."

Sight of Day pointed about five meters north of the hole. The sand sloped away sharply at that point. *{We don't have to wait long.}*

The sand poured inward at the point the Feybrind marked. Geneve approached, Meriwether at her side, his curiosity winning over fear. The sand parted like water into a drain, revealing a narrow, sloping entrance between two walls constructed of the same material the ancients made their roads from.

Armitage was framed in the entrance atop a dome of sand, shovel in hand. "The entrance was filled over. I gave it a kick from this side." He beckoned them. "Come on in, the water's fine."

Geneve followed him. The narrow entrance widened into a cavern of sorts. A door sat at the far end. It was three meters wide and two high, also made of the white stone the ancients built with. "What's behind that?"

"No idea. They don't open anymore. But in here," Armitage spread his arms, encompassing the cavern, "we can wait out the night. Most of the dune creatures don't come close to places like this."

"Is that because they're unsafe?" asked Meriwether.

"Might be," Armitage allowed. "We'd be dead already if this one was a problem. Good news is, no one would see our campfire in here. Bad news is, we've got no wood for a fire, so it'll be a cold night. I hope you like cuddles."

Geneve shuddered at the monster's leer. "You're cold-blooded. It wouldn't help."

"Cuddles help everyone."

She shook her head. The Vhemin wasn't what she'd expected at all. "Why do you have a lantern in your pack? I thought Vhemin could see at night as well as the Feybrind."

"Different. Not better or worse. Isn't that right, cat?"

Sight of Day nodded. *{We see the world in all its colors, but we need at least a little light.}*

"I see heat." Armitage sniffed. "Plenty of places, just like this one, where seeing heat isn't that useful. It's great for hunting, though."

Geneve went to get the horses. She met Beck at the entrance, the bear wanting in, and she stood aside for the beast. It nosed the air as it passed her, as if making sure she was friend, then ambled to Armitage's side. She caught the monster scratching behind the bear's ears.

Outside, Meriwether kept watch as well as keeping an eye on the horses. "Thank you. You know, for before."

She beckoned Tristan. *{Come.}* "I told only truth."

"Truth doesn't always need to be said." He gave a small smile. "Actually, truth doesn't *want* to be said. And you kind of shouted it."

"The monster bothers me."

"Monsters bother everyone." He clicked at Troubles, who tried to bite him. The young man shied away. "Nice try, fiend." The horse let herself be led, Chesterfield coming along for the journey. "I guess I'm not sure he's a monster. This damn horse tries to bite me more often."

"Troubles likes you." Geneve grinned. "She'd have kicked you otherwise."

"Ah." He patted Troubles' face. "I'd kick her right back."

"Meri, we need to help them." She felt the smile slide off her face. "Israel and Vertiline."

He stopped, holding his quiet for a time. "I know."

"No, we need to ... wait, what?"

"I know." He looked back, where the fading light stole details from the dune strewn landscape. "They're two basically good people, trying to do something they believe is right. They're in a desert full of monsters." He had the good grace to not mention they might have died. "They don't have a guide."

"So let's give them one." She scuffed the sand. "We'll mark the shelter for them."

"It won't be enough." Meri looked at his feet. "But I know what might."

⁊

MERI'S PLAN WAS STUPID. BEYOND STUPID, IF GENEVE WAS ASSESSING the situation right. When he'd laid it out for her, she'd laughed, and he'd waited her out until her laughter died away in a sea of incredulity.

Armitage was on board from the moment he'd laid it out. *Fuck, we should have thought of killing you this way two days back*, he'd said, then picked up his club and stalked outside. He didn't profess to love the second part of the plan, but he was happy enough to *let it ride*, whatever that meant.

Sight of Day wasn't okay with it, not at all. The Feybrind had shook his head, saying only, *{Hearts make fools of us all.}* Geneve didn't know what he meant, but since Meriwether was already outside with Armitage, she needed to be there to help him not die.

I spoke my problems, and he listened. I didn't need him to fix them, just hear them. If only I'd kept my mouth shut.

The dark outside their shelter was incomplete. The sky was clear, stars bright above, and the faces of the Three kept their watch above. Cophine's luminance felt especially bright out here without city fires to interfere. A wind picked up, pulling drifts of sand across her boots. The sound was beautiful, if haunting. The dunes sounded like they wept for everything the world lost.

And if you don't get moving, it'll lose a stupid, brave sinner.

Meriwether waited fifty meters ahead. He stood atop a dune, no doubt visible for klicks around, which was part of the plan. He held his knife and Geneve's shield. Of Sight of Day, there was no sign, but she didn't expect the Feybrind to be visible. They came and went like dawn mist. Armitage was a dark shadow about a hundred meters to her left. The brute hulked as low as he was able, but she couldn't mistake the glint of his shark-tooth smile.

Despite Cophine's pale face and Ikmae's gray one, Geneve felt too blind for this work. She wanted a bonfire. A lantern would do in a pinch. The twenty-one hundred patterns taught Knights to fight in all conditions. Where the attacks should come from, and how to defend even if in a pitch-black room. They were drilled over and over until the patterns were second nature. One bled into another, a blade or shield sweeping where the next attack should come from, returning to strike where their opponent was most vulnerable.

In her drills and training, there was room for protecting those needing her shield, but she felt the ancients hadn't made the patterns for moments like this. Geneve wanted light, and a lot of it, so she might better see who she was protecting, and from what.

Meriwether hefted her shield, the movement awkward. He'd not been trained in the use of one, but if he needed the protection all was lost anyway. Saluting to where he thought she was, the gesture made slightly comical by him facing a few meters to her right. *He's not good in the dark either. The monster sees best of all. I hope Sight of Day's arrows fly true.*

The young man hammered on the shield with his knife's pommel. Good Smithsteel, the shield rang like a gong, the sound an accompaniment to the desert's haunting cry. The sound faded, so he struck again. Then once more.

Nothing.

Meriwether sighed. "Come on, you—"

The sand erupted ten meters behind him as monsters boiled forth. He shrieked, then ran like demons were after him. He wasn't far wrong. Five dust hoppers leaped from their nesting burrow beneath the shifting dunes, clawing the ground as they chased him. Their paws dug great furrows, and while it looked like a waste of energy, Geneve saw the intent of the creatures. *They scoop sand like water. They'll be fast and sure.*

She broke from her hiding place, blade held low and ready. Armitage hauled himself up, big arms and legs pumping as he ran for Meriwether, club in hand. Geneve saw again just how fast the monster was over short distances. She was pushing herself as fast as she could, yet he'd get there before her.

The dust devils had other plans. The sand before Armitage erupted, three of the creatures clawing for air. One leaped for him, but the Vhemin swung his club like a bat, knocking the dust hopper aside. Geneve heard the sickening crunch of broken bone and was certain the creature would land in a very dead state.

The other two didn't slow, one lunging with slavering jaws to Armitage's ankles, the other for his shoulder. The Vhemin kicked the low one aside, but the other got its teeth into his shoulder. He bellowed, stumbling.

He can look after himself, but Meriwether will die. *Run!* Geneve pushed herself harder, cursing the sands as they stole her speed. The dust hopper at the head of the original pack was almost on Meriwether, and she was still twenty meters out. The *hiss-chunk* of an arrow finding its mark sounded across the desert's keen, and the creature rolled, an arrow in the socket of its left eye.

Another arrow found the second one, lodging in the skull. The creature screeched but didn't drop.

Geneve was almost there. Meri marked her in the gloom and tossed her shield to her. The throw was bad, the rim wobbling through the air, but she'd carried it for five years. She knew its weight and heft. How it'd land, if left on its course.

She swung the flat of her blade, catching the shield on the edge. Smithsteel chimed in protest, but the shield flew straight up. Geneve passed Meriwether, the young man not slowing in the slightest, and found herself amid a collection of claws and slavering fangs. Her shield fell edge-first into the sand behind her, giving her shelter. A tiny piece of steel that would foul an attacker from the rear. It wasn't much, but she felt the shield would be less useful on her arm against these dog-like creatures.

The Discord of Water. The pattern's name sprang to mind, and she stepped into the movement without giving it a second thought. Water was the enemy of these harsh, dry climes. These creatures were born of earth and ash, and while she didn't know how to fight them, they'd never seen water.

Requiem moved in the first three sweeping arcs. The skymetal glinted Cophine's light back at the moon above. The steel shivered and sang, her weapon slicing low, high, and behind her. A dust hopper fell in two, her blade passing through its neck as if it were made of nothing stronger than smoke. She didn't even feel the resistance.

Sand and grit blew into her eyes, and she blinked to clear them, but it didn't help. Night-blind, sand in her eyes, she stood without backup. Armitage had his own problems, and Meriwether would get in the way. She didn't expect Sight of Day to fire with her this close.

The other two monsters backed off, snarling. *I can't see them clearly. I can't see what they're going to do.* She felt rather than saw the lunge from her left, but the Discord of Water wasn't finished. She raised her foot on that side, sword held in vertical guard before her face, free hand held in bladed strike position. *I don't need to see them.* Geneve fell into the Discord like a diver into a lake. She didn't need her eyes or the confusion they fed her, so she closed them. Geneve felt her hair against her face, dune-sand whispering against her skin.

Requiem sang to the night as she turned the blade into a spinning guard. She swept it behind her, then in front. The Discord of Water was forty-eight perfect moves, and she used them all. From her left, perhaps where Sight of Day lay, she felt a gust of cold wind. The faintest glimmer of a light bloomed through her eyelids and she saw the black-tinged red. She swung her sword as she'd been taught, as perfectly as she could, on shifting sands, with the lonely desert around her.

Done. Other than the sound of her own breathing, she could hear nothing. Geneve's feet finished the Discord of Water in a ready stance, blade held in her right hand, tip toward the sand. She risked opening her eyes but saw nothing except tear-smeared darkness.

"Geneve?" Meri's voice, close by. "I've got water. For your eyes, I mean. They're all dead. Everything is dead. Except us, I mean. We're all fine. I'm fine." He babbled, unable to stop. "I shouldn't be alive! I should be dead. That was a really stupid plan."

She laughed despite the sand in her eyes. "It was the stupidest. Hurry up."

Geneve heard the whisper of his feet drawing close. "Wait. I need a light." *Need a light? One was lit before.* She heard the scratch of flint, and the darkness tinged red through her eyelids again. "Hold still. I'm pouring it now." Geneve felt his hand on the back of her head, shaking, but gentle for all that. She let her head be tipped back and felt the cool splash against her face. Geneve shook her head, and pulled away, rubbing her eyes, then stabbed her blade into the sand.

She held her hand out for the water. Geneve rubbed the grit from her eyes, blinking the last vestiges clear. She took in the aftermath of the battle. Armitage stood by the corpses of three dust hoppers, kicking one with a certain enthusiasm. Sight of Day walked closer, tail lashing, but his golden eyes were bright. He carried his bow in one hand, something else in the other. Meriwether stood so close she could smell him, one hand half-ready to catch her, as if she might fall and break.

At her feet was a mess. Pieces of dust hopper lay strewn on all sides. She saw legs shorn from bodies, the bodies themselves cut in half. All the cuts were meticulous, as if a surgeon dissected these monsters for display.

"That was really impressive," Meri offered. "I don't think I've seen it's like."

"It was the Discord of Water," she said. "It's one of the twenty-one hundred—"

"That's not what I meant." He stepped back, eyes hooded. "But the Discord was fine, I guess."

Sight of Day reached them, handing over what he carried. It looked like clumped white sand. Geneve felt the cold as she took it. "Is this ... snow?" She glanced around. "Here?"

{You have a storm inside you, Daughter of the Three.} The Feybrind gave

a small bow. *{I'd prefer lightning like your friends, but snow in a blasted plague land is good, too.}*

"I didn't make this." She sniffed the snow. It didn't smell like anything except cold air. "I can't command the Sacred Storm."

"I wouldn't call it commanding, as such. Snow's not super useful on the battlefield. No offense." Meriwether held his hand out, and she passed him the melting snow. "Feels like snow. I think we need to do one final test." He turned, tossing the snow at Armitage.

The clod hit the Vhemin, who turned with a roar. "Asshole! That's cold!"

"Definitely snow," Meriwether smirked. He looked at the sky, sobering. "Let's get these monsters gutted and strung up for your friends."

THE PLAN HAD BEEN TO USE MERIWETHER AS NOISY BAIT, THEN CUT down a single dust hopper when it came to see what the noise was. No one thought they'd get eight of the creatures at once. Skinning the beasts took time, slightly reduced by both Armitage and Beck eating pieces raw, bone and all.

Geneve planned to leave out carcasses to dry in the sun, so her fellow Knights would find shelter and food both. They strung meat up to air-dry in the cave, but Geneve wasn't sure what to use as a lure. The cave was difficult to find. She worked her way through her belongings, finally settling on her helmet. If it was Israel and Vertiline on her heels, they'd know it as if they'd seen her face. She didn't want to wear it anymore. Geneve felt too uncertain of purpose to wear the radiant sun on her chest or black sash across her shoulder, and the helmet was just an uncomfortable cherry on the top. Desert heat made the helmet impractical anyway, and when they reached civilization she could get another.

The night brought a cruel cold with it. Armitage nestled with his bear and hot rock both. His injured shoulder didn't seem to bother him. Geneve tried to help bind the wound, but he'd pushed her off. *Just a scratch. Be good as new in the morning.*

Meriwether sat in a huddle of sober quiet for the rest of the night. He chewed a few pieces of dried meat but didn't look like they satisfied. *Terror sits in your belly, taking up all the room, and sometimes it leaves you hungry for life and all things in it*. It sounded like something Israel might have said, but Geneve couldn't remember when.

They were running low on grain for the horses, and water would be a concern before long. The desert was six hundred klicks across, or so said Armitage. In the morning, she'd ask about supplies. Tomorrow would bring time enough to worry about food. Tonight, she needed sleep.

Geneve pulled her cloak about her, watching her companions. Sight of Day took first watch. As the Feybrind slipped into the night outside their shelter she fell into a haunted sleep. Geneve felt demons hunted her, their long claws reaching for her unarmored form, and no blade in the world was bright enough to keep them back.

Chapter Thirty-Two

✦

After Kytto gave her Requiem, he'd told her to get a good night's sleep. Geneve had no intention of doing that. Sleep wouldn't help her now. Wincuf was already completing his Trial, and if the monster didn't need sleep, neither did she.

She snuck into the long hall of combat where the fight would take place tomorrow. Geneve knew she'd stand as Wincuf's last fight. He'd have his eyes on her, working his way down the line of opponents with one thought.

Kill Geneve.

She knew he'd cut her down like a single blade of grass against the scythe. Geneve couldn't use the Storm, and she was tiny. But Kytto taught her well over the years. How to fight with bare knuckles, or using a man's weight against him. He'd said a weapon gave false confidence. Knights were full of it.

Geneve didn't intend to let Wincuf close enough to grapple with him. That would be suicide. Knights of the Tresward were capable fighters without a blade. They trained in all weapons, because they must know what they fought against, and they trained with none, but perhaps not as viciously as Kytto did.

But she had a brain, and hopefully, a good one. Geneve hoped her heart was its equal. She scurried through the Tresward Novice barracks. She found Raja first. Her braids were unbound. "Raja!"

The young girl shot upright, hands in guard, then relaxed on seeing Geneve. "What are you doing here?" she hissed.

"I need a favor."

Raja thought about it. "I owe you, it's true."

"I'm not here to collect payment. That comes tomorrow."

Raja slipped from her bunk, winding strong hands through her hair. Within moments, it was in a rude but functional braid. "Let's go."

Hettie was next. She slept in the same barracks, but ten bunks further in. Geneve padded to the bald girl's side. "Hettie?"

"I heard. You're here for a favor." Hettie's purple tattoos looked black in the half-light. "Are we raiding the kitchens?"

"The stables."

"I'm in."

The three snuck from the barracks, soundlessly moving down the passages. The Tresward didn't train them for stealth, but children knew it as a life skill. Finding Barbet was harder, because he wasn't in his bunk. Hettie smirked. "Kitchens."

They hurried to the kitchens. Geneve felt no fear, only excitement. Tomorrow she'd be tested against Wincuf, and she'd find if Israel was right to have faith in her. If he was, Wincuf would fall.

If Israel was wrong, Geneve would die.

She should be scared, but excitement rode her like a Knight on a charger. Geneve's bare feet slipped along smooth stone floors to the kitchens. They were empty, the huge hearth banked to coals to await the coming of dawn. There'd be fresh bread baked, good eggs and sausages, or porridge for those who wanted it. Jars of honey, preserved fruits, and other mysteries lined the shelves.

A chopping block, knife, crumbs, and a heel of bread marked Barbet's intent. Geneve hissed, "Barbet!"

Silence.

Hettie grunted. "Barbet, we know you're here."

The broken-nosed lad stood from his cozy underneath a bench. He had a giant hunk of bread in one hand. "What?"

"It's time to ... collect," said Raja. "Are you in?"

Chapter Thirty-Three

M eriwether chewed the inside of his lip. "Could you be more specific?"

"There's not a lot of room for confusion, runt." Armitage scratched an armpit. "You want food, we find someone who's got it and punch it out of them."

"I got that part," Meriwether said. They trudged along the sand. The sun's hammer beat the cold right out of him. While the brutal frigid night left him aching, the blasting heat of day wasn't much of an improvement. "The missing piece of the puzzle is where we might find people."

Geneve walked to his left, eyes downcast. "The horses need grain. We need water." It was like she wasn't listening to the conversation. She had bags under her eyes so deep Meriwether thought they might be bruised. *Sleep wasn't good for anyone, it seems.* Only Sight of Day appeared well-rested, which was surprising because the cat hadn't slept at all.

Meriwether's dreams were plagued by Knights who chased him to the edge of a cliff. Each time he jumped for freedom, the fall woke him before he hit the ground. Armitage hadn't offered a clue on his dreams, only saying the ancient's places sometimes brought bad sleep.

"This is what some people call a desert," the monster said, dragging Meriwether from his reverie. "I know it might seem confusing to those who've not stepped on the sands, but nothing grows here. The ground is made entirely of sand. It doesn't rain often, and when it does, people drown in it. The air's poison in many places. No fucken bees, which means no flowers, which means no plants, and we're back to having no grain."

"Hah." Meriwether scratched a little sand out of his hair. "Back to the people with all the grain."

"Right. If we keep going this way," Armitage waved to the north, "we'll get to the temple. The place we're all going anyway."

"There are people there?"

"You might say that." Vertically slitted snake eyes found Meriwether's. "I guess I left some alive when I was last there."

"An encampment?" Geneve looked up, eyes unfocused.

"I hope not. Be a huge pain in the ass if we need to shuck 'em out of their shells. No, last I was there it was a small group. Couldn't be more than twenty Vhemin." Armitage rubbed his ear. "Maybe thirty. I was running at the time."

"Thirty Vhemin is a lot. In my prime, I might have taken twenty on the blade, but today? No." Armitage guffawed, so Meriwether tossed a grin at his feet before continuing. "Why do Vhemin have grain for the horses?"

"Oh, that. Yeah, there's some feebs there too." Armitage shrugged. "Only a couple, but they had horses. I don't know how they got 'em into the desert."

Meriwether stepped around a skull baking in the heat. "Portals."

"Powerful magic," the brute mused. "Means one of the runts is a sorcerer."

"Or Justiciar." Geneve's voice was a croak. Meriwether cast a concerned eye in her direction, but red hair fell over her face, making her expression unreadable.

"That, too. One of them was a woman. Wore armor like a Knight, but black." Armitage shook his head. "Huge pain in the ass keeping painted armor looking right. Gets scratched all the time, unless you're wearing it decoratively."

Geneve looked up at that. "You're sure?"

"I know what a woman looks like."

"No, the black armor." Geneve gritted her teeth.

Meriwether veered off his course next to Armitage and moved closer to her. "Black armor's bad news?"

"I know a woman who wears black Smithsteel. Nicolette." Geneve looked grim, lips pressed into a line.

"She sounds nice. Maybe we should talk to her." Meriwether's smile died on the vine. "It's *really* bad, isn't it?"

"If it's Nicolette, she's a Champion of the order. There is no standing against her." Geneve looked away.

"A ... Champion?" Armitage coughed, spitting sand. "That's like your boss, right?"

"Champions head the militant side of the order. They command the Storm, but also rival Justiciars for mastery of Divine Sway. Israel couldn't stand against Nicolette. Ten Israel's couldn't. If it's her, then she could make us kill ourselves with our blades, or perhaps just stop living." Geneve laughed, a brittle sound. "We're in trouble."

"We're fucked, is what we are," Armitage mused. "Still, not an entirely lost cause, and here's why I think that. The temple's closed. Sealed tighter than a nun's—"

"We get it," Meriwether said. "What's your point?"

"We need a Knight to open it. If she's a Knight, she'd have opened it already." The beast grinned. "So, it probably isn't Nicky. Praise to the Three, all of that."

Meriwether thought the logic held well enough, if you trusted Armitage's view that the temple needed a Knight to open it. "How do we get in?"

"I suggest a tactic called, 'divide and conquer.' You and the cat get the grain. You're small, and wily, and likely to get in tight places. The cat's basically invisible. Me and the Knight go inside." Armitage beamed, the horrible shark teeth showing. "It'll be a piece of cake."

"What's inside?"

"Stuff."

"That sounds elusive."

"It's meant to be. Our deal holds. You get the door open, and we get to the capital in record time. That's all you need to know." The monster looked away, as if ashamed of something. "Just, if I start running, you run too."

"Gee, thanks." Meriwether frowned at the heat shimmer that was north. *Pretty much everything hides like that in this featureless wasteland.* "When will we get there?"

"Tomorrow, maybe. Or the day after." Armitage shrugged. "You can't miss it. Trust me on that."

THEY CAMPED THE NIGHT AT ANOTHER SEALED DOOR OF THE ancients. Meriwether wondered what they'd held close in the days of old. The smooth, white door material was unmarked by time. His dagger couldn't chip it, and no matter how carefully he felt around the seams, he couldn't find a lock to tickle. The thing was closed tight.

This entrance had a previous campfire and a small pile of wood, stacked beside two barrels. One barrel was empty, cracked wood spilling its contents long ago, but the other held brackish water. Meriwether whooped on finding it. The horses would get a decent drink. The party could have blissful treats like hot tea. Armitage said the supplies were probably from a long-dead tribe and suggested boiling the water.

Meriwether bustled about making camp. The horses didn't look happy with their wartime-ration equivalent of grain. Chesterfield in particular looked sour at his share but slurped his water greedily enough.

Sight of Day stood watching the night, back to the cave and campfire. Armitage huddled next to the flames as if trying to get all the heat. Geneve sat apart, head bowed, red trusses guarding her features.

Meriwether set a stew of dust hopper to cook, then made his way to Sight of Day's side. "You okay?"

{*I'm amazing.*} The Feybrind stared at the stars. {*These are the same skies the ancients saw. They're not much different today than eight hundred years ago.*}

"I think I got all that." Meriwether worried at his fledgling beard.

Learning handspeak is coming along nicely. He'd had nothing to occupy this time for two days, and the cat said he'd moved past *talking like a baby* and into *talking like a toddler*. "The ground's a lot different, though. And they didn't have three moons." He pointed to Cophine's pale orb next to Ikmae's gray one. After a bit of hunting, he found Khiton's shadowed sphere. "Say. The moons look like they're coming into alignment."

{They do that.} Sight of Day sighed. He almost seemed contented, as if they could be having this conversation over fine wine, rather than in a desert that wanted to eat them, leaving no trace. *{In a day, perhaps two.}*

"You sound like you spend a lot of time watching the stars."

{They watch us. It seems only fair.} The Feybrind gave him a half-smile. *{Please don't die tomorrow. I quite like you.}*

"Uh, thanks. I like you too. I'm making no promises, though. If we find the temple—"

{We will find it. Can't you feel it?}

"*If* we find the temple, there's thirty Vhemin and a couple of maybe-Knights who stand guard. You and I get to be outside, where it's dangerous." Meriwether scuffed the ground. "Of course, even if we don't find the temple tomorrow, I might still die. This desert sucks."

{The good news is all the violence will be directed toward them.} The cat flicked an ear back at their companions. *{We have it easy.}*

Meriwether glanced inside. Armitage still hunkered by the fire, and Geneve still brooded by the wall. "Would you excuse me?"

The Feybrind caught his arm. *{She is doing an impossible thing each minute, Trickster. Be gentle with her.}*

Meriwether put his hand over the Feybrind's, then tried his own halting handspeak. *{Impossible things are easier when you...}* He frowned. "How do you say, 'delegate?'"

Sight of Day half-smiled, golden eyes glinting. *{I like you more each minute. Try not to undo all that goodwill in the next five.}*

Meriwether left him by the entrance. He didn't go to Geneve, instead charting a course for her bags. She didn't look up, but Armitage did. "What are you doing, runt?"

"It's a surprise." He rummaged through saddlebags. There was tea, wrapped in paper. A small box held sugar cubes, and his light fingers put those in his pocket. At the bottom—*always the last place you look*—he found what he was after.

"What kind of surprise?"

"The kind that will surprise you." Meriwether walked to the horses. He fished out a sugar cube, offering it to Chesterfield. The black charger's lips tickled his palm as the brute inhaled the treat. Meriwether offered another to Troubles, dodged her bite, and then let her nuzzle his palm. "Thing is, we're adrift."

"We're in the fucking desert. No water to be adrift on."

"Figuratively. Nothing's the way it used to be." He gave a sugar cube to Tristan. "Ten days ago, we all lived different lives. Sight of Day lived on the land. Geneve had an order. You had a tribe."

"And you?" Armitage squinted.

"I was free." Meriwether looked into the distance, remembering. It seemed a long time ago. "I don't know if I was happy, though."

He bent, offering a sugar cube to Beck. Armitage growled, "Don't feed him that shit. It's bad for his teeth."

Meriwether ignored him. The bear took the cube, gentle as you pleased, then dropped to the ground with a contented chuff. "The point is, sometimes you need to remember where you came from. These places haunt our sleep. And I've got just the remedy." He fished out a smile.

Geneve looked up. "What kind of remedy?"

"Not the kind I'm looking forward to, but it's a tonic all the same." He walked to crouch before her. "What is the thing you wish for in all the world?"

"This feels like a trick question."

"That's because it is." Meriwether drew out the package he'd got from the saddlebags. It was the pack of Destiny's Supplicant. "You haven't played this since that first night."

"What's Destiny's Supplicant?" Armitage sounded suspicious.

Meriwether stood, hand out to Geneve. She took it, coming to her feet beside him. "It's a training system the Knights use." He felt his smile turn wry. "They sometimes call it Three's Bastard."

"A card game? Is that all?" The monster stood anyway. "How's it work?"

INNOCENT QUESTIONS DON'T ALWAYS HAVE INNOCENT ANSWERS.

All of them played Three's Bastard. Armitage drew the Might card. It was tug-o-war with each other, and to make it fairer, Geneve, Meriwether, and Sight of Day took one end, with the monster on the other. It was a struggle to keep the rope steady, and eventually Armitage pulled them out into the night, dragging the other three through the sand. The monster beamed, bright and happy at his victory, the shark teeth seeming somehow joyful rather than frightening.

Sight of Day selected for Speed. The drawn card commanded they catch arrows. Geneve prepared a wad for the end of a barbless shaft so they wouldn't die on a hit. The cat caught arrows without breaking a sweat. Armitage for all his blazing sprint speed couldn't snatch the shaft from the air, getting hit again, but laughing his great, roaring guffaw. Geneve not only caught the arrow but did it without looking. She said she heard the hiss, and asked Meriwether if he couldn't do the same.

It turned out he could not. Meriwether ended up with more than a few bruises from arrow shafts, but it wasn't the worst thing that happened to him in his life. The pain was minimal, and it made Armitage and Geneve laugh. Sight of Day gave a slight bow at his failures, lowering the bow. *{Sorry, friend Trickster.}*

Agility was Meriwether's pick. The card commanded they walk on their hands. He managed it with a little swearing; he'd hoped for a sleight of hand thing, but it seemed Knights didn't go in for that. Sight of Day aced it, and even Armitage lumbered along on his hands for three or four 'strides' before toppling. Geneve, as expected, managed the Bastard without concern. And by the Three, she did it blindfolded.

The time for Endurance came, and Geneve drew the card. The smile on her face dimmed a little as she placed the card on the ground. It was Prisoner's Punishment, and she said it was always drawn by

Israel. Sight of Day did *not* enjoy the exercise, and even Armitage said he was ready to *puke my guts out* at the end.

Flexibility came last. Simple splits, nothing too hard, but Armitage swore it was a *special kind of bullshit* as he struggled to bend.

They spent a half hour sweating in the cooling night. The fire flicked bright, urgent fingers toward the watercolor sky, and they enjoyed a hot meal afterward. It let them ignore the eclectic makeup of their party: a cat, a monster, and a woman sworn to hunt the man.

It's enough. Enough to let us sleep and be dreamless. Meriwether hurt more than usual, because he wasn't built for this kind of thing, but it was worth it. The price was well paid and bought him something mere coin couldn't get: Geneve's slight smile, and a sparkle in her eyes.

BREAKING CAMP WENT ABOUT AS EXPECTED, RIGHT UP TO THE POINT Armitage came too close to Geneve. It started innocently enough.

Geneve walked past Meriwether toward the shelter's entrance. She had her sword in hand. "I'm going to practice before it gets too hot."

"Sure." He nodded. "Do you need any—"

"You gave me a gift last night, friend Meri." Geneve ran a hand through sand-dirty red hair. "You reminded me of who I am. Today I'll practice, so I don't forget again." She strode out the cavern's mouth. Meriwether watched her go. He'd forgotten what he was doing and found himself with a pan and cloth in each hand and no good idea what to do with either.

She is marvelous. In another life, I could let myself get close to someone like that. In this life, it's a fire that'll burn the flesh from my bones. He went back to pretending to do whatever it was a man did with a cloth and pan.

"Not going to train with her?" Armitage's rumble stole his attention again.

"I don't like getting hurt that much." Meriwether watched Geneve tie a blindfold on, then go to work swinging her sword. The steel glinted in the dawn, and he could hear the hiss as it stroked the air.

"Always gonna be a runt," the monster offered.

{Remember, he's the smart one.} Sight of Day smirked from where he tended the horses.

"Sure." Armitage lumbered outside, but on soft feet. Perhaps he meant to startle Geneve, as a teasing friend might. Innocent, and harmless. But he was a monster, and she was a guardian of the Light, and Meriwether saw what was coming about two heartbeats too late.

Armitage waited for her to finish her set, then tiptoed in. Meriwether sprang up, hand out, but it was a long way away. He still held the damn pan, definitely no idea what to do with it now. If he'd *really* been smart, he'd have called out, but no, he set boot to ground and tried to run between two people who excelled at murder.

He made it half-way by the time Armitage got his hand on Geneve's wrist, another on her shoulder. Blindfolded as she was, it'd be reasonable for a person to step back, startled.

Knights weren't reasonable. Geneve stepped into Armitage's reach, dropping into a sweeping crouch. The monster's feet and head exchanged altitudes, and he slammed onto the sandy ground with the force of a cartful of falling anvils. Geneve continued the motion, hand locked onto Armitage's wrist.

By the time Meriwether got there, she'd spun, the harsh crack of breaking bone carrying on the wind. She swung her blade, that silver-bright edge arcing up and around, other hand sweeping the blindfold free. Meriwether didn't know if he'd seen the direction of the strike or tripped—even in hindsight, he wasn't sure—but he slid on his knees, pot held above his head, to arrive between the Knight and Armitage. "Geneve!"

She tried to pull the blow. The blade rang like a litany of sin, the pan blasting to fragments. Meriwether felt the force of the strike travel down his arms. Pieces of pan rained on his face, and he screamed as they cut him.

He kept his hands up, but there was blood in his eyes. At least that's what he hoped, because his face was alive with agony, and he couldn't see. *Please let it be blood*, he thought. *Please let it just be blood.*

Chapter Thirty-Four

"**M**eri!" Geneve stabbed her blade into the sand, dropping to a crouch before him. His hands were in front of his eyes, and blood leaked down his face. "Let me see."

Sight of Day was beside them faster than thought. The Feybrind's fur soft hands pushed Geneve away gently, but very firmly. He touched Meriwether's face, trying to coax the young man's hands from his eyes. Meriwether hunched away, a low, anguished moan coming from him. Sight of Day glanced at Geneve. *{Keep him calm. Try not to hit him again.}*

She watched him run into their shelter. "Meri? I'm sorry. I ... it felt like I was being attacked." She remembered the flow of the pattern, the weight of the blade in her hand, and the sun on her face. Geneve thought she was at peace for that timeless moment of effort, as step became purpose, and form became intent. She'd been in one of Cophine's patterns when Armitage's hand found her wrist, and Khiton took over. The god of endings snapped Armitage's wrist like a brittle twig, then laid the monster's immense body against the rough sands, out cold. Geneve hadn't felt herself do it consciously. The patterns took over, as they were supposed to.

And now Meri was blind. He coughed snot and a little blood, but kept his hands firmly pressed to his face. "You weren't."

Geneve nodded, although Meriwether couldn't see it. "If I could take it back—"

He gave a coarse, brittle laugh. "How's the other guy?"

"Armitage?" She hunched, unconsciously mirroring the sorcerer. "He's ... out."

Meriwether's laugh took on a manic edge, the pain making it febrile. "You were blindfolded, surprised, and still managed to wreck a Vhemin and a sinner. I bet they don't make them like you anymore."

Geneve shook her head. She wanted to hide behind her hair, but that would be weak in the face of Meri's pain. "That's the problem. It's all the Tresward does. Make more like me. There aren't many of us. Only a few make it out, but we're all the same."

"Ah." The sound was long, drawn out, and laced with the harsh grate of new agony. "Wonderful."

Sight of Day came back carrying his medicine bag. *{Translate for me.}* The Feybrind's golden eyes narrowed. *{I'll be very upset with you, Daughter of the Three, if I've spent the last week training this man to hand speak and he loses the use of his eyes.}* She didn't laugh at the Feybrind's half-smile. *{Ready?}*

Geneve nodded. "I'm ready."

"Ready for what?" Meriwether's face quested in the direction of her voice.

Sight of Day handspoke, and Geneve translated. "Sight of Day is here. He says he needs to look at your eyes." At Meriwether's frantic head-shake, the Feybrind continued. "He thought you'd not like that, so he's brought a narcotic."

"The cat wants to drug me?" Meriwether didn't sound averse to the idea.

{That's not what I said. I said I wanted to knock him out.} The Feybrind's teeth glinted.

"Something like that." Geneve ignored Sight of Day's frown. "Are you ready?"

"No." Meriwether sat back on his haunches.

"Okay. We'll wait until you are." Sight of Day ignored Geneve, rummaging through his pack. He retrieved a small stoppered jar, then gave Geneve a wink. "Meri?"

"Aye."

"I'm sorry about this."

"I know. I'm sorry about it too. Probably more, because I'm the one who can't see."

She winced. "Okay."

Sight of Day balanced the jar on his knee. *{Are you quite finished?}* At her nod, he cracked the seal on the jar, then retrieved a small insect. It looked like a cicada, but without wings. He held the insect in one hand, and as the air flowed past it, its legs spasmed, then began to writhe as if it wanted freedom.

"What *is* that?" Geneve looked at the insect, then the unstoppered jar. "Are there more in there?"

"What's what?" Meriwether's voice took on a frantic note.

"Nothing," she lied. "I thought I saw something."

"Don't lie to me, Red. I know when—"

Sight of Day pressed the insect to Meriwether's neck. There was a click, then the young man stiffened, falling like a poleaxed steer. In a single fluid motion, the Feybrind crushed the insect between his fingers, then caught Meriwether as he slumped, laying the man's head against the sand. *{He'll be out for a while.}*

"What the hell was that?"

{What was what?} The Feybrind's eyes glinted.

"The ... insect thing." Geneve couldn't stop her mouth running away with itself. She'd done a horrible thing, and it seemed her brain wanted to make up for it by filling the world with noise. "You put it on his neck."

Sight of Day ignored her, examining Meriwether. The man's face looked in poor condition. Blood leaked from eyes sightlessly staring at the sky.

"Will he be okay?"

{You are nervous like a child. Go tend the Vhemin.} It was as close to scolding as she'd heard from a Feybrind.

"Sight of Day, I ... did this. To him."

The Feybrind sank on his haunches, favoring her with a jaundiced golden stare. *{Your Tresward would burn him to ash, and you're worried about a little blood?}* He flicked his fingers. *{Shoo.}*

Geneve went, moving to Armitage's side. The monster was starfished on the ground like he'd been hit by a runaway cart. The arm Geneve broke lay twisted like a blade of grass. She bit her lip. What would Kytto have said? *Looks bad, Gen. Try not to fuck it up worse.* Geneve tried to remember her field aid training.

The monster breathed and hadn't swallowed his tongue. There wasn't any blood. The only obvious injury was his arm, and that needed setting before Armitage woke. She didn't want to try it if he was conscious. Vhemin could take a lot of pain, but the arm looked ... horrible.

Stop procrastinating. She set one hand against Armitage's armpit, then grabbed his wrist with the other, and pulled. It felt like trying to straighten steel. Geneve sat, putting her boot into the monster's side, then pulled his arm with both hands. She strained, and then like the clicking of a lock, his bones slid into place.

Geneve grunted, then stood. *I've never healed a Vhemin before. Broke them plenty but setting them to rights is ... different.* Armitage's break didn't feel soft. It felt like all of him was made of steel, and the bone was just a slightly stronger temper of metal. It'd be worth bearing in mind: trying to out-muscle a Vhemin wouldn't work.

She gathered wood from their supply, setting to work making him a splint. *Not too tight. Not too loose, either.* Geneve glanced at the sky, as if any of the Three were watching. "How tight is too tight on a Vhemin?"

No one answered her, but the desert whispered at her back. She scrubbed sand from her hair, put hands on hips, and decided to *not* walk to Meriwether's side. When she found herself there, no one was more surprised than her. "How's he doing?"

Sight of Day made a big show of sighing. {*Do you really want to know?*}

"Yes."

{*Figures.*} The Feybrind counted on his fingers. {*There was a good chunk of iron in his left eye, and two smaller in his right. If you were slightly better at murder, he'd have lost his right eye. It's good you're only an amateur.*}

She laughed. It felt good, because Sight of Day helped her friend, and her friend was alive and would see again. Then she bit her lip, turning away, because she felt she'd encountered a problem with the world. She liked this sinner, and Knights didn't befriend sinners.

"I'll get a fire on," Geneve said after a moment. She trudged away, her thoughts a cloak as she mentally tried to make a square peg fit into a round hole.

⁂

Geneve was by Armitage when he woke up. Unlike a human, he didn't open bleary eyes and ask *wussssup* with a three-day-drunk slur. He sat upright like he'd been stung, snake-slitted pupils wide, looking everywhere at once. They found her, three paces away, sitting cross-legged on the sand by his bedroll. She watched him look around the shelter, only settling once they landed on Beck, who was behind him, snoring.

Apart from the horses, there was no one else inside. Geneve felt the conversation they were about to have needed privacy, and so Sight of Day kept a comatose Meriwether outside, tarps raised to keep the sun off him. The Feybrind fussed over the young man like he was a cub, and Geneve supposed he was. Feybrind lived for hundreds of years, and Meri was about her age. Eighteen, but with scars on his body telling a hard road traveled.

"You," Armitage snapped.

"Me," Geneve agreed.

"Go fuck yourself." He made to rise.

Geneve held a hand out, making no move to stand. "We need to talk."

"I said—"

"Yes, the fucking of myself. I understood that part. There's a missing piece." She leaned forward, resting her elbows on her knees, hands clenched. "It's the part where you don't sneak up on a Knight."

"Baby Knight." He sneered, but there was a little fear around the eyes. She'd not seen it in a Vhemin before. They all seemed to be made of stone and anger.

Geneve kept her face impassive. "I'm only an Adept, it's true. But I passed my Trials, and while I don't call the Storm, I'm trained."

"Yeah, yeah, you can piss gold, and—"

"*Listen,*" Geneve hissed. His eyes narrowed, but he held his peace. "I know twenty-one hundred patterns. For thirteen years I've trained." She shook her head, running a hand through her hair. "I misspoke. The Tresward trained me for ten years. The last three I've traveled, doing as they asked."

"All life's a schoolyard." The Vhemin wrinkled his nose. "Call it thirteen."

"Generous of you." Geneve straightened, gathering her thoughts. She needed to do this right. She wished she was like Israel, for whom this kind of thing seemed easy. "Cophine, Ikmae, and Khiton's teachings show us how to win fights. One on one, or one on many. We know how to fight with one arm, blind, or deaf. The patterns show us the way."

"I felt the fucken pattern. I felt it! It was like—"

"Listen!" Geneve slashed her hand through the air. "You did something you shouldn't have. You tried to—"

"Have a little fun."

"Call it what you like. But I *also* did something I shouldn't have." The Vhemin's eyes widened in surprise. "I struck without knowing the attacker. I felt fear," she touched her chest, "when your hand was on my wrist. The patterns responded, but they're not supposed to be ... in charge." She touched her head. "This is. I hurt you, and I'm sorry."

Armitage blinked twice, like he had a particularly gritty piece of sand in his eye. "Say what?"

"I hurt you, and I hurt Meri, and that was because I wasn't in control." She bowed her head. "Will you accept my apology?"

Geneve waited, head down. The monster grumbled, then sighed. "Yeah." She looked up. "You can still go fuck yourself, though. That really hurt." He flexed his arm, jostled the splint, then tore it off. "It'll be fine. Probably. Good talk, though." Armitage stood, stretched, and faced the exit of their shelter. "You said you hurt the runt?"

"I almost blinded him."

"How'd it happen?"

"He tried to get between us."

Armitage snorted a laugh. "You don't get between two fighting dogs. That's stupid."

"And yet it's what he did."

Rubbing his chin, he glanced in her direction. "We talking about the same guy? Pretty smart most of the time, if I remember our previous talk. About so tall," he jabbed a hand out at Meri's head height, "and kinda follows you around like a lost puppy?"

"He doesn't—"

"The kid's got balls. I'll give him that." Armitage spun, holding a hand out to her. "C'mon. Let's go fuck something up."

She took his hand, letting his easy strength draw her upright. "Thanks."

"Eh." He looked away for a moment. "I guess I'm sorry too."

"For what?"

"Sneaking up on you. Thought it might be a funny trick. Kind of like pulling a chair out from under someone as they're about to sit down, 'cept most people you do that to can't break your arm and knock you out in three heartbeats." He shrugged. "My people aren't nice. But we're trying to learn."

"Your people, or you?" She looked up into the monster's face.

Armitage considered. "You gotta start somewhere."

⁊

THEY WAITED FOR MERIWETHER TO WAKE. IT TOOK A WHILE, AND unlike Armitage he didn't snap awake. He was all the way purebred human, which meant he slurred, head lolling, as he looked around. "Is desert still?"

Geneve felt a stab of guilt. His face was marked by cuts, with evidence of salve over the injuries. But his eyes worked, and he didn't scream in agony.

Sight of Day nodded. {I know you hoped for it all to be a bad dream.}

He looked past the Feybrind to Geneve. "You good?"

Geneve laughed. "I'm ... fine, Meri. Now you're okay, that is." She looked to Armitage. "The Vhemin says we should get on with it."

Meriwether nodded, like all this was fine, then he slapped his neck, scrabbling to his feet. He tangled with the tarp, stumbling sideways. "Insect?"

Sight of Day gave a half-smile. *{That was a nightmare. Nothing like that could exist in the world.}*

"Nothing like what, cat?" Meri pawed his neck. "What did you put on me?"

The Feybrind stood, dusting himself off. *{The patient seems well. I fear we've lost much time.}*

"Time we didn't have to lose," Armitage agreed. "The temple's not far. Let's hustle."

They broke camp. It let Meriwether come to his senses by degrees. Geneve didn't know what the insect was, or why the Feybrind had them, but she admitted it was an effective anesthetic. The cat-people couldn't use the Light to heal people like Clerics, so it made sense they had their own type of healing.

She shuddered, thinking of a swarm of the creatures scuttling over the ground toward her. *Nope. Nope, nope, nope. I don't want one of those things biting me. There's no room in the twenty-one hundred patterns for fighting a cloud of insects.*

The thought made her pause. The patterns were sometimes ambiguous. The movements didn't always make sense, and Tresward Knights spent their lives dedicated to the understanding of their purpose. Interpretations of the stanzas could mean use from horse-back or on foot, armored or naked, running from foes or hunting them. A slight change of wrist posture turned a block into a strike. Israel said, *You'll know when you need to,* but he'd sounded doubtful, like even he wanted to know what the real purpose behind all of them was.

Geneve shook her head to clear it. It didn't matter. She'd lived by the patterns, and they'd saved her life countless times.

They set off north again, leading their mounts. The sand felt less forgiving today, or maybe that was her heart. The desert winds picked up. Hot, dry air swept grit against them. It seemed to get into every crevice. Her canteen seemed about eighty percent silty granules when-ever she took a sip.

About two o'clock they stopped for a rest. Geneve noticed the horizon ahead was broken by a slender spire. She thought it a trick of the light, another heat shimmer. As they resumed their journey, her feet marking distance, the spire became more substantial. "What's that?"

Armitage didn't bother looking up. "Temple."

"It's ... *massive*," breathed Meriwether. "It must be a klick high."

"It's pretty big." The monster shrugged. "Feels bigger on the inside, too. We'll get there by nightfall."

Pace by pace, meter by meter, they approached the temple of the ancients. The sun backed away as it usually did. The Three showed their faces before it'd finished setting. Geneve initially thought there was only Cophine's pale light. "Where are the other moons?"

Meriwether looked up. "I'd bet they're in alignment. Ikmae's behind Cophine, and Khiton's at rearguard."

She nodded. "Tonight's auspicious, then."

"One word for it," Armitage rumbled. "Deadly's another."

Chapter Thirty-Five

The stables yielded Geneve's prize: an ox-wagon front assembly. The hitch was sound oak, linked to two metal-rimmed wheels. Too heavy for her, but with four? Manageable.

They also stole chain and pulleys, a set of hammers, and shovels. Kytto's hand to hand training might not have been good for beating Wincuf, but working beside the Smith taught Geneve a thousand things most Knights would never know.

They hustled the assembly from the stables with whispers and giggles. A few times they had to freeze, fearing a night-delivered noise as discovery, but through the Three's grace no one found them.

They made it to the hall. Geneve directed them on her plan. Hettie shimmied up the walls, the glint of her bald head disappearing into the gloom. Raja and Barbet stayed with Geneve, humping the wagon assembly to the middle of the room.

They made quick work with hammers and chain, tossing ropes above to Hettie. The girl scrabbled like a spider across the roof, looping rope through a pulley she drove into the stone. Novices they might be, but hard training by the Tresward made them strong, and agile as acrobats.

They winched the entire contraption above. It rose as they grunted beneath it. A final step was securing the stay beneath the floor's smooth stone. It involved *lifting the flagstones, digging a trench, and then smoothing all so no eye would be drawn to it.*

Dirt and excitement were on every face. Geneve led them through the clean-up, hiding their actions. The floor was swept, the tools and Novices both returned to their expected places.

She crept to her own bunk and slept like the dead until called to face Wincuf.

WHICH WAS HOW GENEVE FACED WINCUF, BLADE IN HAND, BUT NO FEAR *in her heart. The thug lunged at her, all pretense of form forgotten. He hungered to take her head, hack it from her shoulders, and leave her a corpse.*

Geneve ducked, rolled, spun, and tossed Requiem. The skymetal blade's lightness made this feel effortless. Wincuf watched her blade sail past him, a smile of delight blooming on his face. The sword thunk'd into the wall behind him, right at the flagstone's lip, and severing the rope hidden within.

Wincuf came for her as the wagon assembly fell. The hissing sound of rope under stones was foreign, and he cocked his head at the unexpected noise.

Geneve didn't glance up. She knew what was there and what it looked like. But Wincuf didn't. The entire assembly crashed on the young man, hammering him to the stones like Khiton's fist. His glass blade tumbled from his fingers, shattering as it fell. Wincuf's armor was flattened, crushing him within a vice grip and not leaving him the room to breathe.

Silence held Geneve's hand as she padded past the wreckage to retrieve her sword. Requiem slid from the stone, hissing as it came. She stalked back to the ruin of Wincuf's body.

He gurgled, hand out. Blood leaked from his armor to stain the white stone beneath him. Geneve heard the shouts of Clerics and Knights, the jingle of armor and the whisper of fabric as they ran to help the fallen Novice.

Geneve saluted with her blade, then walked away. Wincuf would never be a Knight. His Trial's failure ensured he'd never be welcome in their halls again.

She hadn't needed the Storm to beat him.

Chapter Thirty-Six

Meriwether lay on his belly, peering over a dune's rise into the encampment below. It looked like a small military setup. He spied a makeshift smithy, complete with bellows and furnace. Horses were listless in a pen with a fabric gazebo to keep the sun off. Tents lay in neat rows, and Vhemin patrolled like soldiers. They were equipped with new-looking armor, but didn't wear it the same way a human might. Many made do with a cuirass, not bothering to strap the breastplate and backplate together. It couldn't be heat, what with them being cold-blooded, but it *could* be plain old laziness.

The horse pen was their destination, but Meriwether couldn't help but stare at the monstrous structure of the temple. From where he lay with Sight of Day on the sand, he could see the main building was a circular structure, perhaps a couple klicks in diameter. It had a smooth finish like polished steel, and he imagined if the sun hadn't set it'd be painful to look at. He felt it was maybe three stories high, but there was nothing like windows on the outside to mark internal floors.

Above the main structure a massive spire reached for the heavens. It was over a klick high, going from a wide base, to narrow like the world's longest hourglass before spreading back out. He spent a lot of time looking at the top, which held a dual-forked tip. The body seemed to be a single piece of shining metal. Unlike the main structure, the winds, sands, or plain old time had played havoc with it. Pieces of the metal were eroded or flaked away, revealing an inner skeleton of struts that seemed impossibly thin to hold such a thing off the ground.

Meriwether marveled at the temple. *Eight hundred years and it's still here.* The temple's top was smooth, without any chimneys or whatever ancients used to get smoke out and air in. It resisted sand, the top a perfect shiny disc. Smaller mounds around the building showed where lesser structures bowed to time's pressure, rotting into the sands beneath them.

The tents around the temple were a respectful hundred meters from the front of the structure. Meriwether labeled it as 'front' because of a thing that might have been a door. It was shiny metal like the rest, but marked around the lip by a seam. He'd not seen it at first; the cat pointed it out to him. Almost too small to make out were small, dull metal discs set to either side of the door.

Sight of Day touched his arm. The cat lay next to him, golden eyes lazy. *{Are you finished ogling ancient wonders? We've got horses to feed.}*

Meriwether nodded. *{I can't believe the ancients fell when they could make things like this.}*

{The ancients were human.} Sight of Day half-smiled. *{I marvel they managed to tie their shoelaces, let alone make this.}*

Meriwether held a snort down. It wouldn't do to make a sound. Their dune hiding place was a couple hundred meters from the nearest tent, and the camp had plenty of its own noises. Bawdry laughter, the odd fight, and shouted orders, even after sunset. *{I can go by myself. The Vhemin hate cats.}*

{Don't be silly.} The cat shook his head. *{You can't tie your shoelaces either.}*

The plan was simple. Wait for Geneve and Armitage to make a ruckus getting inside. Once the diversion started, Meriwether and Sight of Day would sneak to the horse pens and make off with enough grain to keep their horses alive for a few more days. As far as plans went, it had simplicity on its side. It also had the nice advantage of

Meriwether not going against people with swords, because the last time that happened he'd almost been blinded.

He touched his face below his left eye, where a shard of frypan left its mark. *That was close. What was I thinking, diving in between them?* Truth was, he'd been thinking of Geneve killing Armitage, or Armitage savaging her, and he didn't want either to happen.

A shout went up from below. An enterprising soul—probably Armitage—set fire to a tent. Flames billowed, smoke bunting the night sky. Sight of Day tugged his arm. *{Time to try not dying.}*

Meriwether scrambled to his hands and knees, then followed the cat down the bank. They kept low. Meriwether found Sight of Day's pace difficult to match. The Feybrind didn't run on all fours like an *actual* cat, hunching like Meriwether, but still managed to ... flow over the ground. He slipped from cover to cover without seeming to focus on it, and when his hand came to rest on a tent guy-wire, it landed as softly as a night moth. It was frankly embarrassing trying to keep up with someone who did so much with so little apparent effort.

Shoring up next to Sight of Day, Meriwether tripped on a guy-wire. The cat's hand snared his shirt, holding him up while his arms flailed for balance. Once Meriwether's feet were settled, the cat shook his head. *{Remember the not dying part?}*

{I tripped.}

{Which would lead to you falling through the tent, disturbing its occupants, and dying.} Sight of Day shook his finger in a no-no gesture. *{Can you walk the next five meters without killing yourself?}*

{I'll try.} Meriwether curled his lip, then ducked as something explosive detonated a couple hundred meters away, followed by the throaty screams of Vhemin dying. *{What was that?}*

{The oil stores.} Sight of Day shrugged. *{Or a dragon.}*

{There aren't any dragons!}

Sight of Day flicked his ear, then led off again. He kept to the cover of the tents. They made the pens without more guy-wire incidents. The penned horses circled in agitation, liquid black eyes wide. Meriwether counted five of the beasts, all in good condition. They headed for sacks stacked on a wooden pallet, a small tarp drawn over the top.

Meriwether caught the rich smell of grain and hefted a bag over his shoulder. It was heavy, but he'd manage.

The cat eyed him suspiciously. *{Will you be okay with that?}*

Meriwether shifted the load on his shoulder to free his hands. *{Why do you ask?}*

{I've seen Feybrind children carry more weight with less visible effort.} Sight of Day stilled, eyes scanning, then he drew his bow from behind him, notched an arrow, and fired it past Meriwether's ear without blinking.

A *chock* sound came from behind him. Meriwether turned, taking in a Vhemin clutching a shaft sprouting from his throat. Another arrow sprouted from his left eye, and the monster dropped. Meriwether considered the fallen creature. *{I'm curious about something.}*

{Why I'm such a good shot?}

{No—}

{Is it how I heard the Vhemin approach?}

{Not that either. It's about the people here.}

Sight of Day squinted. *{I'm not sure I follow.}*

{Monsters.} Meriwether pointed at the fallen Vhemin. *{Horses,}* he swung his finger to the pen, *{do not let monsters ride them. The black creature of hate and spite we've dragged across the desert would kill Armitage if he got too close. So, where are the five riders?}*

Sight of Day looked to the horses, then back to Meriwether. *{Does it matter?}*

{It might.}

{Does it matter right now?} Sight of Day hefted a bag, then a second one, and a third. He made it look effortless.

Meriwether felt guilty at his more modest load. *{I'll make another trip.}*

The cat said nothing, hands full, but still managed to flow like water away from the pens. No more Vhemin discovered them. Meriwether had time to think about how the horses hadn't panicked when the Vhemin drew near, or at the smell of blood when the monster died. That could mean one potentially bad thing: they were Tresward horses.

Tresward horses came with Knights. *That'd suck.*

They scrabbled over the dune's top, dumping their pile of stolen loot. Meriwether arched his back, but at Sight of Day's wide-eyed astonishment, ducked low. *{Sorry.}*

{Dying! It will happen!} The cat shook his head.

Meriwether was about to offer a witty rejoinder, fit for stories of the ages, when Geneve's cry came from across the camp. "Meri! We need you!"

Ah. His feet were moving before he knew what was going on, tumbling down the dune in a headlong rush to get to her position by the temple. He was a hundred meters into his run before he also realized her position was beset by Vhemin. *This is not how you avoid death. The cat will be upset.* The cat, as it happened, was by his side, running with an easy lope. *Fair enough. I guess we'll die together, then.* The thought was chased by another, less comfortable one.

What could Geneve need me for?

Chapter Thirty-Seven

Geneve approached the temple with her head high, red locks flowing in the desert wind. She'd donned her armor for this, because challenging Vhemin without steel around your heart was foolish, no matter how many patterns you knew. She didn't have her helm because she'd left it on the sands to signpost supplies for old friends, so she'd need to keep her guard up.

At least, I hope they're still old friends.

The desert was uncomfortably warm, the sands radiating the day's heat back at her. Armitage looked happy enough, his leather armor strapped on tight. If his broken arm bothered him, he didn't let it show. His massive club was held loose and easy in both hands.

The plan was simple. Walk to the front door, knock, and enter. When they were still a klick away, Armitage pointed a massive arm at the temple. "There's a path between the tents. Straight as an arrow. In we go."

She nodded. "There's only the small problem of a horde of monsters."

"I resemble that remark," he rumbled. "Also, the woman in the black armor. I'd be more worried about her."

"Are there other Knights?"

"Not when I was here." He sniffed the air. "Just her, and a bunch of other assholes."

"You sure I can open the door?" She felt doubt stir. "How certain?"

"Pretty certain. The woman with black armor opened it first time."

"And you went inside?" Geneve frowned. "With Nicolette?"

"Don't know her name, but sure. Wasn't like we had a choice." He looked away, the untold story standing between them.

"Hmm." Geneve checked Requiem and Tribunal. She'd put Requiem's scabbard at her waist in a rear-draw configuration. Easier to run without getting it tangled in her legs, and she felt there might be running. While Knights didn't run, she'd done a lot of things Knights weren't meant to do, and besides, Nicolette was a Champion. She held Storm and Sway, and there was not even a remote chance an Adept could stand up to her. The scattergun rode on her back, and her shield was strapped to her left arm. "Distractions?"

"I could set fire to something." Armitage rubbed his chin, keeping pace easy enough. "Since we're raiding the place anyway, it feels like the right thing to do."

"Raiding?"

"Yeah. We're going in there, and—"

"I'm not a bandit, sirrah." Geneve shook her head.

"What would you call it, then?"

"You've family in those walls. We're getting them out, and while we're there, you're going to show me how they stole Sight of Day's thoughts."

"Okay, we're liberators and guerrillas then." He lumbered on. "I'm still setting fire to something."

She hid her smile. "If you feel that's best."

"It's just what's *done*, Knight." He picked up speed. "I'll meet you at the door."

Geneve let him go. The night closed in, but she could see just fine. The sands lay smooth and pale under her feet, and the Vhemin's encampment had many burning torches. They weren't hiding. They were waiting.

She felt her heart pick up speed. It always did before a fight. The night smells were sharper, and her eyes picked up every movement.

Calm. Center. The fight will get here without seeking it out. Geneve checked Requiem again, but the blade hadn't gone anywhere. *You're nervous. You're walking into a relic of the ancients with a monster, a sinner, and a cat. Your Knights aren't with you, and a Champion lies ahead.*

"What could go wrong?" she asked the night. It didn't answer.

Fire bloomed, smoke rising. She caught movement, a surge of bodies as Vhemin ran to the disturbance. She heard the *crunch* of wood on bone, and a scream of pain. Geneve jogged, her armor's weight feeling like nothing as her blood pounded in her ears. Requiem wouldn't be denied. The blade shivered as it came free, gleaming under Cophine's pale gaze.

As Geneve made the outskirts of the tents, something detonated in the camp to her left. She ignored it, running faster. A Vhemin loomed from the night to her right and died as Requiem took his head from his shoulders. She didn't slow, barely glancing as she hunkered beneath her shield. A quarrel bounced off, spinning end over end into the dark.

The temple was close. She tried not to look at the spire reaching to the heavens. Geneve ignored the lack of other moons in the sky as Cophine's brilliance stared at her. To be distracted was to die.

Cries broke out, warnings shouted by coarse Vhemin throats. She heard Armitage roar from the left. *"Motherfucker!"* Another crunch, wood on bone, then a body sailed across Geneve's path. It wasn't Vhemin. It was an armored human.

That's a Knight. Geneve's steps slowed, and Armitage broke free from the line of tents ten meters ahead. "You coming?"

"That was a Knight!"

"Looks like it. Hurry up." He turned, heading toward the building. She sprinted after. They left the tents behind, making the short hundred-meter distance to the wall without meeting another soul. A quarrel landed by her feet, spitting sand as it hit. Another *pinged* off her pauldron, a fleck of metal marking her cheek. She barely noticed, pushing herself faster.

They made the door at the same time. Armitage slammed against the smooth metal wall of the temple, and she followed suit. Her Smith-steel screeched as she hit, but the wall wasn't marked by the impact. Armitage pointed to the dull metal circle to her right. "Hammer that."

He moved to the one on the left, putting his big hand over the disc. Geneve didn't understand why putting her hand on metal would do anything, but she did it anyway.

Nothing happened.

Armitage scowled. "Take your damn mitten off."

"How did you beat a Knight?" Geneve kept talking to cover her rising fear. She sheathed Requiem, then tugged the straps on her gauntlet.

"Wasn't a Knight."

"He was."

"Then he wasn't as good as you. Hurry the fuck up!"

That can't be right. He wore the three bands of a Chevalier. The Storm answers his call. No simple Vhemin could knock him aside like a child's doll. She dragged her gauntlet free, metal falling to the sand at her feet. Geneve reached for the disc but felt the lance of agony in her back. She screamed, reaching for whatever it was, but her armor wasn't flexible enough. She couldn't reach it.

Armitage was at her side. "This is going to hurt." She felt the white-hot rip of flesh as he yanked something from her back. He tossed a bloody quarrel to the sand. "Put your hand on the damn disc."

Geneve swayed. *They've poisoned me.* She put her hand on on the metal disc, leaning her head against the cool metal of the temple. Geneve heard a grunt and made the effort to turn to Armitage. A quarrel stuck from his shoulder, another from his leg, but he didn't slow. He slammed his hand on the disc with a shout. "Ha hah, fuckers!"

Nothing happened. Again.

Geneve leaned her back against the temple so she could face the tents. She felt hot, more than just desert heat, her blood pounding. A handful of Vhemin marched on her position, crossbows leveled and firing.

Requiem swept the air before her. She didn't remember drawing it, and the blade felt heavy in her hand. Geneve sliced a quarrel in half but heard another grunt from Armitage. The man had another bolt stuck in his chest, and a fourth in his arm. "Try again," he urged. "Please."

She glared at the Vhemin, then lurched toward the disc. She put her hand against it.

Nothing at first, then a low vibration touched her fingertips. A voice spoke from the wall. *"SANCTUS INVESTUS EST. MAGIA REQUIRITUR."* The voice was loud, the tone hard like an angry god.

Armitage looked lost, his snake eyes searching the wall. "It didn't do that last time."

"No. Last time, it needed one hand. But you broke it, and it locked us all away." Geneve spun at the voice. Pushing through the line of Vhemin was a woman in black armor. She held glass in each hand, the blades catching and refracting torchlight.

"Nicolette," Geneve whispered.

The Champion saluted with one sword, then swept it into a guard. "Do I know you?"

"Do something," Armitage suggested. He sank to the ground, a slick of blood marking the metal wall. It beaded as if it didn't want to stick.

"Me?" Geneve's sword, mean skymetal, was unsuitable for fighting against glass, especially welded by a Champion.

"The door spoke to you, Knight. It tried to tell you something."

"I don't speak..." Geneve shook her head. The door's words were gibberish. The lost madness of fallen ancients, but one word seemed like another she knew. Familiar, even. *Magia.*

Magic. "It needs magic!"

"Fuck," Armitage wheezed. "And here we are, fresh out of wizards. If you assholes hadn't been hunting them down for the last hundred years—"

Geneve gathered her strength. She couldn't fight Nicolette. She didn't know how to get out of this. But she knew how they could get the door open. Propping herself against the wall, she shouted, "Meri! We need you!"

The camp stilled. Vhemin cast glances at each other as they shifted from foot to foot. Nicolette gave a small smile, full of condescension. "Who is Meri?"

Geneve thought about how to answer in a way that would draw this out. To keep the Champion talking, so Meriwether could get here, help her open the door, and then they could slip inside. *He's a sinner.*

No, that was wrong. He was no more a sinner than she was. *He's a friend*. Totally insufficient for what she asked of the man.

And insufficient for how she felt. "He's—"

"Geneve!" A man's bellow cut across her words, hammering them flat. Geneve heard anger, and fear, and more than a little desperation in the cry. Nicolette turned a slow circle, stepping behind one of her Vhemin for cover.

Her sidestep revealed two people. Armored figures, glass in hand. Geneve squinted, trying to focus, but the poison had a hold of her now. She slid down the wall, coming to rest on the ground. The world seemed far away, keeping its distance so she could die in peace.

Nicolette spoke, her voice smug. "Ah, Valiant." She gave a mocking bow. "Come to die, Israel?"

Oh, no. No, no, no. Geneve tried to rise, but the strength was gone from her limbs. Not only would Meriwether fall, but Israel and Vertiline would die too.

Chapter Thirty-Eight

Geneve stood atop the keep's battlements, watching Wincuf walk away. The thug limped. Lucent Eleni claimed his injuries were past her skill with Sway, but she'd re-attached the Novice's arm in times past.

Cleric Eleni wasn't telling the whole truth.

They'd turned him out with silver regals in his pocket, a good Tresward Smithsteel sword, and a total lack of their blessing. The young man cursed them all, and Geneve in particular. She didn't take it personally because she'd won.

Footsteps turned her from the view and her reflection. Tilly walked toward her, armor gleaming in the sun. "Novice."

"Hello." Geneve returned to the wondrous sight of a retreating Wincuf. "That's that, then."

"What's what?" Vertiline placed her hands on the old stone, leaning forward, shoulders hunched.

"No more Wincuf."

The Chevalier laughed. "There will be plenty more Wincuf. He's not dead. And now, he hates you more than ever."

Geneve rubbed her fingers along the stone, feeling its ancient grit. "They could have just expelled him when he attacked me. Gods, it seems so long ago."

"It's not the Justiciar's way."

"Then their way doesn't seem fair."

Vertiline held her peace for a time, wind tousling a stray pale wisp of hair that escaped her braid. "It's the fairest thing in the world."

Geneve frowned. "I don't understand."

"I'm not good at this like Israel." Vertiline hunched further. "There are a lot of bad people out there. We fight them every day."

"So?"

"So, if Knights handle dissent between Novices, what lesson does that teach? That someone will come to their aid." Vertiline brushed the rogue strand back into place. "There is no help out there."

"That's dumb," Geneve said. "Wincuf hurt four Novices."

"He hurt more than that." Tilly shifted from foot to foot. "I'm not arguing. I'm not even sure..." She trailed off.

"Sure about what?"

"It doesn't matter. Let's go get something to eat." Vertiline led the way. Geneve tried for another last glance at Wincuf's retreat, but the young man was lost from view. She hoped he'd leave her alone now. At least he couldn't enter Tresward bastions. She'd be safe here, for a long time to come.

Chapter Thirty-Nine

This is *bullshit. It's a lot of bullshit!* Meriwether sprinted until he couldn't anymore, then tried to push himself to merely run, breath running ragged in his chest. *I need a plan, and I need it fast.*

Fire chewed the camp ahead. Meriwether headed toward it, Sight of Day at his side. The cat's golden eyes were hard, like he hunted dangerous prey. His bow was in hand, and Meriwether was reminded that here he was, with a borrowed knife and no skills.

Hey. I've got some *skills.* He hunkered beside a tent as it verged a makeshift road. Vhemin ran past, heading south. Meriwether almost ducked from cover when ten passed, but Sight of Day held his shoulder. A woman strode by, all black armor and cruel smiles. She was beautiful, but like the sun was to ice. Her face was hard, skin red, hair black, and she carried two glass swords. Meriwether felt his heart stammer as she walked past. It was like the world bent to her will and wanted to carry him away with it.

Sight of Day's hand tethered him. It was warm, soft, and strong. *Peace.* He closed his eyes, swaying, and when he opened them the woman was gone.

Lightning slashed the sky to the south, the boom impossibly loud. Meriwether stumbled, hands over his ears. Sight of Day's eyes were wide, the cat's ears flat against his head. Meriwether looked, and saw dead, charred Vhemin around two Knights. "Fuck me," he breathed. It was Israel and Vertiline. Their armor gleamed, but their skin was sunburnt. She'd had it worse than him, her ghost-pale skin giving way to a lobster's complexion. Israel fared better, but both had windburned faces and the haggard look of a hard trail. They had no horses. Just steel and glass.

Two Knights came from the west, and another burst from the tent line to Meriwether's left. They lined up with the black-armored woman, who could only be Nicolette. Meriwether did the math. *We've got ourselves a road-weary Valiant and a sunburned Chevalier, versus a Champion and three Chevaliers. Not good.* He almost went toward all the trouble, but Sight of Day's hand on his shoulder anchored him to the ground.

The cat snapped fingers in front of his eyes. *{It's the Sway. Do not listen to it.}*

"But she hasn't said anything." Meriwether blinked, confused.

{The Sway isn't always words, friend. It is the thing your heart wants.} The Feybrind turned Meriwether to the temple. *{But your heart* needs *that.}*

At the base of the temple, two figures slumped. Armored Geneve and leathery Armitage. Both were unmoving. Meriwether was running again before he could work out what *heart needs* was all about. His cloak billowed behind him as sand shifted under his feet. He stumbled more than once, but the Feybrind caught his arm each time.

Lightning boomed behind them, and an answering slash followed. The ground shook with the fury of the Light. The air tasted of metal and anger, and his teeth itched. Meriwether slid to a halt beside Geneve as Sight of Day loped to Armitage's side.

Her head lolled, eyes only half open, and blood soaked the sand beneath her. "Meri?"

"I'm here. I'm here! What do I do?"

"Help me up."

"Don't be stupid. You're injured."

Her eyes opened, flashing anger. "Don't call me—"

"And there we have it." He gave her a smile. "You just needed the right motivation." He got a shoulder under her. She grunted, then groaned as he hauled. Geneve's armored body was heavy, but it wasn't the time to compare her to a sack of grain. "Now what?"

"There's a disc, like this one, over there. See it?" At his nod, she gave him a gentle push. "Put your hand on it."

"And then what?"

"Pray," she suggested.

Meriwether hurried to the other disc. Armitage slumped beneath it, head back, but his breath clattered in his chest like a huge baby's rattle. Sight of Day looked up. *{He's still alive. Shame.}*

Lightning cracked behind them, the brilliance reflected in the metal temple wall blinding Meriwether for a moment. The sound of wind came, the tremendous howling of a tornado, and Meriwether's cloak whipped about him. He looked at the disc, squinting through the hail of sand. It looked like dull metal, smooth, worn by time. *What's this supposed to do?*

It didn't matter. He was here, had a hand, and most importantly, Geneve asked him to use it. He put his palm against the disc, glancing to her as he did.

Geneve nodded, and put her hand against her disc. The ground jolted, and a low rumble shook Meriwether's bones. The sand vibrated beneath him, and then it felt like the whole *world* shifted. The wall spoke as it cracked wide. *"ENTER."*

MERIWETHER'S HANDS WERE SLICK WITH GENEVE'S BLOOD. SHE'D fallen after triggering the door to open, so he'd dragged her inside, armor scraping as it skidded across the ancient white floor. Sight of Day pulled Armitage after, and the door sealed behind them.

It closed on a battle between Nicolette, Israel, and Vertiline. They moved faster than Meriwether's eyes could track, and the brilliant slashes of white Light blinded him. It wasn't the warm glow of sunlight, but a bright actinic glare as glass blades clashed.

With the door shut, silence held court. Meriwether knew there was a battle between titans outside, but in the temple? Nothing. Pure, stale calm. The air smelled of age beyond counting. He fussed with Geneve but wasn't sure what to do. Blood ran a trail from the door to her still form. Sand mixed with it, clumping in ruddy patches.

He spared a glance for Armitage. Sight of Day yanked bolts from his body, but the creature didn't respond. Armitage took five times as many hits as Geneve. *He might die. He came here to help his people, and the Feybrind, for all he's a monster. Yet he falls at the finish line.*

Meriwether ran a hand through his hair, and felt it stick because of Geneve's blood. He heaved her over, examining the hole in her armor. The puncture was an uneven, jagged-toothed snarl in the metal. Blood clotted the hole, but at least the leaking seemed to have slowed. *If we can keep her still, then maybe she'll be okay.*

He didn't know what to do. Sight of Day finished yanking bolts from Armitage, then joined him by her side. The cat's golden eyes were gentle. *{She will be okay.}*

"How do you know?"

{Because there is a storm inside her.} Sight of Day shrugged. *{Can't you see it?}*

"I see she's ... *dying.*" Meriwether rubbed his face, then realized he smeared blood across his cheek. It tingled a little, like there was enough poison in her blood to make his skin itch. He wondered what she'd felt like standing by the door as fever's fire ran in her veins. "Can we do anything?"

{You mean, can I do anything?} The cat shook his head. *{There's nothing to do.}*

"What—"

The room spoke. "*Salve.*"

"...the fuck?" Meriwether finished.

Sight of Day's ears flattened against his head. *{We should be careful. There are forgotten evils in the temples of the ancients.}*

The room droned on. "*Welkom. Willkommen. Nau mai. Svāgata cha. Zhelannyy. Velkommen—*"

"Uh, hello?" Meriwether looked to the ceiling, like the Three themselves were up there talking to him.

The room paused before saying, "Welcome."

Meriwether nodded, but slowly, like he'd been hit with a club made of wonder. Now his brain had a few moments to do something other than fret needlessly, it nudged him to take in where he was. The room they'd entered through the massive door was enormous, easily fifty meters to the left and right. The external wall followed the curve of the building, but because the temple was so large, they looked straight at first blush. Walls were of the ancient's smooth white material they used to build their ever-living structures. The interior was a marvel of a glassy wall material, strangely opaque, which reached to the ceiling thirty meters above.

Dust silted in the corners, but surprisingly little for the passage of eight hundred years. There wasn't a cobweb to be seen. Moldering piles of metal and leather were heaped in rows. Meriwether eyed them, trying to guess their purpose. They weren't Artifices. He mentally shook himself. *Time to unlock the secrets of the ancients later. Look for danger.*

An interior wall had a jagged hole punched through it. Splinters of glass lay on the floor. "That looks like how the Vhemin got in."

Sight of Day nodded. *{I wonder if breaking the glass triggered the temple to protect itself.}*

"There aren't any Artifices. Not like at the plague city." Meriwether hugged himself. The temple was cool inside, as if it didn't remember the heat of the day at all. "How does it protect itself?"

{Magic.}

"Maybe." The ceiling gave a trembling glow, then faded. Meriwether pursed his lips. "Where's the light coming from? It seems like it's everywhere."

{The walls.} The cat raised an eyebrow. *{Like a thousand glowworms are trapped deep inside. Which, if true, means it'd suck to be a creation of the ancients.}*

"I've got an idea." Meriwether took a step back from the wall. "Let's find a way out."

He spun at a cough that turned into a retch. Armitage curled over, dry-heaving. "I feel really bad."

"You looked like a pincushion."

"That'd do it." Armitage levered himself upright, glancing at Geneve. "What happened to her? Scratch that. *Who* happened to her?"

"Poison." Meriwether clasped his hands together. "On the bolts."

"Right. Yeah, that stuff doesn't bother me too much." Armitage scratched under his armpit. "I'm feeling better already."

Sight of Day rolled his eyes. *{Which way to your people, my people's salvation, and certain doom?}*

Armitage hauled Geneve onto his shoulders, draping her arms over one shoulder, legs over the other. She didn't fold easily, being encased in armor, but it didn't seem to bother the Vhemin. For all Geneve was a Knight, built like stone and steel came together into one material, she looked tiny on his shoulders. "All three of those things are this way. C'mon."

He led them through the break in the wall, strides sure and steady. Meriwether hurried to keep up. "We should leave her here."

"Don't be a dick." The monster didn't turn to face him. "Soon enough someone'll work out how to open that door. They'll drag another sorcerer from someone's ass crack and shove 'em against the opening disc, and then we'll be fucked. Second, we'll need her hand to open the jail."

"I'm not a sorcerer."

"That's apparent, runt, but the door didn't know that." He stooped to get through the broken wall. Meriwether wanted to urge him to be *careful*, but he didn't knock Geneve against any of the jagged edges. "They'll fire up another portal."

Sight of Day slipped through behind Armitage before Meriwether could follow, and darted to the side. Meriwether gave a last glance at the entrance chamber, it's glowing walls, and floor slicked with a Knight's blood. *Eight hundred years this place stood, and when we got here we bled all over it.*

Once through, Meriwether stopped, struck dumb. The interior of the temple was huge. About five hundred meters in the distance another glass wall bisected the area floor to ceiling. Inside this chamber, the walls held what looked like open-air levels. The middle of the room held a chamber of the same opaque glass as the walls. A dark, immense shadow lay within. "What's that?"

"Dunno. Couldn't get it open." Armitage trudged on, following the curve of the inner chamber.

Sight of Day padded to Meriwether's side, and put a hand on his arm. *{Look. Up there.}*

Following the line of his arm, Meriwether saw lettering on the side of the chamber. It was etched into the material, each letter as tall as he was. He followed the glyphs, trying to work out what they spelled out. They'd started at the final letter, so it took a few steps to get to the start.

SKY FORGE 01.

"What's a sky forge?"

"Ancient's bullshit. Who cares?" Armitage hadn't slowed, his course unchanged.

Meriwether cast a glance over his shoulder at the dark shape within the chamber. "I care a little, I admit. I mean, what's inside it? What's it do?"

"After eight hundred years, seven-eighths of fuck all," Armitage rumbled. "But if you like that, you'll love the next room."

Sight of Day shook his head. *{I don't think the ancients made with wisdom.}*

Meriwether clapped the cat on the back. "If they were as smart as they seemed, they'd still be here."

Armitage led through another break in the glass. The chamber beyond was bisected like the last. This one had shelves of massive proportion, each holding hundreds of miniature versions of the shadow-filled chamber outside. These smaller capsules were twice as tall as Meriwether, and about three times as wide.

{I don't feel good.} Sight of Day looked around, eyes wide.

"This makes me feel weird, too." Meriwether slowed to keep pace with his friend. "We'll get this done, and then leave."

{You don't understand. I feel,} the Feybrind touched his heart, *{wrong. Like how I felt on the raft, or my village, but different. Like someone has a hand on my soul.}*

Meriwether stopped, turning the cat to face him. "Your soul's your own."

A sad, small nod. *{I always thought so, but now I'm not so sure.}*

"Let's get this over with." He shivered. "Why is it so cold in here?"

{Because they fought the sky's might and won.} Sight of Day gave a half-smile, but it seemed forced. *{Then something worse fought them, and all was swept aside.}*

"Hah. Good talk." Sight of Day's words made Meriwether feel colder. "Let's catch up to the asshole."

"I heard that," Armitage called. "We Vhemin have very good hearing."

They picked up their speed, following Armitage through the massive shelves. They seemed empty, but about half were broken open. Inside they were smooth, empty chambers. No materials, or wondrous lights. Just empty, timeless absence.

They'd almost reached the far wall, heading for another break, when Meriwether spotted something in a broken chamber. He swerved off course, jogging over. Laying half in, half out of the glass was a skeleton. Time had withered all but the bleached bones and a few scraps of fur to nothing, but it was unmistakably a Feybrind. It looked like the cat had fallen on the broken teeth of the chamber, perhaps eviscerated itself, and died here.

Meriwether looked around the chamber, rubbing his arms for warmth. "They died here, alone."

{How do you know?}

"Because if they had friends, they'd have carried the body away." Meriwether pressed his hands against the glass beside the sad collection of bones. "I'm sorry you died here. I'm sorry I don't know your name, otherwise I'd carry it to the People for you."

A touch made him turn. Sight of Day stood behind him, eyes sad. *{There is a riddle I'd like you to set your mind to. How did one of the People get in here? The Feybrind and Vhemin couldn't open the temple.}*

"Hmm." Meriwether shrugged. "An eight-hundred-year-old puzzle? My favorite." He tried a grin on for size, trying to hide his shiver. "Armitage is in the next room. Let's stop him doing anything stupid."

{An impossible task, but I feel ready for the challenge.} The cat half-smiled, and there was a little more substance to it this time.

The next room was just as large as the previous ones but was almost empty. Meriwether felt a slight disappointment, like the ancient's cheated him by having an empty box inside his wrapped birthday present. There was a dais in the center, with three large clear panels before it.

Near the west wall was a line of chambers like the ones in the previous room. The difference was these were full of what looked like cloudy water, and each held a humanoid form inside. Meriwether walked to them. The dais wasn't as interesting as tanks with people inside.

He got close, pressing his hand to the glass. The shape inside twitched, a hand knocking the opaque glass. "By the Three! They're alive!"

"I fucken hope so. That's my tribe in there." Armitage marched to the dais, Geneve in tow. "C'mon, wizard. Let's get you plugged in."

"What about the cat's people?" Meriwether hurried to the dais, Sight of Day in tow.

"I figure we get my people out, then we work on that problem." Armitage put a foot on the dais, and the room's gentle glowing walls shifted to red. He froze. "Or not."

"Get your foot off it."

"Good idea." Armitage removed his foot with care, as if he'd stood on a hornet's nest and the only thing keeping the insects inside was his boot. No insects exploded out, though. Nothing much happened at all.

Meriwether made it to the dais. The structure looked big enough for five good friends to share space on it, or two or three people who smelled bad. "How's it work?"

"Step on the dais, and magic happens." The monster laid Geneve on the ground. "Last time I was here, the witch Nicolette did it."

"How'd she get your tribe into the chambers?"

"Other Vhemin." Armitage shrugged. "There were a lot of them and not many of us."

"She's ... not a witch," croaked Geneve. Her face was slack, and only one eye tracked the room, but she was alive. "Knight."

Armitage crouched. "Same difference. Can you stand?"

Geneve shook her head. "Feel ... sick."

"Could you stand if your life depended on it? We're on a ticking clock here." The monster counted on his fingers. "While you were out, Nicolette went against your buddies."

"Iz and Tilly." Geneve seemed more awake on hearing about her friends. What might have been low-grade panic crept into her good eye. "Are they well?"

"I'm not a seer. They're outside, with the dust hoppers, the witch, and some angry Vhemin." Armitage jerked a thumb behind him to the tanks. "There are other angry Vhemin in those things, but they're angry in our favor."

Geneve nodded and made to stand. Armitage reached to help her, but she pushed him away. "I can do it. You've carried me long enough." She rose like a baby learning to walk, teetering, almost falling, but made it to stand, swaying, like a blade of grass in the wind. "Maybe a little help."

Meriwether stepped close. "I've got you. Let's get on the dais. I don't think Vhemin are ... *allowed*."

She nodded. They turned a slow, clumsy circle, like it was their first dance and both were shy. Geneve got an armored foot on the dais. The room didn't shift to red. Meriwether pressed his lips into a line. *Courage. She's half dead and still leading from the front.* He put his own foot on the dais.

Nothing bad happened.

They stepped up fully, and the glass panels glimmered, filling with lines of text. Meriwether's eyes widened. "What is this?"

"Ancient bullshit, like I said."

The floor before them slid aside, and two discs rose on slender rods. Geneve looked to Meriwether. "Are you ready for this?"

"Not even a little."

"It's okay, Meri. I'm here." She seemed so earnest, despite how pale her skin was, and how only one eye worked properly.

"That's what I'm afraid of." The joke fell a little flat, but she smiled anyway, because they were in a temple of the ancients, about to face the legacy of a people eight hundred years dead, and that kind of thing deserved humor. "Let's do this." He pressed his hand to a disc.

She followed suit. For a second, nothing happened, and Meriwether thought maybe the temple was dead, Armitage's people condemned to spend the next eight hundred years inside their chambers. Then the floor gave a savage jolt like the start of an earthquake. Dust shook from above, and he coughed. "What did that do?"

Behind him, the tanks clanked, and that's when the screaming started.

Chapter Forty

Geneve felt sick. It wasn't just the poison. It felt like her soul needed care, a little time out, to just put its feet up and relax. She knew it'd only been days, but Geneve felt she'd run north for what felt like forever. Cut off from her fellow Knights, Geneve had done the best she could. She'd brought the sinner north, and during their time together, she'd learned he wasn't a sinner. Meri wasn't evil, any more than Sight of Day was, or even the monster, Armitage. She'd met evil people before, and none traveled with her.

Iz and Tilly arriving felt like a condemnation of her choices. Israel's voice held such pain when he called her name, and then she'd left his storm to die against the rock of Nicolette.

That's a little dramatic. I was poisoned, dying, and had no choice.

She'd woken as Armitage put her down in a strange room. Sight of Day stood next to the monster, avoiding looking at him. Geneve felt cold, right into her bones, but one thing made her feel warm. When Meri got under her arm, helping her up, it felt like a tiny fragment of her tattered soul started to heal. The Vhemin and Feybrind avoided the dais, but Meri stepped with her into the unknown.

Then the chambers behind them cracked open, viscous fluid spilling onto the ground. The Vhemin inside fell out. She tried to spin about, trying to be ready for whether the monsters would be friend or foe, but only managed a wobble. She wasn't in any condition to fight.

Neither were the monsters.

There were twenty tanks in total. The one furthest from her opened, spilling its contents to the floor. The Vhemin inside sloughed apart like rotted meat, its body disintegrating as it slopped to the floor. The next three were much the same. The fifth was still intact enough to scream its agony as it stumbled free. One leg gave way with a wet snap as it stood, and it fell. The wet crunch-pop of its bones breaking as it hit the ground made her sick.

"By the Three," Meri whispered.

Geneve put her hand to her mouth. There were no words for this horror. Vhemin might be monsters, but they'd been ... *eaten* by something. A rot got to them in the short days it took Armitage to get help. "Meri ... what did they *do* to them?"

"Wait here." He made sure she was steady on her own, then ran to the Vhemin's chambers. Armitage stood, stock still, glancing about with desperation. His shark eyes weren't vile and terrible. They held raw agony. "Armitage! Come on." Meri snared the monster's arm, pulling him toward the dying Vhemin.

Armitage backed up a step. "I ... I came as fast as I could."

Sight of Day's quick steps took him from the dais and past Meriwether to arrive next to a fallen creature. The Vhemin's face was like wax, a malformed dough ready for kneading. The cat's golden eyes looked on, helpless, as the Vhemin sagged on itself, chest collapsing, fluid leaking from its mouth. Sight of Day turned to Geneve. *{I can't help them. I don't know what to do.}*

Geneve spun to the glass panels and their lines of words. "Stop it!"

The floor beneath her vibrated. The room hummed. "Geothermal source at four percent. Biofuel alternatives emptied at your directive."

She screwed up her eyes. *Think. Think! Meri would know what to do.* But Meriwether was fifty meters away, trying to save dying Vhemin from collapsing on themselves. "Heal them!"

"Vehement Systems architecture unknown." The voice hissed and clicked as it spoke, pronunciation strange, as if the ancient thing forgot how words worked.

"What can I do?" she whispered.

"Sky Forge ready. Activate?"

Geneve looked at the dying Vhemin. "What's a Sky Forge?"

"Sky Forge ready. Activate?"

She closed her eyes. A risk either way, but the sky held the Three. Moons of the gods, watching their people below. She opened her eyes. "By Cophine, Ikmae, and Khiton, yes. Unleash the gods' forge."

A handful of seconds passed. It couldn't have been more than five, but the sounds of dying Vhemin made her think it was much longer. "Lunar alignment confirmed. Attitude retrieved. Ready for binding essence."

Her eyes searched the glyph-filled glass in front of her. They gave no clue as to what the ancient temple meant, but the panels lay before her. They hadn't retracted into the floor. Ready. Waiting for someone just like her. Human and whole, the first here in eight hundred years. Geneve put her hand on one. "Here. Take what you need."

The room was quiet for a moment longer. "Both essence types are required."

"Meri!" Geneve turned, feeling panic grab her by the throat. "What do I do?"

He looked to her, then got to his feet. His clothes were foul with sloughed off remains of Vhemin, and he wiped his hands on his shirt. He jogged to her, stepping on the dais, eyes everywhere at once. "It needs us both, Red."

"Will it eat us?" She shuddered. "Like them?"

"I don't know." His voice was soft. "Let me try, first." Before she could stop him, Meriwether put his hand on a disc.

The room shuddered as if hit by a massive hammer. "Both essence types are required."

"Fuck!" he yelled. He knuckled his forehead. "Okay. Okay, we can do this." He shouldered her aside, but not unkindly, then stretched his arms wide.

"Meri, what are you doing?"

He didn't look at her as he put his hands on both discs. Meriwether's body went rigid, jaw locked open wide, eyes staring. A *boom* came from above, and the ceiling thirty meters above cracked, a line widening along its length.

The whole ceiling is opening. The entire temple is unfolding like a flower. Through the gap, Geneve saw Cophine's pale face above, the single eye of the moon staring like judgment. She wanted to scream, *I don't know what to do!* But the goddess was too far away to hear.

Meriwether jerked, then collapsed. Smoke peeled away from his clothes. She bent, shook him, then slapped his face. He didn't respond. His palms were burned, the skin red and raw. Geneve lurched to her feet. "What more do you want from us?" She cast her voice to the heavens, hoping Cophine would hear her. "What did we do wrong?"

The room rumbled around them. "Insufficient essence. Both types are required."

Oh. You need it all. She glanced at Sight of Day, and his wide, haunted eyes. Armitage, shifting from foot to foot, fist in his mouth, blood trickling from where he bit down. The dead and dying Vhemin on the floor. She thought about Israel and Vertiline, fighting for her mistakes on the desert sand.

She dragged off her remaining gauntlet, letting it fall to the dais. The temple wanted her and Meri both. *Two corrupted, broken people, and it needs both of us to make something whole. Three gods, and they do nothing for us but take and take.* "I hope you choke on me," she snarled, and grabbed both discs.

Her back arched. Her eyes locked on the night sky above. Cophine's pale face blazed to brilliance, and Geneve screamed as she felt the razing, burning fury of the Three.

Chapter Forty-One

Geneve's own Trial was a thing she grew to fear. The years marched on, relentless, and still the Storm evaded her. On her fourteenth birthday, it was announced her Trial would be next year.

Kytto said it was 'bullshit.' No one forced a Novice to Trial, but he wanted to help her pass. The Smith never held the Storm, but he eyed her form, and swore it was the best he'd seen from any Novice. Perfection even Chevaliers couldn't manage.

Israel and Vertiline sparred with her. Blades of wood, not glass or steel, but even with a stick Israel could conjure the Storm.

Clerics were brought to assess. Lucent Eleni feared illness, and wise heads nodded in agreement. It was a sickness, but one of the mind. She need only remember what happened before her fifth birthday.

Seal the rift in her memory, and the Three would give her the Storm. They needed Knights who were whole, not broken, crumpled toys.

Eleni worked with her daily, then weekly, but then the sessions dropped to monthly, then almost never.

On the last one, the Lucent sat Geneve down on the padded bed in her clinic. "I can't help you."

"I'm trying," Geneve insisted. "I can't remember."

"Oh, child." Eleni touched her cheek. "I didn't say it was your fault."

"It's my mind. Israel says it's the strongest part of a Knight, but mine's missing a piece." Geneve gritted her teeth. "I don't know what I did wrong."

"It doesn't have to be you that did something wrong." Eleni gusted a sigh, then sat beside her. "Give it time. Your memories will come back. They always do."

"You've seen this before?"

"Many times." Eleni shrugged. "Knights lead a hard life. You keep putting your heads in harm's way! It leads to a lot of forgetfulness."

"How long?" Geneve meant, how long until I don't fear the Trial.

"I don't know," Eleni admitted, meaning, too long.

Chapter Forty-Two

Meriwether's teeth hurt, and that was the good part. He'd grabbed the discs, hoping to give Geneve a rest from burning pieces of her life to ash to help everyone but herself, and that's when the hurting started. It hurt a lot, and everywhere at once. It felt like a hot wire was pushed through his skin, into his bones, but all over his body.

When he hit the floor, his mind drifted. He felt like a leech had sucked something out of him. A component without a name. While his hands were on the discs, he'd felt his life play before him. Not the ridiculous term *flashing before your eyes*, but a blow-by-blow recap of everything he'd done. It wasn't the events that were important, but who he'd been with, and what he'd done to them, or for them. The good and bad, displayed on a podium, an ancient temple reviewing the litany of his sins.

Meriwether drifted for a time, uncertain of his name, or where he was. A red-haired, honey-skinned woman in shining armor stood above him, grabbing two metal plates on spindles. She'd said something before putting her hands on them, but then he forgot what words sounded like. All Meriwether knew was he wanted to stop her holding those discs, because there was a devil inside them and a piece of her would be trapped, just like him.

But that would need those pesky words, and he didn't have any to spare.

She screamed, and the moon above seemed to *shine*, which was weird because moons didn't change their luminance. What was weirder was there was a moon to see, because he could swear there was supposed to be a ceiling above them. Meriwether felt like he should be doing something, but he couldn't remember how his feet worked.

The red-haired girl swayed, then collapsed on top of him, her hands and armor trailing smoke. When she hit, it drove the air out of him, but he couldn't work up the motivation to care. They lay like that, and for how long was anyone's guess.

A shark-toothed man yelled at him. He had snake eyes, scaled skin, and looked to be in a lot of emotional distress. He kept pointing at the sky, like the moon was important, and after a moment Meriwether decided to look.

The ceiling above opened like a flower, and crawling atop one of the petals was a massive monster. Not massive like the shark-toothed man. Totally different scale: huge like a hill. It had a head like a cart, and impressive leathery wings. It climbed from within the temple, from what might have been the southern part. He thought he might have been through there but wasn't sure.

Meriwether watched it for a few moments, feeling his heart pick up pace, because even if his front brain didn't know what that was, there was a hidden yet vocal part that did. "Oh," he said. "That's a dragon."

Then he shot up and dragged the red-haired woman with him. He remembered her name was Geneve, and she was a Knight, and good at killing people who deserved it, and also good at killing people who didn't, like him. It was perplexing he was helping her, but it didn't seem like a settled time for him right now.

She was heavy, but the massive scaled monster above gave him all the motivation he needed. He almost skipped off the dais, drawing her scraping armored form with him. "An exit. We need an exit."

The shark-toothed man, Armitage, grabbed him by the shirt. "That's a fucking dragon!"

Meriwether laughed, a sort of raggedy giggle that wobbled like a three-day drunk man. The dragon roared at the night sky, then blasted a jet of fire toward Cophine. The flame blast was twenty, maybe thirty meters long. "The legends were true. They breathe fire. Who knew?"

A cat man with wondrous golden eyes appeared before Meriwether. Gently, with fur-soft hands, he helped Meriwether put Geneve on the ground. He examined Meriwether with a jaundiced glance, wound up, and slapped him across the face.

Meriwether's head rocked about, and while the room became less steady for a moment, all of his thoughts came into alignment. *There's a dragon. The Sky Forge makes them. The evil witch Nicolette started the process, and we finished it, because we're fools. There's only one way out, and it's past the witch who started animating the dragon.*

"Ah hah," he managed, his voice weak. "I think we've got a problem."

{We have many problems. How do we solve them?} The cat's eyes searched his face. *{There is a dragon above and Knights out the front.}*

"There's always a back door," Meriwether said. "I've got a knack for finding these things. Come on."

❧

ARMITAGE CARRIED GENEVE TOSSED OVER ONE SHOULDER LIKE A drugged-out child. Sight of Day padded ahead on whisper quiet feet, with Meriwether between them. His nose for tavern back exits said *go east*. They ran as best they could. Armitage looked hollowed out, because his tribe was gone. Sight of Day looked frightened, and Meriwether had never seen a Feybrind look that way before. Geneve was lost to them, her mind gone. Her eyes stared, no intelligence behind them.

When they hit a dead end, a glass wall ahead, Armitage adjusted his human burden, lowered his head, and charged. He blasted through the glass wall in a shower of shards that chimed like metal bells as they fell.

The room they found was much smaller. A glass table sat beside a pile of leather and metal. Behind a caged wall stood ten metal plinths.

Seven held metal boxes with a glass front. Two metal boxes lay on the ground, glass fronts shattered, and one was missing.

"Here," Armitage grunted, stopping for a breather. "Those are the things."

"The things?" Meriwether looked through the bars. "Could you be more specific?"

"That steal the cat's minds." The monster waved a vague hand. "They speak, and the Feybrind get really dumb."

"Behind these bars?" Meriwether raised an eyebrow. "How did you get them out?"

"Fucked if I know, I wasn't here. They were trying to stuff me in a glass container and suck my balls out through my eyes." Armitage shrugged. "Don't ask me how it works. It was your ancients that built this place, not mine."

"Fair." Meriwether nodded, then strode to the cage. "Open!" The cage clicked, a section hinging wide on invisible hinges. "Honestly? I didn't expect that to work."

He stepped inside, ignoring the fallen devices. He picked one up from a plinth, shook it, and tossed it aside when it didn't do anything. Sight of Day stepped into the cage with him. {How do metal boxes hurt my people?}

Meriwether picked up another. The glass shimmered, then glowed like the walls. "Huh." He shook it, then held it up to the ceiling, trying to get it to do something. The cat watched him, walking a slow circle as Meriwether fussed. The box came between Sight of Day and Meriwether, and the glass panel shivered.

The voice spoke, but in a smaller voice than the temple did. "Sight of Day." Letters appeared on the screen, spelling out the cat's name. Some of the letters were odd. *SI8HT FF DAA.*

"Uh," Meriwether said. "I think it's damaged." A horrible suspicion took root in his stomach. The device was ancient. Broken, most likely. The letters weren't just odd, they were wrong. But it knew the cat's name without being told. Meriwether knew the Feybrind had a name they gave to everyone, and one they kept just for themselves. It was a special, secret one.

The cat shook his head. {I don't think so.}

Meriwether shook the device, then slapped his palm against it. The box chirped, then said, "Sight of Day. Command key unlock, Roars Like the—"

Meriwether smashed the device against the ground. He slammed his foot into it, then again and again, until there was nothing left but pieces of glass and metal. He tore another box from a plinth, smashing it against the floor, one by one, until all were broken. He panted, chest heaving, fingers hooked into claws, then spun to Armitage. "Are there more?"

"Nice rage out moment. Good to see—"

"*Are there more?*" Meriwether screamed. "Listen, brute. These boxes take the Feybrind's minds away. Your High Priest—"

"Ain't *my* fucken High Priest."

"*The* High Priest has one, and it gives him the names of any Feybrind he's near. Not their called names, but their real ones. The ones they don't tell anyone except those close to their hearts." Meriwether stalked from the cage to stand before Armitage. He stared up at the monster. Meriwether was close enough to smell the musk of him, the animal beneath the leather armor. "Are. There. More?"

Armitage looked at Meriwether, then at Sight of Day. Meriwether didn't step away, which was probably foolish, but he needed the monster to understand. Armitage chewed his lip, then sighed. "This place isn't a temple, is it?"

"I don't think so."

"The ancients weren't nice, were they?" He looked away, something close to sadness or betrayal in his eyes. "They weren't good."

"Not all of them, no." He lowered his voice. "Are there more?"

"I don't know, manling." Armitage shifted under Geneve's weight. "I remember what this place did to my tribe. They're ... *gone*. None died a warrior's death. There was no honor in the fight." He gave another massive sigh. "I don't know if there are more magic boxes, but I would tell you if I knew."

"Good enough." Meriwether stepped away. "One left to destroy. Too easy."

From far off, they heard a roar, and an answering boom of thunder.

Sight of Day perked up a little, one ear flicking. *{There's the small matter of the dragon.}*

Meriwether gave a long, slow nod. "Let's get out of here."

THEY PADDED AROUND THE ANCIENT TEMPLE, TRYING TO FIND A WAY out. The boom of thunder and roar of an angry dragon reached them no matter where they were. Meriwether wondered about the kind of fight you'd have in you if you went toe-to-toe with a giant, fire-breathing lizard. *Those Knights aren't made of paper, and that's the Three's truth.*

Getting outside was hard, until it wasn't. They didn't want to go out the way they came in, because there was a dragon, high-ranked Knights, and Three-knows how many Vhemin. They spent their time looking for a back door. Meriwether felt there should be one. He led them through the warren of the temple. Ten minutes' walk took them to a dead end, which left Meriwether astonished. "This isn't fair."

"It's a wall. Nothing fair or unfair about it." Armitage laid Geneve on the cool floor. She lay like the dead, eyes sightless, only the slight rise and fall of her armor showing she was still with them.

"But who puts a passage to a *wall?*" Meriwether held his hand out to the wall in a *see?* gesture. "There should be a door."

Sight of Day put his ear against the wall. *{It sounds thinner here.}*

"How's something sound thin?" Meriwether cocked his head. "It's a wall. Doesn't sound like anything."

The cat gave a half-smile. *{The dragon's anger is louder.}*

"Out of the way." Armitage shouldered the Feybrind aside, but without rancor. He hefted his club, then took a one-two-three spinning step, swinging with all his might. The club shattered. The wall didn't seem to care; it wasn't even chipped. "Fuck. That was my favorite club."

"Didn't you take it from a dead Vhemin?" Meriwether tried to fit the blade of his knife between where the glass walls met the white stone-like material of the outer wall, but the gap was too fine to get the edge in. "Oh, come *on.*"

"I did. Didn't stop it from being a damn fine skull basher." Armitage dropped the splintered haft, then shouldered Geneve like a sack of yesterday's laundry. "What now?"

Meriwether sighed, then looked back the way they came. He was *sure* this was a back door, but whatever mechanism the ancients had for opening it didn't work, or wouldn't for them. *Eight hundred years* is *a long time*. There'd be another way out, surely? "I guess we head back that way—"

The wall exploded in a shower of white stone. Meriwether took a head-sized chunk to the chest and crumpled to a heap. He saw Sight of Day pirouette beneath a slab the size of a cart that pinwheeled from the wall and vanish in a shower of glass as it tumbled into the temple interior. Armitage curled around Geneve, rocks and chips showering him like hard rain.

The broken wall revealed ... another wall. It was a ridged, dark red affair. Meriwether's brain cycled through the options. He started with *that's weird*, and moved onto *why do they make walls inside walls? The stone's pretty good, right?* Eventually he managed to draw a wheezing breath, coughed out a cloud of dust, and spat onto the chalk-strewn floor. The ridged wall slid to the left a half meter, and that's when Meriwether's brain started working right. He spoke quietly, hearing the fear and urgency in his tone. "That's the dragon. It's *right there*. It's outside, and we shouldn't move or make any noise."

Sight of Day stared at him with golden eyes that said, *you're an idiot. {Of course it's the dragon. It landed here with immense force. Once it's stopped being stunned, it'll probably look for who's making all the stupid comments.}*

"Hah," Meriwether said, then coughed. He clapped hands over his traitorous mouth. *{Sorry.}*

Armitage straightened, then shifted Geneve to his other shoulder. He took a step back from the scaled hide blocking their exit. "I don't want to go out this way."

Meriwether brushed himself off. *Go on. I'll hate myself until the end of my days if I don't.* He stepped past Armitage and Sight of Day, hand out. His footsteps slowed as if his feet didn't want to die regardless of what his brain suggested, and he forced himself forward. Meriwether's heart hammered in his chest so much it made his hand shake, but he reached for the dragon's hide.

It was hard, like steel, but warm, as if the dragon burned deep inside. The scales were smooth, like the finest glass, and were just as sharp where they ended. "Ow!" He yanked his hand back, fingers in his mouth, sucking blood from a cut. With a little more care, and a little less caution, he put his hand against the dragon. He could feel the slow *thud, thud* of a massive heart. Meriwether leaned closer, ear toward the beast, and heard the *hiss, huff* of god's forge bellows breathing. The sound was deep, something you almost felt. He'd never been beside such a majestic creature.

The scales shifted, and Meriwether took five steps back very fast indeed. The dragon slid away from the breached wall. Sand swirled in the wake of its passage. A massive head swung to the hole. Meriwether felt like there was no finer time to wet himself, but no part of him wanted to move, not even his bladder. The dragon's skull was bigger than Armitage's bear, Beck. Its eyes were the size of plates, and glowed a sullen, angry red. Fangs like swords protruded from its jaws. A flanged ridge of bone sat at the base of its skull, and Meriwether saw a line of runes imprinted in the scaly hide. They glowed the same vermilion of the creature's eyes.

Its jaws cracked open, no more than two handspans. Not enough for it to get Meriwether inside, but enough to show more teeth, which took the terror to a new level. It rotated its head sideways like a curious dog, then stepped back from the hole in the wall.

Meriwether tried to say something, but nothing came out except a cough. He held up a hand, steadying his breathing. "Are you ... *laughing* at me?"

The dragon *chuff-chuffed*, shook its head, then vaulted for the sky. Meriwether felt the ground shake as it launched. It made him stumble, and sand swirled like a storm as massive wings beat sky. Then, silence. The dragon was gone.

"Did you *see* that?" Meriwether spun, and found the corridor empty except for piles of rubble and dust. "Guys?"

AFTER SIGHT OF DAY AND ARMITAGE RETURNED, THE FORMER'S TAIL curling about his legs like it was shy, the latter trying to look like he'd just taken a stroll to walk things off, they headed outside. The desert had become chill, and Meriwether shivered in his borrowed clothes. They snuck around the temple's massive circumference, trying to be small and inconspicuous.

They scuttled around a low lump of ruin, regaining sight of the encampment in front of the temple. Or, what was left of it. Where tents had lain in neat rows, lines of burning fabric lit the night. Three people stood amid the ruins. The black-armored Nicolette held two glass blades low and ready. She still wore no helmet, showing a slight mocking smile.

Two others faced her, helmets on, but Meriwether knew who they were by how they stood. Tall, broad Israel was shoulder to shoulder with lean Vertiline. Nicolette was about fifty meters from the temple's entrance. Israel and Vertiline held their peace twenty meters from her, but they weren't there to hug. Israel held a massive two-handed glass blade, and Vertiline's thinner sword caught and held firelight within. Her shield was close to her body, helmeted face peering over the lip at Nicolette.

There was no one else upright. "Ikmae's sometime cock," Meriwether hissed. "Everyone else is dead."

Nicolette stood like she could do this all day. *//DROP YOUR WEAPONS.//* Meriwether felt the command in the words, his own knife somehow suddenly on the sandy ground beneath his feet. Geneve groaned, while Sight of Day's tail lashed, but the Feybrind tightened his grip on his bow.

Vertiline swayed, blade trembling, but Israel shook his head. "The Sway is a cheap trick, witch. The Light knows our cause. It won't let us fall." He took a step forward. *//YIELD.//*

Meriwether felt the same command in the Valiant's words. He wanted to drop to his knees, head bowed, but Nicolette laughed. "The Sway isn't cheap or a trick, but it won't work on me. I'm a Champion of Light, Knight Valiant Israel, and you will do as you're commanded. *Drop. Your. Sword.*"

The massive blade in Israel's hands didn't waver. "The hard way, then."

Vertiline stirred. "I was hoping for something easier."

"Strength, Tilly." Israel didn't look away from Nicolette. "I'm here."

"As you've always been." Vertiline flourished her blade. "No better person to end things with."

Sight of Day tugged Meriwether's sleeve. *{When they are done fighting, the black witch will come for us.}*

"She's a Champion, not a witch." He kept his voice to a murmur.

The cat shook his head. *{The big Knight spoke true. He faces a witch, not one of his own.}*

"Sounds like bullshit," Armitage hissed, but without a lot of conviction. "Looks like a Knight. Talks like a Knight. Uses Knight powers. Seems like a Knight to me."

The three combatants circled each other. Israel and Vertiline stayed close to each other, their mutual orbit bringing them closer to Nicolette. Sight of Day shook his head. *{If she's a Knight, the temple would have opened to her long ago.}*

"They needed a sinner," Meriwether said. "I mean, someone like me."

"Bet they've got one or two stashed away," Armitage mused.

Nicolette let her smile drop like an unwanted baby, then stabbed her blades into the sand. She held her hands wide. She turned a slow circle to keep Israel and Vertiline in view, and as her gaze passed over their position, Meriwether saw her eyes were green. Not a gentle color of the hills, but a rancid, glowing insistence. Her lips moved without sound.

A clank from the right caught Meriwether's attention. A pile of Vhemin lay in a charred heap. One threw its arm high, clawing the sky. "Three's mercy, but he's alive."

Armitage took a step forward, but Sight of Day put a hand on his chest. *{He doesn't live.}* The cat seemed impossibly sad for a moment, his golden eyes carrying the misery of the world for a moment. *{He hungers for death. His pain is without end.}*

The Vhemin shifted his load of Geneve absently. "Are you saying—"

Another Vhemin in the pile moved. It rolled over, got to its hands and knees, then stood with a forlorn cry. Israel and Vertiline stopped their circling, glancing at the monsters. Israel spun back to Nicolette. "It is *forbidden*, Nicolette. Your soul is forfeit for this heresy!"

The black-armored woman shrugged. "My soul was forfeit a long time ago, Valiant."

Israel shook his head as if confused, then squared his shoulders. He and Vertiline charged Nicolette. Meriwether watched in horror as more of the dead Vhemin lurched upright, but they weren't the real threat. A Smithsteel-armored figure, the metal encasing him charred, sprinted from behind Nicolette toward the two Knights. He was joined by another, then a third.

The black-armored witch called the dead to fight by her side. Glass flashed as Israel and Vertiline fought a growing tide of the fallen.

Meriwether hunkered down, beckoning the others down. "Okay, here's what we're going to do."

"We should run," Armitage enthused.

"No." Meriwether rubbed his face. "They'll find us. Tracks in the sand. We're going to sit right here, in plain sight. We're not going to make any noise. We'll do it for as long as we need to."

Sight of Day turned his sad golden eyes on Meriwether. *{Can you do it for that long?}*

Meriwether nodded. "If the option's dying at the hands of the dead, sure."

"Do what?" Armitage looked confused but set Geneve beside Meriwether. The Knight Adept groaned, one eyelid twitching.

"This." Meriwether closed his eyes, picturing what he needed. A sand dune about two meters high, four wide. Big enough to hide beneath. He imagined the sand behind them, once tracked with their footsteps, smooth and clean as if they'd never stepped there. When he opened his eyes, they sat in gray shadow.

Armitage looked around in wonder. "Fuck me."

Sight of Day's ears were flat against his head, but the cat nodded. *{You've covered us in the seeming of a dune. You have some small use after all.}*

Meriwether held his hands up for their attention. *{No noise. I hide what people see, but not hear.}*

Geneve, as if following someone else's script, groaned. Armitage made to cover her mouth, but Meriwether pushed him aside. He laid Geneve as gently as he could. Her legs ran one way, his the other, as they sat side by side. He held her armored body close, lips to her ear. "Hush, Geneve."

The dead fought against the living, and she groaned again. Her arm twitched, as if it wanted to hold steel and fight by her friends. Die beside them, if need be. Meriwether tried again. "Geneve, it's Meri. You're a long way from home. We all are. But it's okay. I've got you."

She didn't answer, but her arm relaxed, and her head lolled against his cheek. *Good enough.*

The sound of massive wings beat the air. Meriwether craned his head, taking in the dragon's black bulk against the night sky. *By the Three, it blocks out so very many stars.* The dragon's maw opened, fire jetting into the night sky. It tucked its wings close, diving for the ground.

The beast landed with a thud Meriwether felt everywhere. It crunched through the melee, raising its head and spewing fire against a horde of the dead. There was so much flame it looked like a liquid torrent. The dead flashed to ash.

Nicolette drew her swords from the sand. "Dragon. You belong to me."

The beast swung that massive head toward her. It seemed to study her for a long time, but Meriwether knew it was only seconds. The dragon reared, then blasted fire on the black-armored woman. Meriwether noticed the runes about its head glowed a brilliant red as it did this. Nicolette's swords held in a perfect guard, blades crossed, and the fire spilled around her.

Israel and Vertiline backed away from the fight. The Knights looked between the dragon and the barbecued dead as they retreated. *Not stupid, those Knights. Wish I could join them, if only they didn't want me dead.*

Nicolette straightened when the fire abated. "You need a lesson, cur." She ran at the beast, blades flashing. The dragon watched her come, head tilted as if curious. Her blades struck its armored fore claw with a sound like a glacier breaking.

A single dark scale spun across the sand, and the dragon surged upright, roaring, then it slammed forward, claws hitting Nicolette. The beast grabbed her, slamming the faux Knight into the ground, then tossed the woman in a pinwheeling arc off into the night. Meriwether watched her body sail a very long way before he lost sight of it.

Sight of Day stroked his chin. *{Dragons can throw things very far indeed.}*

Armitage sniffed. *{Dragons can also take a hit from a Champion without breaking.}*

Meriwether didn't want to let Geneve go to join the conversation, but he agreed with them. He breathed in the closeness of Geneve and focused on keeping their illusionary shelter together. Despite the focus demanded, one thought kept coming up.

How did the ancients, who could bring dragons to life, ever fall?

Chapter Forty-Three

The world swayed, a gentle rolling insistence that kept her mind at peace. Geneve saw light, then dark, followed by more light. Her body hurt, but her soul felt at peace, like she'd given away the piece of herself she didn't want or need. She didn't remember her failure commanding the Storm, how she let Israel and Vertiline down, or why she traveled with a sinner. If she'd died in this state she'd have thought, *it's enough*.

The gentle rolling led to discomfort. Light became heat, and the dark cold, until Geneve was reminded of having someplace to be, and something to do there. Her eyes were dry, and when she tried to rub them, her fingers found cloth. She pawed at her face and pulled away old, rough fabric that smelled of a beggar man who should be king.

Her eyes couldn't make sense of what they saw. The hills should've been green but were rolling heaps of yellow sand. The horizon held the jagged teeth of mountains, but no dusting of snow. She looked at the cloth she'd pulled from her head. An old cloak, worn by time and misery, to be used a few times more before being cast aside. Her hands were well callused, but not covered in armor, which was wrong. They should be covered by gauntlets, holding steel against enemies of the Light.

Geneve swayed, but it wasn't lightheadedness. There was a beast beneath her, a blue roan who pranced too much and didn't take her seriously at all. Leading them was the beggar man. His skin should've been pale, but was burnt a bright red. The shawl he usually wore was in her hands. It protected her from the sun.

She turned, seeing a monster with snake eyes and lizard skin. He led a bear. Both were huge brutes. Geneve's fingers twitched, wanting a blade, but the motion was loose and sloppy. No Storm would answer her call with such imperfection. *He's not a monster, but a man. I broke him on the sands because I was afraid.*

Geneve turned the other way, finding a cat man with golden eyes. The cat watched her, a half-smile on his lips. When his hands moved, they were beautiful, making words in her mind. *{Good morning. How's the hangover?}*

She scratched her head, sand cascading like an avalanche. "Sight of Day?"

The beggar man spun like he'd been stung. "Geneve!"

Her lips moved, trying to find a name. "Sinner?"

His face fell, and he nodded. "Aye."

"Don't be a huge dick," the monster suggested. "He's burnt lobster-red because he insisted on giving you the cloak. Least you could do is return a smile without the insults."

She looked at the rags she held. "I don't remember."

"No, that's because you were walking like the star-touched." The monster scratched his armpit. "Not my business, Knight. I figured myself for the asshole here, is all."

"Are you?" Geneve felt the rebuke, holding it close. *He expects more of me.* "I don't remember a lot of things."

The beggar man gave her a gentle smile, small and bright like a mountain flower. "Not really."

Geneve slid from her horse. *This is Tristan, and he's carried me for two years without failing.* She walked to the sinner. He eyed her, took a step back, then held his ground, chin up, as if daring her to ... what? What was he afraid of? She halted a few steps from him. Geneve could see the burned skin, the cuts on his face where she'd marked him, and knew beneath his rags his body was scarred by others just as ungentle.

The wind shifted, and she caught his scent. Not stale, despite the sand. Honest dirt and road grime, and something underneath that tickled her memory. She remembered his voice: *You're a long way from home.*

She reached for his chin. He flinched, then held still, like a horse that had a bad master before finding a good one. His beard was strong, not the scrabbly wisps most his age got. "I know you."

He took her hand in his, pushing it down. "Aye. We've shared the road." She watched his lips move, remembering them next to her ear. *We all are. But it's okay.*

"And he," Geneve pointed without looking, "is a Vhemin. His name's Armitage. The Feybrind is Sight of Day."

The beggar man nodded. Nervous, wary, but hopeful. "That's right." It felt more than right. She remembered his arms about her as he said, *I've got you.* It felt like the sand beneath her shifted. He caught her as she stumbled, held her upright, and made sure she didn't tumble to the ground. His hands on her arms reminded her of things she'd seen without understanding. Memory returned. The dead, walking. A dragon in the sky. A black-armored witch fighting her friends. Through it all, his voice by her ear. *Geneve, it's Meri.*

"Meri?" At his nod, she grabbed him, pulling him close. Geneve rocked like she was afraid of the dark.

He held her, but after a moment let out a small *urk*. "Gently."

She laughed, pulling away. "You're ... alive? But I saw you fall. The Three demanded us both."

"It felt like it." He left a trailing hand on her arm, and she felt the uncertainty of his touch. "I guess we didn't taste good."

Geneve felt awkward eyes on her and let Meri go. She turned to their companions. Sight of Day stood with a hand on the nose of his horse, Fidget. Armitage scratched Beck's neck, horror teeth bared in a bright shark-toothed grin. She stepped away from Meri, eyes down. "What happened?"

"Two days," Armitage said. "Two days we've dragged your carcass across this shitty desert, that's what happened. The cat said we should toss you in a ditch, but I said keeping you around in case we got hungry was a better idea." He winked, in case the joke wasn't apparent.

Last time he tried a joke, I broke his arm. "Even the Three won't take me."

Sight of Day gave Armitage a little side-eye. *{The Vhemin is confused by the heat. I said we should eat him. Lizard tastes good if cooked just right.}*

Armitage roared his laughter. "Go fuck yourself." But there wasn't rancor in it, and it brought another memory to Geneve. *These two are sworn enemies, but they travel with me. Sight of Day still needs my help, but Armitage already had it. Why is he still here?*

She walked the three steps to the monster's side. He stared down at her, all muscled bulk and unflinching stare. "Your people are gone."

"That's right. What of it?"

"I'm sorry."

"Not your fault." He sniffed, then spat. "That cunt Nicolette, though. She and I are gonna have words."

Meri fussed in Tristan's saddlebags, fetching a canteen and some dried meat. She felt hunger twist her stomach like a fist, and gnawed meat like a feral thing. The water was flat and tepid, and nothing had tasted so good. The beggar man who should've been king laughed, helping her with the canteen. "Easy, Red. *Easy*, I said. Don't drink too fast. You'll be sick."

It didn't slow her much. Once she'd eaten two handfuls of jerky, she took stock. Tristan, Fidget, and Beck were with them. Her sword, Requiem, hung from Tristan's saddle, next to the loose loop of leather that was Tribunal's holster. Her shield was gone, lost to time like her helmet, but the rest of her armor was lashed to her horse. She let her fingers trace the metal, feeling the smooth hardness of it.

Armitage no longer had his club, but it didn't seem to bother the monster. Sight of Day kept his bow and slender blade, and of the four, looked the least touched by the road, despite having seen one of the People's villages destroyed.

A small sack she didn't recognize hung beside her sword and scattergun, but it'd keep. "Where is Chesterfield? Troubles?"

Meri scratched his beard. "Gone."

"Stolen?"

"I don't think so." He patted his shirt, then rummaged in a pocket, producing two small scraps of paper. They were folded, closed with a seal. "These were on Tristan's saddle when we got back to our camp. Half the horse feed was gone, along with the two horses. These were left in return."

She took the letters from him. One held her name in Israel's powerful script: GENEVE. The other was labeled in Tilly's flowing hand: *Gen*. Geneve ran her thumb under the seal of Israel's note, and read.

> *We will lead the dead away, then catch up. Be safe.*
> *—I.*

No demands to surrender the sinner, or changing her path. No calling her out for crimes against the Light. She re-read the note, looking for hidden meaning, before handing it to Meri. "I don't understand."

He unfolded the letter. "Seems pretty clear to me."

"He should be ... angry."

"He's got bigger problems." Meri counted on his fingers. "The dead walk. There's a rogue Champion who commands them. Oh, and let's not forget the dragon."

Fair. Geneve opened Vertiline's note.

> *Thank you for the food. We were dying. Something's not right with the world. I miss you.*
> *—Tilly.*

She looked back at their trail in the sand behind them. Geneve put a hand on Tristan's saddle, meaning to vault aboard and head back. Find her friends—now so close!—who threw themselves against danger for her *again*.

The wind kissed her face. She paused, head against the saddle. Tristan's animal smell surrounded her. His tail swished, the bellows of his lungs working slow and easy. She was exhausted. Lack of food coupled with the Three sucking out a piece of her left her feeling ... *empty*. Geneve didn't have the strength to ride into battle. She doubted she had the strength to do much of anything. "They're going to die."

"I don't think so." Meri sounded tired. "I think if a dragon, five Knights, a Champion, and an army of the dead couldn't kill your friends before, they're not going to drop now. Also, Israel gave you an order. 'Be safe.'"

"It wasn't really an order."

"Shame he's not here to be more specific. C'mon." Geneve felt his hand on her elbow. "Get back on the horse. We're a day's ride from the mountain pass. We might make it tonight."

"And then what?" Her eyes found his. "What do we do?"

"We—"

"I tell you what we do," Armitage rumbled. "We kill a deer and eat it, that's what."

Geneve let a small smile touch her lips. As plans went, it'd do for now.

⚜

SHE WALKED BESIDE MERI, BECAUSE HER BODY CRAVED EXERCISE. "Two days?"

Sand passed, uncaring, while he chewed that over. "Yeah. You were gone for two days. We gave you water. Kept the heat off as best we could. I wasn't... *we* weren't sure if you were coming back."

"Did it happen to you?" Geneve kept her eyes forward on the mountains. She knew they grew larger with each step, but if she watched them they seemed frozen. Geneve didn't want to reach them, because when she did, she'd go back to being a Knight, and him a sinner. *The world will demand its due.*

"Not like that, but I got to talk to a dragon." He dodged her lazy arm-punch. "I'm serious. I was walking stupid for a handful of minutes at best. The temple didn't want much of me. It took more from you."

"I don't know what it needed." Geneve scratched her head. She'd never get the sand out of her hair. "I feel it, but not like a *loss*. Like, a sharing."

"That's it. But, also, oversharing, like one of Armitage's stories."

Geneve chuckled. "What did the dragon say?"

"It didn't say anything. It laughed at me."

"I can understand that."

"What's that supposed to mean?"

She sighed. "What's in the sack?" It looked about the size of a Vhemin's head, but the bag wasn't stained, so she didn't feel like it hid grisly secrets.

"What? Oh, that." He scampered to Tristan's side, fiddling with the bindings until he freed the bag. He returned to her side, holding it out. "It's a souvenir."

"You took something from the temple?"

"From outside, really. But it's not a Knight thing, and Armitage said the Vhemin don't ... just open it."

She looked at the bag, then back to him, feeling inexplicably shy. "It's for me?" At his nod, she opened the sack. Sunlight followed her fingers inside. She saw the glint of metal, felt its cool touch, and drew it out. Geneve held her prize: a helmet, but like nothing she'd seen before. Rather than have a single eye-slit cut in the metal like Tresward armor, this had a piece of black glass. It wasn't heavy like metal and glass should be, as if one of the Three held a little bit of the weight for her. "It's beautiful." She held it to her chest. "I can't keep it."

"Sure you can." He held up his hand to forestall her protest. "You're going to say something like, 'Meri, that's a relic from an ancient temple. We need to give it to the Tresward for safekeeping.' And normally, sure, I'd be on board. But, you need a helmet, and that's the only one that doesn't smell of barbecued asshole."

"Hey," Armitage growled. "Watch it. They weren't my tribe, but they were my kind."

"Also," Meri continued like the monster were klicks distant, rather than in choking distance, "it'll look good on you. Try it out."

She bit her lip, then nodded. Geneve *did* need a helmet, and she could use this for a time. She shook out her hair, then peered inside. The padding in this helmet was still soft, made of a bizarre material that looked like cotton but yielded like a fat man's paunch. She slipped it on, not sure what she'd be able to see with the black glass visor.

From within the helmet, the world looked much the same as before, but both sharper and less bright. Geneve turned a circle, feeling slightly foolish, but also curious. From within, the black glass didn't seem dark at all. Things seemed clearer through it, like an artist drew outlines over the shapes of the world. She could breathe easily, unlike the stuffy draw of her old helm. "It's wonderful."

"Just as I thought." Meri examined her with crossed arms, lips pursed critically. "You look amazing."

She laughed, then removed the helmet and brushed back a wave of red hair. "Thank you."

They walked on, and much to her chagrin, the mountains looked a little larger than before. Geneve wanted to push them away, but she wasn't strong enough for that. Not even Israel could hold back the world.

THEY MADE THE MOUNTAINS JUST AFTER NIGHTFALL. THE VHEMIN and Feybrind ranged ahead, their night sight better for the task. Armitage returned first. "There's a fucked-up hut ahead. I reckon we should stay there tonight."

"What kind of hut?" Meri looked at the cloudless sky. The Three were above, no longer in alignment, and sharing the heavens with the first twinkle of stars.

"Did I stutter? The fucked-up kind. I don't know—looks like maybe an old outpost. Or a trading center, from when you runts thought you could cross the plague lands." Armitage adjusted his pants. "Damn. I hope the cat gets a good-sized deer. I'm losing weight."

The mountain pass was more of a scraggly ravine threading between two monster hills. Geneve knew they'd left the desert behind when she spied a thin wisp of green poking between two rocks. She bent, touching the stray frond of grass. "I never thought we'd see green again."

"You'll love the hut then." Armitage stalked ahead. She stood, following. Tristan, trying to do his part, ate the single stalk before tagging along.

Fifty meters further on, shrubs struggled from the earth. Another fifty, and small trees raised boughs to the sky. Within another hundred they were in a sparse forest, and Geneve picked up the sound of running water head. She broke into a ragged run, Meri at her side.

They shouldered through the growth, arriving at the hut. A stream wound beside it, burbling its course before disappearing underground. The hut was ancient, its wooden walls bleached by sun and time alike. The windows were bare of glass, but still held shutters. A rack held a few stray sticks of firewood.

Armitage bulled his way inside, and after a moment returned. "Looks clear, I guess."

"You guess?" Meri looked between Geneve and the monster. "That's not very specific."

"There's a hive. I'll be fine, but your skin's weaker than a whore's silks. It's in the back room, so don't go there." He clicked his fingers, and Beck followed him in.

"Is he serious?" Meri looked aghast. "*Bees.*"

"Let's make a fire," Geneve suggested. "That won't sting."

He gave her a smile like they were free and went about setting up a meager camp. She joined him, working in companionable silence. Her body was sore and tired, but the stream was peaceful, and she had good companions at her back. Not Knights, but that didn't make them lesser.

Greater, perhaps, if she was being honest. They faced the same dangers she did, but with their ordinary skills. Maybe it meant their hearts were extraordinary.

By the time Sight of Day returned with a steer over his shoulders, they had a blaze going, a pot of water boiling, and the three were seated by its light. The Feybrind and Armitage set to preparing the night's feast.

Geneve looked at the sky, trying not to feel the Three's stare. She had clean water and good food coming. The gods could wait, just this once, while she shared a meal with friends.

Chapter Forty-Four

"There's nothing for it. You're going to have to cheat." Kytto scowled at her, as if his idea was her fault.

Geneve picked up a breastplate from the floor, walking it to a pile. Her Trial was next month. She was out of time. "I don't want to cheat."

"Do you want to die?"

"No."

"Then you need to cheat."

"How?" Geneve dropped the breastplate with a clatter. The Smithsteel never scratched, no matter how indelicate she was with it. "How do I beat fifty Novices who can use the Storm without it at my side?"

"That's not the hard part," Kytto said.

"It feels hard!"

"The hard part is the rest of the Trial, because we don't know what it is. There could be tigers."

"You're not helping."

"Sorry." Kytto hid a grin. "They've never used tigers."

"This isn't funny."

"I think it's funny!" Kytto barked a laugh. "You Knights and your Trials."

"I'm not a Knight." Geneve scowled. "I'm just me!"

"Good," he said, grin fading to an easy smile. "You're one of two people who don't piss me off."

"Who's the other?"

"A fair-haired maiden." He touched the side of his nose. "I'll never tell."

"What will you never tell?" Tilly stood at the base of the stairs, her customary interruption point. Geneve didn't know how she managed to creep up on them in full armor every damn time, but the Chevalier walked on surprisingly quiet feet.

"Truth to a sinner," Kytto said. "What brings you to the dungeon?"

"Not the company." Tilly walked inside with the oiled Tresward precision Geneve was used to seeing. She'd started walking a little like that herself. The Knights taught her perfection, and she learned as best she could. She didn't have Vertiline's slender poise; Geneve was strong like Kytto.

"I hope you get the plague." Kytto coughed.

"That's it!" shouted Geneve.

Vertiline eyed her, one arch eyebrow raised. "You want me to get the plague?"

"Yes! I mean, no. I mean, not really." Geneve pressed her lips into a line so she wouldn't say anything stupid. "I'm going to pass the Trial. I need your help."

"You do?" Vertiline admired a glass blade on a rack. "Why would I help you?"

"Because I know who's kiss it was to give."

Chapter Forty-Five

T hey set no guard. Exhausted as they were, they dropped off where they lay at the fireside. The night approached, cold and hard, waking Meriwether from a dream where he drowned in a sea made of doubts and fears. The night was alive with the sound of small insects singing for a mate, or whatever it was insects did at the border of a blasted desert wasteland.

He got up, eyed the stars, and decided it was about two o'clock. Too early for tea, and too late to return to sleep. Meriwether pottered about the camp, trying to move quietly. He rescued a blanket from their packs before finding Geneve. She slept, head back, one arm over her face, the other cast out as if warding off demons. Meriwether lay the blanket over her, then thought about going for a walk. Armitage lay like a dead thing on the other side of the fire pit, hugging his hot rock. Beck lay at his back. Sight of Day was harder to spot, but Meriwether eventually spied him atop the hut, curled up, tail across his nose.

Any direction was as good as another, so he set off east. The stream burbled behind him, water doing what water did, but the scrubland-meets-forest the old hut hid in was ... *different*. The trees didn't smell like he was used to, and he didn't recognize many of them. His feet led him to the edge of a short cliff, beneath which was a rocky scree.

"Not wise to wander off," Armitage growled behind him.

Meriwether gave a short scream, almost slipping into the ravine. "Khiton's beard! You scared the shit out of me."

"Eh." The monster ambled from the tree line. He seemed thoughtful, eyes hooded, but it could have been a trick of the light. Cophine's pale face watched from above, with Ikmae and Khiton shadowing her watch. "You've seen plenty things worse than me, runt. You put your hand on a dragon and didn't fill your pants."

"That was different." Meriwether tossed a stone into the ravine. It clattered a path down the slope. "Couldn't sleep?"

"Hard to sleep when there's an elephant tromping around the camp." Armitage scratched his head.

"Sorry."

The monster sighed. "No, it's me who's sorry. You're right, I was awake. I was ... thinking."

"Sounds tricky."

"Go fuck yourself."

"Smooth." Meriwether offered Armitage a stone, and the monster tossed it into the ravine, as if rocks were the new currency of thought. "Anything in particular on your mind?"

"We're going to a human kingdom." The creature selected a new stone, tossing it farther than the last. "My kind aren't welcome there."

"That's not it." Meriwether shook his head. "Your kind aren't welcome *anywhere*, friend. No, don't interrupt. You've raided from the top of the world to the bottom and back again. Not you *specifically*, but people who look like you."

"True enough," admitted the monster.

"Problem as I see it is, you're lacking *your* people. Your family died in a temple made by ancient humans like *me*, sacrificed to three gods you've got no time or patience for. You've no hearth to call your own, and that's hard for any man." Meriwether fetched another stone. It was smooth, a vein of quartz running through the surface like frozen lightning. He tossed it after the others, listening to the *click-clack-click* as it fell into the dark.

"That's not it," Armitage said.

"Then what is it?" Meriwether frowned. *I'm usually better at the whole people thing.*

"Don't know." The Vhemin grabbed a rock the size of a human skull, turning it in his hands. "Wish I did."

Meriwether watched the monster, a little uneasy. Sure, they'd shared the trail for a long time, but their alliance should be over. Since they'd completed their business the creature might as easily bash his skull in with his makeshift weapon as hug it out. "Is what's on your mind going to end in you murdering me?"

Armitage guffawed. "Not this week. Maybe not next, either. Haven't decided." His big, scaled hands clutched the rock. Tendons played under his skin, shifting as his muscles bunched. "I ran, you know."

This thing ran? *Impossible.* "From the dragon? I know. I stood in the damn temple alone after you assholes—"

"From the witch." Armitage clenched his damn rock like he was going to pop it open. "She herded us. Me, and my tribe. We tried to fight. It's what we're good at." The rock popped, a shower of stones falling between his fingers.

"She's a *Champion.* You don't fight that kind of thing. You avoid it, or—"

"I know all that." Armitage waved his comments away, then tossed a stray pebble into the ravine. "It was the last of us. We'd been sold out by another, larger clan. Bound up in chains, then tossed into cages that stank of bile and piss. Dragged across the desert. A few died on the way, but not many. Not ... enough." Snake eyes looked down. "No portals for the cattle. Made the temple. Found the doors open. The witch was waiting for us."

"I—"

"I ain't done." Armitage stared up, perhaps at Cophine's cool gaze. His eyes were bright. "When they dragged us inside, we fought. We fought *hard*, because this was the end." His fingers clenched, like he was remembering choking someone. "Didn't help. Too many of them, or too few of us. There were a handful of Knights, but nothing like your one."

"Geneve's not—"

"These were slower. Not as good with a blade. Fuck me, but I've never seen someone as good with steel as that red-haired wench." Armitage sounded like he *admired* being beaten by Geneve. "No clue why she can't call the Storm. Maybe she's like us."

"Ordinary people?"

"The cast-offs. The forgotten. The scrapings from the world's hooves. Vhemin. Feybrind. Doesn't matter. The Three deny us their gifts. Always have." He spat. "Fuckers."

"I can't—"

"Thing is, my tribe fought like demons themselves. We used tooth and fist. I killed two Knights with my bare hands." He held a hand up. "Ain't proud of it."

"Isn't it ... what you do?"

"Not me. Not ol' Armitage." He snarled a sickly smile. "Never been the favorite of the elders. I just don't see the point. You get me? Plenty of reasons to kill a man. See what's on the inside when the fighting starts. Get your hands up to the elbows in red sticky. But when there's no reason? Not much interested in that." He kicked a rock. "Imagine my surprise when the chief tells me to get help. Of all the dumb-ass decisions, she picked *me*." His voice cracked like the stone he'd broken on the last word.

The monster doesn't kill like the rest of his kind. Meriwether chewed that over while Armitage clenched and unclenched his hands. "Seems like it was the right call."

Armitage squinted, face harboring murder and suspicion in equal measure. "How you figure?"

"Most of you wouldn't have done it." Meriwether took a step back as Armitage's shoulders bunched. "I'm not trying to start a fight. Just ... listen. You send a Vhemin to a human town, what happens?"

"Killing."

"Right. Send a Vhemin to a Feybrind village, what happens?"

"Killing. Different kind, but same outcome."

"Exactly. Send a Vhemin to other Vhemin, what happens?"

Armitage growled. "More killing. Where are you going with this?"

Meriwether scratched his beard. "What happened when they sent *you?*"

"I ... got caught."

"But no killing?"

Armitage glowered. "I ain't proud. I should have beaten those runts like—"

"That's my point." Meriwether sighed, wearier than he'd been when they left the trail. "You didn't kill them. You were the *right* choice. The *only* choice. The one Vhemin among all others who wouldn't thirst for blood. Who'd find aid in a world that doesn't lend a hand to the helpless."

"Didn't help." Armitage's chin jutted like a belligerent child.

"It kind of did." Meriwether gave a small smile. "You got a Knight Adept from the Tresward to cross the desert with you. You raided a temple of the ancients. I know you didn't *save* your people, but you gave them *peace*. They saw you'd come back. That their hopes weren't wasted." He took a step toward Armitage. "That you didn't *run away*."

The monster watched him, chest working like a bellows, as if he were racing up a hill with wolves on his heels. "It's not that simple."

"Maybe not. I don't know Vhemin. But I know you." Meriwether bent, retrieving another stone. He offered it to Armitage. "I've never met someone like you, and I don't think I ever will again."

The monster took the stone, turning it over in his hand, then let it drop on the ground. He brushed off his hands. "Good talk. Let's go kill some breakfast."

BREAKFAST WAS ARMITAGE-KILLED RABBIT, AND A FEW ROOT vegetables Meriwether found going to seed behind the hut. He also found the beehive in the hut, which Beck enjoyed, but terrified everyone else. In his roaming the woods he found some wild peppermint, and thought of Geneve. He gathered it for tea.

Armitage rekindled their fire while Sight of Day prepared the rabbits. A pot of boiling water accepted the peppermint, and the smell of roasting rabbit woke Geneve. She ruffled red hair, took stock of the sun's position, and sighed without the appearance of concern.

That's new. We were on the road by dawn in the desert. It feels like we've come through a trial, and everything is less important now. "Tea?"

She nodded, taking a battered cup. The sun climbed its ladder of sky while they sipped. Sight of Day took a cup, perhaps for appearances' sake, and after blowing steam off the surface, clapped his hands. {We should talk about Ravenswall.}

"The human city? It's full of inbreds, liars, and thieves." Meriwether examined his tea. *This isn't half bad.* "I say we avoid it entirely."

{Have you ever been?}

Meriwether shuddered. "No."

{Good. We're going.} The cat swirled his cup. {We *still* have our mission. The Ledger of Lost Souls for the queen. Finding out what's amiss, and fixing,} he eyed Geneve, {what's broken.}

"I feared that's where this was going." Meriwether didn't want to hit the road, and not because Ravenswall was the queen's city. He knew the city meant Geneve donning her armor on the inside, as it were, and he'd be a sinner again. Or another footloose vagrant on the run. "Could we not?"

"Quit whining," Armitage suggested. "At least you won't get shot on sight." He paused, eyebrow raised. "Wait. Are there Knights there? They gonna shoot you?"

"The Tresward has an outpost in Ravenswall." Geneve worried her thumbnail against the rim of her cup. "The Temple Village. It's next to Lesym's Folly."

"The who now?" Meriwether blinked. "Who's Lesym?"

"A Knight, perhaps." She shrugged. "His Folly's a tower of stone beside the Tresward proper. He went in over a hundred years ago and hasn't been seen since."

"They should knock that thing down. What if a kid walks inside?" Meriwether put his tea down. It didn't taste so good anymore. "Ravenswall seems a bad place to go."

{I've been to Ravenswall. I don't remember the Folly.} Sight of Day frowned, ears at half-mast. {I'm sure I'd remember something like that.}

"Were you drunk?" Armitage leaned forward, huddling over his cup. "I forget all sorts of shit when I'm on the beers."

"I've never been either," Geneve admitted. "Tresward records say—"

"Hold up." Meriwether leaned against his pack, trying to find a more comfortable position. "The Folly isn't the real concern. The thing we should be worried about is inbred royalty. From top to bottom, royals tend to cousin-loving. I see no reason this Queen Morgan should be any different."

{You speak as if you've met royalty.} Sight of Day's golden eyes were curious.

"I've seen the world a little," Meriwether agreed, putting a little borrowed authority into his words. "Don't have much time for the blue bloods, though. Never done anything for me, and I don't see that changing." He tried to look at Geneve without moving his eyes. It turned out to be a difficult task. "Doesn't matter, though. I said I'd help, and I will. There's a debt that needs paying, and if the price is meeting a queen with an uncle-dad, I'm fine with that."

"Meri." Geneve leaned forward, then stiffened, working a crick in her neck. "There's a Tresward there. They ... there could be—"

"I know." He looked away from her, trying not to see what was in her eyes. Could be relief, which would make sense, but he didn't know if he could take it if he saw regret. "We'll be careful."

"By 'we' you mean, you fuckers." Armitage shifted, then scratched his butt. "I'm not safe in a city. I mean, I'm good for a couple hundred normal human guards, but eventually I'll get tired. It's a numbers thing."

"I've got just the idea." Meriwether stood. "If you're coming, that is."

"What kind of idea?"

"Are you coming?" Meriwether countered.

"I guess." Armitage looked at the fire. "Just until something better comes along, mind."

"I've been thinking about this a lot." Meriwether took a deep breath. "Meriwether du Reeves, at your service." He bowed, straightening to reveal fresh clothes. Shiny, black leather boots, buffed so fine you could use them as mirrors. Pants, of thick-weave cotton. A white silk shirt, cut in the northern style. Geneve's eyes widened. "Don't laugh."

"I wasn't going to." She hauled herself upright, walking a circle around him. "I've seen it before, but never all at once."

"Yeah, the runt fixes up nice." Armitage glared snake eyes. "I'm not going about looking like a fop. And I'm not going as your prisoner."

"Of course not." Meriwether picked at a ruffled cuff. "You're going as Chevalier Armitage." He held his hands out as if demonstrating wares on a table. "One suit of Tresward armor, just for you."

The air rippled, revealing a complete set of armor fit for a Knight, but in Armitage's massive size, all stacked in a pile. The monster got to his feet, ambling to the pile. He picked up the helmet. "Feels real."

"It wouldn't be a good trick if it didn't." Meriwether watched Geneve stalk to the armor. She hefted the breastplate. "It won't turn an arrow or a blade. Probably not good against harsh language either. But against prying eyes of over-inquisitive guards, it's perfect."

"What about the cat?" Armitage squinted at Sight of Day.

{Unlike you ferals, I'm welcome in human lands.} The Feybrind offered a half-smile. *{They say I'm nice to pat.}*

Geneve squatted by the armor. "I guess there's no need to delay, then." Her voice held something that might have been sadness, or perhaps just weariness.

She'll be happy to see the end of this quest. Even Knights wear out. "No. I can't keep it up forever, but until we get to an inn with a room, it'll be no problem."

"What if you get knocked out or killed?" Armitage kicked a pauldron and watched it spin into the trees.

"I'm not planning on that, and neither should you."

"I said I wouldn't kill you for at least two weeks, but I figure it's an important question. Someone might beat me to it," the monster grumbled.

{I suggest we try to avoid killing each other until we've at least met the queen.} Sight of Day shook his head, like he was surrounded by an imbecile circus. *{Also, do not get too close to humans, Armitage.}*

"I smell bad?"

The cat's tail swished. *{Your eyes will give you away.}*

The monster grinned. "Sure, but it'd be a fabulous fight to go out on, wouldn't it?"

* * *

RAVENSWALL WAS THE QUEEN'S CITY. CAPITAL OF THE KINGDOM OF Ors'en, shining white walls bordering docks that rivaled the best in the world. Beggars shat gold and princes donated time to charity, if you believed everything said about it.

Meriwether didn't. Not even by half. Queen Morgan was beset, or so the whispers said, by incompetent advisors. She had no allies, her throne on uneven legs, and was set to topple at any moment. He didn't really believe that, because the rumors spread like a carpet of rot since her father died. That was a good five years ago, a mighty long time to sit a throne ready for collapse.

No, the real fear was that she was too clever by half, and clever people got themselves into mischief. Meriwether counted himself among that number, so had expertise.

It took three days to reach the city gates. They arrived midafternoon, a warm sun on their backs. North of the plague sands they left the cold winds of the south behind.

Constructing Ravenswall so close to the plague lands was sensible; it discouraged invasion forces approaching from the south. The ocean hugged its eastern approach, meaning enemies needed a navy and a great deal of enthusiasm to get in that way. Main access to the northern kingdoms was, predictably, via the north and west.

The south gate was a massive affair. A wall of stone reached skyward like an accusation against the three. Within this wall was a portcullis that would challenge a dragon, and a group of attentive guards stood out front, pikes in hand, backed up by archers on the walls.

She's showing off. Meriwether would too, if he was a twenty-year-old monarch sitting on her dead father's throne. The principle was a good one, but it didn't help them get inside.

Meri walked in the lead, du Reeves' silk billowing in the light ocean breeze. He expected the city to smell like a two-week-dead carcass, but aside from a slight fishiness, it was fine.

Armitage, Geneve, and Sight of Day rode at his back. The Vhemin sat his bear like it was just the kind of thing Knights *did*, his faux armor reflecting the sun's light just as it should. Geneve wore her Smithsteel. Both had helmets on. Sight of Day rode Fidget without apparent care, his golden eyes seeing everything at once. The only thing betraying any tension was the slight tremble in his tail's tip. It twitch-twitched every minute or so.

The line seeking entrance was not so long late in the day. A few travelers like themselves were ahead. Guards did a cursory check, but didn't put a lot of heart into it, no doubt because they'd been doing this all day, and the Kingdom of Ors'en wasn't at war.

When their turn came, Meriwether stepped up to a guard. He picked one in slightly shinier armor, as they tended toward being in charge. The guard's visor was up, a concession against the heat of the day. "Hello."

The captain eyeballed him. "Name?"

"Meriwether du Reeves."

"Du Reeves. That the fancy family from—"

"Exactly the one," Meriwether assured him. "I'm looking for—"

"I don't care who you are or what you're looking for. This is the queen's city." The guard straightened, hand holding his pike with easy confidence. "The du Reeves family don't have holdings here. Best be polite, if you know what's good for you." He looked past Meriwether, doing a double-take. "Khiton's ass crack! Is that a *bear?*"

Meriwether stepped into his eye line. "It is. This is Knight Chevalier Armitage, with Knight Adept Geneve. They rescued me from bandits from the plague lands. This Feybrind met us on the road, offering his services as a guide."

"But ... he's riding a *bear*."

"He's a Chevalier. Impossible things is their stock in trade." Meriwether tried on a brilliant smile. "I assure you, the bear is quite handy in a fight."

"Will it cause trouble in the city?"

"Depends if you imbeciles keep him waiting in the baking sun," Armitage rumbled. "Step aside."

"Of course, Chevalier." The guard captain took a nervous two steps back, then called to his men. "Let them through! For pity's sake, let them through."

And that's how they got into Ravenswall with a sinner, cat, displaced Knight, and a Vhemin monster: a lie backed by illusion. Meriwether wasn't sure why he was worried in the first place.

Chapter Forty-Six

Queensfane Village lay at the core of Ravenswall's crescent design. Geneve kept her eyes open and her mouth shut as they entered the city. They needed to pass three more walls to get to the hub of the city. Almost fifty thousand souls called this place home, and many would sell out a fallen Knight for a single silver regal.

Her helmet drew the odd passing eye, but not so much as Armitage's bear, Beck. People looked on in awe or scurried away in fear as their personal stock of courage allowed. Children followed in their wake, wide-eyed at first, then with laughter. Geneve felt her shoulder blades tense until it felt like they'd meet in the middle.

"Relax," Meriwether suggested from where he strode by Tristan's neck. His shiny boots walked the cobbles easy enough; she'd never have guessed they were fake.

"I don't—"

"Because nothing draws the suspicious eye like a suspicious person." He winked. "You belong here. Your city, your mission. Trouble will come soon enough without looking for it."

He's right. If the Three meant to cast her down here in Ravenswall, then she'd fall. But their mission was to help the Tresward, weed out corruption at the highest level, and return things to the way they should be. If they failed... *Life without Meri.* She bit her lip, thankful her helmet kept eyes off her face. *He's nothing to me. Just a vagrant conning the world. A sinner, stealing truth from the Three.*

The words sounded so good she almost believed them and hated herself for it. A different, quieter voice spoke at the back of her mind. *He's been a good and loyal friend. Meri's agreed to help the Feybrind no matter the cost to him. He held me in a desert while the dead hungered and hasn't even asked for thanks.*

Those words rang of truth, but her heart felt sick to hear them. A Knight could never be *anything* to a sinner. Not friend, or ... something more.

"This will do nicely." Meriwether broke her train of thought, and she looked up, startled. They'd arrived at the front of a massive inn. It had the look of luxury: drapes were visible through clear glass windows. Lazy smoke curled from three chimneys. The main door was polished oak. A sign inlaid with copper proclaimed it the *Half-full Chalice.* A wide area welcomed their horses in, with clean stablehands ready for their reigns.

Ready, at least, until they saw the bear. Armitage slung himself off Beck's back, shooing a lad away. "I'll tend him."

"What does he eat?" the boy asked.

"Small children," Armitage rumbled. He crouched before the terrified stablehand. "You're too big, though. How about a ham hock?" The boy nodded like his head would pop off, then ran off. Armitage hustled Beck into a stall, ignoring the bear's grumbling. "Be quiet. I'll be just inside."

Geneve wondered how she'd never known Vhemin to be caring. *This one is different. Special, like your sinner.* She cringed. *Like Meri. And like Sight of Day. They don't command the Storm or Sway, but they sit in your heart anyway.*

Meriwether was waiting by the door. "Coming, Knight Adept?"

She nodded, following on his heels. Sight of Day and Armitage brought up the rear. The inn's common room was a confusion of bright light and loud noise, a contrast to the lonely quiet of the desert lands. For a moment, she missed the sand, its desolation, and its peace.

Meri leaned against the bar, a golden sovereign spinning between his finger and the bartop. The innkeeper watched the coin as if hypnotized. Geneve took off her helmet, shook out her hair, and joined his side. "Is there a problem?"

"No problem," Meri assured her. "Keller was telling me about the menu, and I don't think I can decide." The coin continued to spin between his nimble fingers. "What's best?"

The innkeeper—Keller—looked between the coin, Geneve, and Meri. "Aye, uh. That is, I mean. There's boiled mutton and soft cheese. We've had a load of pickled oxen come this morning, and fresh leeks from the docks. My lad's got a brace of pheasant, and we've done those with pear. The lamb stew is excellent, but I'm also partial to the eggs and chestnut bread." The coin continued its travels. "We, uh, also stock a fine selection of regional wines."

"None of that Tebrani nonsense?" Meri leaned close to Keller, as if conspiring. "I can't stand their reds."

"Of course not, master du Reeves."

Meri beamed. "Call me Meri." He cast a glance at Geneve. "All my best friends do."

All his best friends. Geneve tried to find something that wouldn't make her sound like a hick from the outlands. "I like the sound of pheasant."

"So do I, but a bird's not going to go very far," Armitage rumbled. He'd snuck up quietly for a big man, but of course his armor wasn't *real*. It didn't creak like it should.

{*We've not had lamb on the road. I like lamb. Things that stupid shouldn't taste so good.*} Sight of Day's golden eyes held mischief.

"Begging your pardon, but I don't understand the People's handspeak." Keller bobbed his head, as if he'd offended Queen Morgan herself. "Lamb and pheasant, and..?"

He left the question hanging. Meri scooped up the coin in a fist, and when he opened his palm, the gold nestled beside a silver regal. "Why not send up one of everything. We'll need the top floor, of course."

"Of course," Keller agreed, eyes fixed on the coins. When Meri put them on the bar, the innkeeper made them vanish as if by magic.

Meri headed through the crowd. Geneve spied a woman sharing a plate of meat with a shorter man, both intent on a conversation about something *terribly* important. A man leaned by the common room's hearth, looking down his nose at Geneve as if her Adept sash were beneath him. She felt her fingers clench.

"Easy," Meri said, and she realized he'd materialized by her side. "That's Jorni. Perog," he pointed with his chin at a serving boy, "said he's a real jerk, but a wizard at the forge. Don't hit him, because he'll have powerful friends, and we don't. Not until we meet the queen."

"I wasn't going to—"

"You were about to punch him in the teeth," Armitage said. "If you didn't, I was. He makes my skin itch."

{Could be the sand.}

The stairs welcomed them. Two short flights and they were on the top floor. Meriwether turned a key in the lock, and with a click, they were in paradise. Private rooms lay off a central area with its own fireplace. Geneve spied two rooms with what looked like baths. Long couches waited, and low tables held a selection of candied fruits and nuts. "Is this ... heaven?"

"It's a middle of the road tavern in a nice neighborhood." Meriwether helped himself to a fig. "Upper Whitestone Avenue, I think the sign said. Nice place to live if you can afford it."

"It is," she breathed. "I'm going to have a bath."

"We could eat—"

"After a bath." Geneve slung Requiem from her hip, dropping Tribunal beside it. She shed armor all the way to the baths. Hot water, soap, and heaven awaited.

❦

SLEEP WAS DEEP. BREAKFAST WAS DELICIOUS. EGGS AND SALTED pork, thick crusty bread, and cheese. The four ate like it was their last meal. Meri smelled like roses after his bath, and Armitage smelled less like sand, which was a step in the right direction. Sight of Day still smelled like cinnamon, despite not having taken a bath.

"How do we get to the queen?" Geneve spoke around a mouthful stacked with eggs, bread, and pork.

{I think she asked how we get to the queen,} said Sight of Day. *{She's got so much in her mouth it's difficult to tell. Perhaps it was a cry for help.}*

"We call a carriage." Meri slathered too much bread with *far* too much butter. "We don't send a messenger. We just turn up. It's what all the royal assholes do."

{He's right.}

"I'll stay here," Armitage offered. "Look after things."

"Bad idea." Meri shook his head. "If we get too far away, your glamor will fade, and then people will ask questions about how a Vhemin ate an entire Knight."

"I don't think I could do a whole Knight in a sitting," Armitage mused. "You're right, though. Encourages the wrong line of inquiry."

⁂

SHE WATCHED THEIR TRIP THROUGH RAVENSWALL THROUGH carriage windows. It took them down toward the port district, then into the walled enclosure that was Queensfane Village. The Village hugged the water, taking up half the innermost area of Ravenswall.

The other half was—or so claimed their carriage driver—given over to artisans on the queen's whim. He seemed surprised by this, as if giving over the best real estate in the city to a bunch of penniless musicians was craziness.

The castle was what she'd expected. Twin crenelated spires reached for the Three's benediction. Gardens surrounded the keep, tended in what was no doubt a pleasing style. Geneve didn't have time to garden. She knew what grass to feed a horse looked like, and that knowledge served her well.

A man in a rich red robe met them at the main entrance. There were guards *everywhere*. The queen's man eyed Sight of Day, Armitage, then Geneve. "No weapons inside the queen's presence."

"We're not armed," beamed Meri. "Do we look like rubes from the marshes?"

The man sniffed. "Knights like to come prepared."

"And prepared they are. Prepared, I'll say, for the queen's fine hospitality." Meri ran fingers through his freshly trimmed beard. "Where is the old girl, anyway?"

The man's eyes bulged. "Queen Morgan is—"

"Not her, you imbecile. Bela Ernan, Keeper of her Secrets." Meri smiled on, like this was all part of the play.

Geneve shifted her weight. "Lord, uh, du Reeves—"

"Because Bela Ernan is the one who makes sure only the right people get into the queen's presence. You're not her." Meri steamed on. "Unless you've gotten *very* good with the rouge, in which case, I apologize, Keeper Ernan."

The red-robed man swallowed, eyes wide. "Bela—"

"She's listening, isn't she?" Meri turned, arms wide. "Have you seen enough?"

A woman stepped out from the shelter of a decorative suit of armor. She was old, yes, but unstooped by time. She strode forward on shoes that *clacked* against the marble floor. "Du Reeves, is it?"

"Yes."

"And," her eyes roamed them, "two Knights and a Feybrind?"

"Yes. The Feybrind is known to the queen, because she sent him to find *me*." Meri beamed. "I'm so glad we got to the end of this quickly. I'd hate to have spent the day in a waiting room, only to be told to come back tomorrow."

The old woman peered at the Feybrind. "Sight of Day?"

{Hello, Keeper. It's been a long time.} His golden eyes held warmth. *{I come on the queen's orders, but also those of the Feybrind Kingdom. We're here to stop the end of all things.}*

Meri's smile caulked a bit. "A long time? You know each other?"

"Fifty years," Bela said.

Fifty ... years? Sight of Day doesn't look old at all. Geneve stepped forward. It was time to get to business, before Armitage was discovered, or something else happened. "I'm Knight Adept Geneve of the Tresward. We're here to help."

Chapter Forty-Seven

"You want to go to an apothecary?" Vertiline drove the wagon, reins loose in easy hands. "What's this got to do with a kiss?"

"You love Israel," blurted Geneve.

Vertiline snorted. "You're fifteen. You know nothing of love."

"Fourteen."

"Exactly my point." The Chevalier's pale cheeks held no hint of flush. "Out of curiosity, and merely to pass the long, wearying journey, why would you say that?"

"Israel and Kytto don't like each other." Geneve counted on her fingers. "But they work together to help me."

"So?"

"Because you need them to." Geneve looked at the floorboards beneath her feet.

"Oh, wise fourteen-year-old, why would I love Israel if I tried to kiss Kytto?"

"It was twenty years ago."

"Are you going to make my points for me the whole journey?"

Geneve smirked. "You wanted Israel's attention. The Smith is exactly his opposite. You tried to pull him into it."

Vertiline looked carved from marble. "There's no chance that's true."

"There's a small chance," Geneve argued. "It's okay. I'll never tell."

"Good, because spreading lies is likely to get you murdered in your sleep." Vertiline offered a small smile, like a peace offering for words without intent. "There would never be time for me and Iz, anyway. The Tresward needs us to stand against the dark." Her words were bitter.

"Why do you stay?" Geneve swiveled to face the Chevalier. "You don't like it here. You don't agree with how it works."

"Fourteen-year-olds should learn to keep their opinions to themselves."

"Fourteen-year-olds might be dead in a month," Geneve countered. "My dying wish is to know the truth of the heart." Vertiline muttered something like, if-you-don't-die-at-Trial-I'll-kill-you-myself. "What was that?"

"More wishing." Vertiline sighed. "Things are … complicated, Geneve. There are questions the Tresward have no answers to. They don't tell you why a good man won't look at you, or why a bad man won't either."

"Kytto's not bad." Geneve shook red hair. "He just seems that way."

"The wisdom of youth."

"Wisdom is wisdom."

"That sounds like something Iz might say." Vertiline's tone was wistful. "It's a shame I can't leave you in the wilds to die of hunger."

Geneve grinned, facing forward. The wagon rocked beneath her. One less secret to have over her as she went to her grave.

Chapter Forty-Eight

T he path to the throne room wasn't direct. Queen Morgan didn't provide a convenient route from the front door to her throat. Near as Meriwether could tell, she closeted herself behind six sets of vaulted doors, each with six guards. Thirty-six fellows and a lot of wood and steel. It spoke to a learned sense of caution.

The guards were what you'd expect: steely-eyed, hard-faced, and holding weapons in a way that said, *I know how to use this, and I mean to*.

Naturally, they had an escort. The largest man Meriwether had ever seen held the rear. He made Israel look like a dwarf rabbit, but couldn't match Armitage's bulk. The guard kept puffing out his chest and other nonsense if the Vhemin looked his way, as if claiming a piece of him should the action start.

Armitage paid him no mind. The Vhemin trundled along, eyes front, faux helmet on, but Meriwether swore he caught a glint of grinning shark teeth in there somewhere. *By the Three, he's enjoying this.*

The connecting corridors also held ten guards apiece, meaning a standing contingent of ninety-six guards just to get a job interview. Meriwether wondered why Morgan didn't make it a round century until they reached the throne room. The queen sat atop her throne, with four guards at the base of lush carpeted steps leading to her.

And there it is. At least someone here cares about symmetry and order.

The guards at the base of the throne weren't like the lackeys outside. Two men and two women with black armor, bearing the queen's raven crest in bright silver. No helmets, and no welcoming smiles either.

The queen herself looked down on them with all the haughtiness a twenty-two-year-old monarch could. Meriwether admitted, it was quite a lot of haughtiness; she had a talent for it. Morgan was pale-skinned like Vertiline, with hair as black as the ravens on the drapes in the throne room. Ice-blue eyes looked from a face that captured beauty in a way that defied the inbreeding that led to her conception. Her lips were painted red, matching the long gown she wore. It was an elegant cut, revealing nothing, but demanding his attention nonetheless.

A simple silver circlet completed the package. *Silver? Not gold? I guess it goes better with black.* He cast a nervous eye at Geneve and her black sash banded with gold. *Although gold looks better on some people.*

Meriwether walked half the forty meter length of the room, then bent the knee, bowing his head. "My queen."

A slight pause, filled by the silence of Geneve *not* bowing. *Rumors say Knights only bow to the Three.* Morgan answered, her tone full of the hard strength that came from ruling a kingdom since late teens. "Rise."

Meriwether did as he was told. The guards at the base of her throne hadn't moved a millimeter. Sight of Day offered Meriwether a half-smile, then stepped past him. {*Hello, Morgan. I've brought the gift you wanted.*}

"This is the magician who's seen the Ledger of Lost Souls?" Morgan's eye traveled up and down Meriwether. He felt like he'd been measured on the finest scales and found to be a handful short.

{*He is, and so much more.*} Sight of Day's ear flicked. {*The Feybrind honor our pact.*}

Morgan stood, and swept down the stairs. As she reached her guard, they moved with her, two in front and two behind. She made it to Meriwether, measuring him again. This close, he got a chance to measure right back. The gown couldn't hide her youth, and she held a sadness behind her eyes the mask of royalty barely held in check. "Do you have a name, magician?"

"Meriwether du Reeves." He offered her a smile. "At your service. This is Knight Adept Geneve, and Knight Chevalier Armitage. You clearly know Sight of Day."

She gave a slow nod, not taking the smile. "It's curious you travel with Knights of the Tresward. Don't they consider your kind sinners?"

Meriwether felt his smile turn brittle. "Ah. There's a story behind that—"

"We *were* taking him to Judgment." Geneve took a step forward, and Morgan's guards stiffened. "On the way, Sight of Day's family were killed, his village turned to ash. Vhemin hunted Meri. They still do."

"Vhemin are like that." The queen's eyes found Armitage for a moment. "Still, your sacred duty calls for a different outcome."

Geneve took off her helmet, tousled red hair spilling down her face. "There are ... complications." Her eyes found the floor. "Sight of Day promised truth about the Justiciars."

"He offered promises that weren't his to give." The queen's voice was hard as steel. Sight of Day raised an eyebrow, hands moving as if about to speak.

"About that." Meriwether tightened the crank on his smile. "See, that's now how it works. I'm the one who's seen the Ledger. You're not really in a position to bargain."

"You'd put a scattergun to my head when the fate of the kingdom's at stake?" Her tone was incredulous.

"I don't give a shit about the kingdom. Hasn't done much for me, and I don't expect that to change. Knights roam your lands murdering people like me, and you've not lifted a finger. I care about the cat, and..." His voice seized like an old wagon axle when he remembered who he was talking to.

The tiniest hint of what might become, in another thirty years, a smile touched Morgan's lips. "Du Reeves. A northern family, if I remember correctly. A small barony. They make good wine, and poor friends. Friends with the Tresward." The might-be-a-smile fell away. "They lost a boy. Dead, on the Tresward's command." Meriwether held onto his smile like a mother clutches her dead baby to her breast.

"Meri?" Geneve's voice held a softness that cut him to the core. The way she said his name made him want to curl over a sea of memories. "Is that—"

"Probably different branch of the du Reeves family. They breed like rats." Meriwether held his voice steady through sheer force of will.

"Possibly," the queen countered. "Show me the book."

"You won't like it."

"*Show me!*" The queen's voice was like a whip, but Meriwether was used to people shouting at him. He didn't mind it so much anymore. Meriwether rolled his eyes, then held his right hand up, because a little showmanship never hurt. Morgan's eyes followed the motion, and she took a step back when he snapped his fingers.

In the air below his hand a book appeared. Not just any book, but one scholars would call a *tome*. The cover was black leather, but fine, as if made from skin not from cow or lamb. A clever trick of the leatherwork made a snarling face on the front. Green eyes glowed from sockets of malice. It was thick as Meriwether's hand, holding hundreds of pages.

The queen took a step back, hand over her mouth. "The Ledger."

"I guess so." Meriwether snapped his fingers again, and the book vanished.

Morgan pursed her lips, then locked her eyes on his face. "Is it usual to introduce the least-ranked Knight before the senior, Chevalier Armitage?"

"Ooh." Meriwether winced. *That was dumb. I'm slipping.* "My bad."

Geneve's hand clutched, as if seeking a blade. "It's not like that—"

"I'll tell you what it's like," the queen said. Her eyes were hard as stone, but Meriwether could see a glint of amusement in there. "The four of you aren't what you appear. Take off your helm, Chevalier Armitage."

Armitage's voice was quiet. "Ah, fuck."

Sight of Day hurried to Meriwether's side. {*Morgan, that might not be the best idea.*}

She waved him aside. "There are too many secrets, cat. The air is thick with them. I feel them under my feet. They hang behind the drapes in my throne room. Spies are everywhere. Assassins thirst for my blood, because I'm trying to do something *different*. I will trade you one truth for another, heir of the du Reeves estate and liegeman of *my* kingdom. You will tell me who these people are, and I will set you free."

Meriwether considered. "We're kind of fucked either way, aren't we?"

"You put a scattergun to my head, and I've returned the favor." Morgan's guards hadn't appeared to move, but all had hands on swords. It was a trick Meriwether couldn't have managed with the finest illusion. "Sometime, somewhere, some*how* we must learn to trust each other."

Meriwether turned to Armitage. "It's your call."

The monster nodded, shoulders slumped. "We've shared a good road. I'm okay with it ending here." He put massive hands on his faux helmet, lifting it from his head.

The giant guard behind him yelled, "Ware! *Ware!* Vhemin!" He made to draw his sword and managed to get a hand's breadth from his scabbard before Armitage burst into motion.

The monster grabbed the huge man, hauling him off his feet. He slammed a fist into the guard's chest. The man flew back, landing in a clatter of armor and lost opportunity. Armitage roared, spreading his arms in challenge. Sight of Day leaped to his side, standing back to back with the Vhemin. His jaws were bared, tail lashing, and his eyes held goldfire and challenge.

"Hold!" Morgan yelled. She was perhaps a quarter of Armitage's size, but her voice froze the monster and all guards in the room.

Meriwether turned a slow circle, admiring the royal guard's discipline. Some had blades almost fully drawn but froze before striking. Everyone ignored him, which suited Meriwether just fine. Geneve held a guard in a painful-looking arm bar. The man looked nervous, because she hadn't broken his arm or popped it free of its socket, so the future was bright with possibilities.

The queen sighed, as if releasing a burden. "A Vhemin, a Feybrind, a Knight, and a sinner."

"He's not a sinner," Geneve spat. She didn't release the guard.

The queen turned her appraising eye on Geneve. "And you're no longer a Knight, are you?" Morgan shook her head. "Would you release my man?"

"Will he try to kill me?"

"No."

Geneve gave a grudging nod, releasing the guard and pushing him away. "No offense."

"Ah," wheezed the guard. "None taken. And thanks for the professional courtesy of not breaking my arm when you could've."

"My truth is this," Morgan said. "I'm building an army of sinners to overthrow the corruption of this world."

"I've many questions," Meriwether admitted. "Who's the corruption? Where are the sinners? What's the Tresward going to say about this?"

"The Tresward is going to have kittens," Armitage rumbled.

"The Tresward is corrupt." The queen paced, coming to rest before Geneve. "You know this."

"I've seen it." Geneve gave a nod mired in misery. "I feel it."

"But none can stand against the power of the Light." The queen spread her hands in a *what can you do?* gesture. "Sway steals the mind, and the Storm can break castle walls. There are few Knights anymore. Most fell along the way. Do you know why?"

"Because they go in the sharp end," Meriwether said.

"Because they're commanded to go to their deaths. They're the one thing standing between this world and demons, and the Justiciars are corrupted by their foulness."

"Demons?" Meriwether did a double-take. "Fairytales. Children's stories."

"Those children's stories are seeking to rule our world." The queen's voice held fire. "I won't allow it. This is *my* kingdom. These are *my* people."

"And so..." Meriwether coughed into his fist. "You're going to challenge demons with a book?"

"No." The queen shook her head, raven hair like wings for a moment. "I'm going to take away the book that kills Knights. After that, the Knights will do what they do." Morgan gave a nod to Geneve, as if acknowledging an equal. "It's what they were made for, a very long time ago." She looked to Meriwether. "But I need the book first."

THE QUEEN ORDERED REFRESHMENTS. PASTRIES, STUFFED QUAILS, ham and cheese, and thick, crusty bread followed them into a small antechamber off the throne room.

It was cozier, but not small. A small fire crackled to itself. Comfortable-looking chairs were set about a long table able to seat thirty people who didn't like each other very much. That was about how many were here now. The queen retained her four elite guard, and the giant who'd tried to take a bite out of Armitage. She sat in a padded chair with long sweeping arms making it look like a throne, but fun-sized.

Geneve stood by the window, all pensive crossed arms, staring at the darkening sky outside. Meriwether thought he saw a dragon coasting above, but it might have been a gull depending on distance. It wasn't of consequence: if it was a dragon, they were all dead, and gulls didn't matter.

Sight of Day stood near the queen, but nearer the fire, tail curled about his legs. Armitage glowered at the guard he'd hit, who glowered back. Meriwether sat near the queen, cross-legged on a divan that promised him comfort but turned out to be a liar.

Also within the room were a gaggle of men and women who had a mix of looking lost and arrogant. Older, wiser heads tried to look down noses. Younger eyes darted to the door, as if expecting terror. These people were the Queen's Coven, magicians all. Some styled themselves witches, others warlocks. A few claimed they were cunning men, another a hedge wizard.

The queen harbors sorcerers against the Tresward's will. She's gathered as many as she could and kept them secret. Meriwether found himself admiring the young Morgan. Her father might have left her a kingdom in ruin, but she wasn't going down with the ship. If anything, she was single-handedly floating it again.

Thunder rattled the window, breaking Geneve from her brooding. "Your hospitality is generous, Your Majesty. But why are we here?"

"So you can meet the face of tomorrow," Morgan said. "We're remaking the world."

"You don't need me for that." Geneve bowed her head. "I've done too much already."

"I've always a need for good people." The queen pursed her lips. "As does the Tresward. It's your choice."

Meriwether adjusted his position on the unforgiving divan. "So ... how's it work? I show the Ledger, one of these sorcerers brings it here?"

"It's far more complicated than that," an older wizard sniffed. "You couldn't understand."

"Watch it, Sparky," Armitage rumbled. His snake eyes looked hungry. "The runt's not much to look at, but he's clever for a human. Don't underestimate him."

"Thanks, I think." Meriwether scratched his beard. "Then we destroy the Ledger?"

"Then we burn it to ash," the queen agreed.

"After that, we go on our way?" Meriwether frowned.

"You'd be welcome here too, Lord du Reeves. The Queen's Coven has no illusionist, and you'd find teachers here." Morgan sighed. "Perhaps a shred of safety, too."

{*You do have a knack for getting almost dead,*} Sight of Day said. {*Everyone needs a thing to be good at, but you should have chosen something else.*}

"Lord du Reeves?" Meriwether felt Geneve's raised eyebrow from across the room and was entirely successful at not meeting her eye. "Perhaps you'll be at home among your ... family."

Instead of glancing to the eyebrow and all it meant, Meriwether investigated the cold harbor of Morgan's gaze. "Things aren't lining up. Assassins came for me in Calterburry. Or, kidnappers. Whatever." He waved his hand. "Israel said they were assassins, and they used their tools, but they wanted to take me to your man Symonet. The lordling wanted to Harvest my gift."

"He wanted the Ledger," she said. "It gives power over the

Tresward. Imagine the threat of recording a name on its pages and seeing that Knight fall. You could compel a legion with the power of it."

{You haven't worked with many Knights.} Sight of Day's tail lashed while he *also* avoided looking at Geneve. *{They don't bend the knee and will die for the Three. They are singularly stubborn. Some would say willful.}*

Geneve bristled. "I am *not*—"

The queen breezed on. "Some would. Enough, I think, to muster a force capable of toppling a kingdom."

Meriwether nodded. "I've never met a man who couldn't be moved. You just need the right lever."

The door slammed open, a breathless youth who could only be a page coming through. He found himself at the business end of swords, pikes, and a lot of frosty stares. "Your Majesty. Forgiveness, but there is a Knight..." He trailed off, seeing Geneve.

The queen rose, long red gown flowing like water traveling upward. "Take a breath. Then another, and when you're ready, speak."

The page nodded, sandy hair wisping the air. "There is a large Knight who is very angry, and a smaller Knight who is angry at him. They're both at the gates, demanding, uh, *her*." The page raised a trembling finger toward Geneve.

"Israel," Geneve breathed. "Vertiline."

Fuck the man's timing. Meriwether stood, clapped his hands, and beamed. "Let's run."

Chapter Forty-Nine

Geneve felt the throne room was too hot. Too many eyes on her, with far, *far* too many people watching. She waited, unsure of what to do with her hands. Queen Morgan sat on her throne, her Coven arrayed about the room, with her honor guard front and center.

She'd said to Armitage, *Please hide*, and he'd said, *Fuck off*, but she'd held his hands and he'd nodded, hulking back to the antechamber. Sight of Day went with him, tail lashing, gold eyes hard like metal. The Feybrind said nothing, but his eyes reminded her of her duty.

Duty to her Tresward, and to her heart. It felt like she was splitting in half.

She felt someone by her side and turned to find Meri there. His hand found hers, gentle fingers inside her metal gauntlet. "I'm here. Whatever comes, we'll do it together."

Geneve wanted time to talk with him, to work out what this meant, but time wouldn't be held by any woman's leash. The throne room's door crashed open. A guardsman stumbled inside, falling on his rear. Another was held in the armored fist of Israel. Vertiline stalked at his side, glass blade ready to catch the light or a throat, depending on the occasion.

Israel's armor was bright, but his black sash was worn ragged, frayed ends showing the marks of the road. The gold bars were faded almost to nothing. His dark skin was burnt. Vertiline fared worse, her fair skin the bright red of a cheap harlot's hair.

The Knight Champion tossed the second guard atop the first. "Your hospitality is lacking, Morgan." Israel ignored Geneve, his eyes everywhere but on her. They narrowed as they spied Meri at her side.

"Queen."

"Excuse me?"

"*Queen* Morgan. Or Your Majesty. Some call me the Raven Queen, others Morgan the Black. A few brave souls call me Morgan the Fair, but they don't know me very well." Her tone was so frosty Geneve felt the hairs on the back of her neck rise.

Israel's throat worked, but he settled when Vertiline touched his elbow. The big Knight gave a short bow. "My apologies, Your Grace. I feared…" He looked at Geneve as his words choked off.

"She is not my prisoner." Morgan didn't laugh, or cajole, just laid the words like bricks of explanation.

"You silly man," Tilly said. "I've tried telling you for three days."

Geneve ran, armor clattering. She crashed into Israel as he curled her into a bear hug. She held him tight. "I've been so lost. I wasn't ready. I'm so sorry." Geneve tried to hold back tears, but they wouldn't be denied.

She felt his armored hand on the back of her head, smoothing her hair. His voice was thick when he spoke. "It's me that's sorry, Geneve." He didn't say what for. It didn't matter.

Geneve didn't know how long they stood like that. Perhaps seconds. Minutes, maybe, but time urged forward. Meri gave a soft cough behind her. "I, uh."

Israel released her, then set her back, both hands on her arms. His eyes were bright as he pushed her aside, marching toward the young man. "Sinner, by the authority of the Tresward, you will—"

"No!" Geneve stormed past Israel, stepping between the Valiant and Meri. She shoved her hand against his chest. "He is no sinner, Iz. He is kind, and decent, and … he took us from the temple of the ancients. His gifts kept me safe when you left me with the Vhemin.

He's been at my side when the wise thing would be to stick a knife in my throat. Meri's given his all to come *here*, so I could find what was wrong with *our* Tresward. He's helping the Feybrind, because the monsters destroyed their family. It's all connected. The Vhemin, their priests, and our, our..." She ran out of words, chest heaving.

"Knight Valiant Israel, you might want to listen to your Adept." Vertiline joined them, her blue eyes deep and calm. "What do you mean when you say there's something wrong with *our* Tresward?"

Israel's jaw clenched as he stared past her at Meri. Then he let his anger go, calming like sea after a storm. "What have you seen?"

"The Vhemin take the will from the Feybrind. They are hunting Meri, because he knows about the Ledger of Lost Souls—" Israel laughed, then cut off like a tightened faucet at Geneve's glare. "The Ledger is *real*, Iz. The queen will bring it here and destroy it."

"With more sinners?" His tone was ominous.

"With whatever I deem necessary," Morgan said. "It's my kingdom, after all. Or did you forget?"

Geneve didn't look at her. She kept her hand on Israel's breastplate. *Listen to us. Please just* listen. "Would you like to see it?"

Israel shook his head. "I count you and the sinner, but we followed four sets of tracks through the desert. Where are the other two?"

"Sight of Day, and, uh, Armitage." She dropped her hands and her eyes. "It's complicated."

"Uncomplicate it," he suggested.

"She means I'm a monster," Armitage said, in the door of the antechamber. "She thinks you'll kill me soon as look at me, and to be honest, so do I. Been waiting for death since I got to this pissant castle, no offense Your Grace, but no one here looked up to the task until you walked in." The monster rolled his shoulders, striding forward. "So, shall we have us a little fuck-up party? Just you and me."

Israel's mouth opened and closed before he faced the queen. "You harbor *Vhemin* in your kingdom?"

"No, he just turned up." Geneve swore laughter hid in the queen's tone. "With the other three. But I'm of no mind to turn away honest help. There's precious little going around, and more than enough fighting and backstabbing already."

Thunder rolled from less far away. The storm drew closer, the hiss of rain sliding across the tiles above. Geneve bit her lip. "Iz, please. Let us find what's going on."

The Valiant looked about the room, counting the people there. The four honor guard he skipped over as unimportant, but he lingered on the Coven. "Are these all sinners?"

"They're not your concern," Morgan said, as another toll of thunder rumbled across the throne room. It sounded closer, angrier. "They're—"

The throne room door banged open again, but with far less force, as the young page from earlier returned. His hair was slicked wet, eyes wild. "Run!"

Israel blinked. Vertiline raised an eyebrow. Queen Morgan descended the steps. "Take a breath. Then another. What's—"

"The dead!" the lad wailed. "The dead walk the streets!"

Chapter Fifty

Geneve 'borrowed' good silver regals from Vertiline before heading for the apothecary. The Chevalier said she was going to 'get drunk' and ambled off, leaving their wagon in the care of a stable boy who looked struck dumb by her pale beauty.

It made Geneve grumpy, because no one looked at her that way. Her amber skin and red hair were not a thing people seemed to want. No Novice at the Tresward paid her attention. Boys and girls snuck off, but none took her hand.

I must be plain. She shook her head, locks lashing in anger. I'll never be pretty like Vertiline.

The apothecary's door banged open as she barged in. The little bell atop the frame jingled in panic. An old man harrumphed from the back of the shop. "What? Who's there?"

She stormed forward. The old man watched her approach, unimpressed with her anger. Geneve put the small sack of regals on the counter between them. "I need to poison someone."

The apothecary gave an apologetic smile. "I deal in healing. The odd love potion. That sort of thing. No poison."

Geneve sighed. "I'll be dead in a month if you don't help me."

"Sounds serious."

"It is!" Geneve nudged the sack of coins closer to the old man. "Here."

"I'll admit to curiosity. Young lass. Twelve or thirteen?"

"Fourteen. Almost fifteen."

"Close enough," he smiled. "At my age, that's a rounding error."

"A what?"

"The thing is, if I sell poison to a Tresward Novice—"

"How do you know I'm Tresward? I carry no sash." Geneve felt her scowl deepen.

He snorted. "It's writ larger than the Three moons above, girl. You walk like a killer. There's a storm inside you."

Geneve slumped. "That's the problem. There's no Storm."

The old man rubbed his nose. "I think you should start from the beginning."

"My Trial's in a month. I can't use the Storm. I need to fight fifty Novices and kill my tree." The last words came with a slight hitch. Geneve realized she held a sob in check. "I don't want to kill my tree."

"You don't mind fighting fifty Novices?" A blink.

"They can fight back."

"Uh-huh." The old man opened the sack of coins. "This is a lot."

"I need a lot of poison."

He closed the coin purse, hefting it. "Tell me your plan, and then we'll see what can be done."

Chapter Fifty-One

I t wasn't thunder. It was the Storm, held by a Champion's leash. Nicolette marched on Queensfane Village. The Witch Knight held an army of the dead on a tether of lost souls, burning a choking, corrupted path through the belly of Ravenswall. And she really, really wanted Meriwether.

Screams made faint by distance carried on the wind. They may as well have been the cries of gulls. Lightning lashed the sky, cracking the Three's whip as Nicolette came to finish them.

The dragon hadn't managed to kill Nicolette. Israel hadn't bested her, even with Vertiline's help. She wanted Meriwether, or at least the knowledge he carried. When she got it she would tear the righteous from the Tresward, corrupting it into a force for evil.

Which means she'll write names in the damn book, including Geneve's. Meriwether clenched his fists. "Remember when I said we should run?" He scratched his bearded chin, which made him look up. Just in time to see black-clothed people high above, clinging like limpets. Four held the roof like spiders. Meriwether wasn't sure if he or they were more surprised, so he blurted, "Assassins!"

The four dropped. The throne room was twenty meters floor to ceiling but the assassins landed like they'd hopped off a stool. Meriwether saw blades, steel's brightness dulled by lampblack, the weapons hungering.

Two went for the queen, the others for Israel and Vertiline. Meriwether wanted to *do* something, but he wasn't fast, or strong. Morgan's guards weren't fast *enough*, blades barely a handbreadth from scabbards when the first assassin's padded boots hit the floor.

Luckily, Geneve was.

She'd moved at Meriwether's alarm. Her hand found the hilt of a guardsman's sword, and she kicked the man back, sword drawing as he tumbled to the floor. Her borrowed steel rang as she parried a cut to Morgan's neck from the left, then chimed again as she blocked the other assassin's thrust to the queen's chest.

Israel's glass blade didn't make a noise as it parted an assassin's sword, then its wielder's skull and chest to exit through his groin. Vertiline didn't appear to change her posture a millimeter as her glass licked once, twice, three times to leave her opponent in four separate pieces on the ground.

Geneve spun, steel sluicing red rain as an assassin's head left his shoulders. She kept the motion flowing as the final assassin struck. Her borrowed blade cracked, steel splintering. The assassin's eyes were bright with glee as he lunged. She accepted his advance, one hand closing about his wrist, other driving the broken teeth of her sword through the man's skull.

His wet slump was followed by silence.

"About that running thing," Meriwether said, just in case people hadn't got the idea the first time.

Israel shook his head. "There is no point." He retrieved a small glass globe about the size of a child's fist from an assassin's pouch. "All-Seeing Eye."

Vertiline growled. "So Nicolette knows who's here, and what we said? Perfect." Her eyes frosted over like hard southern ice.

The queen's guard, eyes wide, gathered around their ward. Morgan's eyes were a hard, glittering match for Vertiline's. "This Nicolette and I need an accounting." She glanced at her guardsman who'd lost his blade to Geneve. "Get another blade. And one for the Knight Adept, too." As the man scurried to comply, she held up her hand for his attention. "Two things, guardsman. Do not take it to heart you were bested by the best. And make sure your new blades are the best steel possible. I feel they'll be tested many times today."

"This is sinner's magic." Israel glanced from the All-Seeing Eye to Meriwether. "I mean no offence."

"Of course you do." Armitage sauntered to the body wreckage pile, kicking a headless corpse with enthusiasm. "You can't help yourself, but you definitely mean offense. You want to cut him down, or put him in a cage, but what's really grinding your gears is knowing without his warning you'd have three feet of steel in your belly. They caught you flat-footed, Tresward man."

Meriwether looked between the two hulks, decided it wasn't really about him, and turned to the queen. "Your Grace, do you have a back way out of here?"

She eyed him with the cool disdain of someone with secrets they didn't want to share. "No."

"Okay, where are they?"

"I said—"

"I was there when you said it." Meriwether scratched his beard again, but the ceiling shed no more assassins. "We're going to split up, but," he held a palm out to Geneve as she looked ready to get in the middle, "only for a little while. I'll get you safe. The cat's with me. We'll send the B-team to face the witch of doom, and once we've got you squared away, the cat and I will return, and he'll shoot her in the eye."

Armitage narrowed his eyes. "Who's the B-team?"

"Easy, champ," Meriwether said. "They're the ones who can't make illusions or move silently."

Queen Morgan pressed her lips in a line. "How do you propose to spirit me away?"

"Out the back, like I said." Meriwether offered her another smile, this one a little gentler. "This isn't the first time I've run from the law, you know."

THE 'BACK DOOR' WAS BEHIND THE THRONE. QUEEN MORGAN RAPID-fired instructions to her Coterie. *Assist the Knights. Protect your friends. Run if you have to.* Then she touched a stud on the back of her throne, and it rotated aside revealing steps into the dark.

They'd ducked inside and hurried along a narrow but not disreputable corridor. Two of Morgan's honor guard roamed ahead, two behind. Sight of Day was with Meriwether and the queen, a borrowed bow in hand. Stone walls free of cobwebs led straight ahead. Spheres set in sconces lit at their approach, lending a clean warm light to their passage. Morgan touched one. "The benefits of having wizards."

Meriwether marveled at the spheres. *Such a simple thing would do so much for so many, but the Tresward hunts us like dogs.* "I hope you can stand against the Tresward."

"I hope I don't have to." She stood close to Meriwether, because the tunnel wasn't roomy. He smelled lavender and tried to ignore it. "War isn't what I want."

"Got it." Meriwether worried at his beard. Since this morning's trim, it'd reverted to the itchy phase. "You'll need to send your guards elsewhere."

"You're joking, of course."

"I'm definitely not. We're trying to hide you, Your Grace. Once we're outside, anyone with four guards looks like someone important."

She considered it. "And where are we going?"

"Dockside inn." He looked away. "We'll get a room—"

"We will not."

"And once we've got the room, you'll stay there, and we'll go watch while the Knights save your kingdom." Meriwether felt his smile lose a little balance in the face of her hard, dark eyes. "Trust me."

"Unlikely."

WHICH WAS HOW THEY ARRIVED AT THE *SAILOR'S ARMS*, AN INN three copper barons above seedy. Meriwether entered with the queen after attiring her with illusions to look like a doxy he'd seen outside:

tawdry skirts replaced the magnificent red gown, and a blouse with too many ruffles completed the picture.

As a concession to the situation, Meriwether had two of her guards nurse mead in the taproom below, after shucking their honor-black armor. Their blades came with them, but a sword was a sword and everyone here had one.

Speed was of the essence. He needed to get Morgan hidden before everyone ran for their lives. The streets already surged with panic, but no one was sure what they should be panicking about.

He scattered coins on the bartop, one possessive hand on Morgan's arm, and demanded a key. "Hurry, sir." He put a little wheedling in his tone as he danced from foot to foot.

The innkeeper, a man almost perfectly spherical, swept the coins aside with a leering wink, and put a key in Meriwether's hand. Meriwether hustled Morgan upstairs, kicked the door of their room open, and gave her the key. "Lock yourself in."

She eyed him, and he was certain frost spread across the floor between them. "After this we'll talk about how you handle the royal person."

"After this, if we're alive to talk, you can shout all you like." He pulled the door closed, dashed downstairs, and headed for where everything he held dear waited. Sight of Day followed, barely a step behind, his golden eyes on everything at once. He hurried through Ravenswall as panic swelled. Smoke blackened the sky from the south, Nicolette's army of dead hungering for the living.

Meriwether ignored that, because he couldn't fix it. He needed to get to the Brook District.

To Geneve.

Chapter Fifty-Two

Geneve marched with Israel and Vertiline to the Brook District. It had been a sleepy enough settlement within Ravenswall. Not too wealthy, not too poor. Artisans made it their home. Nothing was tactically significant about it, except for one thing.

It was right in Nicolette's path.

Meri's plan made sense: head to the Brook District and meet Nicolette head on. Aside from the warm comfort of her old friends Iz and Tilly, she had the bulwark of Armitage's presence. Nicolette nearly bested two Knights, but an Adept plus a very large Vhemin might make all the difference.

Geneve doubted it. She figured the secret weapon of Meri's plan a better idea. He'd said, *Your job is to draw Nicolette's eye. Be in her face. Be angry. The seen thing. Hide the idea of wizards from her until it's too late.* His eyes had found the floor. *But also the living thing. Come back alive, Red.*

She didn't know if she could. It didn't feel like that kind of fight. Geneve knew what the Sway felt like and fighting a Knight Champion with its full power at her command felt like suicide.

"This feels like suicide," Vertiline said. Her shield hung ready off her arm, but her glass was safely scabbarded.

"I was thinking the same thing," Geneve said. "How did you beat her before?"

"I remember a dragon," Iz said, a faint smile on his face. They paused at an intersection, marking the direction of smoke blackening the sky. He fingered his crystal necklace. "There was definitely a dragon."

"We did okay against the dead, though. Once Nicolette left, we spent a day or two on mop-up." Tilly took her helm off, scratched her head, then put it back on. "I wonder what she did on the way. We managed to beat her here."

"Recovering?" Geneve shrugged. "Maybe the dragon hurt her. She probably holed up somewhere to use the Sway."

Iz rolled his shoulders. "More than we did, I think. Still, now we are three again." He gave a tight grin, and Geneve saw a hint of the young man he'd been when they first met.

"Four, motherfucker." Armitage twirled a wicked-looking halberd like it was a twig. "Learn to count." He ignored Israel's bulging eyes.

"Technically, there are twelve." Vertiline pointed at a furtive figure in an alley to their left. "Four of us, and two groups of four sinners." She gritted her teeth. "Sorry, Geneve."

"It's fine," she lied. "At least the burning city's distracting people from the Vhemin we're walking with."

"How can you *not* see him?" Vertiline looked sideways at the monster. "He's a two-meter tall monster with horror teeth, snake eyes, and scaled skin."

"You're just jealous," Armitage said.

THEY FOUND A MARKET SQUARE IN THE DEAD CENTER OF THE BROOK District. Stalls were set up, but unattended. Awnings fluttered in a wind the south sent to remind them of where this started. Rain fell, heavy, insistent, and with teeth of ice.

"This is perfect." Iz removed his helmet, slicked water from his face, and beamed. "We'll set up here. The square provides even ground and good sight lines for the sinners." He slammed his helmet back on. "I hope they know who the enemy is."

"I'm sure they do." Armitage used his halberd to scratch his back. "It's the four of us, and everyone the witch brings. Lots of fish in this barrel."

"Will they fire on us?" Tilly scanned the rooftops, sighting a hooded figure. The figure tossed a wave, then ducked from sight.

"I don't think so." Geneve removed her own helmet, thankful for the ancient's light design. One less thing to wear her down. The black glass didn't mark with rain's legs like windows did. It remained clear despite the weather. "Or, not until later."

"Please don't try and cheer us up again." Armitage winked. "How you want to play this?"

Israel pointed with his sword. "We'll set up here—"

"Wasn't talking to you." Armitage turned his back on the Valiant. He seemed to size up Geneve and found her weight to be just right. "You're my chief. You tell me where to go, and I'll be there."

Vertiline's eyes were cold within her helmet. "She's just an Adept."

"Wasn't talking to you either, Frosty. You got to wonder, though. Bunch of sinners up there? They know the runt's sweet on Geneve. She talks with his word, and he's one of 'em. She's the perfect person to lead all of us to death." Armitage hunkered a bit lower. "So, Adept. What'll it be?"

"I don't want to lead."

"Not always about you." He grinned horror teeth. "Sometimes it's about pissing off the Valiant."

Iz snorted, and Geneve smiled, then donned her helmet. "Iz?"

"A teachable moment, for all of us," he admitted. "If this were your battle, what would you do?"

Geneve scanned the market square. A hundred meters a side, littered with mercantile goods. Smoke warred with rain for who got to walk the skies. There was a *lot* of smoke, suggesting how Nicolette got her army: she burned people from their homes, killed them, then raised the lost as revenants. "If we stay here, her forces will wash over us like a wave. We need to lure her into a smaller area."

Israel pursed his lips. "I only thought of going blade on blade against her. You're right, of course. Where do we go?"

Geneve pointed to a low stone building to the north side of the square. "That looks like a bank. Stone walls and barred windows. Inside, her dead can't swarm us."

"We'll be trapped, though." Vertiline bobbed her head, considering. "She could sweep the walls aside with the Storm."

"As could we." Geneve sighed. "Well, two of us, at least. But her dead can't use Sway or Storm."

"Meat for the grinder," Armitage grumbled.

"We keep four sorcerers out here and bring the rest with us. The ones here can contain the dead. Inside, we use them against the Champion." Geneve nodded with a certainty she didn't feel.

"Will four be enough?" Israel considered the smoky sky. "Can you bring your dragon here?"

"What? No. It's not my dragon." Geneve shook her head. "The dragon is long gone, Iz. It's just us."

"Then we will do." She saw the glint of his teeth through his visor. "It's always been enough before."

⁘

Tilly was the bait. She was the fastest of the four of them. The Chevalier stood in the rain, gleaming Smithsteel dripping, glass ready.

Geneve, Armitage, and Iz waited inside. The bank had smooth stone floors and polished wood walls. It oozed wealth, the kind of money merchants touched but only royalty really knew. The back half held a vault. Barred windows allowed customers to talk with bankers.

There was no one here but them and their mages. One, a young woman of perhaps twenty-five summers, approached Geneve. "Where do you want us?"

"The vault." Geneve put her hand on the woman's sleeve. The arm beneath was thin, half-staved. *These people ran from mine, and have been running for over a hundred years. Here we are at the end, only to discover we need them.* "I'm very sorry."

The witch yanked her sleeve free. "We're here because the Tresward comes for us, as it always has. Black sashes and gold bars mean death. Your words mean nothing. I hope they make you gag." She stalked away, beckoning with an angry hand to her three companions. So unlike Meri, with his gentle words and kind eyes. Geneve thought of the queen's comment.

They lost a boy. Dead, on the Tresward's command.

Which boy had they lost? Meri's brother? If true, why didn't he hate her like he should? *Oh, Meri. What happened to you?* Geneve shook her head to clear it. *There's no time for that.*

"You good?" Armitage looked after the young witch. "That looked like a dry fuck if ever I saw one."

"She holds anger in her heart. It'll help." Geneve spread her hands. "And she's earned it. I wear the Three's burnished sun. If I scrubbed until my fingers were raw, I couldn't get the blood off my hands."

"She's a sinner. Pay her no mind." Israel joined them. He glanced at the monster. "Can we count on you?"

"You mean, in the middle of the fight, will I stick this halberd up your ass, or the enemy's?"

"Yes."

"How about this. I promise I won't try to kill you until tomorrow. Good enough for you?" Armitage bared shark teeth.

"Good enough, Vhemin." Israel gave a tight nod. Armitage gave Geneve a lazy salute, then sauntered after the witch. "Things have not been ... easy."

"I know, Valiant."

He took off his helmet, smoothing his hair. Geneve saw it was shot with gray, but still thick as ever. "Stay behind me. Don't listen to her words."

"I know how to fight the Sway." Geneve nodded all the same. "But thank you for the reminder. After this, I will need ... more reminders."

Israel shook his head. The necklace at his throat glittered. "I don't think so." He put his helmet on. "It's time. Can you feel it?"

Geneve cocked her head, listening not just with her ears, but her heart. The sounds of panic outside had faded, leaving an eerie quiet, filled with the hush of rain. Within the rainsong, Geneve heard something else, deeper, hidden within the stillness. "The dead walk." She hurried to a window, looking outside.

Men and women flowed from the lanes leading to the market. Some looked hearty, if a little pale. Others were charred, misshapen, or missing limbs. Their eyes tracked nothing, a shuffling gait marking their steps through the city.

She spied a girl in their number, holding a cat. The girl had gnawed the head from the cat, blood slicking her chin. A man behind the girl walked, head high, oblivious to the hammer lodged in his skull.

Hundreds of the dead filled the market, unseeing eyes fixed on Tilly and her vigil before the bank. One walking corpse, a woman who may have been thirty-five before her corruption, ran for the Chevalier.

Vertiline spun aside from her charge, three perfect strikes cutting the woman to pieces. The parts tumbled past her until starved of momentum. She resumed her silent stance, watching, waiting.

A minute later, the crowd of dead shifted as if they were a lake someone dropped a stone into. The ripples spread, parting to reveal a black-armored woman. She carried twin blades of glass. Unlike last time, her helmet was on, no doubt hiding a sneer.

"Hello, Nicolette," Vertiline called. "It's time for you to stop this."

"Where is your man?" Nicolette scanned the market. "Where is Israel?"

"I'd be more worried about me."

Nicolette laughed. "Hardly, Chevalier." *//DROP YOUR SWORD.//* Vertiline swayed, glass trembling in her hand.

Israel growled, looking like he wanted to leave. Geneve clasped his arm. "Not yet, Iz. Trust Tilly. Has she ever let you down?"

His eyes flashed, but he gave a grudging nod. "Not once."

Vertiline steadied, then flourished her sword. "You're losing your touch with the Sway. Or reality. I can't work out which. Come and die, Nicolette."

The black-armored woman ran. Tilly waited, a cell of quiet in the rain, until Nicolette was ten meters from her. Then she spun, sprinting for the bank.

She came inside, and Geneve slammed the door behind her. It didn't slow Nicolette. The Champion swung a glass blade with such perfection it made Geneve's heart ache. There was a golden flash, and the bank's door blew to kindling, flames licking the wood as it scattered inside.

Nicolette entered, a squall on her heels. She took Israel's measure as he stood with his great glass blade before her, gave a quick salute, and lunged.

Israel roared, charging. Tilly yelled her defiance, blade hungering. Armitage barged forward, halberd low. Geneve felt the weight of her borrowed steel and screamed defiance as she leaped.

Chapter Fifty-Three

The day of Geneve's Trial dawned like any other. Perhaps a little more sun, a little more fear. She made her preparations, then went into the mess to eat.

Breakfast was big and hearty. A scrap of folded paper was delivered to her by a Postulant while she ate. She felt her belly grow cold as she opened it.

TRESWARD'S TRIAL OF NOVICE GENEVE

THE CHARGE OF FREEZING

THE CHARGE OF BEASTS

THE CHARGE OF FIFTY

THE CHARGE OF THE TREE

That was it. Two tests other than the expected fights and killing of her tree. A single day's Trial. She wondered if Israel had asked Justiciars to be lenient. Whether Vertiline spoke in their hallowed presence, demanding balance. If they remembered Wincuf and his terror.

She crumpled the paper, tossing it to the table. Pushing her bowl aside, Geneve stood. "Let's begin."

THE CHARGE OF FREEZING INVOLVED A STONE LINED PIT. IT DESCENDED *a claimed thirty meters into the dark. Rime lined the walls for five meters, ending at a frozen skin.*

A crowd gathered. Two hundred Tresward souls, wanting to see her fail. This Novice without the Storm couldn't hope to pass the Trial.

Lucent Eleni stood beside her. "The Charge of Freezing is to retrieve your sword, Novice."

"You stole my sword?"

"All you have is the Tresward's. We can't steal what we own." Eleni winked. "But yes. I took it from your store this morning."

Geneve ran a hand through red hair. "It's at the bottom of there?"

"It is."

"It looks cold."

"Wouldn't be much of a Charge of Freezing if it wasn't." Eleni held her hand out, in an after you *gesture. "Please don't die. I'd miss you."*

Geneve nodded her thanks at the older woman, then disrobed to her underclothes. Her Novice whites landed at her feet. The southern cold whispered against her arms, and she shivered. "Thirty meters?"

"Maybe more."

"Great." Geneve rubbed her arms. Fifteen years old at the dawn, about to dive into a frozen pit. It hadn't been here yesterday, and she wondered how the Tresward dug a pit thirty or more meters down, lined it with stones, and filled it with frozen water before she woke.

Stop avoiding. Finish the Trial.

She stepped onto the stone lip, focused her mind, and jumped. Geneve brought her heels down at the precise moment she impacted the ice's surface, cracking it with the sound of a thunderclap.

The cold took her. She almost screamed, but Geneve needed the air. She descended into the dark. After five meters, it felt like night. But after ten meters, all light was gone. Geneve looked up at the dwindling circle of hope above her. Tiny bubbles escaped her nose as she fell.

Geneve calmed her mind as she descended. Tresward taught her to control her body. She made her pulse slow. Time dragged its long legs across her heart. She wanted to breathe. A fire would be nice. But Requiem was below, and she'd earned that blade.

Her feet hit the bottom. Geneve almost screamed but held onto her air. Her limbs were sluggish with the cold. It felt a part of her now, ice in her chest, ice in her veins. Ice enough to coat the world. She cast about, looking for Requiem. There was no light.

Geneve didn't want to cut herself against the blade's edge. Had Eleni tossed it here with the scabbard? No time to worry about that now. If she got up, they could fix her cuts.

Her foot hit something hard. Geneve's leg snared in cold, clammy leather. She felt about, finding the familiar hilt of her steel. Geneve boosted up, hands against the wall, clawing for the tiny dot of light above. Her lungs ached, but the rest of her was numb.

Peace. *She repeated it to herself.* You dived in here. Now you've got to dive back out.

She rose, moving faster as the water pressure abated. Her ears popped. Geneve wanted air. She wanted warmth. She would die down here.

Her head broke the surface, and she raised Requiem above the water in triumph. Geneve clawed her way onto the ice, teeth chattering. Her usually amber-honey skin was pale like a corpse's. But she couldn't stop her grin.

Eleni helped her out of the pit, draping coarse wool about her. "Well done. Now let's see those beasts."

KYTTO WOULD BE SURPRISED IF HE WERE HERE. THEY'D FILLED A PEN *with tigers.*

Apparently starved, ready to eat. The other end of the room held a scatter-gun. Hers, if she made it. It held two shells. There were three tigers.

Eleni looked pale, her voice thin. "Try not to die—"

"You'd miss me, I know."

"Not that. Cleaning up after this would be ... difficult." The Lucent swayed.

Geneve put a hand on her arm. "Are you all right?"

"Fine."

Geneve stepped into the tiger's enclosure. The cats were huge things. Teeth and claws, all powerful muscle and hungry intent. She didn't know how to pass this Charge. Tigers couldn't be reasoned with.

The first tiger saw her, snarled, and charged. Geneve held up her hand, snarling back. "Stop!" The cat slowed, watching her. It's tail lashed. She held up her right hand, knuckling her left. {Kneel.}

The tiger growled. Geneve stalked forward. {Kneel.} She pressed her fingers into her palm harder, more insistent. {Kneel!}

The cat growled, but crouched. The second followed suit, then the third. Geneve walked past them with the caution they deserved, taking the scattergun from its perch.

She faced the tigers and astonished onlookers as she brandished the weapon. "Got it."

A tiger rumbled its agreement. Geneve walked past them and left the enclosure.

"The People's handspeak." Eleni was ghost white. "How did you learn that?"

"I don't remember," Geneve admitted. "But you know that."

※

THE CHARGE OF FIFTY WAS A PIECE OF CAKE. GENEVE ARMORED herself, this time the Smithsteel fitting her frame better. She named the scattergun Tribunal, in honor of her Trials. It sat in a holster on her thigh. Requiem waited in rear-draw sheath, but if all went well she'd need neither.

She'd named her fifty. None of them turned up.

Geneve walked the hall of the Trial, looking for opponents. Raja was missing. Bald Hettie was absent. Broken-nosed Barbet she'd chosen as her final fight, the youth's bulk a sufficient challenge.

All missing.

Geneve stalked to the door at the far end. She opened it and marched for her tree.

※

THE TRESWARD FOREST WAS AS SHE REMEMBERED IT, EXCEPT ONE SMALL detail. Her tree was gone.

A massive hole sat where it used to be. Earth was strewn about in clods. Geneve walked to the pit, all onlookers absent. She was alone.

She crouched, picking up dirt. It sifted through her fingers, and she smiled. Geneve hadn't had to kill her tree, and that was exactly as she'd planned it.

Geneve stood, arms wide. "I've finished my Trial!"

No one answered. It didn't stop her smiling all the way to Kytto.

"You what?" Kytto's eyes bulged.

"I poisoned the Tresward," Geneve said. "Every last one."

"I'm fine!"

"Are you a Knight?" She eyed him suspiciously. "I didn't see you in the refectory this morning."

"But—"

"They'll get over it. Explosive vomiting, unstoppable diarrhea, and cramps. Two days at the most. But I turned up." Geneve smirked.

"You poisoned everyone?*" Kytto looked to the stairs, and Vertiline's absence. "What about Tilly?"*

"Every. One." Geneve brushed her red hair back. "It was your idea."

"No."

"Yes. You said to cheat." She grinned. "I'm a Knight, Kytto. I'm a Knight."

Chapter Fifty-Four

Meriwether and Sight of Day made good speed for about ten minutes until they hit a snag.

The snag was about two meters tall, clothed in shabby robes. The Vhemin High Priest stood in the middle of the road, wearing a scowl that shifted to a mad-tinged grin when he caught sight of Meriwether. "You!"

"Ah." Meriwether offered a small bow, then darted down an alley to the left. Sight of Day, initially on his heels, paced past him almost effortlessly.

The Feybrind vaulted onto a fence to the left, spun, and held his hand out to Meriwether. Scrambling over, they tumbled to land in a pile of rotten vegetables on the other side.

"Marvelous," Meriwether said.

The cat clicked his fingers in front of Meriwether's face to get his attention. {*The High Priest can unmake me. I feel it in my blood. A weakness the ancients could exploit. I will join my people soon. You must run, friend.*}

"Then we keep running together." Meriwether brushed pieces of moldering cabbage from his pants. "After all, if I leave you here, who's going to look after me?"

The wall behind them shook, a Vhemin roar behind it. A guttural voice snarled, "I smell them!"

Sight of Day's golden eyes were full of shame, but he nodded. The cat lurched into motion, some of his grace left on the floor behind them. He wasn't as fast as before, and Meriwether had no trouble keeping up with him.

There was a crash behind as the Vhemin broke through the wall. Meriwether grabbed the cat's hand. "Hold tight. Don't ever let go."

They kept the pace up through a confusing array of streets. Meriwether saw abandoned inns beside smithys where fires burned in untended forges. A bakery blazed, the ovens spilling fire and soot. A washhouse lay abandoned, wet laundry scattered out front.

Sight of Day lurched to a halt. {*I feel it calling me. I can't resist. I must stop.*}

Meriwether glanced around for options. He didn't need a big one. Just a sliver of hope. Was it too much to ask? He snapped his fingers. "Got it."

Sight of Day dropped his bow from slack fingers. Meriwether snatched it up, then hustled the cat down a short alley. He pinned the cat to a wall. "Hold still. Be quiet. Like the woods, right before dawn. Do you understand?"

The Feybrind gave him a long look full of pain but nodded. Meriwether held the cat. He smelled cinnamon and fear. He squeezed his eyes shut, remembering an outhouse they'd passed not two streets back. It had walls of old, untreated wood. A stain on the door, perhaps blood. The unmistakable crescent moon cut into the door stated its purpose better than any sign.

When he opened his eyes, they huddled inside old timber walls. Vhemin footsteps hammered dirt in the street beyond the alley. A familiar voice roared, "I know you're here, manling! I can smell you. And the cat, too. Bring him to me, creature."

Sight of Day lurched. Meriwether put his lips to the cat's ear. "It's just you and me. Listen to my voice."

Golden eyes full of fear found his. The Feybrind shook his head, then shoved Meriwether back. He stumbled through the illusory wall of his imaginary outhouse, falling to the alley ground.

The walls of the outhouse shimmered like a mirage. Meriwether tried to hold the illusion in place, to hide his friend inside, but a Vhemin's boot found his back. He arched in pain, and the outhouse vanished.

Sight of Day huddled against the wall. *{I'm sorry.}*

"Run," Meriwether hissed. "*Run!*"

"Don't run, cat. I command it." The High Priest stood at the alley's entrance. He held a metal box, glass glinting under the glowering sky. His lips split into a shark-toothed leer. "I've been hoping we'd meet again, manling. Waiting for it, you might say. You cost me a great deal."

"Take an IOU?" Meriwether wheezed.

The monster laughed. "I could almost like you, if you weren't so weak and feeble." The High Priest toyed with the box that commanded Feybrind. "Should I make the cat kill you? Or watch while I do the butchering? Which do you think would be worse?"

Meriwether spat bile, then got to his knees. "I think a long, slow death by starvation would be best." Vhemin huddled around him. First a couple, then five, and before he knew it the alley was full of muscled biceps and scaled hides.

The High Priest guffawed. "You have *spark*, manling. We've come to help liberate your fine city, and most of your kind run, or scream, or die silently on the blade. But not you." He shook his head. "You want to *live*."

Meriwether got a knee under him, and when no one kicked it away, lurched to his feet. He ran a hand through his hair. *Khiton's balls, but I can smell my own fear.* "Who doesn't?" He cast a glance at the sky, which continued to rain on him. His shirt stuck to his lean frame, and with so much angry beef around him, he was never more aware of his lack of strength, size, or martial skill.

"True enough. You want it in the head or the chest?" The High Priest stalked closer.

Meriwether closed his eyes. *I don't want either. But I'd take both, if I could say goodbye to Geneve. Tell her I tried my best, but I wasn't her, and that's why the cat died.* He opened his eyes, and by weird chance he had an unrestricted view of Sight of Day.

{I would have you know my all before we go.} The cat raised a weak hand. *{Roars.}*

"What's he saying?" The High Priest squinted at Sight of Day, suspicion writ on his face.

{Like.}

"It's a prayer," Meriwether lied.

{The.}

"It going to take long?" The High Priest leered, and his fellows chortled in vile accompaniment.

{Singing.}

"I think he's just about done," Meriwether said. The cat sagged against the wall, weakness taking the very heart of him.

With a last grunt, the Feybrind straightened. A Vhemin slammed a fist into the cat's belly, dropping him to the alley floor. Meriwether tried to run to him, but a Vhemin punched him in the jaw with a hand the size of a ham.

Meriwether dropped, seeing stars. He saw boots, mismatched, old, worn. Borrowed from the dead, people the Vhemin had murdered. The feet shifted aside for a moment, and he saw Sight of Day on his knees. The cat's golden eyes met his. *{Sun.}*

A hand found Meriwether's throat, and he choked as a monster hauled him to his feet. The creature punched him in the gut, and he curled over the pain, but the Vhemin wouldn't let him be. It slammed him against the wall, placing a knife to his throat.

The High Priest stood behind Meriwether's captor. "So, runt. Head or chest?"

Meriwether gestured to the hand holding his throat. At the High Priest's grudging nod, the Vhemin released him. Meriwether choked, gagged, then held a hand up in a *give me a second* gesture. He stood, shoulders straight, and looked the High Priest in his snake eyes. "Those are my choices?"

The High Priest nodded, picking his teeth with a knife, the ancient device for controlling Feybrind held in his other hand. "Seems simple enough."

"Okay." Meriwether reached deep and found a smile he didn't know he owned. It was all sharp edges. You could cut yourself on the blade of his teeth. *The cat gave me his name. The secret thing inside him that he doesn't let anyone see. Let's see if I can give him a gift as worthy.* "Roars Like the Singing Sun, please kill these motherfuckers."

The High Priest's eyes went wide, then blood fountained from his lips as a long, ugly sword tore through his ribcage. The sword twisted, exiting sideways in a spray of gore. The monster teetered, then slumped, revealing Sight of Day standing tall and unbowed.

He held Vhemin steel. A dead monster lay at his back, another to his left. The Vhemin about them surged back as if noting the toddler in their midst brandished a live, loaded scattergun.

The cat's golden eyes met Meriwether's. They were still gold, but no longer warm. They were hard as the sun, as unforgiving as the desert. They weren't human, nor Feybrind. They were primal, atavistic, and so very hungry.

Sight of Day spun like a dervish. Blood sprayed as he dismembered Vhemin with a ferocity Meriwether had never seen the cat display. A monster stabbed him through the shoulder, but Sight of Day didn't appear to notice, merely snatching the blade with his bare hands, slicing the soft meat of his palm as he yanked it free.

Ah, Meriwether thought. *Now he has two swords.*

The Feybrind twirled, blades licking left, then right. Two-bladed strikes to one foe, then a single-blade strike to two. Sight of Day hacked the head from a Vhemin, then split it in half with his other sword. In eight seconds, it was done. The Feybrind stood in the alley, dripping red. His borrowed blades weeped remembered misery.

Meriwether walked to his friend. "Are you okay?"

The cat tossed the blades to his feet. *{Command me.}*

Meriwether looked about. He hauled bodies aside until he found what he was after: the ancient's control box. He grabbed a discarded blade, hammering on the device until it wasn't anything more than glittering pebbles. "There. No more commands."

{Command me.} Sight of Day's eyes were still unearthly, alien, and hard.

Meriwether shook his head, then held his hands up for attention. The Feybrind watched him, eyes locked on Meriwether's fingers. *{Roars Like the Singing Sun, you must be free.}*

The cat shuddered, dragging a great, sobbing breath. His hand went to his wounded shoulder, and the Feybrind swayed. Meriwether caught him. "You're okay. You're okay! Well, you got stabbed, but you'll *be* okay." He got Sight of Day's arm over his shoulders, then walked him to the alley mouth.

The sky was gray and hard, but Meriwether felt the wind change. It shifted around, and for a moment, he caught the slight warmth of the northern breeze.

"I thought we were going to die," he admitted.

The Feybrind unlimbered himself. *{So did I. You're terrible in a fight.}*

Meriwether sighed. "Thank you for trusting me with your truth."

{You were worthy of it.} The cat looked away. *{What happened to me?}*

"Nothing we'll speak of again." Meriwether combed hair with his fingers. "The ancient's command boxes are gone. We broke them all."

Sight of Day nodded. *{How did they make them? Were you the enemies of the People?}*

"I don't know." Meriwether sighed. "It was a long time ago. I'm sorry if we were. Humans can be dicks."

The cat considered him for a moment that held like the silence after a bell's toll. *{Not all of them.}*

Meriwether grinned. "Chin up. We've still got work to do."

{I've been stabbed. I need to lie down.}

"What, and let Geneve and Armitage get all the glory?" Meriwether paced to the wash house, finding a clean shirt. He tore it to strips for a bandage.

The cat waited, sitting on a bench, but his eyes were warm again. *{You're right, of course. Armitage is quite likely to screw everything up.}*

Meriwether set to bandaging his friend. He kept his smile in place, his tone light, even though one thought kept running through his mind.

Where's Geneve?

Chapter Fifty-Five

The air tasted of copper. The hair on Geneve's nape rose. Her fingers felt thin, too weak to hold her borrowed blade. Or perhaps it was her soul, too weak to hold her body upright after the compromises she'd made to get here.

I'm no Knight. I'll never be Israel and can't touch Vertiline. And here I am, standing with them, against a Champion.

Nicolette's poise was faultless. Her stance was exactly as written by the Three. Her glass blades moved with precision even clockwork couldn't give. Every part of her was matchless perfection. The Three walked not *with* her, but *in* her. She was their Champion in the world. A tiny dragonfly appeared on one of her sword's edges, glittering with inner heat, before taking flight to circle her head. Another joined it, then four more, giving her a crown of flying fire.

Israel, Vertiline, and Geneve took equidistant positions. Iz faced the Champion. Vertiline and Geneve had her flanks, three precise points of a invisible triangle. Three points, three sides: the gods' scripture. Iz held his great glass blade two-handed, the point exactly one centimeter from the ground. His stillness was a kind of perfection. The Storm was in him. Geneve saw the glitter of gold in his eyes.

When he smiled, the light in his eyes intensified. "Nicolette, insects won't save you."

Vertiline held her blade above her head, point forward over her shield. She stepped forward into a stance so precise it made Geneve's heart groan. A crackle of gleaming electricity walked the unforgiving edge of her sword, arcing to the ceiling.

Geneve smelled ozone. She held her steel in both hands. The Storm wasn't with her. It never was, no matter how perfectly she stepped, or the exacting precision of her bladework. She had nothing but steel against a demigod.

Why do Iz and Tilly trust me to have their backs? I'm the weakest of us. Worse than useless: I'll distract their thoughts.

Israel struck. He was so fast Geneve almost missed it. The great glass blade went from low to high as the Valiant charged. It cut a slice through the ceiling as the overhand swing yearned for Nicolette's head. Gold fire burst to life along its length as he swung.

Nicolette blocked it with a cross guard from her blades, and three glass weapons sang a note. High and pure, it made Geneve's teeth itch. The windows on the north side of the bank blew outward.

Israel's strike was a feint, not for him, but for Tilly. The Chevalier moved forward, seeming to slip between one point to another without stepping through the intervening space. Her blade lanced a perfect line for Nicolette's unprotected back.

The Champion flowed a pirouette, evading Tilly's strike. Her sword cut Tilly's shield in half, and the Tresward steel screamed apart in a shower of gold and red. Vertiline gave an answering scream, falling to the floor, glass shattering as it hit beside her. Her shield gone, Geneve saw her arm ended at the wrist, blood flowing a fountain of ruin.

Israel's eye twitched. Barely a whisker, a thing no one but those closest would notice. But it was imperfection, and the Storm dimmed in his eyes. He swung his glass once, twice, and a third time. Geneve sidestepped to her fallen friend, standing ward over Vertiline's body. A quick glance showed pale skin ghost-white, as if her soul left already. But the Chevalier snarled, "Help him!"

Geneve spun to the conflict. Nicolette's blades answered each of Israel's strikes, but she couldn't mark him. His form was almost as flawless as hers. She was faster; he stronger. Her small, agile body was starved of reach. His bulk cost him speed but gave height. Almost matched warriors, Tresward-trained, the Storm lighting their blades. A blocked strike hit the ground, shattering stone in a long rent through the floor.

Geneve darted forward, blade ready, looking for an opening. Nicolette was distracted, half-turning, and Israel swung. His blade caught one of hers, glass against glass, but instead of the perfect note of before, her glass *crunched*. The edge chipped, the blade fracturing, the entire length crumbling to the floor.

Lunging, Geneve tried to put her steel into the Champion's heart. Israel's strike from the opposite side held the force of a falling star. Nicolette sidestepped, Geneve's steel keening along her black armor. Her other glass blade licked out once, twice, and a perfect third time.

Israel stumbled, swayed, and let his blade touch the floor. Blood trickled from his mouth, the rivulet turning to a torrent. Nicolette's strikes hit his chest above, below, and through his heart. Her eyes gleamed malice, her arm rising for a final strike.

Geneve grabbed Nicolette's arm. It felt like holding a bison. Damnation and power filled the Champion. An Adept may as well try to hold back the tide. It was a tiny gesture, but unexpected. The move wasn't in any of the seven hundred moves Cophine gave for a battle's beginning. Ikmae might have pursed their lips while reflecting on their patterns, and Khiton would have laughed as Geneve ignored his final teachings for the ending of things.

It was enough. Israel swung his blade, the last of his strength in the movement. Geneve thought she heard an angel's song as nightingales took flight in the wake of his sword. His sword cut Nicolette's blade in half, then fell to the ground, shattering into a thousand brilliant pieces.

The blow shook the room. The force of the Valiant's strike, given will by the Storm, knocked Geneve back. Nicolette slammed against a wall. Then the opposite wall buckled, the dead thronging around the building clambering and clawing for a way inside. One got in, then another. A crowd, then a torrent. Ten became twenty in a fraction of time measured by the slowing, seeping red coming from Israel's chest.

Iz met her eyes. His dark skin seemed almost as pale as Vertiline's as the life left him. His right hand, wet red over steel, clutched at his amulet. He gave Geneve a tiny, fragile smile, fingers spasming over the crystal, crushing it, then he toppled to the ground.

Broken fragments of the necklace *tinked* beside his body. Light wisped from the fragments, and Geneve screamed, a cry without ending, as five lost years of memories flooded into her.

Chapter Fifty-Six

Meriwether stood atop what might have been a nice taverna, if not for the dead milling in the courtyard out front. To his left, a woman with dead-white hair glared hate at the risen below. To his right, Sight of Day stood with a bow, arrow nocked, but no apparent desire to use it.

It wouldn't make much difference. There's a thousand dead below, and he's got maybe thirty arrows.

White-Hair sniffed. "You want to go in *there?*" She pointed at the bank, around which most of the dead's attention focused.

"Want? Hell, no. Need? Yes." Meriwether flexed his hand. It felt strained after smashing the Feybrind control device. *Won't kill me, though.* "We just saw a Champion enter. I'm going to help."

"And you want us to lay down covering fire?" She held up fingers hooked into claws. Arcs of electricity danced between her fingertips.

"No, I want you to lay down covering fire *and* avoid burning me alive." He gave an encouraging nod. "Thin their numbers. We'll need a way out the front door, so maybe focus on that."

"Don't be stupid!" she called after him, but he was already slipping off the roof to land amid the risen in the courtyard.

Be like them. A life of hiding in plain sight made Meriwether a better actor than any troubadour. He didn't spring to his feet; instead he lurched up with a raspy groan. Dead eyes passed over him, then focused on the bank.

It wasn't hard to make out. The bank was raised atop steps, and if that wasn't enough, lights blinked in the windows. *Am I sure about this? I'm going into a fight between people using the Storm. Mortals can't stand against the Tresward.*

Geneve can't use the Storm, and she's in there. He shuffled across the square. The throng pressed close, and he smelled old blood, shit, and fear. The fear was his; the rest belonged to the bodies. No rot, but it didn't look like these had been dead long.

Eyes down, idiot. A semblance of curiosity sparked in a man's eyes to Meriwether's right. Meriwether groaned, gnashed his teeth, and lurched on as the man's eyes slid away.

In normal circumstances it'd be tricky to push through a crowd this large, but each of the risen lacked intelligence. They shuffled, shambled, and ambled, but none dropped the elbow, barged, or scuttled low. Meriwether did, guilt-free because there were no witnesses. Well, aside from the cat, but he figured the two of them were past that. He hoped Sight of Day marked his progress through the throng.

Sure enough, when a clammy hand grasped his elbow, a dead mouth opening into a slavering maw, a feathered shaft sprouted from the thing's head. It slipped from Meriwether's side. The ones about him turned to the taverna, a few heading back that way.

Hurry up. He dropped his shoulder unto a woman's back, and unashamedly kicked a small boy aside. The kid was already dead, so the usual rules didn't count.

The sky rumbled, then a massive pillar of lightning slashed the ground. Dead bodies blew apart. Some turned to ash instantly. Those on the periphery of the strike burst into flame. Meriwether risked a glance back. The taverna's roof held White-Hair, her hands raised in supplication to the heavens. Another bolt of blue-white smashed the market square, tossing bodies like sand.

A wizard atop a clothier's touched fingers to brow, saluting Meriwether, then clapped his hands together. Wind swept from the sea, not rising gently but howling into the market with the wail of a hungry typhoon. It carried ice and the smell of old salt. The ice flensed the dead, shredding flesh from bone, and bone from sinew, destroying the bodies where they stood.

These are the echo of powerful sorcerers. The Tresward beat them all. Herded them to nothing. But the Tresward have gods at their beck and call. The Storm beats this every time.

While the magi culled the dead, Meriwether went back to the task of getting inside. The risen were thinnest on one side of the bank, so he headed there. *Screw going in the front door. That's a portal to suicide.* He ambled between two women, one who looked to have eaten everything ever, and one who looked starved. They were reaching for the bank's boarded windows. The thin one cawed, then twisted her head on a creaking neck to face him.

Arrows *thunked* into her eye sockets, a one-two punch, and she dropped. Meriwether took her place at the wall, peering inside.

The Knights were well into it. Vertiline was on the ground, bleeding out, or perhaps dead. Geneve rushed the black-armored witch. Meriwether wiped rain and salt from his eyes. *I've got to get in there!*

Too fast for him to see the specifics, the witch carved her name in Israel's chest. The Knight Valiant fell, and by some magic Meriwether couldn't tell, a shockwave blasted from his fallen body. *Did the magi on the roofs strike inside?* Meriwether couldn't see exactly, because he was torn from his feet by the larger woman.

He would have screamed, but the wall shook, bricks showering the alley. The large woman took about forty in her back, stumbled to the ground, and—Three be praised—loosened her grip.

Meriwether got to his feet. The dead were everywhere. They lurched inside, and he was drawn on the current of their passage. Inside, he cast about for Geneve. Meriwether saw a tousle of red hair chalked by dust and ran for her.

The mages inside burst from the back room. They hurled fire and ice at the dead. A chunk of stone nicked Meriwether's cheek. Another chunk hit his knee. Armitage was at their head, a massive club in his hands. He swept it like a broom, giving the mages room. Dead swarmed the Vhemin, and the monster laughed. Gleeful, delighted to die this way. Meriwether ignored all of it, falling to Geneve's side.

Her eyes were open, staring. He touched her face. "Geneve!" Nothing. He winced, then slapped her face. *No response. Is she dead?*

He wanted to bend an ear to her lips, but the storm of magic as wizards fought the dead wouldn't allow it. Meriwether could barely hear his own thoughts. He twisted, looking for a solution, and locked eyes with the black-armored woman.

She was embedded in a wall but creaked her way free. Her face was partially ruined, cheek crushed, but no blood ran from her face. She arched her back, then smiled crooked, broken teeth at Meriwether.

The enchanters blasted dead back outside. They slung lightning and flame like whips, leaving a burning trail of limbs as they pushed the dead back. Armitage roared his defiance, keeping them safe from stragglers trying to flank. The Vhemin bled from a hundred cuts and bites but didn't look like they bothered him. They fought on, taking the battle outside.

Leaving Meriwether alone with a Knight Champion.

Fuck, fuck, fuck! Meriwether fumbled through chalk dust and rubble, fingers coming against cold metal. He raised Geneve's borrowed sword, then stood, feet astride her body. "Come get some."

She chuckled, a broken sound like fractured clockwork. "You're the sinner?" Nicolette drew a length of steel from a back sheath. It was a simple dagger, ordinary metal not glass, but Meriwether had no doubts. She might have the smaller weapon, but she had years of service to three relentless gods on her side.

"We prefer the term, 'gifted.'" Meriwether turned as the Champion walked a circle.

She shored up at Israel's body. Nicolette nudged him with a boot. He didn't respond, but she bent, sticking him over and over with her knife. Job done, she straightened. "Where's the other one?"

Meriwether cast about, spying Vertiline not three meters from Geneve. He'd missed her in all the excitement, but possibly also because her skin was the same color as the chalk coating her. The giveaway was the red paste her blood made of the dust.

He stepped between Geneve and Vertiline, blade ready. Meriwether saw how the point wavered, mirroring his fear. "She's not for you."

"And who's to stop me, little one?" Nicolette felt in her mouth, and with a *pop*, straightened her jaw. "Not you."

Meriwether frowned. "Are you ... *dead?* Is that what's going on?" She nodded, smile even wider now her jaw was settled. "Is that why you couldn't get into the temple?"

Nicolette shrugged. "I don't know how the ancients worked. I could get in, then I couldn't." She tossed her knife from hand to hand. "How do you want it? Head or chest? If you like, I could make sure you never saw it coming."

"Don't you want the Ledger?" Meriwether felt his breath coming faster and faster, fear speeding everything up. "You know, the book."

She considered him. "I think we can get you to give it to us after you're dead. Death isn't the end, sinner. It's the start of so much more." Nicolette took two steps forward, then stopped, her eyes wide.

Meriwether felt strong fingers on his hands. He startled, turning to the side, but was disarmed effortlessly. *No, not effortlessly. Perfectly.* Geneve took her sword back. "You came."

"Hah. I mean, sure."

She nodded, something sad and relieved in it at the same time. "You stood when all else didn't. Step back, Meri. I've got this."

"But ... the Storm," he said. "You should run. Get away, while you can."

Her eyes glinted gold. Her smile was warm, like the dawn. Geneve swung her sword in a three-strike flourish. The first time, her blade glimmered with Cophine's pale face. The second, ash-gray light seeped from the metal. On the final, Khiton's dark light rippled down the blade. "Oh, Meri. I didn't believe Sight of Day. But he saw it, from the first day."

"Saw what?"

She faced Nicolette, sinking into a ready stance. "I'm a daughter of the Three, and there's a Storm inside me."

Chapter Fifty-Seven

I t wasn't her first memory, just the first to arrive. Geneve felt it slot into place like a wooden piece from a child's puzzle. It had the same bright, lacquered edges children love, painted in brilliant vermilion.

She stood in a town square. Or above it: her feet were on wooden planks, coarse cut and rude. To her left and right were the tall faces of her fellow slaves. Tall, because she was five, but for all she was young she felt something was terribly wrong.

A slave to her right was Feybrind. Worn, faded pelt. Patchy, because even they got old. Emerald green eyes undimmed by time, because the People weren't made to cower. Her name was Time of Waiting, and she'd volunteered to be here, because Geneve's mother wasn't.

No, that wasn't right. Geneve's mother was below in the square. Her throat was cut ear to ear, lending more dramatic red to the sea of it soaking the cobbles. Sightless eyes searched for everything and nothing. Her hand clutched the air, clawed it, trying to work a way back to life, but her time was done.

{Don't look,} *Time of Waiting* said. {Don't see.}

To Geneve's right stood a pale-haired woman, terrible as Cophine, final as Khiton. She held glass in one hand. A circle of empty lay about her, a perfect margin scribed in the bodies of the dead. The dead wore mail. Their fallen weapons were cut, shattered, and bent, as if they'd been thrown by a giant to break against a wall. Her name was Vertiline, but then-Geneve borrowed that name from now-Geneve.

The slaves with Geneve on the auctioneer's stand were frightened. They tugged at their chains, striving for freedom. Doom approached, and the doom was a dark amber-skinned man with hard, unforgiving eyes. He held a massive glass sword, his Tresward armor gleaming in the afternoon sun.

When he looked on Geneve, his eyes softened, and she wondered why she cried.

GENEVE'S NEXT MEMORY WAS YEARS EARLIER. ONE OF HER FIRST, perhaps when she was two or three. She was in a small house. Not poor, nor fancy, but for servants. A great lord owned this place, and her mother was one of his lady's attendants.

Her mother held the giant, dark amber-skinned man close. This time, he wore no armor and carried no sword. His eyes were softer than before, and so very warm. But sad, and also afraid. Geneve didn't know why, but it made her want to hide her face.

The big man crouched. "I'm—"

"Don't tell her," her mother warned. "For your sake, and hers. The Tresward don't have children. It's forbidden."

The man tousled Geneve's hair, then rose. "It's not forbidden, Elvige. It's impossible. Our girl is a miracle."

"Still."

"Still," he agreed.

Her mother—Elvige—sighed. "You must help us."

He frowned. "How?"

"Come away with us."

"I can't leave the Tresward." His words were like stone, heavy and unbreakable.

"But you can leave your daughter?"

"It's different."

"That's right," snapped Elvige. "It's different because it's wrong. It's fine to turn your back on those who need you, and serve those who don't."

"I'm not—"

"Because it's evil," she hissed. "What would your Tresward say if they knew?"

ANOTHER MEMORY, PLAYING IN THE SUN WITH THE BIG MAN. HIS EYES *were kind, but shadowed, like he was so very tired. Elvige was the same: always tired, always on edge.*

{YOU LEARN FAST,} SAID TIME OF WAITING. {PERHAPS YOU SHOULD become one of the People.} *Emerald green eyes sparked with humor.*

{I can't be a cat,} *Geneve laughed.* {I'm too little.}

{Size doesn't change perfection.} *The Feybrind's eyes left her for a moment, and Geneve felt cold.* {Hush now.}

The lord walked toward them. No, not them, but their house. Geneve and Time of Waiting played outside, while the man opened the door. He considered Geneve for a moment before entering. She remembered him as ancient, over a hundred years old, but that wasn't right. He was a little older than Elvige.

The door shut, but Geneve didn't forget. The lord came to their house many more times. Ten. Twenty. A hundred? She didn't know how to count, but a hundred sounded right. It was a big enough number.

Whenever he came, Time of Waiting played with her. Geneve didn't know what her mother did while she learned handspeak.

SHE WAS FIVE AGAIN. ELVIGE WAS DISMISSED. HER MOTHER CRIED A LOT. *She said they didn't have enough regals, or even barons.*

There was no money. Elvige's face was old and tired, cracked by hardship. The big man didn't come any more.

*I*T WAS THE MORNING OF THE AUCTION. *S*HE WAS IN A CAGE. *I*T WAS HARD *and cold. Others were with her, including Time of Waiting. They were to be sold for coin. All were unwanted, castoffs, worthy of a handful of regals at best.*

Her mother sobbed fifteen meters away but took the money anyway.

⁊

*B*EFORE THE AUCTION, *G*ENEVE HAD IRON CLASPED AROUND HER THIN *wrists. She'd kicked the man who'd bound her and got a slap for her troubles. The iron around her wrists was so heavy she couldn't raise her arms. They'd padded it with sheepskin because her wrists were smaller than anyone else's. Maybe they didn't put children on the platform very often.*

Her mother was below her, arguing with the big man. His armor was sunbright, brilliant, radiant. Geneve wondered where he'd been. A pale-haired woman stood at his side. Her face was young, teeth bared. "Iz, what's going on?"

"Is this your new whore?" her mother spat. "Is this why you never came back?"

"I wasn't allowed." The large man looked at Geneve. "This stops now."

Her mother cackled a broken smile. "They won't get the money back."

"Perhaps both of us share enough evil for the world," the big man mused.

"Iz," said the pale-haired woman. "We can't be here."

"That's right." He swung toward Geneve, climbing the steps toward her. She remembered the way his armor hurt to look on, how bright it was, how perfectly he walked.

A guard made to stop him, and fell, broken. Geneve didn't understand how it happened. One minute the guard was alive, hand out, face hard, then he was gone, a tumble of limbs that didn't work anymore.

Someone in the crowd screamed. Someone threw something. It flew fast and true. The big man drew his sword fast as thought and cut down the missile. Two halves of a crossbow bolt landed at Geneve's feet.

The big man stood before. "I want just this one!"

Geneve didn't remember what happened next. She didn't want to.

⁊

THE CART TO THE TRESWARD CHAPEL TOOK A LONG, WINDING PATH *through cold countryside. The pale-haired woman left her with the big man. She rode on ahead, to "fix this tremendous fuck-up."*

The big man nodded, his eyes back to being happy and sad. Geneve rode beside him, the cart's seat smoother than the slaver's docks had been beneath her feet. "Are you a Knight?"

"Perhaps," he said. "I thought so."

"What are you now?"

"I'm your father." He glanced at the sky, looking for rain. "I'm Israel."

ANOTHER MAN MET THEM ON THE ROAD. HE WORE WHITE ROBES, A *silver sash with nine bars across his chest. Israel stepped from the wagon, walking to meet the newcomer.*

Geneve remembered how deeply Israel bowed. So low, his forehead touched the wet and muddy ground. "Cleric Justiciar Ambrose."

"Israel." Ambrose held a hand out for Israel's. "Who's this?"

"This is Geneve." Israel sighed. "She's my daughter."

"Impossible."

"And yet," Israel said, neither agreeing or arguing.

Ambrose answered Israel's sigh with a heavier one. Bigger, and full of weary sight of the future. "I can help you." At Israel's startled look, the Cleric Justiciar held up a placating hand. "She must never know."

"What do you mean?" Israel's voice broke on the last word. Geneve thought she knew why. He'd done so much to get here.

"I mean exactly that. You can't be her father, Chevalier. You're a Knight of the Tresward. You must think of the Three above all else. But she can join us. We'll protect her."

Israel clenched his hands. "You want her to become a Cleric?"

"No. She will be a Knight, like her father. To protect the land. Its people, under the Three's protection. Perhaps, even, to undo some of your terrible ... mistakes." Ambrose said the last word like killing people was an accident.

"What of me?"

"She must never know you, Israel."

"But—"

Ambrose held aloft a small crystal on a silver chain. "This will keep a piece of her separate. Everything from this moment back, to the time of her birth. It will be as if she's made anew in the Three's eyes, and in their service."

Israel's throat worked. "But she will never know ... me?"

"Never." Geneve thought she saw a curl of malice in the old man's face, quickly gone, or maybe never there in the first place. "But she'll live. And so will you. This is the line of our secret. You, and me, and the child. We take her memories. Does anyone else know?"

Geneve thought of the pale-haired woman, thinking to speak, but Israel shook his head. "No one else, Justiciar."

"Then it is done." Ambrose strode to the wagon, holding a hand for Geneve. She took it, joining the Justiciar on the muddy road. The dirt didn't cling to his robes. Her feet were muddy and small beside his. He crouched low, holding the necklace before her eyes. "It'll be our little secret."

Chapter Fifty-Eight

Geneve's eyes snapped open, breath dragging through her
chest. Her body felt raw, her mind bloody.

Memory after memory *snicked* into place, pieces of a
puzzle, fragments of a person, held apart from the rest of her for thirteen years. Each one hit with the force of a punch.

Israel is my father.

Vertiline knew.

My mother sold me.

She stood on weary legs. The witch Nicolette faced Meriwether.
He held Geneve's borrowed steel with trembling arms. She could see
the fear in him, burning like a bonfire. Terrible, and wonderful, that he
would bring his beautiful, fragile self between her and a demon.

Geneve stepped to his side as she'd been taught. Cophine's third
stanza, for closing distance. She took the sword from Meriwether,
feeling a gentle strength in her hands. A feeling she'd never had before
because she'd always been imperfect. Broken. But it hadn't been *her*.

She'd had a piece missing. A terrible, frightening part. Her father,
the murderer. Her friend, the accomplice. They were her broken,
bitter family, and she loved them. "You came."

"Hah. I mean, sure."

Geneve looked into Meriwether's face, seeing his pain, his fear, and his anguish she would die. "You stood when all else didn't. Step back, Meri. I've got this."

"But ... the Storm," he said. "You should run. Get away, while you can."

The Storm. Geneve knew what it felt like now. Her steps were always perfect. She'd been *right* for so long, it was a part of her, waiting for the rest to return. Geneve swung her sword, welcoming the gods with each swing. Cophine, Ikmae, and Khiton's colors lit the steel. "Oh, Meri. I didn't believe Sight of Day. But he saw it, from the first day."

"Saw what?"

She faced Nicolette. Geneve saw behind the dead mask at what lay behind it. A corruption. This was no Champion. Nicolette was impure. She'd welcomed a demon into her soul. "I'm a daughter of the Three, and there's a Storm inside me."

⚡

NEITHER OF THEM HELD GLASS. FOR THE FIRST TIME GENEVE COULD finally use a Tresward blade, she didn't have one, and Nicolette's were broken by Israel.

Oh, Iz. Father.

Nicolette held a short steel knife, blade against her forearm. Geneve held her blade in Scorpion's Guard, sword above her head, other hand forward in a knife edge. The circled like dogs. The sound from outside as wizards fought an army of the dead sounded far away, like a battle happening on another world.

Meri crept back, looking for anything to help, but he couldn't help her here. She was a Knight of the Tresward, and the Three put her here, at this point at time, to kill a demon.

//DROP. YOUR. SWORD.// Nicolette spoke with Sway, the command in the words begging Geneve to lower her blade.

Instead, she laughed. "I don't think so, witch. Let's finish this with steel. No glass. No tricks."

"A Champion against an Adept."

Geneve nodded. "Or a demon against a Knight."

"You can see it? Israel couldn't." Nicolette stopped moving left, returning to the right. Her blade danced, trying to catch stray light, but the skies above were the gray of Ikmae's cloak. No sun came inside.

"Demons aren't real," Meri said, like he wanted to believe it.

Nicolette smiled wider. "They're as real as sinners. Now." //BE. QUIET.// "I'll get to you in a minute."

Meri's lips snapped shut, and he clasped his mouth with both hands, denying any noise.

Don't look. It's the distraction she wants.

Or, look. Distract her.

Geneve glanced to Meri, and Nicolette leaped forward. Her blade cut light from the air, a short swath of brilliant gold. Geneve stepped aside, her own sword slicing heaven's door. She'd trained for perfection when perfection never answered. Pattern after pattern, time after time. She'd worn a blindfold as often as her eyes were open. Never before had the Storm answered.

It came now.

Her sword cut Nicolette's blade in half. No chime of metal, no ring of an angel's cry. One moment Nicolette held steel, then nothing but the haft of a dagger. Geneve swung again, and Nicolette danced back.

The Storm followed Geneve's strike, a roaring wall of force tearing the floor apart. A shower of stone blasted Nicolette, and the Champion tumbled back as if Khiton himself tossed her aside.

Geneve knew moves in the patterns that had no purpose without the Storm behind them. Now she felt the Three's power in her arm and used it to break the witch knight. She swung overhand. Nicolette caught her blade against her armor, but the strike was too good.

The blade sheared through Nicolette's arm. The wave of force following Geneve's swing crushed the Champion to the ground, flattening her to a crumpled mess. Geneve swung again, then once more. Both blows rang with the tone of a massive bell, peals ringing out, calling for all to bear witness as a fallen Champion was cast down.

Smoke. Dust raining from the ceiling, then rain, wet and cold, as the roof collapsed. Silence, broken only after three heaving breaths. Geneve ran to Israel, sank to her knees beside the dead Valiant, and wept.

Chapter Fifty-Nine

When Nicolette fell, so did Meriwether's hands. The compulsion to not speak was gone. He scrambled to his feet. *You saw the divine. Geneve brought the Storm. She beat a Champion, blade on blade, and saved, like, everyone.*

She knelt in a crumpled huddle beside Israel. The pool of red beneath the Knight didn't grow. He was well dead, so Meriwether didn't go there.

He found himself by Vertiline's side. Blood still flowed from her arm. How she was still alive was a mystery. Maybe the Chevalier was too ornery to give up. He yanked off his belt, then worried the buckles on her greaves. The metal was twisted, the cut edge melted as if a great heat passed through it, but nothing burnt the flesh beneath. *Tresward mystic Smithsteel shit. Ignore it.*

He lashed his belt around Vertiline's arm. She stirred, eyes widening, nothing but delirium behind them. "Iz?"

"No. Just a sinner." He tugged the tourniquet tight, and she moaned, slipping back into unconsciousness. Meriwether wondered if it'd be better if she died here. He didn't know what lay between her and Israel, but he felt it would hurt enough to break the world.

Meriwether felt a gauntleted hand on his shoulder. Geneve sank beside him. She leaned forward, smoothing Vertiline's hair from her face. "Don't ever say that. You're no sinner, Meri."

"She's dying."

Geneve nodded. "The Tresward holds Knights as servants to the Clerics. We answer their orders and do the great works they demand." Her smile was twisted and bitter. "This is what it leads to. Dead Knights, and corrupt Clerics."

Meriwether got to one knee. "I'll get help."

"She's past help."

"There's a Tresward here, Red. I'll ... find a Cleric. Someone with the Sway." Meriwether ran a dust-caked hand through his hair. "Someone useful."

"Someone useful? You were the only one who stayed. If you go to the Tresward, they'll kill you. And where are they now, as the city burns?" Geneve closed her eyes, head bowed. "Tresward scripture says when the Three left this world, they left us to hold the door against the darkness. Knights as the good right arm of Light. Clerics to Sway the night. There's crossover. The best Champions use Sway, like Nicolette. My father..." Her voice cracked, but her eyes were clear when she opened them. "Iz could do it, a little."

"I know."

Geneve put her hand on Vertiline's stump. She leaned close to the Chevalier's ear, whispering. For three heartbeats nothing happened, then Vertiline spasmed, breath rattling in her lungs. Her eyes snapped open, wild like a terrified stallion, good hand clawing the air.

Geneve grasped it, held it to her chest. "Easy, Tilly."

Vertiline looked at Geneve, then Meriwether, and finally roamed the room. "Iz?"

"His Light is gone." Geneve's voice was so tight it could snap at any moment.

"Wait." Meriwether scratched his beard. "Israel is ... was your father?"

"Peace, Meri." Geneve held Vertiline's hand, like they both might drown. "Save your questions for tomorrow. Today we honor our valiant dead."

THE DEAD WERE NOT JUST VALIANT, THEY WERE A CARPET.
Meriwether picked his way through the market square. A mound larger
than most demanded his attention. He heaved bodies aside, uncov-
ering scaled hide, shark teeth, and snake eyes. "Armitage? Get up."

The Vhemin groaned. "I'm dead."

"If you say so." Meriwether walked on, looking for Sight of Day. He
spied the cat, bent over a fallen mage, tending as best he could. "Are
you okay?"

{You burn your frail lives for so little.} The Feybrind wept. *{So many of
you. Gone, like morning mist.}*

"Aye. That's about right, cat." Meri put his hand on Sight of Day's
shoulder. The Feybrind clutched the hand like a lifeline, stroking his
skin with a lightly-furred hand. "Shh. It's okay."

The cat nodded, then stood as the mage he'd been tending rattled a
last breath. The dying ... no, *dead* man had a hole in his chest, the
wound a bloody ruin. The Feybrind couldn't fix this. He'd just stayed so
the mage wouldn't die alone.

Meriwether watched the Feybrind walk to the pile of bodies,
unearthing more from around Armitage. The Vhemin sat upright,
looked around, and said something to Sight of Day. The Feybrind
nodded, head bowed. After an awkward moment, Armitage put his
hand on the cat's head. Meriwether left them like that.

He had someone to talk to.

MORGAN WALKED AT HIS SIDE BACK TO THE QUEENSFANE. DEAD
littered the streets, but fewer the farther they walked. Good
guardsmen stood against the dead, sheltering Ravenswall citizens as
best they could.

Meriwether saw tear-streaked faces. Astonishment that the dead
had fallen like broken tools. Joy mixed with sorrow. Men and women
helping children not their own. People stacking the bodies.

The queen hadn't asked stupid questions. Her red robe swept

beside Meriwether's rags, both their disguises gone. She'd been quiet as she saw the aftermath. Her honor guard was down to one man, the same Geneve had disarmed. He kept looking at his side, as if his companions might come back to life, but it wasn't that kind of day.

"What happened?" The queen didn't sound angry or sad. Just curious, and a little tired.

"Fallen Champion. Maybe a demon invasion. One Tresward, dead. Another crippled. A third ... I don't know." Meriwether raked his hair back from his face with a savage hand. "Broken worse, maybe. Or fixed. Too soon to know."

"They came to my capital, Lord du Reeves. I want to know who they are. I want them stopped."

"It's nice to want things."

She hissed, then subsided. "Perhaps that's fair. It's been a trying day."

"I'm sorry." Meriwether rubbed his chest. His heart ached for no good reason. "It wasn't fair. Can you ... give me a day or two?"

"You need to talk to your friends." She nodded, as if understanding.

"I need to help them grieve, Your Grace. Today was a bitter victory."

Chapter Sixty

T he queen gave them more than a day. She put them up in her
keep. People had made a fuss about Armitage until Geneve
stared them down. She didn't know what to say, so settled
for glaring. Rumors spread about the Adept who'd cut down a Champion, so the glare was enough.

Armitage said he thought it funny but didn't laugh. He watched
Sight of Day a lot and spent time with the Feybrind when he thought
no one was looking.

Geneve needed answers. She left the castle alone, on foot. No one
had seen Tristan, and she feared him dead, especially after Beck and
Fidget were brought to the castle stables. Her weary feet led her
through Ravenswall. Geneve wore no armor. She couldn't stand the
golden sun's weight today.

She carried a black sash with five gold bars. It was tattered and
worn, the black faded to white in places. Blood stained it, but the
black hid it well.

Geneve found the Tresward chapter house empty. No Knights
guarded its doors. No Novices tended the kitchens or trained in
the yard. She didn't know what to make of it as she walked the
deserted halls. It felt like it should be familiar, but she was an

imposter here. She'd welcomed a sinner into her life, and a city almost died for it.

He's not a sinner. And I fought to save the city. Stop moping. She straightened, wondering where that inner voice came from. It sounded like something Meri might have said, and so she trusted it.

The inner sanctum was empty, the three torches snuffed. She walked to the altar, draping Israel's sash across it. "Goodbye, Iz. Father. Friend. I'm sorry I let you down."

When she left, Meri was on the steps, back to her, waiting. She smiled, although he couldn't see it. *Of course he knew where I was going.* "Well met, Meri."

"Hey, Red." He stood, facing her. He clutched a book. "I guess we won, but it feels like we lost."

She nodded, hair hanging like tears. "There is no joy left."

"I don't know about that." He sat, patting the step beside him. "I've got to show you something."

"You shouldn't be here." Geneve sat anyway. "If the Tresward were still here—"

"You'd get me out." He leaned against her for a moment, a small smile on his face. She leaned right back for a moment. He straightened, and she immediately missed it. He patted the book, now in his lap. "I bet you're wondering what this is."

"It's a book."

"Hah. You're very clever." He smoothed the cover with a hand. "This is the Ledger of Lost Souls."

She goggled. "But ... we saw the Ledger. It had a face on it!"

"That old thing?" He scoffed. "No, that was some gaudy thing I saw at a market. This," he patted the leather cover, "is the Ledger. I showed it to their conjurer, and viola, here it is."

"I thought the queen wanted to destroy it."

"She did." Meri winked, and she felt warmer despite her heavy heart. "So, I stole it."

"You *what?*"

"Stole it," he admitted. "I wanted to read it."

"You wanted to read about dead Knights?"

"I wanted to know if it was true, Red." He opened the book about two-thirds through. Name after name was writ on the pages in the same perfect, flowing script. There were hundreds of names with lines through them, and others after unmarked. The last name with a line through it was hard to read.

~~KNIGHT VALIANT ISRAEL~~.

She keened, looking away. He touched her arm. "I'm sorry. That's not what I wanted to show you, but I can't show you without ... *showing* you."

Geneve blinked tears. "By the Three, Meri—"

"Here." He traced a finger over the name prior to Israel's.

~~KNIGHT ADEPT MANDER~~.

"What of it?" She followed the line of his finger, reading a few names.

"Well, it *should* say something like, 'High Bitch Nicolette.'" He flipped back five or ten pages. "It took me a while to find it, but I did. Here." He pointed to a name.

~~KNIGHT CHAMPION NICOLETTE~~.

Geneve took the Ledger from him. "This makes no sense."

"It kind of makes a really bad kind of sense." Meri stood, pacing. "She's been dead a long time. Years and fucking *years*, Red. We fought her, but she hasn't been a Knight in a long time."

"Resurrected?"

"Risen," he corrected. "Dark sorcery. All that." He waved a hand, then pursed his lips. "True sin."

"Don't—"

"Hey, I'm not raising the dead. I get it." Meri stretched. "But I'd be interested in knowing who else is in that book who's walking and talking but apparently dead. You know, no one's asked me where I saw the book."

Geneve nodded, finger holding her place. "I figured you didn't want to say."

"It's not like that. I mean—"

"But I think I know." She sighed. "This is from your father's library, isn't it?"

He sagged, like all the air went out of him. He gave a miserable nod. "Yes."

"It's okay." She met his eyes. "It wasn't *your* library."

"Don't you want to know what happened between me and dear ol' dad?" His voice was bitter, his smile crooked.

"Yes, but not until you want to tell the tale. You know I'm here." She looked away, letting him gather himself.

It didn't take long. Meri was used to scraping himself up with dustpan and broom. "Thank you. I want to, but ... not today."

"I understand. The world cries while we sit."

"Not that. I ... think we should remember our friends, not our enemies, today." He sank back beside her. "But soon. I promise."

Geneve nodded, head on his shoulder for a moment, then hunkered over the book. She went back farther than Nicolette's name. Years beyond counting, thousands of names of fallen Tresward under her fingers. "Uh."

"Uh?"

"More like, uh oh." Geneve offered him the book. "There."

He read the name. "Who's this guy?"

"Someone with answers." She stood, dusting off her pants. "Will you help me get them?"

He considered her question. Looked her up and down, a slow nod following. "Where are we going?"

"To hell and back."

"More specifically?"

Geneve thought about that for a while. "North, I think. That's where he was last."

"What about the dragon?"

"It'll turn up." She offered him a smile and beamed wider as he gathered it up and returned it. "Are you with me?"

"Always." He took her hand, open book in the other. "But really. Who is this guy?"

"A very bad man, I think." Geneve led Meri from the Tresward, and into the city beyond. They had work to do. The name she held in her thoughts, one she'd never forget again. Someone with answers.

~~CLERIC JUSTICIAR AMBROSE~~.

THE END.

THE CROWN TEETERS.

Geneve barely survived the truth. Now, **assassins come for the Queen.**

While burying their dead, Geneve and Meriwether are attacked by killers who can **be anyone, wear any face—including the one she loves.** Their goal? **To break the kingdom, one blade at a time.**

The rebellion is burning. The Feybrind and Vhemin are at war. And in the north, a madman whispers to a dragon, gripping a power even the ancients feared.

Geneve's skymetal blade has felled many foes. But against **fire and legend**, steel alone won't be enough.

Turn the page to begin *The Storm Within*.

THE STORM WITHIN
A DARK FANTASY ADVENTURE

Facing the Night

They came for Geneve while she buried her dead.

The air of Ravenswall smelled of smoke and rot. A sky forged of lead and sorrow hung overhead, threatening rain. It was cold, as cold as the south was, but with a malice that got into the bones. Geneve stood within the city's Tresward keep. Its walls held supplicant hands to the clouds, but the Three didn't answer. The gods had been silent for so long, she wondered if they were real.

The city mourned. Thousands died, and her losses were tiny compared to that. *Just one man, and perhaps not a very good one. Why am I here?*

The keep's courtyard was empty of anyone except her closest. Armitage glared snake eyes at the pyre, the torch in his hand a licking, hissing statement of anger. Sight of Day clasped hands before him, head bowed. Geneve didn't know if he prayed, or who to. The Three had forsaken his kind long ago. Vertiline leaned on a cane with her remaining hand, a bloody bandage covering the stump of her other. It was stained, but couldn't come close to the redness of her eyes. Tilly hadn't cried in front of Geneve, but the evidence of her grief was written on her face.

Meri stood out of sight behind her, but she could *feel* his presence.

Still reed-thin, shivering in borrowed, tattered clothes. But here all the same, because he had her back when sense suggested he should run. Or hide, to get away from her, and those like her.

The pyre waited. It held two bodies. Nicolette, Knight Champion, and Israel, Knight Valiant. Both were Tresward, but so much more. Nicolette died a long time ago and walked as risen.

Israel was her father.

Both seemed peaceful. Sight of Day, Armitage, and Meri dressed them in Smithsteel, because she couldn't bear to, and Tilly couldn't anymore. The burnished sun on their breastplates stared at the heavens as if demanding an accounting from Cophine, Ikmae, and Khiton. The gods didn't seem to care. Not about their shield for the world, or perhaps the world itself.

A scuff of shoe on stone, and then a touch at her elbow. "Would you like to say anything?" Meri's voice was calm, even, and stronger than she felt.

"I have nothing to say. Burn them." Geneve nodded to Armitage.

The monster's snake eyes looked past her to Meriwether. The young man's hand left her elbow. "I have a few words. If nobody minds."

Geneve swung to him, voice dry as old leaves. "They're not your dead."

He nodded, not arguing, but not stepping back. "I don't know who Nicolette was. A Champion for Light? We've seen it. But corrupted by the dark, dragged low. Forsaken. She doesn't deserve our anger, but instead, our pity. Our memory of the good she did." He sighed, a bellows running low on wind. "I know who Israel was, though. Dedicated. Honorable."

"He tried to kill you a handful of times," Armitage grunted. "This torch isn't getting any lighter."

"Who's to say I didn't deserve the killing?" Meriwether shrugged. "I'm no god. But I think Israel wasn't guided by the Three."

{The Justiciars,} Sight of Day suggested, his golden eyes soft. {They are just people.}

"Maybe. But I'm not talking about him hunting me. I'm an accident of thought here. A red herring to cloud the mind." Meri stepped away from Geneve, holding his hand out as if to display her as an exhibit. "His most important thing in all the world wasn't his honor, or his dedication. It was something more ... precious." Meri's hand fell. "I would have liked to know him better. I feel the lack is mine." Geneve felt something in her chest give, just a little. "He gave up love," Meri's eyes found Vertiline's, "and duty," he turned to the keep, before finally looking at Geneve, "to pursue something more."

"Treachery?" Geneve felt the anguish in her voice.

"No, Red." Meri's eyes turned sad, but she saw the understanding there. "Hope."

"A time when he could leave the Tresward?" Tilly's coldness rivaled the cloud's. "He was their man. He was—"

"*Here*," Meri insisted. "*Right* here. Always." He tried for a lighter tone. "Trust me. As a man with an absentee father..." The joke died on his lips. "But this isn't about me." He raised his eyes to the keep's walls. "This is ... hang about. Who's that?"

Geneve followed his gaze. Standing atop the keep's walls, frozen against the skyline, stood a hooded figure. They held a bow. In a single smooth motion, they raised it. "'Ware!" she screamed. "We're under attack!"

Vertiline spun, the motion no longer smooth enough. The loss of her hand unbalanced her. She swept her glass blade from its scabbard. The figure loosed, Vertiline sidestepping, slicing the arrow from the air. But she wasn't perfect. Not anymore, and the Storm didn't answer her call. The arrow and blade both shattered, the clatter of the shaft against stone accompanied by the tinkling bells of glass rain.

More assailants boiled from the shadows. Geneve counted five, Requiem finding her hand like a lover in the dark. An arrow spat toward Meri, and she swung the steel in a beautiful, wondrous arc. A flight of vermillion sparrows fluttered skyward in the blade's wake, the arrow shattered to fragments.

Sight of Day turned, tail swishing. He met an attacker head-on. His assailant leveled a pike, but the Feybrind slipped around the thrust like his body were air. The cat disarmed his opponent, spun, and beheaded his foe, golden eyes seeking others.

Two rushed Armitage. The monster laughed, using the torch like a cudgel. Flame and justice hammered the face of one using a short blade. The second used a rapier, darting in, hoping speed would be better against bulk. *He's not seen the monsters fight.* The Vhemin jinked left, then clotheslined his enemy. He followed the man to the ground with brutal punches.

Two came for Vertiline. Geneve called, "Tilly!" then tossed Requiem. The skymetal hungered across the distance, turning in a vicious spin. It collected one of Vertiline's attackers, knocking the woman from her feet. Tilly followed the sword's path without looking, putting her hand on hilt as the blade thrummed in the corpse. She drew Requiem from the body, swinging low, then high. Her strikes no longer held perfection, but that didn't stop her attacker losing his left leg followed by his head.

Geneve looked up. The bowman still stood on the walls. Tribunal's range would be insufficient. She ran forward, eyes resting on Armitage's dropped torch. Geneve grabbed it, felt its weight, and eyed the distance. One of Khiton's seven hundred patterns came to mind. *Return What is Owed.* Her stance was faultless as she wound up, throwing the burning brand.

It spun, arcing across the distance. She heard the song of the Storm, the scream of vengeance, the cry of justice. The torch burned brighter, exploding as it hit the archer. His body erupted into burning fragments, charred gristle and ash hurrying away on the cold wind.

"Fuck me," Armitage said.

Sight of Day walked past her, eyes on the battlements. {*I always said there was a storm inside you, Daughter of the Three.*}

"I'm not their fucking daughter," Geneve spat. She whirled, red locks angry. Vertiline met her glare first and tipped her head, half tiny bow, half acknowledgment.

Armitage's eyes were wide, slitted snake pupils still on the burning ruin above. He held an assassin in one hand, but almost like he'd forgotten about the man. "Lemme get another torch."

Behind them all, Meri. The still calm in the eye of the storm. The young sorcerer walked past Vertiline, and sidestepped Armitage to stand before Geneve. "You're not their daughter, no. You're his." A slight nod to the pyre, and Israel.

He held his arms out as if he knew what was coming next. *Israel doesn't deserve my tears. He lied to me my entire life. He turned his face from my mother. He and Vertiline slaughtered a village. They conspired with a Justiciar to keep everything from me.* But those were just words, and words were nothing against what she tried to keep inside. *Tresward don't crack. We don't break. We are the world's shield.*

Meriwether didn't move. His eyes were kind, and sad, and asked nothing of her. His arms were still waiting for ... for what? For her to bend? To fall apart, for a man who didn't deserve it, in a city that didn't care?

Her heart didn't care what she thought. Geneve felt the crack in her chest break open, and she huddled into Meri as the tears came. He put his hand on her head, stroking her red hair. "It's okay," he said. "It's okay."

But it wasn't. Geneve sobbed by the pyre of a man she'd never really known. She'd thought him a friend, a mentor. A guide through life. But she'd not known him as her father, and she never would.

It wouldn't be okay ever again.

❦

TIME PASSED. THE MINUTES SEEMED INFINITE, YET INSUFFICIENT.

Geneve walked the halls of Ravenswall's Tresward bastion. Things felt familiar enough, yet she was a foreigner here. She didn't know why. It wasn't the emptiness. Geneve remembered the smell of oil and sweat. Could almost hear steel on glass, the huff of breath, the cry of the Storm unleashed. The training halls here were smaller, designed for Knights to practice rather than train Novices, but they had the same equipment. Heavy things to lift. Solid wood and stone to hit. Ropes, and unsteady bridges. Blindfolds and shields, spears and Smithsteel. Glass if she wanted it.

Her fingers trailed over a wooden mannequin. The face was pitted and scarred, rough under her fingers. It felt like bark, not the polished training dummy that'd been delivered here, shiny and new.

Geneve left the training area. She found the barracks. All cots were empty. Possessions, gone. Drawers held no keepsakes. *Have they aban-*

doned me? The city? Or the world? Whatever called the Tresward away at Ravenswall's hour of need, they'd left no trace. She found no books in the Cleric's library, the shelves empty. The kitchen ovens were cold, and bathing water was freezing.

Her armored boots clacked against the stone floors. Geneve's echoes kept her company. She'd left the burning pyre behind. The regard of her friends felt too heavy to carry, so she'd walked inside. *I look for solace where I don't belong.*

Am I still Tresward? I command the Storm. But my brothers and sisters left me.

Her feet knew where to go. They led her down steps worn with use. The Smithy was empty. Gloom lay like a gray blanket, broken by shafts of dusty light from small windows set high in the walls. It smelled of a man she didn't know. Not Kytto and the warmth beneath his anger, but someone like him. It was as familiar as dirt. The armory held no glass or steel, but the air remembered the scent of hard work. Her fingers ran across the empty racks.

They didn't even leave dust.

Geneve's fingers ran along her sash. The black strip, and its single bar of gold. *Knight Adept Geneve.* Her lips twisted into a sneer, fist clenching around the sash.

"Don't do that."

Geneve whirled at Meri's voice. He stood in the Smithy's gloom, face shadowed, but she heard the care, layered brick by brick, in his voice. Cautious, because this was her place. *Maybe he fears his voice isn't welcome here.* "Do what?"

"Your sash." He moved through the shadows, rags whispering as he came. He touched her armored hand above the fabric. She couldn't feel his fingers but wanted to.

"I'm no Tresward."

"You are all the *way* Tresward."

"We hunt sinners." Geneve jerked her hand away. "You've no idea what that means."

He sighed, lowering his fingers. "Maybe I don't. I thought it meant someone who was strong but kind. Brave when it made no sense. A person who put shoulder to the heaviest weights, giving all, letting nothing go."

Geneve fingered the sash, then slipped it over her head. She let the black puddle to the floor. "I didn't earn that, you know."

"Hah. Oh, you're serious." He paced. "Tell me, then."

"I drugged my opponents before my Trial. I couldn't use the Storm. They'd have swept me aside like pieces from a board." Geneve hung her head.

"So?"

"So, I cheated!"

Meri laughed for real this time. "Everyone cheats. *Everyone*. You just feel bad about it. Tell me, oh doubtful Knight, what's so wrong about using your mind?"

Geneve sighed. "It wasn't ... honorable."

"But you passed the Trial?"

"The Clerics thought it an amusing trick. They let me carry my single gold bar." She nudged the sash with her boot. "But Vertiline and Israel had to carry the rest of me. Until—"

"Until you saved a city. Yeah, I was there." He scuffed a hand through unruly hair. It'd grown longer on the road. It had a curl to it Geneve liked. "Why are you here?"

"I miss him." Geneve unbuckled her gauntlet. "I can't stand it, this, this..." Her words ran out as she tore the metal glove free. It hit the ground with a clatter. Her fingers found the clasps on her other gauntlet. "This *cage!*"

Meriwether was by her side. Hands over hers. "What are you doing?"

"Will you help me?" Eyes on his. Heart hammering. Chest pounding.

"Always."

"Get it *off* me." Piece by piece, he helped her take off her Tresward armor. The golden sun clattered to the ground, face down. Pauldrons, greaves, and gauntlets. Steel, chain, and leather, all in a heap. She stood in the cellar, wearing only padding. Feeling her heart grow lighter with each piece removed.

Kytto wouldn't be pleased at the mess. Geneve picked up the armor, returning it to the racks. Last of all was the sash. She felt the fabric in her hands. It was almost new, holding the black like a moonless night. Vertiline's was a little frayed, and Israel's had been gray.

"You should keep that, at least." Meri tried for a grin, but it was sickly, born feeble. "You never know. You might need something to guide you home."

She fetched holster and scabbard, then turned to the stairs. "Come, Meri."

"In a minute." The young wizard lingered, eyes roaming the room. "I'll be right behind you. I just want to ... understand."

Geneve nodded, leaving him to his peace. But she took his advice, clutching the black sash in her fist. Its single gold bar felt almost as heavy as the steel she'd shed.

Chapter One

It took a while for Meriwether to find everything he needed. The Tresward did an excellent job of stripping the place of anything that wasn't nailed down, but it wasn't the first time he'd robbed someone. A cabinet in the scullery, forgotten by even the spiders who'd woven ancient silk above the lock, yielded a suitable sack. It'd held desiccated remains of what might once have been onions, but there was no one to ask, and Meriwether wasn't an archeologist.

Geneve was long gone once he'd collected the things he thought they'd need. Armitage and a glowing pile of coals waited in the courtyard. The Vhemin grunted when Meriwether emerged, hauling his sack. "You need a hand with that?"

"I got it." Meriwether joined the monster by the pyre's remains.

"Good. I wasn't going to help anyway." The creature reached a scaled hand into the coals, rooting about. He pulled free a burnished gauntlet. No soot clung to it. It wasn't the blackened Smithsteel of a fallen Champion, which meant it was Israel's. "That Tresward armor's really something, isn't it?"

"It's the people within it that are the real marvel."

"Don't be a dick." Armitage tossed the gauntlet back into the glowing heap, then brushed soot from his hands. "That's not what I meant, and you know it." He eyed Meriwether's sack. "What's in the bag?"

"Something I think we'll need."

"Weapons?"

"Of a sort."

"I heard it's legal to kill a man for being an asshole," the Vhemin warned. "The guard don't come looking or nothing."

Meriwether laughed. "This isn't for you. Not for me either, really."

Armitage sniffed. "Smells like bullshit."

"Could be." Meriwether headed toward the gates, avoiding the fallen bodies of their attackers. "I feel we should be worried about these guys."

"Worrying won't help," the monster warned. "They know where we are."

"Who?"

"Whoever's behind all," Armitage waved his arm at the sky, "this shit. We got undead fuckers. We've got turned Knights and fallen heroes. Some asshole's even worked out to get my kind," he slapped his chest, "working together. And then we kicked 'em in the balls. That's a thing a man doesn't soon forget."

Meriwether paused half-way to the gates. "We did, didn't we? Kick 'em in the balls, I mean. Geneve killed their Champion."

The monster squinted. "You got a point, or are you just seeing if your teeth still meet in the middle?"

"Why would you send six normal people against the Savior of Ravenswall?" Meriwether eyed the battlements where smoke still curled from the remains of an assassin. "It doesn't make sense. Not unless..."

They both stood like posts for a handful of heartbeats. Armitage scratched his armpit. "Oh, fuck."

"That's what I was thinking." Meriwether turned for the gate, putting a little curry in his stride. "Why didn't I bring a horse?"

THE JOURNEY TO THE QUEENSFANE WAS A HURRIED AFFAIR. Meriwether's burden was too heavy to run with, and he wouldn't surrender it to Armitage. The monster jogged at his side, glaring snake eyes at any humans who got too close.

Vhemin weren't welcome in Ravenswall, and it was a wonder he hadn't been murdered. *Still, plenty of time for that. It's only mid-week.* Meriwether didn't know why Armitage was still with them. Or Sight of Day, for that matter. The cat had promised to bring Meriwether to the queen, and he'd delivered. The Vhemin's deal was up, too. They'd opened the temple, and he'd taken them across the desert.

We're worlds apart, the four of us. A sinner, Knight, monster, and house cat. But Meriwether admitted he was glad of the Vhemin's company. Armitage might've been a murderer, but he was *their* murderer. And being a wizard in a city brought low by vile magic wasn't the safest place to be.

The streets wound toward the Queensfane. The pair ducked through the Artists Borough, ignoring the misery they found. No actors practiced for play. No artists painted. The city mourned, and none felt it so plain as those tuned to the heart.

The castle was quiet enough, no alarms crying a warning. That didn't mean they weren't too late. Meriwether puffed. "We need to hurry."

"Gimme the sack, then."

"Get your own." Meriwether flashed the Vhemin a quick grin. The monster answered with his horror-show teeth. "The only reason to attack us was a diversion. There's only one target more important than the Savior of Ravenswall."

"The queen," the monster agreed. "Don't know why you runts bother. The woman can't lift a sword. She'd die in three days on the plague lands. Maybe it's a mercy to rid you of weakness at the top."

"Sometimes it's not about our outer strength." Meriwether ducked around a cart. "It's what's inside."

"Blood? No?" Armitage shook his head. "I've no idea what you mean, then."

"I think you do, monster."

"I think you need to run faster, runt."

The sack didn't get lighter, or the breathing easier. But that wasn't the worst thing that would happen today. So, they ran.

THEY CAUGHT UP WITH GENEVE AND SIGHT OF DAY OUTSIDE THE castle. Vertiline was nowhere to be seen, her pale skin and almost white hair absent. Geneve marched with purpose toward the castle gates. The Knight's hair was teased into red strands by the wind. The cat appeared unruffled by the wind and current events both. "Geneve!"

She turned, a smile touching her lips as she saw him. "Meri." Her eyes found the sack. "What's that?"

"Why's everyone worried about my luggage?" Meriwether paused, sucking air. He waved at Armitage to continue, as the monster didn't seem winded at all.

"The runt … your pardon." Armitage wiped his mouth, starting again at Geneve's glare. "I mean no disrespect, and you know it. It's just, we've got a thing going on. He calls me monster, I call him runt, and neither of us knifes the other in their sleep."

"Wait, there are knives involved?" Meriwether adjusted his load, expression astonished.

{We're going to die, and we won't even know why.} Sight of Day rolled his eyes.

"Shut it, cat." Armitage scratched his gut. "Here's the thing. You don't attack the Savior of Ravenswall—"

"The who?" Geneve glare turned to an overcast scowl.

{He means you.}

"I'm not—"

"This will go faster if you shut up," Armitage suggested. "You don't attack the slayer of a Champion with six grunts. Doesn't matter if you've got the element of surprise or not. The only way you kill a Knight, and take this from someone who knows for sure, is from a distance, with an arbalest."

"The queen," Geneve hissed, whirling to the keep. Her fingers clutched her empty scabbard. "Vertiline has my sword."

{She'll probably need it more than you. They will send many, and in great

numbers, against a Chevalier.} Sight of Day's tail swished. *{I hope her shopping expedition is important.}*

Shopping? Meriwether frowned. "She's going to get drunk?"

{That's what I said.}

"She's not a Chevalier. None of us are what we were a week ago." Geneve looked to the castle. "Let's get inside."

⁂

THEY BURST INTO THE QUEEN'S THRONE ROOM. QUEEN MORGAN WAS in deep conversation with one of her Coterie when they slammed the doors open. The queen's house guard arrayed before her throne came to attention, blades already out of scabbards before recognizing Meriwether and Geneve.

Maybe we should've knocked first.

Morgan's eyes widened, lips pressed into a line. "Knight Adept Geneve. Lord du Reeves." Morgan looked across the monster and cat. "And ... friends. I trust this intrusion has purpose?" If she was surprised at Geneve's appearance, all white cotton and no armor, she didn't let it show.

"Assassins," Geneve said. "They came at us at the Tresward bastion."

The man the queen was talking to straightened. Meriwether didn't recognize him, but there was a lot of that going round. His robe said *I'm a wizard, stand back* better than the small silver broach the queen gave to her favored. The broach was fine and all: the Coterie's symbol was a stylized lightning bolt, which Meriwether felt overemphasized the benefits of evokers, but everyone needed a mascot. "And yet ... we are perfectly safe."

Meriwether glanced at the ceiling. *That's where they came from last time.* The rafters were free of clinging assassins. "This is ... unexpected."

"Not at all, Lord du Reeves," the man oozed. "While you've been playing at wizardry and grandstanding, a few of us are trying to save the kingdom. I thought you might try a little more showmanship. It's what your kind is," he sneered, "good for."

Geneve bridled, but Meriwether touched her arm. *I've got this.* Gentle fingers, a passing touch, but she stilled. "And how many Champions have you killed, hmm?"

The man cleared his throat. "That's hardly—"

"Or risen dead?" Meriwether leaned forward, ear cocked. "Is it more or less than one?"

"Lord du Reeves." Queen Morgan stood.

Meriwether winced. "Please don't call me that."

"My throne room, my rules." A smile, a hint of the young woman behind it. "Please, let me introduce Vikander. He is the new head of the Coterie. He holds sway over the elements."

Meriwether felt his gut churn. *This asshole?* "I'm sure he'll be fine. Back to the assassins—"

"That means you report to me," Vikander said.

Meriwether frowned. "What a curious notion. What gives you that idea?"

"I, uh, am in charge of the—"

"The Coterie, I know." Meriwether waved his hand. "You're under some kind of fantastic illusion I'm a member of your special club." Geneve snorted. "I've got friends aplenty."

The queen patted the air with her hands. *{Calm down.}* "I meant to make this offer more formally, but since you're here..." The queen's eyes slid off Meriwether, finding Geneve at his side. "I've need of people with specialist skills. Those who can hunt threats against the kingdom."

"The kingdom, or the throne?" Geneve's voice was clear, betraying none of the morning's emotion. If she felt self-conscious without her armor, white cotton hanging in soft lines down her frame, she gave no hint.

"They are the same thing." The queen's voice held a little ice mixed with steel.

"They are fucking not," Armitage said. "One's a person, who might be an asshole. The other's a group of people, which I'll admit, might mean a group of assholes."

Morgan spared the monster a withering glare. "Both, then."

"I'm not working for him." Meriwether eyed Vikander. "I don't think anyone else will, either."

Vikander's eyes held amber fire, the faintest hint of power deep within. "You'll come to heel, you little—"

Geneve took one perfect, flawless step forward. When her foot landed, a distant peal of thunder touched the air. Her eyes were locked on Vikander.

"Hi," Meriwether said brightly. "Look, before this gets out of hand, I think it's worth finishing the introductions. I'm Meriwether, this is Sight of Day," he pointed to the cat, "the warlord Armitage," the Vhemin cocked an eyebrow but said nothing, "and the Savior of Ravenswall, Knight Adept Geneve."

Vikander's throat worked like he was swallowing a live cockroach. "That's the—"

"Knight Adept, yes. Keep up, man." Meriwether beamed, then faced the queen. "You want to offer us a job?"

She nodded. "I need people..." Morgan quieted, raven locks framing her face, then eyed Armitage. "I need humans I can trust."

Geneve shook her head. "If one of us works for you, all of us do."

The queen's smile faded. "Perhaps I could ask the Feybrind Kingdom, but the Vhemin—"

"All or none, your majesty." Geneve glanced to Meriwether. "I've friends aplenty, too."

"Also, we need to think about it," Armitage said. "The cat thinks so too." Sight of Day nodded. "Mostly, we need to get drunk."

Before the queen could answer, a bell pealed, high and clear. It wasn't the regular cadence of a clocktower, but the panicked frenzy of an alarm. More of Morgan's house guard streamed into the throne room, readying to whisk her to safety.

Armitage sighed. "I guess that's a no to the drink."

"I need steel." Geneve faced Meriwether. "Go with the queen. Stay out of sight."

"I can—"

"I need you *safe*," she hissed. "I've lost so much already." Red hair lashing, she stormed from the room, Armitage and Sight of Day on her heels.

Meriwether watched them go. "But I need you safe, too."

Chapter Two

Geneve knew the castle wasn't under attack. The alarms came from outside, the high peal carrying across the sea air near the keep. She ran through the keep, seeking anyone with a sword who didn't look like they needed it.

A mace would do.

She didn't find any conveniently laying about. The three made the keep's main portcullis. It rumbled closed behind them as they squinted in the overcast glare. Geneve visored her eyes with a hand, trying to work out where the crisis was. The bell tolled from the Artist's Borough, but she couldn't see the cause. "Where do we go?"

{Over there.} Sight of Day arrived at her shoulder, pointing. *{See the flame?}*

The cat's golden eyes were sharp. She'd missed it at first: a tiny plume of smoke was chased heavenward by licks of fire. A fire could be disastrous, but didn't explain the alarm. The sound demanded *attack!* not, *get a bucket!* "Let's find out what's going on."

They ran from the keep. Soldiers and the queen's house guard readied defenses in the grounds. People hurried, but none seemed to have clear purpose. Panic was everyone's constant companion after the living dead walked these streets.

The roads outside the keep were more choked than usual as some ran toward the alarm, others away. Armitage bellowed, bulling his way through the crowd. Sight of Day slid between people like water around rocks, and found an underused alley. *{This way.}* He waved them over. *{As happy as Armitage looks bashing skulls, it'll be faster if we avoid people.}*

Geneve and the monster joined Sight of Day. She clutched useless fingers over her empty scabbard. "I need a blade."

Armitage snorted. "You also need armor, but you had to go all melodramatic."

{The creature speaks truth. There's a first time for everything.} Golden eyes found hers. *{We could leave this to those with arms and armor.}*

"Tilly's out here somewhere. Knowing our luck, she'll be at the heart of the ruckus. Come on." Geneve headed down the alley at a run, eyes up to the roofs for danger from above.

The Feybrind paced past her, making her speed look like the slow amble of a racing snail. He leaped up a wall, bounced to the other, then hauled himself onto a balcony. Another jump, a ricochet from the opposite wall, and he was on the roof. He peered over, then pointed north. *{That way. I'll guide you from up here.}*

"Fucking cat." Armitage glared. "Always running away."

Geneve headed north. She felt light without her armor. Faster, more fluid. *The feeling is dangerous. I've nothing between my heart and harm but a thin cotton shift.* Their path crossed a busy street. Armitage stampeded through, parting people like a ram through a rotted gate. Geneve followed on his heels, ignoring scared eyes and more immediate cries of alarm. *Vhemin!* and *monster!* filled her ears, and then they were past.

Sight of Day waved from a rooftop, directing them to the west. Geneve rounded a corner, finding a short alley and a closed door. She slowed, but Armitage didn't. The Vhemin sped up, shoulder down, barreling through the closed door as if it were parchment. Geneve jumped debris. Her eyes said *you're in a kitchen* and her mind screamed *no time! Run!*

Another door, and into a small shop front. The smell of pastry and panic. More cries, and a blade bared, steel hungering for the light. Armitage slugged the man who'd drawn. Geneve grabbed the dropped shortsword—*at last!*—in passing. Her hand measured its weight and said *this is a flimsy weapon*, but there were no others.

With the Storm backing her swing, she didn't need strong steel. Geneve could fight with brittle glass and carve apart the Three's enemies.

Except I don't know if these are enemies of the Three. I've no idea what's ahead.

She brushed rebellious hair from her eyes. Geneve's heart said something terrible was coming, and her heart hadn't lied. The same heart told her Meri was a good and true friend, the Vhemin wouldn't turn on her, and that Sight of Day would stand with her.

The street outside clotted with people. Two broken carts lay tangled ahead. One was lashed to a horse, which lay on the ground on account of being dead. The other was headed by a donkey, braying in pain, while people milled about in confusion. Armitage slowed, charting a course for the trapped animal.

"Armitage! No time!"

"We make time," the monster roared, not slowing. He slammed into a man in argument with another by the tangled donkey, knocking him into the broken cart. A scaled fist dropped the other, and the Vhemin grabbed the fallen man's belt knife. A few slashes, and the donkey was free of bonds, but still trapped by the wreckage.

Armitage got beneath the cart's seat, shouldering the weight. He heaved, feet skidding against the cobbled ground. *We don't have time for this!* But Geneve saw the monster's eyes as he looked on the donkey. Something like remembered pain, or borrowed sympathy.

She vaulted the wreckage, getting to the other side. Geneve got her hands under the cart, heaving. Wood splinters fought against callused palms, but she ignored them. She strained, and the cart rose. The donkey brayed, back legs spasming, then it was free.

Armitage dropped his side, Geneve following suit. He reached for the donkey, but it kicked, hitting him in the chest. He staggered, and the beast used the time to make a quick getaway. Armitage righted himself, horror teeth split in a grin. "Got a good kick, that one."

"Didn't it hurt?"

"Hurt plenty. Not the worst thing that'll happen to me, though." Snake eyes found her own. "Why are we standing around?"

She bared her teeth, half snarl, half grin, then looked for Sight of Day. The Feybrind waved them on from the rooftop corner of a building by an alley. Geneve ran, passing a gentlemen's clothier, a barber, and an empty store before hitting the relative quiet of the alley.

The Vhemin will kill people without pause, but stops to help an animal. Her mind wouldn't leave it alone. The monster chugged along beside her, snake eyes front, paying her no mind. *He is like that with his bear, Beck.*

Her thoughts were waylaid as they burst into a small courtyard. It was the type used by carts to deliver raw materials and pick up finished goods. Back to a wall, pale face a contrast to the bloody bandage at her severed wrist, leaned Vertiline. The Chevalier held Requiem steady enough, but Geneve had seen enough people lose blood to know Tilly was standing on grit alone. Requiem's fang tasted the enemy, the blade a ruddy, wet red.

Arrayed before her like the scattered leaves of a deadly flower were black-clad bodies. None moved, because Tresward didn't strike to injure. Vertiline might not hold the Storm on a tight leash anymore, but she knew the blade, the body, and how the former was the key to the latter's lock. Release, and you free the soul within.

An open door to Geneve's left disgorged thick, black smoke. The building's windows vomited flame. *This is where the fire is. But also, enemies intent on Tilly's murder.*

The dead were many, but still outnumbered by the living. Geneve's quick count said *ten still breathe*. Armitage, never one for complex math, charged into the fray. He grabbed a man by his belt, then swung him like a club into another.

Tribunal was in Geneve's hand, the scattergun roaring like a lion, calling all eyes to her. *That's right, ignore my friend. Pale Vertiline trembles like a leaf in a storm.* The gun's first bite chewed a woman's arm and shoulder to the bone, the second tearing the jaw from another.

She threw her shortsword, the blade whistling through the air to lodge in the skull of a man preparing to throw a spear at Vertiline. The hilt snapped off as the blade hit, confirming her belief it was a shoddy weapon. Geneve followed the weapon's path, halting her charge in the middle of the courtyard. Weaponless, and with five opponents still standing.

They spread around her, ignoring—*blessed Three*—Vertiline. Two went for Armitage, three still on Geneve. A *snick-thud* announced the arrival of Sight of Day's attention, an arrow shaft sprouting from the skull of a man with hard, gray eyes. The Feybrind was invisible in the pall of smoke above, but his arrows still found their mark.

A woman to Geneve's left threw a javelin. Geneve caught it, letting the momentum take her arm back, then tossed the shaft on the same path back to its owner. The Storm trembled along the javelin. It hit, shearing the woman in half like the hand of Khiton himself knocked her apart.

Three left. A crunch and a scream behind her suggested Armitage had dropped that number to two. Geneve faced her remaining opponent, nothing between her heart and his stiletto but thin cotton, stained with sweat and blood. His eyes roamed her, then he turned on his heel to flee.

Another arrow *snick-thudded* from Sight of Day's vantage above, hitting behind her. Armitage's last opponent gone, with but one remaining. A whirl of bloody skymetal, the unmistakable flash of Requiem as it spun past Geneve, hitting the man in the chest. He gurgled, fingers clutching steel as he fell.

Geneve turned, seeing Vertiline so very pale, her stump dripping blood through its bandage. The Chevalier gave a crooked smile. "You throw your sword so often, I wanted to see what it was like."

The burning building's heat was like a forge. Geneve shielded her eyes with her hand, coughing at smoke that hadn't found the heavens. Armitage kicked a woman at his feet. She had an arrow through her neck. The monster squinted at Sight of Day, who gave a cheery wave. "That one was *mine*, cat! You don't steal another man's kill."

The Feybrind landed cat-perfect on the ground beside Geneve, bow in hand. *{You looked like you could use the help.}*

"It's just not done!" The monster kicked the corpse again.

Geneve made it to Vertiline's side before she could slide to the ground. She held her friend up, one hand on her shoulder, the other resting light fingers above her stump. Vertiline's breath hissed through clenched teeth. "It stings."

"You shouldn't have exerted yourself. It's not healed, Tilly."

"Tell them. I just..." She trailed off, eyes unfocused for a moment. "I came here to get—"

"Drunk," Armitage snarled. "While the rest of us were working for a living."

"Armor." The pale woman sighed. "I need to sit."

"Hold her. Don't let her sleep." Geneve waited for Armitage to step in. The monster's snake eyes met hers. His look said, *She's probably going to die.*

Geneve turned aside. She didn't want to hear it. A quick rummage among the dead yielded a strong leather belt. She bound it around Vertiline's wrist, closing off the blood flow. *I used the Sway on her to stop the bleeding before. Can I do it again?* She leaned close to Vertiline's ear. The Chevalier smelled of smoke, sweat, and a sickly kind of fear, but mostly of regret. Geneve tried to ignore Tilly's feelings, reaching inside herself.

It was difficult to remember what happened when—

Don't think about it.

—the Valiant fell. Geneve felt into the core of her, the place where she kept her feelings locked away. Her mind's fingers found one that felt like terror, then discarded it for one that tasted of love. She whispered, "Vertiline, your body doesn't bleed. You know this to be true." Geneve drew back, then kissed Tilly on the forehead. *//BE WELL.//*

Vertiline's eyes were closed, her breathing shallow. She'd passed out. But Geneve liked to think her skin looked a little less pale, her skin less pinched in pain.

"Well, hell, I'm glad you did that. We should wheel you out to kiss everyone better on the battlefield." Armitage hefted Vertiline, but gently, so carefully, like she was made of the glass she used to wield.

"Don't get any ideas." Geneve retrieved Requiem, then slipped shells into Tribunal. She scanned the courtyard. "Why was Tilly here?"

{Why did someone set fire to this perfectly fine building?} Sight of Day's tail swish, swished. His golden eyes squinted against the blaze's heat. *{Perhaps we should get clear. Fire is bad.}*

Geneve made a quick search of the dead. As expected, they had no papers, no convenient scrolls showing their mission, and no helpful tattoos or clan markings. Clean skins, near as her hurried search could tell. Professionals, sent for one purpose. She eyed Vertiline, who looked like a child in Armitage's massive arms.

They were sent to kill a Knight, and they almost succeeded.

Geneve almost gave up, then saw a too-familiar wave of hair defying the constraints of a hood. She knelt, pushing the hood aside, then stumbled back, hand to her mouth. Geneve wouldn't mistake that face, not in a thousand lifetimes. The hair her fingers wanted to feel, the beard that never seemed short or long enough.

It was Meri, sightless eyes staring skyward.

The Assassins Have Struck.

THE KINGDOM BURNS.

Geneve has fought monsters before. But this time, the enemy hides in plain sight.

The Queen's rule is crumbling. **Rebellion spreads.** The Feybrind and Vhemin **march to war.** And in the north, a madman wields the power of a dragon. If Geneve and Meriwether can't stop him, the throne will fall—and the kingdom with it.

Her blade is sharp. Her enemies are sharper. And time is running out.

Grab *The Storm Within* now!

Because once the killing starts, no one is safe.

About the Author

Richard Parry worked as a senior marketing manager in one of the world's top tech companies. It sounds cool, but it wasn't all cocaine parties. He lives in Wellington with the love of his life, Rae. They have two cats, Harry and Friday, who chase birds. The birds, who have the power of flight, don't seem to mind.

WAIT. DON'T GO!

Thanks for reading my book. If you enjoyed it, let's keep the party going:

📖 Join *Roll for Narrative* for reviews, storytelling breakdowns, and writing misadventures:

https://rollfornarrative.parrydox.com

✏ Lurk, judge, or say hi:

https://www.parrydox.com

P.S. An angel still gets its wings for every five-star review, but I'm told they're on backorder.

🅰 amazon.com/author/richard.parry

🄌 goodreads.com/richard_parry

BB bookbub.com/authors/richard-parry-6ffc3911-9f2c-43ef-8ab4-13dc-cd7f5874

▶ youtube.com/@parrydigm

🦋 bsky.app/profile/parrydox.com

in linkedin.com/in/therealrichardparry

Also by Richard Parry

DAWN'S WARDEN

The Three Faces of Fate

The Undefeated Throne

The Fury of the Betrayed

THE SPLINTERED LAND

THE EZEROC WARS

The Ezeroc Wars universe is big (and growing!). Get the reading guide here: https://www.parrydox.com/ezeroc-wars-reading-guide/

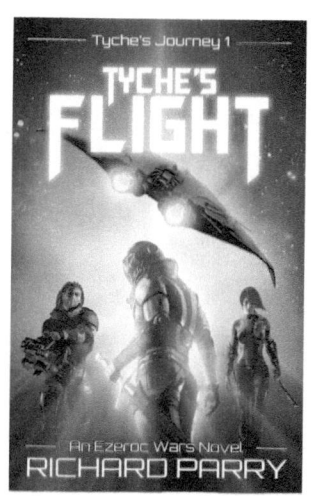

The Empire's Rogues: Volume 1

FUTURE FORFEIT

Not sure where to start? Get the reading guide here: https://www.parrydox.com/future-forfeit-reading-guide/

Chromed: Upgrade

Chromed: Rogue

Chromed: Restore

City Stories

Chromed: Consensus

Chromed: Delilah

Chromed: Meltdown

NIGHT'S CHAMPION

www.ingramcontent.com/pod-product-compliance
Lightning Source LLC
Chambersburg PA
CBHW021839010726
47493CB00005B/1465